A THREE-TURTLE SUMMER

A THREE-TURTLE SUMMER

Janelle Meraz Hooper

Writers Club Press
San Jose New York Lincoln Shanghai

A Three-Turtle Summer

Writers Club Press
an imprint of iUniverse, Inc.

For information address:
iUniverse, Inc.
5220 S. 16th St., Suite 200
Lincoln, NE 68512
www.iuniverse.com

Any resemblance to actual people and events is purely coincidental.
This is a work of fiction.

ISBN: 0-595-24375-4

Printed in the United States of America

For Mom and Dick

"If we don't save our mother's stories, who will?"
Jim Bodeen, *With My Hands Full* (*Con Mis Mano Llenas*)

Contents

Acknowledgements

First books are a lot of work and stress—for a writer's family and friends. I'd like to acknowledge the support of the following people: my husband Dick, and my daughter Chanel, who both read the many drafts of this story. Also, the support of my Aunt Norah, Uncle Ben, and cousins Danny and Bob who are a part of my Oklahoma family. Feedback from my Aunt Violet in Washington was invaluable. Also to brother-in-law Doug, for helping me to remember the lyrics to the song *High Cotton* (written by songwriters Scott Anders and Roger Murrah). Jane, thanks for sharing your memories.

I'd also like to thank my fellow writer, Ginger Foglesong Guy, who gave so freely of her time, and two writer's groups: The Writers Roundtable, whose members are too numerous to mention; and The Brutal Writers Group: Don Sellers, Jim Muri, Rob Miller, and Gale Truett Richardson.

Elizabeth Lyons and Carol Craig worked with me on the first version of this story. Rob Miller and Val Dumond did the final editing.

Credits also go to The Grand Ole Oprey and Ernest Tubb's performance of *I'm Walking the Floor Over You* and Hank Williams's performance of *Your Cold, Cold Heart*.

Sometimes I Feel Like a Motherless Child was written by Harry Thacker Burleigh.

Janelle Meraz Hooper

CHAPTER 1

A Sister in Trouble

Fort Sill, Oklahoma, July, 1949

It was too hot to play cards, especially if someone were keeping score, and Vera *was*.

"*Ay, carumba*! You can't stand to go two hours without beating *someone* at *something* can you?" Grace Tyler playfully pouted.

Vera ignored her little sister, and began shuffling cards as she gleefully announced, "*Senoras*, the game is canasta, and we're going to play according to Hoyle." She began to deal the cards like a Las Vegas gambler while Pauline laughed and pointed at her mother, a notorious and frequent card-cheater.

Everyone was hot, but in her long-sleeved shirt and long skirt, Grace was sweltering. Sweat beaded up on her forehead and neck and she kept stretching her legs out because the backs of her knees stuck to her skirt.

"Gracie, for God's sake, go put some shorts on," Vera said.

Grace ignored her sister, pulled her shirt away from her perspiring chest and asked, "Anyone want more iced tea before Vera whips the pants off of us?"

Momma and Pauline both nodded and Grace poured tea over fresh ice cubes while Vera got a tablet and pencil out of her purse.

The room was almost silent as each woman arranged her hand. Only Momma barely tapped her foot and softly sang a song from her childhood under her breath:

> *"The fair senorita with the rose in her hair…*
> *worked in the cantina but she didn't care…*
> *played cards with the men and took all their loot…awh-ha!*
> *went to the store and bought brand new boots…"*

"Awh-Haaa!" Grace's five-year-old daughter Glory joined in.

Unconsciously, the other two women started to hum along while they looked at their hand. About the second "Awh-Haaa!" Vera abruptly stopped humming and looked at her sisters with a raised eyebrow. Something was fishy; Momma was *much* too happy. Barely containing their amusement, they watched as she cheerfully arranged her cards.

Finally, unable to suppress her laughter any longer, Vera jumped up, snatched the cards out of her mother's hands, and fanned them face-up across the table.

"*Ay, ay, ay!*" She cried out, "Momma, tell me how can you have a meld *and* eleven cards in your hand when we've just gotten started?"

The fun escalated as Vera rushed around the table and ran her hands all around her mother and the chair she sat on to feel for extra cards.

"Stand up!" Grace and her sisters said as they pulled their mother to her feet. They shook her blue calico dress and screamed with laughter as extra cards fell from every fold.

"Glory," Vera told her young niece, "crawl under the table and get those cards for your Auntie Vera, okay?" Grace moved her feet to the side so that Glory could scramble under the table. Her childish giggles danced around the women's feet as she scrambled for the extra cards that dropped from her grandmother's dress.

"Momma," Vera laughed, "you're a born cheater. How did you know we were going to play cards today?" she asked.

"I'm not the only one in this family who's been caught with a few too many cards," Momma said in her defense.

"Yes, but you're the family matriarch. We expect better of you than we do our good-for-nothing brothers," Pauline said.

"Huh! Matriarch, my foot. You girls never listen to a word I say," Momma grumbled.

"Maybe that's because we can't trust you," Vera said.

As another card dropped from Gregoria's dress and slid across the floor, Vera added, "We'll strip you down to your rosary before we ever play cards with you again, Momma."

"Yeah," Pauline, chimed in, "the next time you'll play in nothing but your lace step-ins and a bra made from two tortillas."

"Well, at least I'll be the coolest one at the table," Momma chirped.

Vera reached across the table to gather all the cards and reshuffle them. "We're going to start all over, and we'll watch you every minute."

Grace felt a sharp pain in her stomach when she looked up and saw her husband's scowling face through the screen door. Why was he home so early? She didn't have to look at him again to know his normally handsome blond features smoldered with disgust.

Dwayne hated for Grace to have her family over. There would be trouble once her family left, since the room was heavy with the smell of pinto beans and tortillas. When they visited it was bad enough. It irked Dwayne even more when her dark-skinned family stayed for meals.

"Gawd almighty!" Grace had mimicked earlier in Dwayne's high twangy voice to her sisters, "A Texan breakin' bread with tacos! What will folks be thinkin'?"

The minute Grace's family saw Dwayne, their laughter died, and they quickly packed up their cards, crochet cotton, and magazines that had filled a hot afternoon with laughter and joy. One by one, they lined up to leave through the back door.

Grace said a quick goodbye to her mother and sisters and moved away from the narrow doorway as the women filed past Dwayne. She held her breath as Pauline and Vera passed the loathsome soldier. She never knew what her sisters might say. All she could count on was that her mother would deliberately say something sweet to him. Always gracious, she wasn't one to pick a fight.

"Poor thing, you look absolutely beat," Gregoria Ramirez said to Dwayne as she winked at Grace. "We're going to get out of here so you can take a nap before dinner."

Her mother's words were mollifying, but Gregoria didn't walk around Dwayne to rush out the door. Instead, she stood her ground and looked him straight in the eyes until she intimidated him into stepping out of *her* way.

When Grace's mother stepped onto the porch she leisurely adjusted the plastic tortoise shell combs that held her long, dark hair in a bun. Then she fished her clip earrings that matched her outfit out of her dress pocket and put them back on her ears. Grace gasped when she saw her mother nonchalantly slip another extra card that was also in her pocket into her purse before she stepped onto the sidewalk.

Pauline was next in line. "Dwayne, this heat's too much for you, it's over a hundred today, you'd better take it easy," she cautioned. The sound of her high heels click-click-clicked on the shiny kitchen floor and made Dwayne cringe.

From the beginning of her marriage to Dwayne, Grace had been caught in the ferocious sandstorm that swirled around him and her sisters whenever they were together. Raised on a cattle ranch where his father's booze bottles almost outnumbered the cattle, Dwayne didn't know what to think of Pauline's high-heeled shoes and frilly clothes. He just knew he didn't like them.

For her part, Pauline never considered making any changes to accommodate the manipulative soldier her sister had married.

Dwayne clinched his jaw and refused to let himself look down at Pauline's high heels as she passed him, but she knew that he knew that she wore them. Always playful, she did a quickstep on her way to the door.

The ruffles on her colorful full skirt moved to the music her heels made as she walked. Before she passed Dwayne, she adjusted her peasant style blouse with the elastic around the top to make sure her bosom wasn't exposed. It was a subtle movement; only Grace noticed it.

Pauline lingered in the doorway as she said goodbye to Grace, then glided out the door and tossed her long, wavy black hair. The movement jangled her large, golden earrings as she crossed the threshold. "*Adios, Muchacho!*" she called to Dwayne, as she gave him a backward wave. Grace's eyes flew to Dwayne to see if he noticed that her middle finger stayed up longer than the others. He didn't. He was already looking at Vera.

"You look like hell," Vera said as she passed a sweaty and wrinkled Dwayne, "and you could use a shower. Phew!" she added as she marched out the door. Grace saw her mother give Vera a sharp look when she got to the porch, but her oldest daughter just shrugged her chubby shoulders, as if to say it was the best she could do. This cowboy had used up all of his good graces with her.

Grace wasn't surprised that Dwayne had remained quiet while her family left. She imagined that he had plenty to say; he just didn't dare say it. Not with these women, who weren't as meek as she was. She couldn't tell which woman he feared the most: the mother, quiet but cunning; Vera, outspoken, tough, and fearless; or Pauline, who could cut a man to ribbons with her tongue and flirt with him at the same time.

As Vera reached the sidewalk at the bottom of the porch stairs, Pauline broke into a sprint ahead of her across the yard to Vera's car and jumped into the back seat, still giggling. Pauline had given her first *gringo salute* when she held up her finger to Dwayne, and she was tickled with herself. Even her mother's look of disapproval couldn't dampen her glee.

When Gregoria opened the car door on the passenger side to get into the front, Pauline buried her face between her legs in her ruffled skirt, to muffle her laughter. Vera opened the door on the driver's side and stopped outside the car to light a Kool and let some of the hot air out of the car before she got in. She waved a final goodbye to Grace just before she slid behind the wheel and started the old blue Cadillac.

Grace's heart ached when she saw Vera's car move out of the parking lot. To avoid raising dust in the neighborhood, Vera drove so slowly that Grace thought about grabbing Glory and making a run for the car. But if she left now, it could make Dwayne mad enough to file custody papers for their daughter. She could leave her marriage anytime. The trick would be leaving with Glory.

She was convinced that the courts often awarded custody of mixed blood children to white fathers because their perception was that the children would be more educated and better off economically in a white environment. It was much like the theory that Indian children would be better off if they were forcefully separated from their Indian culture and raised away from home in white schools.

*   *   *

Vera headed the old Cadillac for the highway and blew her cigarette smoke out the window as Gregoria halfheartedly said, "Vera, you must show respect to the men in the family, the way we did to Poppa."

"When he acts like Poppa did, I'll show respect," Vera answered. "Did you see how mad he was? He just can't stand to see us have a good time. I'd like to see our baby sister dump that pain-in-the-ass sourpuss. He'll never treat her right."

"Look where they're living, on the far edge of the post, in old converted Army barracks. It's worse than Dogpatch out there," Pauline joined in.

"Yeah, it breaks my heart to see Grace married to that awful slouch. Momma, how did Poppa ever allow that?" Vera asked her mother.

"*Ayyy*, Vera, by the time Gracie met Dwayne, Poppa was already sick. He couldn't stop Dwayne, and you girls were off with your new husbands," Momma groaned. "Dwayne made your Poppa so miserable. Juan worked so hard to fit in here, and Dwayne did everything he could to make him feel like he didn't belong. He always refused to believe your father had a college degree in engineering from the University of Mexico. He treated him like he was nothing but a cotton-picker. Your poppa only picked cotton when it was the Depression, and he needed to put food on the table." Momma dabbed at her eyes.

The women nodded their heads in agreement, as if they'd never heard the stories before.

"Yeah, I remember that gun he used to carry for rattlesnakes in the fields," Pauline jumped in. "Poppa was a perfect shot. BAM! Those snakes were dead as sticks."

"Pauline, you don't really believe that?" Vera laughed as she looked at her sister in the rearview mirror. "Poppa couldn't hit the broad side of a barn with that old gun. It was loaded with snake shot. He couldn't miss because the pellets sprayed everywhere. That's why he always told us to stand way back."

"Really?" Pauline asked. "I thought it was so we wouldn't get snake blood all over us."

Just before they dropped Pauline off at her tiny garage apartment, Vera asked, "Sis, do you and Boyd want to come over and listen to my new records tonight? I've got all the new ones, even Nat King Cole."

"Naw, Boyd is off somewhere, he may not even get home for dinner," her eyes avoided Vera's staring suspiciously at her in the rear view mirror.

"Come without him. Benny is going to show us how to samba. You can come as you are, no one else will be there. I want to learn a new dance before Rudolf takes me to the officers' club Saturday night." Pauline was obviously uneasy, but with Momma in the car, Vera couldn't dig any deeper. Besides, if her sister were having trouble with Boyd, she'd handle it. Pauline was tough.

Grace was the sister Vera was worried about. Her little sister was in over her head and too stubborn to admit it. Momma's favorite, Grace had been kept so close to home that she'd never had any experience with men when she was growing up. At the time, Dwayne must have looked good to her naive sister. Anyone else with more savvy would have thrown him head first into a creek and never looked back.

"Maybe. Will Grace come?" Pauline pouted, as she sank further into the back seat, her mind still on Grace's cranky husband.

"I asked her and she said she'd ask Dwayne," Vera answered. "But you know Dwayne doesn't like us or our music, and he has never been a dancer. He doesn't even two-step to that country music he loves to torture us with."

Her mother and sisters gone, Grace braced herself for the latest tirade from Dwayne as she started dinner. She didn't have to wait long. Dwayne stood behind Grace and ranted at her as she breaded perch with a combination of flour and cornmeal. When she moved back and forth from the countertop by the sink to the stove, he followed her so she wouldn't miss a word.

"The fish you caught look good, Dwayne," Grace chatted as she tried to soften his anger. It was an honest compliment. Dwayne had a lot of faults, but he was one heck of a fisherman. The day before, he'd gone fishing on the way home from work and had caught a whole stringer full of perch before it started to get dark. They didn't eat them that night because Grace already had dinner on the table when he got home. Dwayne was only briefly pleased at the compliment. Soon he was back to running down Grace's family as she peeled potatoes to fry in one of her big wrought iron skillets.

"Why the hell can't you keep your family out of here?" Dwayne yelled as he jerked his fatigue hat off his head and threw it across the room. "What if I'd brought one of the officers from the battalion home? Do you think one of *them* would want to see a bunch of women sittin' around playin' cards and gibberin' in Spanish the minute he walked through the door?"

"I'm sorry, Dwayne, I never thought you'd be home so early." Grace's lower lip quivered, and her words tumbled out on top of each other like potatoes that rolled out of an overturned sack. "But we weren't speaking Spanish, Dwayne, we weren't!" Grace hustled around the kitchen to get Dwayne a goblet of iced tea.

She desperately wanted to go to Vera's. Not only would it be fun but it would also keep Dwayne away from her for the evening. She knew she didn't dare ask to go until he was in a better mood.

Grace held her breath as he looked around the kitchen and gave the air an arrogant sniff before he sipped his tea.

"It's a good thing you pepper-bellies just eat beans. Otherwise, I'd be in the poor house," he sneered as he lit a Camel.

It wasn't just the food. Dwayne even resented her mother and sisters when they brought the food with them. He never hid the fact that he felt her family wasn't worth his time. Only Rudolf, Vera's husband who was an Army colonel, ever got more than a few grunts from him.

"I'm sorry, Dwayne. It's just that they were here all day, and we got so hungry, and Glory had to eat something. I just warmed up some leftover beans and Momma made a few tortillas. It was nothing fancy."

"It's a dog-eat-dog world, Grace." Dwayne lit another cigarette from what was left of the last one. "And we're not rich. We've got to spend our time and money on the people who can do us some good." Dwayne finished his iced tea and left the glass on the table, where a puddle of condensation formed at its base and crept like a bleeding wound across the old table with the red, marbleized plastic top. The pattern of the moisture disturbed Grace and she hurried to wipe it up.

"Okay. Vera invited us over tonight. Everybody will be there. Benny's going to be there to show Vera how to samba, and I haven't seen him for awhile. But, if you don't want to go, I'll call and say we're staying home."

"We were invited to Vera's? Is Rudolf going to be there?" When Grace nodded yes, she noticed his interest perked up. "Call them," he urged, "tell them we'll be over as soon as we eat. In this man's Army, it could come in real handy to be on good terms with a colonel."

On his way down the hall to change out of his uniform, he said loudly over his shoulder so Grace could hear, "And I've got a business idea to talk over with your mother." Grace, who was at the stove serving the fish and fried potatoes on plates, rolled her eyes. *Just what made him think her mother would be interested in one of his screwy business plans?*

"Call her," Dwayne shouted again from the bathroom.

Grace went to the bathroom and stood outside the door. "There's no need to call her. She said to come if we could," Grace explained. "I think she's just serving drinks and that cocktail cereal-mix she makes up in the oven. It'll be an early night since everyone has to work tomorrow."

As soon as they ate, Grace ran to get herself and Glory ready to go before something happened to change Dwayne's mind.

❧   ❧   ❧

Even though she hurried, when the Tylers pulled into Vera's driveway, everyone else was already there. Her brother Benny was in the large living room of the old house with Vera, demonstrating his latest dance step. Vera, who'd always been a quick study, followed right along.

"Gracie," Benny called to Grace, "come dance with me. Vera's already got it."

"Is this the samba?" Grace asked, bubbling over with excitement.

On his way to Grace, Benny grabbed Glory and twirled her around the living room before she ran to play with her cousin Carlos, Pauline's son. Carlos was underneath Vera's large dining room table busily building a skyscraper out of dominos and cards.

"Glory, you'll be a great little dancer someday," Benny called after Glory, "just stick with your Uncle Ben."

Glory turned and giggled as she joined Carlos.

Grace wasn't surprised to see that Rudolf and Vera's two boys hadn't stuck around. Her nephews were already in high school and seldom hung around for their mother's impromptu dance parties. They often teased their mother and Grace by going out the door while they sang, "*It must be jelly 'cause jam don't shake like that*," lyrics they'd heard on one of their mother's records.

The whole family—even Dwayne—laughed as Benny playfully grabbed Grace and dipped her all the way to the floor before they even started to dance. Used to her brother's antics, she followed the movement gracefully and came up following Benny step for step, with her eyes on her brother's feet.

Rudolf sat in a corner of the living room in a big easy chair, reading the paper. When the dancers stopped to change records, his twinkling eyes peeked over the paper and he called out encouragement to Vera. Rudolf was never an enthusiastic dancer but he liked a wife who looked good on the dance floor. Vera told Grace she could always count on Rudolf to dance the night away—as long as they played nothing but waltzes. A popular dancer, Vera was never short of partners at the Officers' Club so she was content to let Rudolf sit and visit with their friends when they went out for the night.

With barely a nod to the other members of the family, Dwayne headed for Rudolf. He was too dense to notice that the colonel pulled his paper up over his face when he saw Dwayne coming his way. Before Dwayne could sit down in an easy chair next to the colonel, he had to move a pile of fabric and carpet swatches that Vera was using in her latest redecorating project.

"Jesussss-Christ," Dwayne said as he looked for a place to lay the handful of samples. "You oughta kick Vera's butt for spendin' so much of your money."

Rudolf put down his paper and gave him a stony stare. Dwayne could barely hear him with the music blaring, so Rudolf was sure no one else heard him say, "What my wife and I do with our money is our business, Dwayne." He didn't say anymore before he picked up his paper and began to read again.

That put Dwayne's tail between his legs and he didn't know what to do next. How could Rudolf not be mad as hell about the money Vera spent? He wasn't prepared for such a rebuff. He should have shut up, but Dwayne blundered on, like a cannon rolling downhill and picking up speed as its metal wheels banged over the rocks.

"Well, if it were me, I wouldn't have no use for a woman who spent my money and did nothing but play bridge all day." Rudolf made no reply as he gave Dwayne another icy stare and went to make himself a fresh drink. He didn't bother to offer his brother-in-law one. Dwayne didn't even notice the slight; he was so dumbfounded that his last statement hadn't turned Rudolf around and made him see things his way. It was all so clear to *him*. Couldn't Rudolf see Vera would drain his bank account dry?

Rudolf never came back, and instead disappeared without a word into his bedroom. Left alone with his gangly legs jutting out from the low couch, Dwayne finally made an awkward move to the other side of the room to talk to Pauline. He looked down at the high heels she wore. Well, if Rudolf wouldn't listen to him, at least he could straighten Pauline out.

"Pauline," Dwayne said as he pointed to her feet, "the only other women I've seen wear shoes like that were whores. You'd better stop buying those things. People will start to talk."

"Oh, tell me, Dwayne, have you seen a lot of whores? Where?" she asked as she rolled her eyes at her mother. Dwayne was the only man who made her husband Boyd—although he was absent—look good to her. In Spanish, she said something to her mother about Vera and snakes. He was pretty sure Pauline was telling her mother that Vera had said he was a rattlesnake. Dwayne didn't understand the rest, but he'd heard the Spanish word for snake—*serpiente*—often on post. Momma nodded, and pretended to talk about Glory in Spanish, but Dwayne wasn't fooled. He knew they were putting him down again.

Dwayne was beside himself, but he didn't want to go home until he'd accomplished his main mission: to get money from Grace's mother for his ranch. Grace was still dancing with Benny. Vera and Pauline had joined them, so Dwayne rushed to the kitchen and poured two cups of coffee. It should be easy to get the old lady to do things his way. She didn't even know how to read English. For sure, *she'd* do what he told her.

"Momma, I've been thinkin'," Dwayne said to his mother-in-law as he handed her a cup of coffee. "Why on earth are you still living in that big ole house by yourself? You should sell that thing and move into an apartment."

"Why, what would I do with myself in an apartment? I'd have no garden. Besides, I'm happy where I am; all of my memories of Juan are there in that house. It's the only home we ever had that was ours."

"Momma, you'd better think about it, you're getting old, and one of these days you're gonna fall in that house and there won't be anyone there to help you. Besides, you could get a ton of money for that old place. Property values are going through the roof around here."

"Dwayne," said Momma, puzzled by Dwayne's forcefulness, "I don't need money. I live simply and I have everything I want."

"Well," Dwayne pushed on, "you should be thinkin' of Glory. She's gonna have to go to college someday, ya' know, and if you took the money from the house and invested it in my cattle ranch, you'd have a nice little nest egg for her when she needs it." Dwayne thought it was a pretty convincing argument; everyone knew that she adored Glory.

"Oh, so you want me to sell my house and give you the money?" Dwayne saw the beginning of a smile at the corners of Gregoria's lips. "My coffee needs more sugar. Would you get me some?" She handed her cup to Dwayne who was glad to have an excuse to escape to the kitchen. He needed to think. What should he say next?

When Dwayne could think of nothing else to say, he couldn't control the anger he felt. He had to get out of that house before he started to beat the shit out of everyone there. In fact, if the two men hadn't been there, things could have gotten real ugly.

What makes these women so damned uppity? he wondered. When he was growing up on the ranch, his mother never dressed up and wore high heels and spent all kinds of money to decorate her house like these women did. His dad would have beat the livin' tar out of her and told her to go feed the cows. He always told Dwayne that women who didn't do what their husbands told them were whores, and should be treated like whores. Clean and simple. No ifs, ands, or buts.

With no warning, Dwayne came back to the living room and shouted, "Grace! Time to go home. Get Glory and let's get started. Gotta work tomorrow." He walked over to the phonograph and dragged the needle off the spinning record, putting a long scratch in it.

Startled, Grace gathered up Glory and raced out the door, while Dwayne pushed them from behind. As they got to their car, they heard the music start up again, louder than before; he was sure it was Pauline who turned the music up as a final salute to him.

        ❦   ❦   ❦

In the car, Grace listened to Dwayne's opinions of her family all the way home. He'd worked himself into a real good lather as he went on and on about what whores her sisters were. Grace was afraid to take her eyes off of the tall, blond soldier. At any moment, she thought, he might hit her.

Dwayne held off his anger until they were in their quarters. Then his anger flew out of control. While he yelled, he pulled Grace into the hallway, where she was trapped in a space just wide enough for one person to pass. First, an arm flew out from his body and he backhanded Grace across the face and sent her into a spin to the opposite wall. When she bounced off the sheetrock, he was there to catch her. He twisted her arm behind her back and jerked it up each time he spoke.

"Damn little whore. You're just like your sisters, you're *all* nothing but whores." He pulled up on her arm again so hard that Grace cried out, but he didn't loosen his grip.

"And look at your skin. It's as black as a colored's. What do you do, bake in the sun while I'm at work?"

He pulled up on Grace's arm a third time. "I don't know why I even bother with you. You're more useless than a tit on a bullet."

Grace crumbled in the hallway. "Stop. Please stop. You're hurting me."

"Damn little pepper-belly," he raged, "I'll show you how a real man treats whores."

"I'm not a whore, Dwayne, and you know it," Grace cried as she shielded her face.

"Don't you talk back to me, don't you *dare* talk back to me. I hear what the men in town say about you and your sisters."

Grace had heard it all before. Felt it all before. Belittling her made Dwayne feel important.

Made him feel more like a man.

Made him feel like sex.

When he pulled her into the bedroom, Grace's battered mind scurried away like a prairie mouse under sagebrush. Only the faint smell of Dwayne's Camel cigarettes and unwashed underarm odor managed to creep underneath the mental barriers she put up to survive.

Grace didn't bother to ask anymore what the men had said; she'd heard it all before. In past fights, she had asked which men said bad things about her and her sisters, but Dwayne would never give her a name. She finally figured out that there were no "other men," just the mean and crazy ramblings of a Texan who looked for any excuse to use his fists and feel superior. Now, she didn't even listen to the words; she only tried to protect herself as much as she could.

As he pulled Grace back to the bedroom, she saw Glory run for her closet, carrying a plate of leftover perch from the table. Grace had been so anxious to go to her sister's that she'd forgotten to put it in the refrigerator.

"Glory," she screamed, but Dwayne pulled her back when she tried to run to their daughter. "Dwayne, let me go. Glory has the fish. Dwayne, please, she'll choke on the bones."

Dwayne didn't even look Glory's way as he threw Grace on the bed and started to unbuckle his pants.

It broke Grace's heart to know that their daughter had begun to hide in her closet as soon as she started to walk; she began to take food into the closet with her as soon as she could reach the plates on the table.

Tonight, Glory ate leftover bony perch while she hid on top of a pile of her father's duffel bags in her dark closet. But other nights,

Grace had found her in the middle of the night curled around a plate of fried chicken, or cold biscuits—whatever she could grab before she ran for her bunker.

When Dwayne's anger and lust finally exhausted him, he began to cool off. Just before he went to sleep, he told Grace, "I love you Grace; I'll try to never hit you again."

He said the same thing every time.

Every time, it was a lie.

And, every time, she talked herself into believing him. Why did she think he'd ever change?

In the middle of the night, Grace dragged her aching body into her daughter's room, moved the sleeping Glory from the closet, and put her in her Army-issue metal bed. She shivered even though the heat was over a hundred degrees as she crawled back into bed next to Dwayne. She could have slept with Glory on her bed, but it was too small for an adult to be comfortable, and Grace was already hurting. There was no place else to go except the couch in the living room, and the one time she'd slept there, Dwayne got angry all over again. It just wasn't worth it.

Once, the morning after a bad night, Glory asked Grace if her daddy would come after her next, and cried, "What'll I do, Mommy? What'll I do?" Grace looked at her panicked little face and promised her that she'd protect her if her father ever did come after her, but deep inside, she didn't know how. She couldn't even protect herself.

The next morning, Dwayne was gone before Grace put on the coffee. She sat down in the morning sun that seeped through the worn window shades and began to sew. As her machine clicked over pins and fabric at a comforting, soothing pace, she began to pull herself together. *Not much longer, she told herself. Not much longer.* At times, she winced as her sore ribs accidentally rubbed against the edge of the table.

Grace didn't hear well, so she was startled when an excited voice right next to her shouted, "Mom, what are you makin' today?"

With great effort, Grace turned and lifted her daughter onto her lap. Her ribs were throbbing, so she gave her a careful but affectionate hug. While they cuddled, she pulled out the clips that held Glory's blond hair in dog-ears. Grace ran her fingers through hair that was sticky with a combination of tears and fried fish from the night before.

"We have to wash your hair today. Might as well wait until you come in for your nap, okay?" She quickly pulled Glory's hair back into a low ponytail. Without a shampoo, there wasn't much else she could do with it.

"Okay." Glory readily agreed because she was anxious to go outside and play.

Grace marveled at this creation with light skin, green eyes, and darkening blond hair that she'd given birth to. Her skin and hair were dark. How could a child of hers look so little like her, even with Dwayne as the father? Other children from similar marriages were a lot darker, although Dwayne *was* exceptionally light—he almost looked like an albino. The only other explanation was the Spanish blood on her mother's side of the family. She knew that many of them had light hair.

Strangers assumed Glory was Dwayne's from another marriage, and Grace always smiled and said she didn't blame them. But, deep inside, she resented it. Glory was hers, even if everything about her, from her blond hair to her long legs, looked like Dwayne.

"Hon, are you hungry?" Grace gingerly rocked Glory on her lap to avoid bumping her sore ribs into Glory.

"No, what are you makin'?" Glory asked as she looked at Grace's machine on the kitchen table.

"Well, I thought my girl could use some cooler play clothes. It's starting to get hot."

"For me? Can I see? Oh, boy, can I have pockets?"

"You want pockets?" Grace laughed at Glory's excitement.

"Yes. Pockets and lace."

"Where shall I put the lace?"

"On the seat, like Linda Joy has. Her mom got her these panties with ruffles all over the seat so when she bends over all you see is ruffles, ruffles, ruffles. I *love* ruffles." Glory bounced off Grace's lap and danced around the kitchen floor, as she bent over and patted her bottom with both hands.

"What else do you want?"

"Could I have a turtle?"

"A *tortuga*? Where did you get that idea?"

"Linda Joy has a turtle. She calls it Fluffy. She's teaching it to talk."

"I'll have to think about that. Are you sure you're not hungry?"

"No. Sew, Mommy."

Grace smiled to herself as she put the tiny pieces of material together. Glory was so small she could make her a whole outfit from the odds and ends leftover from the sewing she did for her relatives and friends. That was how, even on a very limited budget, Grace had filled Glory's closet with lacy dresses, colorful play clothes, and even a rabbit fur coat. The coat, made from a couple of old rabbit stoles that Vera bought at a church bazaar, looked "Damn dandy," Vera had said.

"When will it be finished?" Glory wanted to know as she pulled herself up over the edge of the table to get a better look at her new outfit.

"Before you know it, if you eat some breakfast and go outside and play."

"Okay." She stood on tiptoes to see what was on the counter, "Can I have that tortilla?"

"Yes. Why don't you put some oleo on it?"

"If I eat it all, *then* can I go outside?"

Yes," said Grace. She watched Glory sit down on the cool floor with the flour tortilla and a small glass of red Kool-Aid; their food budget didn't allow for extras like juice. Although, somehow, when Dwayne went to the commissary, he always found enough change for *his* favorites: coffee, tea, and cocoa for chocolate cakes and home-made fudge.

Mostly Dwayne spent every penny he could scrounge to build up his mother's shabby cattle ranch in Texas, even if it meant they had to cut down on food items that Glory needed, like milk and eggs.

When Glory started to eat her tortilla, Grace went back to sewing. As she eased the material under the presser foot she felt a wave of anger wash over her. What kind of a breakfast was that for a little girl? Shoot! She and all her brothers and sisters ate better than that during the Depression, Poppa saw to it.

"If Poppa could feed all of us, why can't this good-for-nothing-son-of-a-gun feed one little girl?" Grace muttered. "And how can he think he's such a big shot when he has money to buy food for a bunch of dumb cows, but none for his only child, who doesn't even have milk or orange juice?" She mumbled over her sewing machine.

The machine answered with *click-click. Click-click.*

Since Grace didn't drive, she'd have to ask her sisters to get some of the sewing money she hid from Dwayne at her mother's and pick up a few groceries for her. Dwayne only gave her extra money for food when he felt like it—usually when he had friends come over that he wanted to impress.

Sometimes, in frustration, Grace would complain that Dwayne spent too much on his ranch, but she was always fearful that she would go too far and make him angry. Besides, she told herself, any day now he'd be sent on another overseas assignment. Whole units of soldiers shipped out every day from Fort Sill on post-war assign-ments to occupy Japan. Most would be gone two to three years.

Her plan was to wait until he left, then divorce him. Once he was out of town, it would be easier to keep custody of Glory, so why risk getting beaten again? *Any day. Any day now,* Grace told herself as she rested her forehead on the cool metal of her old Singer sewing machine and tried to steady her breath.

Daily, Grace held onto the dream of her and Glory in a little house, living happily alone, just the two of them. She would start a sewing business; Glory would play in the backyard by the flower garden. Her heart skipped a beat whenever she dared to think she might even have a car. It wouldn't have to be new, just something to take her to the grocery store. On the way, she pictured, she'd stop by her mother's for coffee. Someday, she promised herself. Someday. All she had to do was be smart enough to keep Glory, and get out of her marriage alive.

While she held on from day to day, Dwayne strutted his six-foot, two-inch frame around the small Army quarters and acted as if he held all the cards. His favorite threat was to tell her, "I'll take Glory away from you if you ever try to leave me. All the judges are white," he liked to say, "and they'll do whatever I tell them to do."

From the stories about the judges that she heard in town, Grace didn't doubt it for a minute.

CHAPTER 2

Sorry. Sorry. Sorry

When Grace sent Glory out to play that morning, the heat was already in the nineties. Not even eight o'clock yet, the parched yard was alive with children who played while sleepy moms held toys in one hand and coffee cups in the other. Even her friend and next door neighbor, Sako, was there talking to her neighbors while she poured her leftover coffee from her cold cup over a scorched plant that was too far gone to be saved with moisture. She'd given up all pretenses that she was outside to watch Ronnie run around in circles, and visited with the other mothers who were as hot as she was.

Meiko was there, Sako's childhood friend that she talked about all the time. She and Sako had been inseparable at the internment camp at Poston, Arizona. By a twist of fate, the soldiers they'd married were both assigned to Fort Sill when the internment camp was closed. Meiko had spunk, Sako once told Grace.

Named Cathy by her parents, she had paid twenty-dollars as soon as she got out of Poston to change her name to Meiko.

"If I'm Japanese, I want a Japanese name," she told her surprised parents. Sako said she was relieved Cathy hadn't changed her name to Poston.

Grace could imagine that the women talked about the same old stuff they talked about every morning: the weather, the latest rumor about which company would go to Japan next, and the ins-and-outs of quarters' inspections. The few times she had joined them, the conversation always steered toward the same topics. Not that she blamed them. The lives of Army dependents were regularly turned upside down by the latest hot spot on the globe.

Most mornings, Sako stayed inside to keep a close watch on Daniel. Bedridden with muscular dystrophy, he was the older of her husband's two sons by an earlier marriage. When Sako was outside, Grace knew that Daniel either felt much better, or he was asleep.

Soon, Grace knew, the moms would flee the blazing heat and run for their shadier, if not cooler, kitchens. Before they ran inside, the women would beg their children to stay in the patchy shade, and to try to keep their hats on—although they knew full well that their pleas would go mostly unheeded.

She seldom visited with the women in the mornings. The heat in her kitchen built up fast in the summer, so she tried to get her sewing done before it got too hot. Also, she worried that if she joined the coffee klatch, one of the women might ask about what went on with Dwayne at night. What could she say? "Sure, my husband beats me, but he always says he's sorry, so it's okay." How could she expect them to understand that?

From inside, she watched as her daughter tried to figure out what game the other kids were playing. Glory was the youngest child in the neighborhood, and Grace always made sure she was playing with the other children, to keep her from wandering off alone. Each morning, early, Grace patrolled the yard between her place and Sako's to make sure a snake hadn't moved in during the night. Snakes—usually rattlesnakes—had a particular fondness for the cement patios over in the officers' quarters where they'd stretch out on the warm cement to sun themselves. So far, none of them had found Grace's small porch appealing. Spiders and wasp nests were about the most dangerous things her patrols had turned up. Luckily, the play area was surrounded by the housing units, so it wouldn't be easy for Glory to wander out of the neighborhood, where she *could* run into a snake.

"Glory, Glory, Gloriiia! Glory, Glory, Gloriiia! Glory, Glory, Glori-iia!" Ronnie, Sako's youngest stepson, chanted as he galloped by on an old broom and threw a rope around her. Glory grinned when she saw the game was cowboys and Indians, one of her favorites. Grace waved to Sako and went back to her sewing. All of the children in the neighborhood were good kids. Glory would be fine. Grace sat back down at the kitchen table and began again to ease the material through the machine.

While she sewed, it occurred to her that Dwayne was the only one who ever called their daughter Gloria. Even the priest at St. Mary's called Glory by her nickname. *Does he use Gloria's given name as a way to keep from getting too close to her?*

Again, her machine answered, *click-click, click-click.*

Later, after a rollicking game of cowboys and Indians, she put Glory down for a nap. Out of habit, Grace felt her forehead even though she knew that Glory's nervous stomachaches were caused by Dwayne, and not some germ that was going around.

"How do you feel, Sugar?"

"I'm okay, Mommy, I'm okay."

"Does your stomach hurt?" Grace asked when she noticed that Glory held it.

"A little."

Grace let out a soft curse in Spanish as she walked down the hall. How much longer until this bastard ships out? she asked herself. Her marriage to Dwayne had turned out to be the biggest mistake of her life, and if Dwayne didn't ship out to Japan soon, she didn't know what she'd do; he got meaner by the day. *If he hated Mexicans so much, why did he marry her? Just to have someone to beat so he could feel superior?*

When Glory woke up, the first thing she saw was her new play outfit, complete with lacy bloomers. Grace didn't bother to tell her she'd sewn the outfit with recycled lace from one of her Aunt Pauline's old outfits. Glory wouldn't have cared anyway.

"You did it, Momma. Ruffles. Just like Linda Joy's!" Glory danced around the room, and stopped only long enough to hug her mother.

"Can I put them on now?"

"Yes," Grace answered. "Put the whole outfit on. I want to make sure it fits."

"It'll fit. I just know it."

After Grace checked the waistline to make sure it wasn't too tight, she patted Glory on her ruffles and sent her out to play.

Deep inside, Grace knew that she sewed for Glory as a way to say she was sorry. Sorry she had picked such a lousy man to be her father. Sorry for the lack of food. Sorry for the terror-filled nights. Sorry for the whole mess.

Sorry.

Sorry.

Sorry.

Before she left Glory's room, she looked at the sparse furnishings. All the rooms in the old converted barracks had drab walls, linoleum floors, yellowed window shades, and metal beds. The only other pieces of furniture Glory had were an Army-issue chest of drawers and a wooden toy chest her Uncle Rudolf had made for her at the post wood shop. Grace longed to paint the walls a pretty shade of pink and cover the bed, windows, and doorless closet with a pink-flowered print, but she knew Dwayne would never allow it, even if he weren't about to ship out. A project like that would take yards and yards of fabric. Even if she just used gingham at seventy-cents a yard, they couldn't afford it.

       ❦   ❦   ❦

Grace had put away her sewing and started dinner when Vera sauntered through the front door carrying her bowling bag and practicing her swearing. From Vera's observations, officer's wives did two things that made them stand out from other wives: they swore and smoked. Learning to smoke had been easy, but she couldn't seem to get the hang of swearing. Grace thought it was because no one else in the family swore—Momma wouldn't allow it—so Vera didn't have an example to follow. More often than not, when she swore, people just laughed.

"*Ay, ay, ay,* goddamn! It's hotter in here than the inside of Momma's bean pot."

"Nice outfit, Sis."

Vera's bowling clothes, a bright pink shirt with a matching plaid skirt almost vibrated with their loud color. Even her socks were shocking pink.

"Thanks, I got it at The Parisian," Vera said, her voice full of pride. Ever since Rudolf got his last promotion, she acted like she owned the two fancy department stores in town. The funny thing was, she enjoyed shopping at Kress just as much. Once, Grace found a Kress sack, full of the kinds of trinkets that a kid would buy, in the back seat of Vera's Cadillac. Tiny plastic dolls, key chains, little pencils and notebooks to put beside the phone, and packages of clay. All the things, Grace guessed, that Vera wanted when she was small but never had the money to buy.

Although she was a little overweight, Vera golfed, swam, and bowled day and night with all of the other officers' wives, so she looked good. Good and tanned. She was never one who worried about her skin not being light enough. If she wore a hat it was because the sun was in her eyes, and she couldn't see the next golf hole without it. It would never be because she was trying to keep her face from getting brown.

Her short hair had red henna highlights and was perfectly groomed with the newest hair dressing that she swore by; she said just a little bit made her hair shine and kept it from "flying away" when she was out on the golf course. She told Grace it came in a tube like toothpaste, and Grace couldn't wait to try some as soon as she got to town to do some shopping.

"Vera, why did you bring your bowling bag in here? Are you afraid someone will steal it?"

"I'm more afraid someone will steal what's *in* it." Vera unzipped the bowling bag and dumped its contents onto the kitchen table.

"Okra! Where did you get it?" Grace asked as she rushed to the table to get a better look at the slightly curved green pods covered in a soft, white fuzz. It was fresh, and just the right size. In the stores, if you could find it at all, it was usually too big and tough to have much flavor.

"At Uncle Joe's." Vera took her Kools and silver Zippo out of her shirt pocket and lit up while she talked.

"Oh, how is Poppa's older brother? I haven't seen him for ages." Grace scooped up enough okra for a meal, and took it to the sink to wash it. While Vera chatted and smoked, Grace sliced and breaded the pods in a combination of flour, cornmeal, and salt.

"I don't know, he wasn't there, so I helped myself," Vera teased. "Sis, you should see what he has back there. Tomatoes as big as watermelons and watermelons as big as the moon!" She raised her tanned arms upward and out, as if she were holding a huge melon up to the sky. All of her brightly colored bangle bracelets raced for her chubby elbows when her arms were on the way up, and tumbled just as fast for her wrists when she put her arms down.

"*Ay, ay, ay.* I wonder how he does it. Everything around this stinkin' place has dried up and turned to dust." As Grace talked, she pulled another wrought iron skillet out of the bottom drawer of the oven. She placed a big spoonful of Crisco in it and put it on the stove.

"He says he's been collecting rainwater off his roof in old barrels before it has a chance to run down the street. Then he put in spigots near the bottoms of the barrels and attached his garden hoses to them. He's also using something he calls mulch, but it smells like rotten combat boots to me." Vera shuddered at the thought, then pulled out a kitchen chair and pushed away enough okra pods from the edge of the table to make room to pull a mirror out of her purse and put on fresh lipstick.

"I wonder where he got the idea about the rainwater. We'll have to tell Momma; she's always worrying about water for her garden. She says the city is going to ration water again this year. Where do you think we could get her some old barrels?"

Vera shrugged. "I don't know, but Rudolf will." After some thought she added, "Let's not tell Momma the part about the mulch. Oklahoma stinks enough already."

"Okay. Do you want some of this?" Grace asked, as she stood over the table full of okra.

"No, I've got a trunk full. I'll call him tomorrow and have him over for lunch."

"I hope you're not going to feed him okra."

"No. I also took a mess of black-eyed peas. I'll cook that up with some corn bread."

"He'll like that, but I wish you wouldn't take things without asking. You know Momma will have a fit if she finds out."

"Aw, Sis, I was just kidding. Do you think I want to hear Momma scold, 'Ain't you got no *shame*?' like she always does? No, Uncle Joe was there, I don't think he ever leaves; he begged me to take some of this stuff off his hands because he always grows too much."

"Why doesn't he sell it?"

"He says he promised himself he wouldn't work after he retired. Poor thing, it's not as if he couldn't use the money. When he's finished in the garden, he just sits on his porch all day and rocks with a big pitcher of iced tea sitting on the railing. He says that's what he wants to do. He even bought an extra rocking chair, but I've never seen anyone in it."

"Maybe he's planning on getting a girlfriend. Vera, can I ask you something?" Grace had hoped her sister would stop by so she could ask her about her plan to open a sewing business as soon as Dwayne left for Japan. Vera's opinion meant a lot to her. If she said she thought it was a bad idea, Grace would believe her and start to look for another way out of the mess she was in. Although she didn't know what else she could do, unless she cleaned people's houses.

"Ask away. I have until six o'clock when I have to leave for bowling." She took a long drag on her Kool cigarette as she swept the rest of the okra off the table into a large bowl with the inside of her arm.

"That stuff is going to make your arm itch," Grace warned. "Vera, do you think I could make enough money sewing to make a living after Dwayne goes?" She turned and faced the sink to pour her sister a glass of Kool-Aid so Vera wouldn't see the desperation in her eyes.

Grace held her breath. She turned just in time to hear Vera mumble a stream of swear words worthy of a general's wife as she rushed out through the front door. She couldn't hear everything her big sister said, but she heard enough to guess Dwayne was home. She glanced out the kitchen window and saw him pull into the back parking lot. Grace sighed, and placed the cold drink on the table.

A fresh stack of flour tortillas sat on the counter. Grace quickly fried the okra, put on the macaroni noodles, and made some home-made salsa. What a strange combination. She wished Dwayne wouldn't use so much of his puny paycheck to try to revive that piti-ful patch of ground he called a ranch in Texas.

Outside, Dwayne parked his old Ford and stopped to chat with a neighbor. He oozed with charm when he talked to people outside the family; Grace wondered if he really thought they were fooled. They know what you are, you *gringo* jerk, Grace thought as she watched him through the window. Do you think they can't hear you yell at me at night? One of these days, she threatened, "I'm going to sew your prick shut and make you pee out your nose."

Surprised that she'd uttered the vulgar statement out loud, she turned around quickly to make sure Glory hadn't heard her. She didn't usually talk like that, and she sure didn't want Glory to pick up such language. If Glory swore when she got to school, her teachers and classmates could say it was because she was Mexican, and they might use her bad language for another excuse to dislike her.

Judy, one of Grace's cousins, had trouble fitting in at school. She went her first six years of school with no friends. Grace remembered how, before Valentine's Day, she'd spent days crafting little valentines, counting them over and over to make sure she had one for each schoolmate. The whole family had helped her decorate her shoebox with rows and rows of crepe paper. The top was decorated with red hearts cut from construction paper. When the big day came, everyone opened their boxes and the valentine greetings overflowed the tops of their desks. She opened her box and it was almost empty.

By the time she had reached the third grade she no longer expected or even hoped for seasonal cards or party invitations. The school dances were a nightmare that she dreaded for days before and after until she gave up and started to stay home, saying she was sick. By the time she got to high school she was so traumatized she just dropped out. Grace was determined that Glory would fit in better than her cousin had.

Because Dwayne always left their quarters before she woke up, Glory hadn't seen her father all day. Grace had to shut her eyes and turn away from the window so she wouldn't see Glory rush out the door to get attention from the very person who was making her sick. The worse Dwayne treated them, the more Glory clung to him; Grace shook her head and gave up trying to figure it out. She peeked out the window and watched Glory reach out to grab Dwayne's legs in a big hug. Dwayne gave her a quick pat on the head, and then ignored her.

"It wouldn't hurt you to put your arms around her," Grace hissed at the window.

Soon, the neighbor made an excuse to go on his way and Dwayne put out his cigarette and rushed for the back door, not noticing that he left a bare-footed Glory standing alone on the hot, parched grass. Grace looked at him in disbelief. Why didn't he pick her up and bring her in? She ran to the screen door and yelled, "Dwayne, go back and pick up Glory!"

As he came through the screen door with Glory under one arm and a green bundle under the other arm, he swore, "Jesus, it's hot!" His heavily-starched dark green fatigues stuck to the back of his body and left dark wet spots that spread until they joined the wet spots underneath his arms. Another wet line followed his webbed belt down the back seam of his pants, where it traveled to places Grace didn't want to think about.

"Grace. Tea. Lots of it," Dwayne said as he entered the kitchen.

"We're out of tea, Dwayne. I made Kool-Aid." She handed him the glass she'd poured for her sister as he headed for the couch for his daily siesta.

"A quick twenty-winks and I'll be ready for dinner. Oh, first, look what I got."

Grace went to the kitchen table where Dwayne laid down an old Army green towel. Whatever it was had Dwayne in a high state of excitement. The last roll of the towel revealed a gun—a big chrome pistol with a pearl handle.

"What is that for? Hunting?" Grace asked.

"Naw, I got hunting rifles. This is for shooting people."

"What people? Where?" Grace nervously asked.

"Well, you never know. I got it just in case from a sergeant on post who was broke but wanted me to work on his car. I might take it to Japan with me, if the Army will let me."

Dwayne went to strap the pistol to the head of the iron bed in his and Grace's room. Grace followed him, weakly protesting that it wasn't a good idea to have a gun around Glory.

"She won't touch it. I'll whip her butt," he growled.

The discussion over, he went to the couch and laid down for his nap. Grace's knees felt weak. *Why the gun? This wasn't the first crazy thing Dwayne had done, but it was the most dangerous. Maybe he was going to take it to Japan with him. But, then, why did he have to strap it to their bed?* Feeling helpless, Grace pushed the gun out of her mind and finished supper while Dwayne napped.

The one thing that Dwayne seldom complained about was the meals. A lot of times, though, there wasn't much to cook. While she covered the food to keep it warm, Grace dreamed again about the day she'd drive herself to the grocery store and buy everything she wanted. *What would it feel like to just get in the car and drive herself to the store—to open her refrigerator and see cartons of milk and orange juice?* On the second shelf, she dreamed of a small package of hamburger and a box of strawberries.

Maybe, when Dwayne got a promotion, he'd give her more money for food.

She just hoped he didn't spend it all on that crazy cattle ranch he told everyone was his but really belonged to his mother. Whenever anyone was around, he'd always loudly tell Grace that the fences needed to be repaired, and he needed to buy more cows, a new tractor, and put in a pond. What a blowhard.

It took her years, but Grace finally figured out that Dwayne had three priorities: his ranch, his sisters, and his white friends. Lots of times, Grace knew, Dwayne beat her after he got a burr under his saddle because he felt his white friends thought she wasn't good enough to pal around with them and their wives.

Actually, Grace and her family were a mix of Mexican, with French and Spanish ancestors on both sides of their family tree. But Grace and her family understood early on that the "one drop rule" applied to all races in Oklahoma, not only to people who had one drop of Negro blood in them. It took just one drop of the wrong blood color to shut doors to nightclubs, country clubs, and even some churches. Tired of trying to explain their heritage to people who already had their minds made up, Grace and her family had given up years ago. They were Mexican. Period. Take it or leave it.

From the beginning, Grace had tried to get along with the white women who were married to Dwayne's friends. She found that they were nice as pie to her when the men were around, but the minute the men left, they wouldn't talk to her—especially if they were out in public.

For her part, Grace was just as prejudiced against them. She often told her sisters that the women Dwayne's friends brought to the house were sloppy, vulgar, booze-drinking riffraff. Not only that, but they thought nothing of their unkempt nails or the shoes they wore with run-down heels. Grace would forgive that in a minute in a poor person, but these women had husbands who made good money. *Why couldn't they fix up a little? Maybe do their nails? Shave under their arms?*

The food would soon be cold. How long was he going to sleep? Maybe a few subtle noises. She cautiously dropped a pan lid on the counter. It wasn't a loud noise, just enough to wake him up.

"Oh Dwayne, did I wake you?" Before he could answer, she added, "Dinner's ready, are you hungry?" Grace spoke carefully, and tried to put a lilt in a voice that had had the lilt beaten out of it months ago.

She really didn't care if she woke him or not. She didn't care if he were hungry or not. She just desperately wanted to avoid Dwayne's fists. Maybe now, she also had to avoid Dwayne's gun.

❧   ❧   ❧

Dwayne was sure the noise was an accident. She wouldn't dare do it on purpose—he'd jerk a knot in her tail, by God. Anyway, he *was* hungry. The captains and majors he liked to kiss up to had gone to lunch today and hadn't invited him to go along. They probably went to the officers' club, and he didn't fit in there. Embarrassed that he wasn't invited, he had stayed in the motor pool through lunch and worked on an artillery mock-up.

A bunch of foreign officers were due to visit this week to look at Fort Sill's artillery, and they'd all parade through his area. Yessir, they'd be lookin' at all the weapons and jabberin' in some foreign language to each other and saying God-only-knows-what.

He didn't know what country they were coming from and he didn't care. It just frosted his butt that, so far, he'd been sent to England, France, and even Africa to teach artillery classes. He didn't think they should give America's secrets away to foreign armies, even if they *were* allies. Who knew which side they'd be on in the next war? There was even a rumor about maybe bringing Germans over here to train. Germans! Jesus Christ, where the hell did the Army get such crazy ideas? Why don't we just send them over some new tanks and guns so they can start another damn war with our own artillery?

At the table, Dwayne looked at Glory's dark face and got even madder. He just couldn't get through to Grace that he didn't want a daughter who looked like a little pickaninny. *Keep the kid inside, for God's sake.*

And was that hair of hers turning darker? It had better not, or there would be hell to pay. She used to be such a pretty little girl, but now the kid's coloring looked more like her mother's every day. Damn. He looked at Grace. Oh, well, no point in making a fuss. He wasn't dealing with a Mexican Einstein here.

What had he gone and gotten himself into? Was his dark-skinned wife the reason he hadn't been invited for lunch? Nah. They'd known about Grace for a long time, but he was sure she would hold him back eventually. To get anywhere in Oklahoma you'd better be the right color, live on the right side of the tracks, and be Baptist. Jesus, it was hot.

Dwayne had scooped a spoonful of fried potatoes into a tortilla to make a warm fragrant bundle when he spied the bowl of noodles. Without putting down his tortilla, he reached with his left hand for a spoonful but lost control of the spoon and the noodles before they got to his plate.

Glory saw the noodles do a surprise swan dive into Dwayne's beer goblet full of red Kool-Aid. Her eyes widened as the white noodles bobbed up and down in the cold red drink and mixed with the frosty ice cubes. His chest filled with rage as she giggled and clapped with glee. Dwayne was hot, hungry, tired, and already pissed off from a bad day at work. He did not see anything funny about his dinner noodles floating in a sea of red liquid. He looked at Grace, but she was smart enough not to laugh. She'd better not. He'd knock her silly.

Glory wasn't old enough to be that smart. On its way across the table to slap a little face too brown for its own good, Dwayne's hand knocked over his goblet and spilled a waterfall of Kool-Aid, noodles and ice cubes all across the table. This was too much. The sound of his anger exploded, bounced off the kitchen wall, shot over his family's heads, and out the rusted screen door. It didn't stop until it bounced off the far wall of Sako Hill's kitchen next door.

Dwayne was too busy throwing a fit to notice his frightened daughter grab a plate of homemade fudge and beat a hasty retreat to her closet. He didn't care that Grace and Glory hadn't eaten; *he* wore the pants in this family. Dinner was over when *he* said so, and if they didn't like it, too bad. As far as he was concerned, he could do whatever he wanted with his family, just like his dad did. They belonged to him. They'd damn well eat—or not—when he said so.

Without warning, he jumped up so fast his chair slammed against the wall. He grabbed Grace by her arm and dragged her back to their bedroom. The thumping began. What a day. As if being snubbed at work weren't enough, he was laughed at in his own home. Well, he wouldn't take any more shit from anybody. Especially Grace.

Thump. Grace's back hit the wall as Dwayne took out the frustrations of his day on his wife, the only person that he dared to hit. His friends were too big. Glory was too small.

Thump, thump.

Thump, thump, thump. Every time Dwayne hit Grace, she hit the bedroom wall and bounced back into his open hand, like a rubber ball attached to a wooden paddle with a long rubber band.

       ❧   ❧   ❧

Next door, Grace's cries of pain traveled like mortar shells and landed in Sako's kitchen. Sako and her husband Sergeant Hill caught their breath and tried to talk louder to distract their children from the fight next door. A small Japanese woman raised in much more elegant and well-mannered surroundings before her family's wartime internment, Sako had uneasily adapted to her new surroundings since she had married her soldier husband and moved to Oklahoma—a place, she had decided, that was nothing more than another internment camp, only with oil wells and assorted Indian chiefs. If the Indians had *really* stopped crying when they arrived in Oklahoma, the end of The Trail of Tears, she was sure they'd started back up again when they'd had a chance to look around.

Quickly, Sako turned the big radio in the living room up as loud as she dared to keep Daniel from becoming upset, while the sergeant hugged Ronnie who sat next to him. As soon as they did the dishes, they'd all settle down to listen to their favorite radio shows. It was the best they could do. They would have moved long ago if there were any place else they could afford to live, but their sick son used up every extra penny; they were lucky to find this place.

Her husband told her that reporting Dwayne to the military police was out of the question. An inquiry might somehow backfire, especially with a Japanese wife. If they were forced to leave military quarters, Sako and her husband didn't know where else they could afford to go. Housing in town was scarce right now because so many troops were moving their families back to town before they shipped out.

Also, Sergeant Hill had explained to Sako that it was too soon after the war, and the landlords in town might not rent to a soldier with a Japanese wife. It made no difference to them that Sako was born, raised, and educated in the United States. In fact, it made things worse; their own government had said the Japanese couldn't be trusted when it moved them away from the coast and set up internment camps for them.

Sako and her family experienced the war next door for the first time after they'd just moved in, several months ago. Then, they had shut the windows, but it was too hot to do that now. The quarters didn't have fans, much less air conditioners. To make matters worse, the windows in some of the quarters had been painted shut by sloppy maintenance men. Hot humid nights had been known to drive sleepless soldiers to grab a beer bottle and break out the panes, just to get a breath of air. Sako liked to joke that there was no danger of letting in mosquitoes, because they were all too big to fit through the broken glass.

Right after they'd first moved in, there was a fight next door. Sako had gone into her living room with a cup of coffee and studied its floor plan. Soon, she had begun to rearrange the furniture. Some of the mahogany furniture supplied by the army weighed more than she did, but she was in no mood to wait until her husband got home. She decided the first thing to do was move Daniel's bed into the far corner as far away from the Tyler's as possible. Next, she moved the big radio next to him.

Then she arranged the chairs into a small listening area to surround the radio and the hospital bed. Just minutes later she stood back and looked at the wall of heavy chairs and tables she'd created. "Sort of like being in a ruckin' bunker," she mumbled, mimicking the Japanese soldiers she saw in the '40s wartime movies Hollywood produced to support the war effort.

❦   ❦   ❦

Hours later, back at the Tyler's, Grace opened the curtain to Glory's closet. There was Glory, who'd fallen asleep where she'd hidden on top of the pile of duffel bags, her sweaty little body wrapped around what was left of a plate of fudge. Most of it was melted onto her new play clothes.

Grace curled up next to her on her bed, though it was uncomfortable. She was unwilling to sleep with Dwayne. Sometime during the night, Dwayne turned on the light and Grace thought he might come to look for her, but she went to the door of their bedroom and said that Glory had gotten sick, and she was going to stay up and watch her. There was little chance that Dwayne would get up to check on Glory himself.

He growled some more, but had little argument to make. Grace heard him mumble something about "That damn kid." Then he rolled over and went back to sleep.

CHAPTER 3

Leave For Texas

The next morning, Dwayne couldn't wait to get leave from his First Sergeant and head for Texas. The way things were going if he hung around home much longer, he'd end up in jail. The first hurdle would be the toughest: Sergeant Ortiz, the company clerk, had a desk right outside First Sergeant Howard's door.

If a troop wanted to see the First Sergeant, he had to go through the clerk. Not very many made it past the feisty Puerto Rican who was all spit and polish. He regularly sent troops back to the barracks to polish their brass or shine their shoes before he let them get past his desk. Soldiers he didn't like were sent back to their barracks so often they just gave up and forgot about whatever it was they wanted to ask him.

Dwayne looked down at his dusty shoes and tarnished brass and knew he'd never get past Sergeant Ortiz, so he hung around in the hallway until he saw him head for the bathroom with a cup of coffee and the newspaper. As soon as the clerk rounded the corner, Dwayne barged through the door to First Sergeant Howard's office.

The old artilleryman glared at him, and mumbled into his coffee cup, "Oh, Lord, I haven't even finished my first cup of coffee yet."

Sergeant Howard was one of the few men Dwayne had never been able to butter up with his funny stories and Texas twang, and his superior had long ago given up trying to hide his comments about Dwayne's sloppiness.

He could be in for a rough time. In the Army, the First Sergeant controlled his troops' lives twenty-four hours a day. He decided when they slept, when they got up, when they reported for work, and when they went home. Leaves were the same. The First Sergeant told them when they could go on vacation and when they had to be back. Period.

This was the Army, and in some ways, it was a love-hate relationship with Dwayne. The Army gave him the only security he'd ever had. The other side of the coin was that he was always being told what to do. Dwayne *hated* being told what to do.

"Uh, Sarge, I need to talk to you about getting some leave. Uh, I really need it."

"What's the problem, *now*, Sergeant?" asked Sergeant Howard. Every night he went home and swore to his wife that there were no soldiers in the Army anymore, only chronic whiners.

"It's my mom, Sarge," Dwayne lied. "The fence on the ranch is all broken down and she's got cows runnin' all over the road. You know, since my dad died…" Dwayne counted on his sarge not knowing that his dad had died years ago, and his mom had lived in a mental institution since just before Dwayne joined the Army. The weary man raised his hand to stop the spiel.

"Sergeant Tyler, you're a sorry excuse for a soldier, and if it weren't for those good-for-nothing officers you hang out with, I'd bust your sorry ass 'til it was lower than a horny toad's," he took a swig of hot coffee and went on, "and I'd sooner spit on my own birthday cake than let you have any time off, but every soldier in this unit had better have their personal problems settled and be ready to ship out. Even you. Can you do it in a week?" he asked.

"Yes Sir, I think I can, Sarge."

"Well, do it and get back here. Remember, you also have to find housing for your wife and daughter. They won't be able to stay in military housing after you've gone. This whole damn fort will be on its way to Japan in two weeks," said the First Sergeant.

Normally, each soldier earned thirty-days of leave a year, but this year most wouldn't get it, unless they wanted to take it in Tokyo. As much as he disliked Dwayne, giving him a week to take care of personal business couldn't be avoided.

"Yes, Sir, I'll be back in a week."

"One more thing," Sergeant Howard said as he stood up and leaned over his desk. He lowered his voice, and growled threateningly, "don't you *ever* come in here without the company clerk's permission again. And don't you *ever* address me as "Sarge" or "Sir" again. You've been in the Army long enough to know you are to address me as First Sergeant, and *only* First Sergeant."

"Yes, sir, First Sergeant Howard!"

"Now get out of here, I don't want to see you in here again. You're a disgrace to the battalion."

Dwayne felt his First Sergeant watch him leave the office. When he turned away, he smirked and said aloud to himself, "You might not like me, Sarge, but you can't touch me. All the officers love me, and they'll kick your butt all the way to Tallahassee and back if you even think of laying one hand on their fishing buddy. I'm *in*, Sarge, and there's nothing you can do about it."

To himself he grinned over how cleverly he'd made friends with the officers. Dwayne was working himself to the top with a fishing pole. He hadn't figured out yet just how he would profit from their friendship, but how could it be a bad thing to be on a first name basis with an officer? Somehow, eventually, all of his fishing know-how would put an extra dollar in his pocket. Had to.

On his way out of Sergeant Howard's office he passed Sergeant Ortiz on his way back to his desk. It was obvious Dwayne had been in to see the First Sergeant; there was no other office at the end of the hall. Just as he called Dwayne back to question him, Dwayne scooted around the corner. If he were ever asked why he didn't stop, Dwayne could say he didn't hear him. The clerk wouldn't be fooled, but there would be nothing he could do about it.

As he slid behind the wheel of his old Ford, he took a deep breath, and wondered why in hell he had to put up with so many people tellin' him what to do? "Be back in a week," he sneered. "I'll be back when I want to be back, by God." But deep down, he knew he *would* be back in a week, because Sarge said so. It made Dwayne mad as hell.

He shot into the motor pool building where he kept his artillery mock-ups. He had to get all of his equipment ready to be shipped to Japan. He estimated that if he kept at it, he could have his work organized and be ready to leave for Texas right after dinner.

He wasn't totally lying about his mother needing help. When he'd moved her to that crazy hospital in Houston, he'd hired a ranch foreman to take care of the place, but without funds to make the fence and equipment repairs the man said were needed, there wasn't a lot he could do.

None of his brothers and sisters had shown any interest in the land their parents had spent their lives building up.

At first, Dwayne had kept his siblings informed about what was going on at the homestead his parents had turned into a ranch. He'd even sent them certified copies each year that proved he'd paid the taxes. In his mind, he thought his brothers and sisters would want to chip in for all of the expenses so that they would always have a home to go back to. A letter from his sister one day made it clear he was on his own. He had the letter right there in his glove compartment, but he didn't have to dig it out to read it; he had it memorized:

ॐ

Dear Dwayne, our visit to the ranch was the first in many years. Bertha and I couldn't believe the mess it was in. Funny, but when we were kids it never bothered us that the house is right in the middle of the pasture. The flies out there are so big and thick Sis and I couldn't even go out on the porch to cool off.

We never saw a snake, although your foreman warned us they were all over. But both of us got eaten up by chiggers when we tried to go out and pick some roses off of Mama's climbing rose bush that grows on the back side of the old chicken house. And the spiders! They were everywhere. Bertha says they're black widows, although I wouldn't know.

Cord says the raccoons find a way into the henhouse no matter how much screen he puts up, and it was a bloody mess when we were there. Not only that, but wild wolves or coyotes or *something* came right up to the bedroom screens at night, and looked right in at us. They scared us to death.

And those are the sorriest-looking cows we've ever seen, Dwayne. They're so dirty I'll bet they sleep on their own cowpies, and I'm sure they're full of fleas, maybe even ticks.

We say the best thing to do is let the whole place go. Save yourself the trouble. If you decide to keep it and want our help, we have to honestly say that we'd rather raise scorpions under our beds in old shoe boxes than put any of our money into cattle ranching.

If you want it, it's all yours, as far as we're concerned. Most likely, our brothers will feel the same way. We wish you all the best, Dwayne. Give our love to Grace and Glory.

Your Sis, Helen

P.S. Before we left, we did take some cuttings from Mama's roses. We thought that they were the only things we wanted to remember about home. Everything else there brought back too many painful memories. Helen

After that letter, Dwayne had given up on any hope that they'd ever pay their share of the taxes or any other expenses for the ranch. As far as he knew, the ranch would belong to his mother until she died in that mental hospital in Houston, but after that it would be his. Then he could really start to build it up.

In the back of his mind he knew the constant beatings his father had given his mother had caused her to have a mental breakdown;

but he justified his father's actions against his mother and his own with Grace, by telling himself that the two women deserved a good beating. For what, he wasn't sure. Unless it was like his dad always said, "Any woman who doesn't do what her man tells her is a god-damned whore."

When Dwayne got home he was ready for the fight he didn't dare have with his First Sergeant.

"Grace," he yelled, "I'm packin' my bag and goin' to Texas tonight. Is dinner ready?" He stuffed his leather satchel while he talked as if he were running from the law.

"Yes, I fixed Spanish spaghetti, it's on the stove. I'll call Glory," Grace answered as she turned and left the hallway. He didn't see the relief on her face.

At the table, Dwayne loaded his plate with spaghetti noodles fried Mexican style with tomatoes, onions, and garlic, and two buttered Mexican biscuits. He still itched for a fight, so he repeated the same old story he had told Grace from the beginning as he ate. "I hope you don't go and beg me to take you two with me. You know my family doesn't cotton to Mexicans. We lost a lot of our good men down there to Santa Anna. My family sure as hell wouldn't look fondly on me if I brought a Mexican and a half-breed kid to the ranch."

As he ate the noodles, he looked up at Grace's face. She showed no emotion and made no sound. Dwayne looked at Glory. She looked as if she might ask what a half-breed was, but he started to talk again before she could get the words out.

"Oh, no, there is no way I'm taking a pepper-belly to Texas." He looked at Grace again.

Still no reaction.

He tried again, just begging for a fight, "You can just stay home and make cute little outfits for Glory on that old sewing machine your sister dug out of the trash and dragged over here."

"Would you like some more spaghetti, Dwayne?" Grace smiled sweetly, but underneath the table, her fingers dug into her leg. He nodded yes, and she got up and refilled his plate at the stove.

Just before he went out the door, he turned and told her, "And you'd better not be sewing stuff for that family of yours. I'm not running a goddamned charity here," Dwayne said smugly.

"I won't, Dwayne," Grace promised. She pulled Glory onto her lap and buttered the last biscuit for her as he left.

Women who worked, he had often told her, were nothing but whores, like most women nowadays were anyway. He wouldn't have people talk about his wife behind his back. Deep down, he knew that his beliefs weren't about religion, truth, or even culture. Dwayne wanted control.

If Grace worked and earned money, she might figure out that she could leave him. She *might* even begin to believe she was as good or even *better* than he was. He could never allow that to happen. Grace would do things his way; he was the boss in his family. "If the other men her sisters married want to let those crazy women walk all over them, well, they can do whatever they want," Dwayne muttered out loud as he hurried to his car. "Those bastards just better not come crying to me when they discover they aren't the boss of *anything*."

With one hand he absentmindedly tucked his cowboy shirt into his jeans. He didn't have a cowboy belt with a big silver buckle, or boots. In their place, he wore a plain black leather belt from an old suit. On his feet he wore old black low-quarter Army shoes that originally were worn with his dress uniform. At least he had a straw cowboy hat. He'd really need that. For now, he didn't care about the rest of what he wore, as long as he got out of there. When he got to the ranch, he'd change into his black Army combat boots to work on the fence.

Dwayne looked back over his shoulder as he rushed across the backyard. He'd heard those sisters of Grace's tell her that she should pack up a bag and jump in the back seat with Glory whenever he headed his car for the ranch. He knew *they'd* do it, if it were them; they were so goddamned pushy.

He wasn't sure about their mother, either. All those women had a way of smiling and agreeing with him and then going ahead and doing things their own way. Since he'd gotten into this family, Dwayne had never been agreed with so much and obeyed so little.

And that damn Spanish they used. People in this country should speak English. He suspected they used their language to hide things from him; he was well aware that when they were alone they spoke English most of the time. Grace told him once that they only spoke Spanish when they were around her mother because she preferred it. It was a matter of respect. He wasn't buying that. What kind of joker did those women take him for?

None of the white men in the family spoke Spanish, but it didn't seem to bother the other husbands that they couldn't understand the women the way it did him. He wanted to tell them that they'd never get anywhere if they kept on spending so much time with the girls' family and letting all that foreign talk go on right in front of them, but he didn't figure it'd do any good. Someday, they'd wake up and smell the coffee, but by then, He would already be on his ranch sittin' on a big ole pile of beef cows.

He figured it would take him the most of a week to get the fences fixed even if he had some help. The trip alone was eight hours each way. He threw a carton of Camels on the front seat and his leather satchel in the trunk of the old Ford. He hardly bothered to wave goodbye to Glory as he left in a cloud of red dust, with never a thought about his neighbors' open windows. He was also in too much of a hurry to notice that his secret savings book, one that Grace didn't know about, had fallen out of his back pocket and lay on the ground, already half-covered in dust.

As soon as he left, Grace went back to their bedroom to see if he'd taken the gun. It was still there—so it wasn't for the ranch.

❧   ❧   ❧

On old Highway 44, Dwayne was too excited to get sleepy. By morning, he'd be on his parents' old homestead with his cows. No captains or majors there to boss him around. In Texas, he was the boss. Someday, he'd have the ranch built up to where he could just retire there and raise his Herefords.

Grace and Glory never entered into his future plans, but neither did anyone else. Dwayne always had trouble imagining just what sort of woman he'd end up with after he dumped Grace. He tried and tried, but he could never fill in that part of the picture. All he knew was that she'd be pretty and white, obey his every wish, and not get in the way too much. One more thing: she'd have to live on the ranch with him and not hang around with her family all the time. Whoever she turned out to be, he'd lay down the law.

Traffic was light on the highway that led to Wichita Falls. When darkness fell, there wasn't much to do except keep the car on the road and watch out for deer and coyotes. This would be a hot trip during the day; even now it was ninety-two degrees. Dwayne rolled all of the windows down and turned on a country station that played the twangy kind of music he grew up listening to. Good old Hank, Ernest, and the other Grand Old Oprey singers. He knew all the words by heart: *"Your cold, cold heart will tell on you"*—*"I'm walking the floor over you, I can't sleep a wink that is true…"* Dwayne sang along in his weak, creaky voice and dreamed about the pretty blond he'd met at a honky-tonk off post. Now there was a lady a man could take most anywhere. Yep. She had it all. Pretty. Tall. Blond. She was probably even Baptist, though things like that didn't often come up in taverns, so he didn't know for sure.

He didn't ever carry a thermos on these long trips. He preferred to make frequent stops at dusty little run-down coffee shops along the highway. He spotted one up ahead with just a few cars in the parking lot. Joe's Java, the sign said. He wondered if they had any chocolate cake to go with their coffee?

Dwayne loved these road trips. He was a good listener and people told him the damnedest things. More than once, he had been dragged down to a basement somewhere to admire a collection of rocks or guns or some such thing. He was interested in everything. Before he'd joined the Army, he'd never gotten off the ranch, so he liked to get a peek into other people's lives, especially if he thought they'd made a lot of money. Each time, before he left, he'd made a friend, shared some laughs, and told a few stories of his own.

No one could deny that Dwayne could tell stories with the best of them. Maybe that was why he liked to travel so much like this: to find new people to hear his stories and to hear that laughter all over again as if he were telling the story for the first time.

Back in his car, still headed toward East Texas while the radio hummed in the background, his thoughts went back to Grace. What was he going to do about her? When her parents had forbidden their marriage he'd married her anyway just to prove to them, especially that puny little old father of hers, that no Mexican would ever tell *him* what to do.

He'd pushed Grace into becoming his wife even though he'd always known his family outside Athens, Texas would never accept a pepper-belly. She was as sweet as she could be, and sexy, too, but she was all wrong for him. He had plans to live on the ranch someday, surrounded by his relatives, and she would never be accepted down there.

Dwayne couldn't admit, even to himself, he had married her for another reason: when he joined the Army, he found himself away from home and lonely. Dwayne had never taken the union seriously, and the vows taken in a justice of the peace's office above the old Murrey's Movie Theater had never slowed down his pursuit of pretty blond women who were crazy about him—for a short while. Fresh off the ranch, he'd met Grace right after he'd gotten to Fort Sill, before he found out how attractive he was to women. If he'd only known, he could have had one of those long-legged Texas gals with blond hair and big tits.

Actually, he couldn't. Dwayne had soon found out it would be hard to keep up with a white gal who knew what was what. He could spend a little time with a woman like that, but when they'd been with him awhile, they'd get a sense there was a lot lacking in Dwayne.

"Sure," one girl had flat-out told him, "you're good-lookin' Hon, but you're unpolished, uneducated, backward, and bossy." After a few dates, other savvy white girls as much as told him there was no way they'd ever take him home to meet Mom and Dad.

Because of his drunkard father, Dwayne had a childhood so twisted and cruel he could never fit into a normal family. Down deep, he knew that. His dad drank from sun-up to sundown and usually beat the tar out of his mom before he passed out. There were relatives all around but none of them would step in and interfere with what a man did with his own family. They were his; he could do what he wanted with them.

Grace's mom and dad were different. They didn't speak much English and were easy to push around. Once he and Grace were married, they knew they were stuck and quietly accepted him. Besides, Grace's father, Juan, was too sick with cancer to raise much of a fuss. It was easy for Dwayne to keep them a little afraid of him, to keep them in their place. It wasn't unintentional that he never knocked when he went to their house, always made fun of their backgrounds, and laughed at them because they had to sign an "X" on their legal documents. Someday, another family that wasn't Mexican would be a lot harder to control, but he could deal with that later.

Well, for sure, he decided as he drove down the narrow highway, Grace and Glory had to go sooner or later. Might as well make the break when he went to Japan. That way he could start to put all of his extra money into the ranch as soon as he got back. He knew her sisters would help her leave him if they ever found out what all was going on, but when anyone left, it would be him, and if she didn't watch out, he'd put her in that crazy house with his mother before he left. He could do it too. All it would take was a few phone calls. One of his friends on post had told him just how to set it up. Then where would Gloria be? he smirked.

Who knew if Glory were even his? Maybe Grace had whored around just like her sisters; some other guy might be Gloria's father. Everyone said she looked just like him, but maybe they just said that to his face, and laughed behind his back. All that stuff he told Grace about taking Glory away from her was all a bluff; it was one of the ways he kept her in line. He had no use for that kid. Hell, she was already turning dark; she'd probably grow up dumb as a rock.

Yes, he might as well wait until he shipped out to tell Grace he was kicking them out. No use in having every Mexican in town after him. Dwayne especially dreaded the thought of having to fight with Grace's sisters, and their mother wouldn't be any easier to deal with. He swore she was getting more like her girls everyday. Like the night at Vera's when she'd said she would keep her house. Those women wouldn't put up with any of his crap once they found out he was leaving Grace.

Shit. He'd rather fight the Japanese than Grace's sisters. He wasn't worried about the brothers in her family, though. They wouldn't dare cross him, he'd send them to jail quicker than a jackrabbit breeds and they knew it.

Darkness swallowed up the little black car as it drove into the night on a highway hugged by a sandy shoulder that stretched on either side for miles. Songs on a hillbilly radio station droned on and on about love that had gone wrong and then gone wrong again and finally went to the grave, still goin' wrong.

Dwayne hardly noticed when it finally began to cool off. It was late and the road was straight; there wasn't another car in sight any-where. He could have floorboarded it and no one would have cared. The only thing that stopped him was the fact that his old car was already going almost forty, and that was as fast as he had ever dared to push it. He was in no hurry anyway; if he got there too early, everyone would still be asleep and he wouldn't even be able to get a cup of coffee. He reached over and grabbed a pack of cigarettes from the carton.

He had just lighted another Camel and looked out the window when his eyes caught something in the headlights. There, in the middle of nowhere, on a dark night with a sky full of big ole Texas stars, a huge cougar playfully kept pace with the glow from the car's headlights as it moved along the side of the road. The big cat, spotlighted against the darkness, stretched its long, golden body in a short race against speed and light across the desert sand. Its muscles flexed and rippled as it nimbly leaped over tumbleweeds and rocks. He saw it for just a few seconds before it dropped back, unable to keep up with the car for long.

Luckily, it hadn't tried to cross the road in front of him. It'd be a shame to kill it, although he briefly wondered how his new pistol would have handled a cat that big. Maybe he should have brought it. If he hadn't left in such a hurry, he would have.

Even if he didn't want to shoot cougars, he could have sighted it in. The ranch was a good place to do something like that.

Dwayne smoked his cigarette and turned up the radio; the large animal was forgotten before the song was over, even though cougar sightings were no longer common in Texas.

Truth be told, he usually pretty much forgot everything that didn't put money in his pocket, one way or another.

CHAPTER 4

Sewing Her Ticket to Freedom

Just as Grace was waking up the next morning her hand bumped the leather holster that held Dwayne's new pistol to the bed. Once she woke up enough to realize what it was, she sat up in bed and stared at the pistol. Glory came running in and found her mother looking fearfully at the firearm.

"Daddy's got a gun like Ronnie's! Can I play with it?"

"No! Glory, it's not a toy gun. It's real. Promise Mommy you'll never touch it." The urgency in her voice puzzled Glory.

"Okay, Mommy, I won't." Glory seemed to lose all interest in the gun after that. Grace never saw her look at it again, even on mornings when she crawled into bed with her mother. Grace thought that must be the difference between little girls and boys. She was sure Ronnie would have had that gun strapped on and fired before Sako had finished her first cup of coffee.

Grace attacked her chore list with a panicky fervor to keep her mind off the pistol. On the way to her kitchen, which was already hot, she pulled her long, thick hair back into a ponytail to keep it off her neck. First, she had to wash and starch Dwayne's fatigues in the kitchen sink so that they could dry while she sewed. If they weren't hanging in his closet when he got home, "There'd be hell to pay," she mumbled to herself, picturing Dwayne as he threw one of his fits.

Long ago, she'd stopped wondering why he insisted on his uniforms being perfectly starched and ironed, only to lie down on the couch in them at lunch and take a quick nap before he went back to work. Didn't he ever look in the mirror? If there ever was a contest for sloppiest soldier on post, Grace was sure Dwayne would win it.

Once, she'd washed the fatigues in the kitchen sink after dinner and hung them outside at night so that she'd have more time to sew in the daytime, but the next morning, they had bug eggs all over them. She didn't know which bugs and she didn't care. She just knew a lot of hard work had almost gone down the drain. Luckily, she'd been able to spot clean the egg stains and iron right over them. Of course, she never told Dwayne; he would have insisted she wash the fatigues and start all over. What he didn't know wouldn't hurt him. Ever since the egg-laying trouble, she'd done her drying in the daytime. Early. Before Sako filled up the shared clothesline between the two buildings with *her* husband's fatigues.

Grace's mother had brought over Aunt Lilia's fabric earlier in the week. Grace always hid her sewing projects in Glory's toy box until she was ready to work on them. Since Dwayne paid little attention to Glory, there wasn't much chance that he'd find material hidden in her room.

She laid a paper pattern on the kitchen table and smoothed it out with her hands. She'd sewn the same pattern for Aunt Lilia before, so all of the size adjustments were already made. She found the little green print at the bottom of the paper sack and took it to the kitchen sink where she dipped it in hot water to preshrink it.

It would be faster to dry it outside, but the hot Oklahoma sun would fade the material as fast as it dried it. Besides, in this heat, the lightweight fabric would dry soon enough inside. While she was at it, she dipped the zipper and bias tape in the hot water too. She knew from experience that if she didn't, the material would pucker around them after the dress was washed.

There were many tricks in the dressmaking trade, and Grace mastered most of them when other girls her age were in high school.

❧   ❧   ❧

Grace had always liked school and had cried when her mother said the younger children had to stay home after the third grade because the local school in Cyril had begun to charge a fee for each student, and their mother and father could only afford to send the oldest girls and boys. To make herself useful, she began to help with the chores and the younger children. Some of them weren't even her mother's, but babies and toddlers that were dropped off by aunts and cousins on their way to live their own life, while they took away hers.

So, while her brothers and sisters went to the cotton fields and school, Grace turned the big red barn connected to the house into a nursery; she even got her poppa to hang a makeshift cradle with rope from the big beams that ran the length of the building. She used it to rock her brother Benny when he was an infant. The closeness of the barn to the kitchen also enabled her to be available to help her mother with the cooking. In the evenings, she crocheted lace on sheets and pillowcases for her mother to give away as gifts.

Since she seldom left the farm, there was no need to spend money or time on her appearance. When her hair got too long, her mother would put a bean bowl over her head and quickly chop around the edge of it with a pair of old kitchen shears that were so dull they shredded the hair more than cut it. She wore hand-me-downs several times over that she often held up with a belt made from a thin piece of rough rope her father had found in the barn.

Even as a child, Grace hadn't had much to look forward to. Once, on a particularly bleak day in the barn, Grace had worn a pair of high heel shoes that belonged to Vera. By the end of the day, the shoes were ruined. She had known what would likely happen to the shoes when she put them on, but she didn't care. The feeling she got from wearing them was worth anything her sister could do to her when she got caught.

As she thought back, she couldn't remember how Vera got the shoes, or what had happened to her when Vera caught her with them. Perhaps Poppa had stepped in to protect her. Today, she still didn't have much, but she'd turned out to be the prettiest of the four sisters, even if they did have fancier clothes.

❦   ❦   ❦

She had long ago gotten over the pain of being kept out of school. But sometimes, especially after a bad night with Dwayne, she thought about what her life would have been like, not only if she'd gone to school, but if she had been born someplace else, like New York. Maybe she could have gone to a fancy art school and become a famous dress designer. Places like that had teachers who knew it all: tailoring, sewing on lingerie fabric, and even hat-making. Magazines were her lifeline to the fashion world, and her sisters kept her well supplied with theirs.

While the fabric dripped onto a pad of old newspapers on the floor, she tried to mentally calculate how much, if any, material would be leftover to make something for Glory or herself. She could use a new blouse. The one she wore actually had little holes worn in the middle of each side on the front where her nipples rubbed the fabric from the inside.

Her sister, Pauline, came to the door pleading, "Gracie, open the door."

Grace turned to see her sister loaded down with one of her mother's large pans.

"What is that?" She asked as she rushed to open the screen door.

"Watermelon. Vera went to see Uncle Joe and he gave her the biggest one in the garden. Sixty-five pounds, we weighed it on Momma's old scales. He said it was too big for him to eat. Sis, we just barely touched it with the point of the butcher knife and it snapped open. It's the most perfect melon I've ever seen."

"But why did you peel it? We could have just sliced it ourselves."

"Well, after we divided it up, Aunt Lilia called and when she found out about it she put dibs on the rind to make watermelon pickles. Momma cut it off and we took it to her."

Just then, she looked down at the two holes in the front of Grace's clean, freshly pressed white blouse.

"Grace, what's wrong with your shirt?"

"Pauline, this blouse is so old I've worn holes in the front," Grace said as she held the blouse away from her body to get a better look.

"*Ayyy*! We've got to take you shopping while Dwayne is gone," her sister laughed.

"No, that would raise too many questions."

"Like what?" Pauline asked as she poured a cup of coffee.

"Like when did I leave the house? Who was I with? Who did I see? And what was I doing spending money when things are so tight? And not only that, but just who was I dressing up for? Had I been running around while he was gone? It will be easier to just sew some pockets over the holes."

Pauline shook her head. That man was hopeless. And maybe, so was her sister. She decided to change the subject.

"So Aunt Lilia's getting a new dress," Pauline said when she saw the green print fabric dripping dry.

"How did you know it was for her?"

"She picks out the same type of material every time."

"Yes," Grace admitted, "she does like small-flowered prints. I tried once to get her to pick a larger print so it would be in better proportion to her size, but she's very sentimental. Her mom used to buy this type of fabric for her when she was a little girl."

"Grace, she's sixty-years old."

"To each his own. Wasn't it you who had me sewing a dress with huge shoulder pads, just like Barbara Stanwyck's, last month?" Grace kidded.

"Yeah, that was me, and I look darn good in it. I guess we all have our fantasies."

"Well, all right, then. Did you see Glory when you came in?"

"Yes, she's out in the hot sun, playing cowboys with the neighborhood Jesse James. I hope she doesn't get heatstroke out there."

"She never seems to notice the heat." Grace changed the subject by asking, "Pauline, do you know anyone who would like to have some sewing done when Dwayne goes overseas? I don't know how much money he'll send me and I have to be able to take care of Glory." She hadn't told anyone in her family that she planned to leave Dwayne as soon as he got sent overseas. There would be time enough to drop that bombshell later.

"Not now, but I'll ask around. Well, I've got to go. I'm putting your milk and orange juice in the refrigerator with the watermelon. I'm going to have to get a little red wagon to carry all of the groceries if Uncle Joe keeps gardening."

When Pauline opened the door to the refrigerator, the air that rushed out was hardly cool. She touched the stored food to see if it was cold. It was, but just barely. She added the milk and juice to the other foods and was glad Grace only asked her to buy a quart of milk at a time. Hopefully, it wouldn't last long enough to spoil.

"Oh, I almost forgot. I brought a pair of Uncle Joe's pants. Can you put in a new zipper before he gets arrested?"

"That's easy. I even have some extra zippers on hand. I'll fix them tonight."

"Good. It's either that, or he'd better move to the back porch."

"Are you working at the USO again today?"

"Yes, and today's payday, so I don't want to be late. They only schedule me three days a week for three hours a day, but it's better than nothing, and at least I know how to use a cash register now.

Momma asked me if I was selling cigarettes. I was afraid she was going to ask me to quit."

"Well, *are* you selling cigarettes?" Grace laughed.

"Not you too. When is your ranch dude due back?"

"In a week."

"I hope a bull throws him over a fence and knocks a little sense into him."

"Can't. The fence is down, that's why he's gone."

Pauline raised her cup and grinned, "A toast to downed fences! You, know, in Europe, they throw their cups into the fireplace after a toast."

"Sis, you've been reading those romance novels again. Look around. Do you see any fireplaces?"

"If you'd listened to me, you would have married better."

"Yeah," Grace cut her off, "better and more often."

"I could have kept the first one," Pauline laughed, "if I'd been willing to get a bigger apartment to accommodate all of his girlfriends."

"Get out of here. I've got work to do," Grace said.

"How much money is Mom holding for you now?" Pauline asked as she left.

"I'm not sure. Maybe around three hundred dollars. I keep telling her to take some out for her groceries but I don't know if she ever does. Do you know where she keeps it? In the top drawer of her chest in her bedroom. *Ay, Caramba!* I hope some *bandito* doesn't come in and take it all."

"I'll see if I can get her to hide it better. You know she'll never open a bank account. She's too embarrassed to have to sign an "X" for her signature in public."

"Yeah. I also heard her ask Aunt Lilia how would they know her "X" from a forger's when the check got back to the bank?"

"You know, that's a darn good question. Our little Mom isn't so dumb," Pauline laughed as she went out the door and headed for her car. The next thing Grace saw was her sister's old Packard slowly creep out of the parking strip in the alley; it barely raised any dust.

She grinned as she thought about how Pauline had decided one day to get a car and learn to drive and the next day she drove up in front of Grace's in an old gray Packard. That was just the way she was; she always seemed to come out on top. No man ever messed with her, and she never took any crap from anybody.

Actually, both of her older sisters had the nerve to tell an Apache warrior how the cow eats the cabbage. Her older sister, Vera, seemed to lie in wait for opportunities to tell some hapless man or woman where to go and how to get there without a map.

Where was her gumption? Why couldn't she be like her sisters? Just the thought ran chills through her body and she crossed herself and said a quick prayer. Like always, Grace told herself that she was trying to work out the problems in her marriage, but she knew better. She'd gone from the safety of Momma's home to live with Dwayne, so she'd never been on her own.

Even though living with Dwayne was a living hell, she didn't have to support herself and make decisions. In an unexplainable way, it was comfortable. A lot more comfortable than going out on her own was going to be when she left him.

Someday, she'd have to support herself and Glory, and find a place to live. A part of her wasn't looking forward to the responsibility of earning a living, and she kept hanging back, hoping for a way to avoid sticking her neck out. Either one of her sisters would have already lit a fire under Dwayne's butt and poured gasoline on the flames.

Tired of waiting for the fabric to dry, she decided to iron it dry the rest of the way. Even though she had lots of time, she didn't want to waste any of it. While the iron heated, she looked at a page torn out of a magazine her brother Frank, a musician, had sent over to her. He wanted to know if she could make a shirt like the one in the magazine. Grace snorted to herself. Like it? She could make one much better. She'd make him a fantastic shirt. If he dressed better when he was on stage, maybe he'd get more jobs. The local country western bands didn't seem to have much modesty in the clothing department, and Grace suspected that they hoped their loud shirts would make up for their lack of talent.

Unfortunately, their bright clothes also made them a better target, and Frank had told her he'd ducked more than one Hamm's beer bottle as it flew past him on stage. So far, he'd never been hurt, but he said the audience was like an angry bull—you never turned your back on it.

Sort of like Dwayne, Grace thought.

CHAPTER 5

The Neighborhood

Grace got carried away sewing and lost track of the time. It was almost two o'clock. Why hadn't Glory come inside for something to eat? Where was she? She went from window to window, but the play yard was deserted. If she didn't have so much trouble hearing, she would have noticed it was awfully quiet for an Army neighborhood full of kids. She turned off the iron and slipped on a pair of sandals; she'd better look for her.

She didn't have to go far; she found Glory right outside the kitchen door, out of sight of the kitchen window, gagged and tied to the clothesline pole—a forgotten cowgirl in a game of cowboys and Indians. Grace hurriedly untied her and took the cowboy hanky out of her mouth. Glory sobbed and gasped for breath as she fell into her mother's arms.

"Glory, why are you all tied up? Where are Ronnie and the rest of the kids?"

"We were playing cowboys and Indians," Glory sobbed, "then they all went inside for a drink and forgot to come out again," Glory blubbered as she threw her arms around Grace and wiped her wet nose on her mother's shoulder.

"When?"

"Before Aunt Pauly left."

"You've been out here all this time? You could have been burned to a crisp. Did your Aunt Pauline see you?"

"Yes, but she thought we were just playing."

Grace bathed her cowgirl in cool water, and then gave her a big glass of Kool-Aid and a bologna sandwich before she put her down for a nap and went back to her sewing.

Dwayne would have a fit when he saw his little girl as brown as a pinto bean. *Ay, ay, ay!* She'd have to talk to Sako about Ronnie and his antics. *If he were going in, why didn't he take Glory with him? Or bring her home?* He wasn't a bad boy; he just didn't think. Luckily, Glory wasn't seriously sunburned, but only because Grace had found her in time.

A mother with normal hearing would have noticed right away that something was wrong. She'd never forgive Dwayne for damaging her ears. Sometimes she thought he hit her there intentionally, having discovered a place he could hurt her that wouldn't show. It wouldn't do any good to ask a doctor about it. She didn't need a medical expert to tell her what was wrong with her ears.

She had to get away from him—but how? How would she support herself? She had little schooling and no training. She had to be able to support and care for Glory; otherwise the courts would take her away from Grace for sure. She cringed when she thought how Dwayne would tell a divorce judge about this cowgirl incident. He could make her look real bad. It would make a great example of how Grace was unfit to care for their daughter.

A few days later, Grace was watching the children play at her kitchen window when Ronnie announced to his soldiers that he would lead them on a dangerous mission to gather wild gourds for their Indian camp. His loud voice echoed between the buildings and caught Grace's attention. She couldn't understand everything he said, but she watched as all of his little troops lined up, prepared to follow Ronnie wherever he commanded them to go. Glory was at the very end of the line. Grace couldn't imagine what was going on, but it created a huge amount of excitement among his troops, so she decided to slip on her shoes and follow them.

She sneaked along behind them at a distance as the children chanted, "HUT, one, two, three, four. HUT, one, two, three, four," as they obediently followed Ronnie across the street. Down the road they went, right past the "US Government, Do Not Trespass" sign, and into off-limits territory over by the railroad tracks. It was off-limits for a good reason. The area held a maze of tracks that trains rolled over all day. Grace, and all of the other mothers had told the children over and over that they mustn't ever go in that area, but there they were, blindly following Ronnie wherever he led them.

A twinge of fear crept over her as she passed the warning sign and crouched in the tall grass to watch the children. What if the military police pulled up with their red lights flashing and arrested *her*?

Grace cringed when she saw that Glory couldn't keep up with the older kids, so she found an easier path, right down the middle of the railroad tracks. When the children heard a train in the distance, Ronnie lifted her off the track, but she'd dropped a sandal, and he didn't notice she'd gone back to get it. Just as Grace was ready to scream, Ronnie turned, saw Glory, and quickly snatched her off the track. Grace watched each car pass over the sandal—bam, clack-clack, bam, clack-clack, the heavily-loaded cars rocked from side to side as they were pulled by the engine along the worn, overused tracks. It wasn't difficult for Grace to see how the incident could have been tragic, but the children hardly noticed how close Glory had come to being run over by the train. They were on a maneuver, just like their soldier dads.

The kids stopped and pointed at the ground. Grace got on her knees and moved through the tall grass until she was close enough to see the huge rattlesnake skeletons the group discovered, coiled like they were ready to strike, underneath the large leaves of the wild gourd vines. The snakes were easily over four feet long when they were alive. She watched Glory skip around and pick little bouquets of buttercups and paintbrushes; sometimes the grass was so tall Grace almost lost sight of her. The flowers were laid in front of the makeshift grave-markers Ronnie made out of rocks for the snakes.

What had killed the rattlers? Grace wondered. She could see that the Army had sprayed a wide path of weed-killer that had killed the grass and left a broad brown path on each side of the track. Could the spray have killed the grass and the snakes, but not the gourd vines? She looked down and realized she was crouched in the same high grass the snakes had been in before the Army sprayed it. Panicked, she looked around to see if there were any snakes near her that she hadn't been able to hear. She broke out in a cold sweat even though she didn't see any.

Her first plan had been to stay hidden, but now she had a new plan: to get herself and the kids out of there as quickly as possible. While she raced to the children, she waved her arms and screamed real loud. It felt darn good, and might even have scared some snakes away.

The gourd-gathering forgotten, the kids reluctantly followed her back to the housing area empty-handed. They were all puzzled over a hysterical mother screaming about a few snake skeletons. "What's the big deal, anyway?" Ronnie whispered to Glory. "They were dead, weren't they?"

When she got the kids back to the housing area, moms all over had started to look around to see why it was so quiet. Over glasses of iced tea, Grace told them about the railroad tracks, and the moms shared their own horror stories. Like the time the kids had all decided to sneak household cleaning agents out of their houses and play chemistry. Luckily, they did it outside where ventilation was good. Or the time the boys decided to make their own rockets with leftover firecrackers and coffee cans, and almost set fire to one of the roofs.

The girls were no angels, either. There was a time, the women laughed, when almost every dog and cat in the neighborhood sported a very unauthorized, very rough, military haircut. And the time they decided to play movie star and took all their mom's makeup outside and left it all in the sun to melt. Once, one of the girls—they couldn't remember which one—had opened the doors to all of a neighbor's bird cages when they'd been left on the porch to get some sun. For days, parakeets and cockatiels sat on the chimneys and flew above the clotheslines…just out of reach of their desperate owners. Then, one morning they were gone. The women tried not to think about which predator might have eaten them: the snakes? the hawks? maybe even an eagle?

❧   ❧   ❧

Next, Sako took center stage and told the story about the time Ronnie broke Glory's Mickey Mouse watch. As the women sat lined up against Grace's quarters in a tiny strip of shade in the backyard, she had all the women in stitches as she played the parts of both children in a story pieced together from Ronnie and other witnesses.

"Glory wanted to wear her new Mickey Mouse watch outside to play and against her instincts, Grace said, 'yes.'" The other women moaned because they were sure that trouble was coming. "She found Ronnie outside playing ambulance with Daniel's wheelchair and wanted a ride, but Ronnie kept rushing past her. Finally, she held up her wrist with the new watch on it."

"Oh, no!" the women chorused.

"Oh, yes!" Sako rolled her eyes.

"Where'd ya get that?" Sako mimicked Ronnie, while she rubbed her nose on her arm the way Ronnie always did.

"Daddy gave it to me," Sako hugged her arm to her chest and snuggled herself in her best Glory imitation.

"Where'd *he* get it?" asked Sako. Her rough, cowboy voice sounded just like Ronnie's. The women rolled with laughter as Sako pulled an imaginary cowboy hat over her eyes and rested her fists on her waist.

"I don't know," Sako played out Glory being coy and batting her eyes.

"I bet he got it at the PX!" Sako said as she slapped her thigh.

"Do *you* have a Mickey Mouse watch?" Sako asked in her sweetest Glory voice.

"No, but I could *fix* one."

"Mine isn't broken," Sako continued in Glory's voice. Now, the women howled. Ronnie had the reputation of being the neighborhood booger, and the women couldn't wait to hear what would happen next.

"Well, then, I could take it apart," Sako said in her best, most confident Ronnie voice.

"Uh-uh," Sako said in Glory's whiny voice, with her hand over her wrist.

"Chicken!" Sako flapped her arms and pranced around in a circle. Now the women were out of control. The ultimate insult among Army kids was to be called a chicken.

"So," Sako continued in her normal voice, "they sat down on the curb and Glory took off her brand new Mickey Mouse watch and Ronnie took it apart and—of course—he broke it."

Women who hadn't heard the story before thought they'd reached the end of a classic Army brat story. But there was more.

Sako caught her breath and began again. "Ronnie was so frightened he climbed up on our roof, holding the broken wrist watch in one hand and shouting, 'No one come near me or I'll jump!'"

The women wiped the tears from their eyes while Sako continued, "That's when he fell in."

"Fell in what?" One of the women asked.

"The chimney," Sako answered, and all of the women gasped as they turned to look at the old brick chimneys on the two story buildings that rose twenty-feet above their roofs.

"Hellp! Dad, hellppp!" Sako yelled in her frightened son's voice.

"It took all night, and a whole bunch of engineers and firemen to get him out. I thought they were going to kick us out of housing." Sako had done a good job with her little play. The women were exhausted from laughter at the end of her story.

"He could have been killed," one of the women said weakly.

"Yep," Sako answered, "almost was, the next morning when his dad got ahold of him."

The women roared again. There was nothing like a good story on a hot day, told by a master storyteller like Sako.

Grace was grateful that Sako didn't mention that the reason Ronnie was so frightened was because he was afraid Dwayne would beat him with a stick because he broke Glory's watch. She had found out later from her sister-in-law that Dwayne hadn't even bought the watch. Some blond hussy in a honky-tonk had given it to him because she'd won it in a bingo game and didn't have any kids of her own to give it to.

After the stories, Patty, who was from New Jersey, was curious about the snake skeletons.

"Grace, take me over there. I'd like to see those snake skeletons for myself."

"Patty, no. You don't know how big those snakes can be. It's dangerous over there. We could get bitten." Grace started to shake and sweat again. As a child she had heard enough about the snakes in the cotton fields to fear them forever.

"Grace, you're shaking—you stay here, relax and don't worry about it. I can find those snakes by myself."

Grace marveled at the gutsy young mother as she headed off in the direction of the railroad tracks wearing her shorts and sandals and armed only with a stick she'd picked up in the yard.

The next time she looked out the window, she saw Patty come home, then leave again with a box big enough to put snake skeletons in. *Lordy, lordy, Patty is going home soon. I guess she thinks she has found the perfect souvenir to take back to New Jersey.*

CHAPTER 6

Leaving on a Pony

It didn't take Grace long to forget all about the snakes. With Glory down for a nap, She started to lay out the pattern on Aunt Lilia's material. Grace had a deal with everyone she sewed for that she could have any leftover fabric, so she was precise when she placed the pattern on the cloth.

When the pattern pieces were pinned, Grace walked around the table and checked the placement of each piece. Once the fabric was cut, it was too late correct errors. In her nightmares, Grace made dresses with two fronts and no backs. It was funny how in her dreams, it was always an officer's wife whose bare butt flapped in the wind. Officers' wives were her pet peeve because everything seemed to come so easily to them. Especially cars. If there was an officer's wife on post who didn't have one, Grace was sure it was because she was blind.

Anxious to look at the material for Frank's shirt, she put the almost-finished dress on a hanger and twisted the wire hook so she could hang it over the top of the door that went into the living room. The toy box that hid the shirt fabric was next to Glory's bed, but there was little danger that her daughter would wake up when Grace went to get it. She was the type of child who could roll off her bed, hit the hard linoleum floor, and never wake up. Just like her mother. Even before she started to lose her hearing, Grace could sleep through a powwow, even if her pillow rested on the drums.

Back in the kitchen, Grace opened the bag and looked at the red and white striped cotton. At the bottom of the bag, a note from Frank told her he wanted to wear the shirt on the Fourth of July. She knew she had an old flapper costume of Vera's with rows and rows of red fringe as good as new that she could reuse. She'd also put stars on it. They should be shiny; maybe she could find some used ones on another of Vera's old costumes. Her sister's costume trunk was full of old party getups; officers' wives loved costume parties.

One of the many costumes Grace had made for Vera was a "Dorothy" outfit from *The Wizard of Oz*. Her sister had almost killed herself when she tried to ride an old bicycle with a basket in front of the handlebars into the officers' club. She'd never ridden a bicycle before, but she'd said, "How hard can it be? Kids do it all the time." While she recuperated with a bandage over her head, Grace had brought her an old stuffed dog of Glory's she'd renamed "Toto." She told Vera it was short for "**Toto**-lly dumb."

Grace chuckled at her sister's antics. A little past midnight she glanced at the phone; Dwayne wouldn't call. She never asked him to and he never did. She vaguely understood it had something to do with him being able to come and go as he wanted. To her, he came and went and went and went, so what was left to prove?

Soon, she would show Dwayne that he wasn't the only one who could leave. Oh, she might not go with Dwayne's flare, and drive his old car out the back alley throwing red dust all over, but she'd go, for good. Maybe she'd go on a bus. She chuckled and imagined herself carrying Glory and her sewing machine in her arms onto the city bus.

Or, better yet, on one of those ponies that men brought door to door so kids could have their pictures taken. Even though it was slower, she was leaning toward leaving on the pony because she wanted the photo. She could just picture herself and Glory all dressed up in red cowboy outfits with lots of white fringe. They'd both sit on top of a brown and white pinto pony and wave big white cowboy hats and shout *"Adios!"* to Dwayne. Maybe she'd even strap the sewing machine to her back, like a guitar.

"Stop, Grace! This isn't a laughing matter," Grace scolded herself out loud. "That's why you're in this mess, you keep sweeping your problems under the rug."

Under Glory's bed, she'd hidden a cardboard box of red and white checked material to make table linens for her cousin Tia's new Italian restaurant. She'd give this job her full attention the next day because it was important to get it out of the house; there would be too much of it to hide from Dwayne the way she did the smaller projects. Besides, Tia wanted to open soon. Her mother had been making Mexican wedding cakes for days for her daughter to give away as free desserts. No one questioned why an Italian restaurant would give away a Mexican pastry during its grand opening.

Things were like that in Oklahoma, where Negroes, Mexicans, and Indians mixed happily and naturally with the women from other countries brought home by Fort Sill soldiers. White people in town, of course, kept their distance as much as possible, murmured polite refusals to mixed race social invitations, and only revealed their true disdain for the foreign, darker skinned, and poorer class to each other. Why, butter wouldn't melt in their mouths. Outside their elite circle, only the chance meeting with a minority who had light skin and undetected descent revealed their true feelings. There wasn't a light skinned colored person in town who hadn't experienced a hair-raising conversation with a white person who'd stopped in the middle of a very pleasant conversation about roses or some such thing to point at someone who walked by and whisper, "There's so and so. He's got colored blood in him, you know, and he's got the nerve to strut around town as if he's as good as us. Everybody knows, just *everybody.*" Grace had grown up hearing the stories, and had come to suspect, expect, and accept the prejudice. After years of being treated as less than equal, she'd even come to believe it was deserved.

Except for the parties that Dwayne insisted that she throw so that he could impress his officer friends—parties that they couldn't afford—she was careful to move in her own circles unless she knew the white people she would be mixing with. That way, she and Glory avoided having their feelings hurt. She was especially uncomfortable around Dwayne's officer friends.

Grace believed the officers came and dragged their snooty wives with them because they had one thing in common with the uneducated sergeant: they loved to fish, and Dwayne was the battalion expert on fishing. They needed him to show them where the good spots were and how deep to set their line at the lakes. The officers also depended upon Dwayne to provide the appropriate bait and wade out in snake-infested creek waters to load up the catfish hooks. She often wondered just what part of fishing they did for themselves.

Dwayne's friends accepted his and Grace's invitations, but they never reciprocated. At first, she set a few outfits aside in her closet just in case they were invited somewhere, but in the end, she just wore them to town.

She didn't care much for herself, but she worried about what would happen to Glory when the little blond Mexican went to school. She knew they wouldn't keep Glory from attending class, but she wasn't sure whether she'd have any real friends, the kind that would come over to play and spend the night. She had never had any friends outside the family when she was growing up, and it was one of her fantasies for Glory to be wildly popular. She imagined fixing after-school snacks for Glory and her friends, and making animals from leftover material for them to play with on rainy days.

Grace could sketch a rabbit or turtle on material and have it sewn up and stuffed almost before Glory could pick out buttons for its eyes. Her instant stuffed animals were a big hit among Glory and her cousins. Grace hoped that, someday, her school friends would like them too.

She turned her attention back to Aunt Lilia's dress. She always saved the handwork, like sewing the buttons on dresses and hand stitching the hems, for evenings when she was too tired to do more complicated sewing. The buttons for Aunt Lilia's dress had been cut from one of Uncle Miguel's old shirts, and her aunt had sent them over with the dress material, strung together on a piece of white cotton crochet thread. They were real mother-of-pearl, so they resembled a pearl necklace. Grace smiled; her aunt must have had the buttons around since the 1930s. They went on in no time, and Grace hung the finished dress in Glory's closet.

Before she went to sleep, she cut out a paper pattern for the napkins for Tia's restaurant from a piece of old newspaper. Even though she was sure Dwayne must be in Texas by now, she put everything away, just in case. He always threatened to come back unexpectedly to catch her with some man. Although Grace was lonely, she was much more worried that he'd catch her with a kitchen full of fabric.

There would be time to think about other men later, after she and Glory had their freedom, a house, and a car. If Dwayne were to walk through the door some time during the night and try to surprise her, he'd see nothing unusual. Certainly not a man. She even swept the floor to remove all the loose threads. Then she wrapped them in a piece of newspaper and pushed them way down into the wastebasket.

Secrecy had become so much a way of life for Grace that she hardly thought about it anymore, but deep inside, her spirit was taking a beating. Her heart was beginning to feel like one of her brother's footballs that had been kicked around the block, finally coming to rest underneath a truck wheel—ready to explode at the turn of the ignition key.

As a final disguise, she put a plate of leftover tortillas in the middle of the kitchen table next to some old uniform patches of Dwayne's she was recycling. It took a long time to take them off the uniforms and pull off all of the little threads around the edge. Some of the patches were worth fifty-cents apiece, a lot of money to Grace and Dwayne. After she starched and ironed the new fatigues, she'd sew on the recycled patches.

Everyone in the housing area did this. Here in the barracks-style quarters for lower-ranking soldiers, there was more time than money. It was different in the officers' quarters, where women had no time and lots of money. They took their washing and sewing to the post laundry.

Once, Dwayne had told Grace about an officer's wife who did such a poor job when she starched and ironed his fatigues that her husband begged her to spend the money and have them done in a laundry. *Begged* her. He had told the story to her as just another dumb officer's wife's tale, but secretly, she thought the woman was definitely the smartest woman who lived in the fancy red brick quarters on the other side of the post. Dwayne had never complained about the job she did on his fatigues. She could only dream about being so deliciously sloppy.

Grace surveyed the living room and kitchen one more time before she turned out the lights. Mentally, she scored her day: one finished dress and two unfinished sewing jobs. Every stitch she sewed brought her one step closer to leaving Dwayne. She would have to pick up speed to get all of her work done before Dwayne got home. She could save half a day on delivery to her customers if her sisters would drop them off for her; delivering her sewing on a city bus would take up more than a morning. Worse, she'd have to drag Glory all over town on a hot bus.

CHAPTER 7

Grace's Leg

Another day, another tortilla, Grace kidded herself. She put away the material for Frank's shirt and began to cut out large squares of red and white checked fabric for tablecloths. Next, she would stack the scraps and cut out the napkins several at a time.

She dialed her cousin's number. "Tia, this is Grace. I have a lot of fabric leftover. I could cut some more napkins, but I really think you have plenty. How about if I make you some spaghetti bibs?"

"Grace, what a good idea, could you do that? Where will we find a pattern?"

"I can make my own pattern. There's nothing to that. Then, it's okay?"

"Okay? It's great!"

"*Bien!*"

When Grace turned around she saw a sleepy bundle of pajamas with tangled hair and blistered skin standing behind her.

"*Ay, ay, ay.* Here is one little girl who's not going outside today. You, kiddo, are going to stay inside and color. Does it hurt?"

"A little. Can I have some coffee?" Glory asked while she rubbed the sleep out of her eyes with her fists.

"How will coffee help? How about some milk? Aunt Pauline brought you some yesterday." Glory had been trying to get a taste of coffee for days. If it weren't for the polio scare and its mysterious causes, Grace would have just let her have some.

"Is *milk* a cure for sunburn?" Glory asked, peeking through one of her fists.

Grace turned back to her machine so Glory wouldn't see her grin. "Quiet, or I'll sew all your crayons together."

By four o'clock, Grace's table was stacked with linens ready for Tia's restaurant opening. "I had a good day's work, Momma," she said over the phone, "why don't you and the girls come out for dinner tonight?"

It would be good to have some company. Grace changed into her long cotton skirt to hide the bruises on her legs from Dwayne. Also, she'd be able to get the restaurant job and the dress she'd made for Aunt Lilia out of the house. Dinner was never a problem. She had a pot of beans on the stove and she would make a stack of tortillas at the last minute. Some salsa would be good. She would have one of her sisters bring a pepper to put in it.

No one ate dessert in the Ramirez family, so she didn't have to worry about that. Rarely, when Momma got a sweet tooth, she'd get a piece of white bread and put it in the middle of a plate and pour molasses over it. The rusty, sweet smell sent the rest of the family running from the kitchen holding their noses. Proud of her statuesque figure, Pauline would sooner put a gun in her mouth than eat sugar; and chubby Vera, who was always on a diet, never had dessert before eleven o'clock at night when everyone else was in bed and couldn't see her eat. Rudolf called the late night snacks her "fat infractions." Grace never thought much about food at all, much less dessert. Since she'd gotten married, she had trouble when she ate anything, especially if Dwayne were at the table.

That night turned out to be better than expected: Vera not only brought a pepper, she brought her sister a handful of shiny red stars.

"Where did these come from?" Grace asked.

"I found them in my fabric trunk still wrapped up with the price tag, so they're new. I don't even remember why I bought them."

Grace was familiar with Vera's trunk full of fabrics she'd purchased in her travels around the globe with her military husband. It was so full of Irish tweeds, Scottish plaids, and other souvenir yardage mixed in with plainer material from local fabric sales, that it took two people to cram the trunk lid shut.

Once, she told Grace, Rudolf told her to get rid of the trunk and its contents. He said it was just an extra burden on their weight allowance each time they moved to a new post, but Vera said she told him the fabrics were an investment, just like his stocks. Someday, they'd be worth a fortune.

"I hope you're charging Frank for his shirts," Vera wondered aloud.

"Oh, Vera, he always pays me what he can, but that crazy Benny owes me for three pairs of golf pants."

"No, he gave me twenty-dollars for you today. Don't mention it yet. He did it while he was in the shower," Momma said.

Shocked, Pauline asked, "Momma, you *took* it?"

"Well, if he didn't want me to take it, he should have kept it with him. Besides, you know he won't have a dollar left after he runs around this weekend."

Surprised, Grace and her sisters laughed at their mother's sneaky approach to bill collecting, but they let it go because they knew she was right. Most of Benny's money from his job at the local Coca-Cola bottling plant *would* be gone by Monday morning. Besides, the beans were getting cold. Pauline threw up her hands and said, "Let's eat."

The bowl of beans was making its first round when Pauline dropped her napkin. When she reached down to get it, Grace realized her black and blue legs were uncovered under the table. Too late, she tried to pull down her skirt.

Pauline straightened up; her anger exploded like cold pinto beans thrown into hot grease. The conversation turned immediately to Spanish. "Momma, Vera, come over here. Grace, show them your legs," she shrieked. Grace couldn't say no; there were three of them against one, and one of the three was Momma. She pulled her chair away from the table and slowly pulled up her skirt.

"Why, Grace, what is this?" Momma asked, her troubled eyes filled with tears. Suddenly, no one was hungry. Grace, found out at last, sat very still while tears dropped onto her plate of beans.

"Good-God damnit to hell!" Vera yelled, when she finally put all of the clues together. "Another one of your falls down stairs, or maybe you tripped again getting out of the car? I always thought you had too many accidents."

Grace trembled as she watched Momma's eyes tighten around the edges, and the blue her mother had inherited from the French side of her family flashed from light to dark lapis. "Grace, Dwayne hits you! For how long?"

"Always, Momma," Grace kept her head down and wrung her hands as they lay in her lap.

"Why didn't you tell us?" Gregoria asked.

"I was ashamed," Grace broke down all the way, and sobbed, "and once he said he'd hit Poppa. I was even afraid he might hit you. You don't know his temper. And he's so strong."

Pauline, always the feisty one, pushed up the sleeves on her blouse, made a fist and said, "Let him hit *this*."

In a voice low with fury, Momma said, "Grace, you must leave. Pack your things; you and Glory must come home now, before he comes back." She'd never liked Dwayne, but she never dreamed he would hit Grace. "Why would he do such a thing?" she asked Pauline and Vera. "She can't be doing anything wrong, she's always with us." Grace knew that never in a million years would her mother guess that Dwayne beat Grace because of her color. Her mother had always shrugged off comments about "pepper bellies" and "wetbacks" as just the rough humor of a Texan who'd never learned any manners.

With a cry in her voice, Vera demanded to know, "Shit, does he hit Glory?" All eyes turned to Glory, her face troubled by questions she didn't understand.

"No, but Vera, she hears him yelling at me and hitting me. The doctor says if I don't leave Dwayne, she'll have a nervous break-down."

"*Ayyy!* Can kids have nervous breakdowns?" Pauline wondered out loud.

"I don't know, but that's what the doctor says," Grace answered.

"Jesus H. Christ-on-a-bicycle. That son-of-a-bitch. I'd wondered why you were always taking that girl to the doctor. I thought you were worried about her not gaining weight," Vera said.

"Her weight is just part of the problem, Vera."

"You must leave," Momma begged again.

"No, Momma," Grace reasoned. "If I do that he might hurt you. I want to wait until he gets his orders and goes to Japan. Then he'll be gone, and he can't hurt anyone."

Grace looked into the women's faces and continued to plead her case. "The other night he told me he could take Glory away from me anytime he wanted to. He says all he has to do is go to a judge and tell him I've been running around with other men. He says he can get men on post who'll back him up. I can't take that chance. Let him go, I can get set up in town and in three years when he gets back, I'll fig-ure out a way to tell him I'm leaving him." She talked fast. She had to convince them her plan was the best.

"Grace, what ever made you marry this guy?" Pauline asked, her hands held over her face to hide her despair.

"Oh, Pauline, he was so nice to me at first. He took me to movies and bought me little presents. No one had ever done that for me before. Then one night, he asked me to go to the movie at Murrey's, and when we got there, he forced me upstairs to that justice of the peace with a peg leg who has an office over the theatre. Before I knew it, we were married. He never proposed. I wasn't even sure what was happening until it was over. I thought there must be more to it than that. It only took five minutes. I was so dumb."

Vera rushed over to comfort her sister and wished she had arms long enough to comfort her mother too. She'd hadn't seen the woman in such despair since they'd lost Poppa. What could they do? They couldn't turn to the police; they couldn't prove that Dwayne had broken any law. The church couldn't help her. Glory was already five; it was too late for an annulment. If they got someone to beat the crap out of him, they could be the ones who went to jail. What good would that do?

"Grace, does he drink?" Vera asked.

"Not a drop. He's just mean," Grace groaned.

"Good. They don't need some drunken soldier running around Tokyo causing trouble. If he were a drunk, they might keep him here." Vera took a long drag on her cigarette while she thought things out. "Grace might be right," she finally said, "her plan might be the best. Let the army ship him out of here." Vera gave her sister a big hug before she blew her nose into a paper napkin.

Pauline, her voice on a slow boil added, "Maybe some Japanese will practice his *hara-kiri* on him and he'll never come back." With that, she made a twisting motion with her finger that made Vera and Grace laugh. Then, she squinted her eyes together in her best Japanese impression and said, "Ahhh, soooo, passa-re-beans, rady-son." Grace stole a glance at her mother to see if Pauline had made her laugh, but her mother's face was blank.

There was no joy in her eyes.

No peace in her heart.

Gregoria reached into her purse for her rosary; she never touched her food.

CHAPTER 8

Sako's Nightmare

Even though Sako's kitchen door was open, she didn't hear the goings on at Grace's. She was busy getting her two boys bathed and put to bed. In better times, when a young woman had more choices, people might have questioned the wisdom of a young girl marrying a man who already had two children, especially when one of them was bedridden. But Sako looked at her charges as a sacred trust—victims of a war they had no part in. How strange that they were caught in the vice of a decision made by a president hundreds of miles away.

When President Roosevelt signed executive order #9066, it destroyed lives far beyond those it was meant to affect. The net that Roosevelt, Herbert Hoover, General John De Witt, and others threw out over the land caught not only Japanese, Germans, and Italians who were considered to be potential threats to national security, but others who were not even on the subversive list. It was like a salmon net cast out over deep waters that caught a hundred other unwanted species of fish in its seine.

This time, the net brought in a whole array of victims: American wives of immigrants who had their citizenship stripped away by the Cable Act of 1916: old women who had lost sons when the Arizona went down and then were forced to move to internment camps. German and Italian men who were separated from their families and scattered in camps all over the country, and children, like Sergeant Hill's, whose mother died from fear, even though she wasn't meant to be caught in the net at all.

Roosevelt.

Hoover.

De Witt.

Sako always looked through the paper when Sergeant Hill wasn't around, so he wouldn't see her bite her lip and twist her hair tightly around her finger as she skimmed every news story for their names. She looked for numbers too. Numbers like 9066 and 1916. Any number that could mean future trouble for her or her family. She didn't believe for a minute that it could never happen again.

❦   ❦   ❦

Elizabeth Hill, Sergeant Hill's first wife, had become paralyzed with fear when she read about the internments on the front page of her hometown newspaper. She had an Italian grandmother on one side of her family and a German grandfather on the other. Although they'd held citizenship papers for years, Elizabeth became obsessed with the fear that they would be rounded up and stripped of their citizenship. She even feared for herself.

She worried so much about being labeled an enemy alien that she began to drink. Next came Elizabeth's nightmares, Sergeant Hill had told Sako. Night after night, she dreamed about government men who took her away in the middle of the night, never to see her boys again. Over and over in her dreams, she awoke to men in dark suits with their hats pulled low over their foreheads who dragged her out of her home by her foot, her nightgown trailing behind her. One G-man always had her Philco radio tucked underneath his arm, and said it was proof that she was a spy.

Sergeant Hill tried to reassure her that she was safe, and that the stories she heard about government men who broke down doors in the middle of the night and took away men and their short-wave radios were largely exaggerated. It wouldn't happen to her; all of her relatives had been citizens for years.

One night, government men broke into the house across the street one night, and the Italian man who'd lived there with his family for years was hauled off. Weeks later, his family got a letter postmarked Ft. Missoula, where an internment camp for Italians had been set up.

Elizabeth was on the edge. One morning, after she saw in the morning headlines that more citizens had been rounded up, the weeks and weeks of no sleep and too much booze drove Elizabeth to leave her boys and drive her car off a cliff. Soon after that, Sergeant Hill was ordered to report to a new assignment in Arizona. The assignment turned out to be the Japanese internment camp at Poston.

For the Army, the tenderhearted sergeant was the worst person they could have sent to Poston. For the captives, he was a blessing. During his assignment, he adopted several Japanese families, one of them Sako's. He made each one as comfortable as possible and earned a place in their hearts forever.

Just before the camp closed in 1946, he and Sako knew they were in love and were married in front of the whole camp. Sergeant Hill, a small man of thirty-six years with dark hair and thick eyeglasses, wore his uniform. Sako had a real wedding gown sewn from white satin with seed pearls around the neck, a purchase made from one of the Sear's catalogs that the interned community shared. In fact, her trousseau and the clothes for the entire wedding party came from the mail order catalog. It was the only way the internees could shop.

And now, each night, as Sako tucked the two boys into bed, she would say a prayer for Elizabeth, Sergeant Hill, and the two boys she guarded with her life. On her way out of their room, she always put her hands together and made a tiny bow in front of the little gold frame that held Elizabeth's picture that hung on the wall near the light switch. "Your children are safe for the night," she would whisper, "may God give you peace."

In the hottest part of the day, when the women sat behind their makeshift quarters in the only available shade in the neighborhood, Sako could count at least three other women who must have felt Elizabeth's fear: two German women, and one Italian, but none of them ever mentioned Executive Order #9066, or the Cable Act of 1916. It was a secret shame that made them feel helpless. Made them feel like second class citizens.

Besides, who knew who could be trusted? Best not to talk about it. It was easier for Sako to talk about what had happened with someone who hadn't been there. Someone who didn't come to the conversation with a head full of memories and a heart full of sadness. Maybe someone who had her own problems, like Grace.

Not that the subject often came up. But one time, when Sako sat in the shade with the other women, one of the newer, uppity wives managed to get Sako riled up.

"Where were you when the atom bombs hit, Sako?" she asked.

"I was in Poston," Sako answered.

"Is that near Hiroshima?" the young woman asked.

"Poston was an internment camp in Arizona. Our government *invited* a bunch of us to stay there during the war. Where were *you*, Palm Springs?"

"Oh," the young wife stammered, still confused, "I thought you were Japanese."

"I'm as American as you are," Sako snapped, "Maybe more. I'm American enough to have seen the dirty side of freedom—*American* enough to have seen my mother lose her home, her heart, and maybe her soul." Sako became more and more upset and let all of her anger and hurt out. "*American* enough to have seen my father lose the straightness in his back when he saw *our* government put his wife and children behind barbed wire." Tears ran down Sako's face, but she couldn't stop, she had to go on, "*American* enough to have seen jealous white farmers walk away with our land. *American* enough to have seen strangers come into our home, paw through our personal possessions, and take everything we had worked for." Sako stopped to breathe and then spat out one final sentence, "Oh, don't you *dare* treat me as if I don't belong here."

The woman ran home, but Sako stayed in the shade and drank her iced tea as if she'd just made a toast to newlyweds. The rest of the women, especially the German and Italian ones who had war horror stories of their own, were quiet. Sako spoke for all of them and had said what they had been unable to say. Sako thought she could see a grin peeking around the edge of their lips even though their eyes were tearing up.

"Good for you, Sako. You got her told!" a German woman finally said after she caught her breath.

Unlike some of the other Japanese who were interned, Sako was smart enough to grasp the wider picture. She didn't have to go to college to know the history of fear, jealousy, and hate. From her network of fellow former internees scattered around the country, she had learned all she needed to know about how Italian fishermen had their boats confiscated in California without any payment or apologies. She'd also read about the Japanese-Peruvian fishermen, who were snatched off the coast of Peru and, after the war, dumped unceremoniously in Japan, a country that hadn't been theirs for generations.

Fortunately, because she was young and in love, Sako was usually more positive about her circumstances than older past internees. Besides, what was done, was done.

Her problems now were the heat in her quarters, the red dust, the snakes, the scorpions—and that creepy black widow spider that was

weaving a web in the corner of her back porch, right above her mop
bucket.

CHAPTER 9

Down On the Ranch

Dwayne hadn't told anyone at the ranch he was coming to Texas, and no one was around when he got there.

He drove down the dusty road that ran along his property and got angrier at each passed fence post. The fence was still in the same sorry shape it was when he was there last. Posts leaned every which way, and barbed wire sprawled on the ground in a lot of places. Before he ever got to the ranch, he had to stop his car and shoo five of his own cows off the road. "Where the hell is that foreman of mine?" he cursed. He only had a few days to help him get things in order before he had to go back to the post.

Back in his car, he raced up the road to Cord's shack, ready to read him the riot act, only to find he wasn't there, either. "I'll just have to get a rope and pull the damn cows back over the fence myself," he muttered. He tried the doorknob on the tool shed and let out a yell. "The son-of-a-bitchin' door is locked!" He kicked the door on the shed until the boards cracked. "Cows roamin' all over the place—lucky they weren't run over—and the son-of-a-bitchin' shed that holds a two-dollar rope is locked up tight." Dwayne all but frothed at the mouth. He hollered and swore in every direction, "God damn it to hell!"

As he yelled, the cows moved in on him, mooing with every step. It was certain Cord hadn't gotten around to feeding them yet, and they were looking for dinner. "Damn cows would've starved to death," Dwayne shouted into the sky, "if I hadn't showed up." He stood and beat his fists on the hood of his car out of pure frustration and anger. The cows seemed to take his pounding as some kind of dinner bell; they moved closer and closer until their wet, slimy noses pushed against him.

Totally frustrated, he broke down the door to the shed, grabbed a bag of feed and a rope, and went to work. As he pulled each loose cow back over the downed fence, each one broke into a trot and headed for the feed bin. "Damn almighty!" He yelled after them. "You can walk over a broken fence to get out, but you need help to get back in over the same damn broken fence?" He couldn't decide if they were ornery or just plain stupid. Maybe a lot of both.

And where was that useless foreman he'd hired? Dwayne looked around at the tractors and bulldozers he'd borrowed from Aunt Bett so that Cord could dig a pond for the cows. Far as he could tell, they'd never even been moved since he brought them over. Well, Cord would have to explain to Aunt Bett why the machinery was starting to rust. Damn. She was gonna be mad, and he couldn't blame her. Not one bit.

With the cows fed, he began work on the fence, but it was really a two-man job, and it was hot, so he decided to wait for Cord in his shack. Another burst of anger erupted from him when he tried to turn the doorknob. The shack, too, was locked. He peeked in the window and swore again when he saw the floor, littered with empty beer bottles, crumpled cigarette packages, and other assorted garbage.

Just then, he saw a green pickup pulling a trail of lazy dust behind it, headed his way. He watched it as it leisurely made its way down the road, like a cow walking away when the feed bin was empty. He was more than annoyed that Cord didn't even speed up when he saw Dwayne's car parked in front of his place.

Dwayne crossed his arms over his chest and leaned against the fender of his Ford and waited impatiently for his foreman to drive up. His narrowed eyes seethed with disgust as he smoked his Camel and stared bullets through Cord's windshield.

He expected that Cord would be ashamed of himself, like a little boy who got caught when he skipped school. He wanted to see fear in Cord's apologetic eyes.

"Why didn't you call and tell me you were coming?" Cord demanded to know as he jumped out of his pickup.

Surprised, Dwayne fell back against his car, threw his cigarette to the ground, clenched his fists by his sides and shot back, "What do you mean, 'Let you know I was coming,' you son-of-a-bitch? This is *my* ranch and I can come any damn time I want to, by God. It's not my fault you got caught with your pants down."

Dwayne was angry, but he didn't want to actually fight Cord, and he was relieved when he saw his Aunt Bett driving her John Deere tractor up the road. What was that thing that hung over her head? At closer look, he saw that she had tied a big pink umbrella to her tractor.

No one bothered to try to talk until she parked the big machine and shut off the engine that roared like the mechanical king of the fields that it was. Dwayne lifted her tiny body down from the high seat.

"Aunt Bett, what are you doing out in this heat in an open tractor?" He asked as he lifted her down and hugged her at the same time.

"Have to drive the tractor. They took away my driver's license after they tricked me into taking that eye test." She followed his gaze to the umbrella and explained, "The umbrella helps a little. Besides, got to keep my face from wrinklin'."

Dwayne looked at the weathered and leathered face that was so old people had lost track of its years. Was she eighty-nine? Ninety-two?

"Your face looks fine to me, Aunt Bett. You should stay out of this heat, though."

"Would've, 'ceptin' I saw you drive by. Whyn't ya stop? Could've cooled ya off with something cold to drink."

Before Dwayne could answer, Cord stuck his hand in front of Dwayne's face and said, "That's a good idea. Give me a coupla bucks, Dwayne, and I'll go get us some cold beers."

Dwayne didn't bother to answer, he just turned and stared at Cord. The long, hateful stare hung in the hot air until Aunt Bett broke the silence, "No matter, ya'll come over ta my house. I'll cool ya both off with some iced tea and black boy cake."

"You still bakin', Aunt Bett?" Dwayne asked as he headed to his car. When he saw her heading toward her tractor he called to her and said, "You ride with me; we'll fetch your tractor when it cools off some."

When Aunt Bett pulled the car door shut, she turned to Dwayne and laughed, "No, I don't bake no more. Haven't for years. Not since I put a batch of strawberry jam on the stove to can, and took a nap. Boy," she laughed, "I had myself a mess then. There's still jam on the kitchen ceiling, don't have any way to get it off. But gettin' back to the cake, your brothers' bratty girls bring me something right regular nowadays, always tryin' to sweeten me up so I'll give them a piece or two of my antique furniture. I never do, of course. The minute I start giving away stuff, they'll never go home and I won't never get no peace."

"Better watch those spoiled nieces of mine, Aunt. They're used to gettin' their way. Don't know for sure if anyone's ever told them no. And I ain't never heard of them liftin' a finger around any of my brothers' ranches, have you?"

"No. Can't say as I have. Don't know as how they'd work in them fancy clothes they got anyway. I don't even think they really cook all that stuff they bring me either. I'm bettin' their moms are abakin' it for them."

"I just can't figure out why they built those big new houses, now they want to go fill 'em up with old furniture. No offense."

"None taken. I told them all that stuff was so old it came over in a covered wagon."

Dwayne parked the car next to Aunt Bett's kitchen door.

"What'd they say?"

"Asked me if I still had the wagon." They both laughed, and Aunt Bett waved away his help to get her out of the car.

Before they went into the house, Cord slowed his car down and yelled out his window, "I'm gonna grab some beers. Be back soon." Off he drove in a cloud of thirsty dust.

Dwayne went into the kitchen and sat on one of Aunt Bett's two kitchen chairs. After she poured the iced tea and put a bowl of fresh strawberries on the table, she moved the extra chair next to the wall and brought out an old wooden pear crate to sit on. Aunt Bett never sat on any regular seat that wasn't painted John Deere green; she'd had back trouble for years. When Dwayne looked at the empty chair his aunt had moved out of the way, Aunt Bett cautiously said, "Most likely, Cord won't be back tonight. He's got lots of friends at the tavern."

Damn it was hot! Dwayne gulped his iced tea that had the distinct flavor of East Texas well water, like a combination of rust and oil. He tried to make Aunt Bett think he didn't care where Cord was by announcing, "Long as he's there at sun-up tomorrow, ready to work."

Aunt Bett got real quiet and looked down at the sugar crystals that were spilled on the table when Dwayne had sugared his iced tea. She moved them around with the tip of her finger from one spot to another, carefully avoiding Dwayne's eyes. Dwayne got the idea that the chances that Cord would be up bright and early tomorrow and ready to work weren't very good, either.

"So how's the family?" Aunt Bett finally asked.

"Fine. They're getting ready to move back to town when I leave for Japan." Dwayne knew Aunt Bett wasn't really interested in Grace and Gloria, so he didn't say anymore. He wanted to tell her he was leaving Grace, but he just didn't know how. Besides, he really wasn't ready to get into an I-told-you-so conversation.

"How was the trip?"

"Hot. Long—there was one thing different—a cougar ran up along the side of my car for awhile."

"You should have run over him. All those mangy cats do is chew the legs off of cows."

"Have any around here?"

"Naw, run the cougars and wolves off long ago. Texas is changing. You can be in Dallas now in under two spits of a cricket."

Aunt Bett and Dwayne talked half the night and he finally bunked on Aunt Bett's couch that was about two feet shorter than Dwayne. Before he went to sleep, he looked over the furniture that his nieces wanted so bad. Just looked like old junk to him. That old pie safe, for instance. With its pine construction and punched tin doors, it was about as useful as a light bulb on a bale of hay. To his way of thinkin', anyway. And that ugly old oak china cabinet must be over a hundred years old. Who in their right mind would want that? Now, that bed of Aunt Bett's was special and probably worth quite a bit. Its headboard almost touched the ceiling, and it was heavily carved out of solid black walnut.

He had always wondered about that bed. It must have come through Aunt Bett's side of the family. No Tyler that Dwayne ever heard of had furniture like that. Aunt Bett was originally from New Orleans. 'Course that was years ago. Maybe that bed had come out of a southern mansion somewhere.

Before the sun was up the next morning, Aunt Bett banged around the kitchen and boiled coffee in an old tin pot while she fried eggs in her favorite wrought iron skillet. The smell of the fresh eggs mingled with the spicy aroma of the home-cured, thick-sliced bacon and slowed Dwayne down for over an hour. After he ate, he helped his aunt clean up the kitchen and wiped up some of the jam on the ceiling left from her last canning adventure. The ceiling was, after all, just inches above his head. It was easy for him to wipe a soapy rag over the dried red splotches.

As he cleaned the ceiling, he asked, "Aunt Bett, you've got a mess of black walnuts out there on the ground. What are you planning to do with them?"

"I never can use them all. I just beg everyone who comes to my door to take a bagful home with 'em. There's paper sacks by the door if you want some."

"Might take some to Glory. Not much else to take her from around here."

"Help yourself. They taste real good in cookies, but they're such a pain to crack. Ya gotta really want 'em. Some fella stopped by the other day and offered to buy the tree from me. The whole tree! Said it wasn't worth much, but he thought maybe he could sell it for a few bucks to the lumber companies."

"What'd you tell him?"

"I run him off, like I did that joker who wanted to buy my land for hardly no money just so he could build a lot of cheap stick houses on it. Imagine. Land I've spent my whole life buildin' up the topsoil on and he wants to cover it up with asphalt. Thought I'd have to get the shotgun after him just to get him off my property. Then he said he 'understood I needed time to think it over,' and he'd be back. The jackass."

Alarmed, Dwayne asked, "Why don't you call Cord or one of the other men around here to take care of those city-slickers?"

"There's never any time. They hit the door so quick, and then they're gone quicker than water in a well. I never even have time to load my shotgun. I'd get me a mean ole dog, but he'd probably crap on my strawberries and I'd get so darned mad I'd end up shootin' *him*."

"Well, a dog probably isn't a good idea. He might knock you down and make you break a hip or something. You don't need that." Dwayne gave his aunt a quick hug before he went out the door.

"Better go start that fence. First, I have to go into town and buy some more posts and wire. Good thing I cashed a check before I left. I can't find my savings book anywhere. Must have left it at a truck stop on the highway."

"Come back for supper tonight. I figure I can git a meal cooked as long as I stay awake and in the kitchen. I'll bring you men some sandwiches and lemonade at noon."

"Thanks, Aunt Bett." As he left the kitchen, his aunt was beginning to knock the fat off a piece of smoked ham with an old butcher knife before she put it in a pot with some fresh black-eyed peas. He knew she'd make some corn bread later to go with them. Always did.

The heat built up right fast, and when Dwayne stepped off the porch, he decided he'd leave that tractor of Aunt Bett's where it was. He and Cord would just drive over to her house for lunch. No use in her getting out and maybe getting heatstroke.

He felt a pain in his chest every time he thought that something might happen to his aunt. After he'd lost his parents, one to an accident and the other to the mental hospital, he and his brothers and sisters had been homeless. The girls found a home right away with his mother's sisters. Aunt Bett had taken in the boys when no one else wanted them. She'd been good to them too. But one night, in a fit of anger because Aunt Bett yelled at him for not feeding the pigs when he was supposed to, he'd run away to Fort Worth to join the Army. He was only fourteen, but he was big and strong for his age. At six feet tall, no one ever questioned his age.

He always did regret that he'd left Aunt Bett. Soon after that, her husband died, and the rest of the boys left to join the Army too. Guess they were all anxious to be on their own. Dwayne would have never left if he'd known his brothers were going to leave and she was going to be left all alone.

The fact that, as good as she was to Dwayne, she'd never accepted his Mexican wife and child hadn't changed his feelings toward her none. Folks were just like that around here. "If only I'd never left," Dwayne said softly to himself over and over. "I'd have my ranch right down the road from Aunt Bett, a normal family, and everything would be okay."

Thinking about his aunt made the short car ride to Cord's shack even shorter. Before he knew it, he was in front of the outbuilding he let Cord live in. He'd been so deep in thought about his childhood that he didn't notice until he was out of the car that Cord's truck wasn't there.

"Damn." Dwayne muttered to himself. "That good-for-nothing bastard knows we have to start work so I can get back to Fort Sill. Where the hell can he be?"

Dwayne didn't know where Cord was, but he had a pretty good idea what he'd been doing. Cord was always popular with the local girls. Anger mixed with jealousy. Dwayne was about ready to go into town alone and get the fence supplies when he saw Cord's pickup as it sped down the road, dust flying everywhere.

"Damn, you're gonna scare the cows to death," Dwayne said to him when he drove up.

"Naw, they're used to me," Cord grinned. "Ready to go? Let's take my pickup."

Dwayne climbed onto the high seat of Cord's truck and slid his feet around so the empty beer bottles wouldn't be underfoot. The empties rolled back and nestled around his feet like eggs around a hen.

"Damn almighty, did you drink all this beer yourself?"

"Naw, I had help," Cord grinned. "A lot of help." He grinned some more.

Dwayne couldn't help but grin a little himself. "I'm glad to hear it. We've got a lot of work to do, and it's gonna be hot. Aunt Bett's making us sandwiches for lunch. I've got to be out of here early next Sunday. Thought we might have some time to dig some on that pond after we finish the fence." There was a total lack of enthusiasm on Cord's part, but he let it go. No sense startin' out in a pissin' contest before the day even got started.

It took no time at all to pick up the fence supplies; they were the only customers in the feed store. "Most other people are smart enough to stay home in this heat," the man behind the counter groused as he took Dwayne's money and sat down again in front of the fan. He made a half-hearted gesture with his gnarled hand at the door. It was clear the cranky old codger wasn't going to help them load their purchases into the pickup. On his way out, Dwayne looked at the old rusted and bent thermometer hanging on the wall and whistled when he read: a hundred and one—and it was still early. For once, Dwayne didn't stop to chat the way he normally did with strangers. Best to just get in and get out and get to work, to his way of thinkin'.

On the trip back, Cord made a quick swing into the same tavern he'd just left a few hours before.

"Gonna get us some beers and ice for the cooler. We're sure as hell going to be sweatin' it off today. How's about I pick up some orange pop for Aunt Bett? She must be runnin' low."

Dwayne nodded and reached into his shirt pocket to hand Cord a twenty. Well, if he knew what Aunt Bett's favorite pop was, he must be checkin' in on her some, and Dwayne liked that. Maybe Cord wasn't more trouble than he was worth, after all. His hostile feelings toward his foreman began to melt away like the crushed ice that clung to the outside of a cold beer on a picnic table.

By the time Cord came out of the tavern with the ice and drinks, it was hotter than a barbecue pit inside the truck, and Dwayne didn't complain when Cord handed him a cold beer that had been iced down for a couple of hours. Cord joked that there were too many to fit in the ice chest anyway.

They were on the road by Aunt Bett's place when Dwayne looked out and saw Aunt Bett bouncing on her tractor as she drove around and around in circles in her south pasture. He watched with alarm at the pink umbrella furiously bobbing over her head as she raced the machine around in tight circles.

"What the hell?" Dwayne asked. He didn't have to tell Cord to head for the nearest opening in the fence.

"She must have walked down to your shack to get her tractor," Dwayne moaned. This was all his fault. He should have known she wouldn't sit still while they worked.

"What's she doin'?" Cord asked. "She don't have no work to do out there. Plantin's over."

"Looks like she's got heatstroke." Dwayne didn't take his eyes off his aunt. "Aunt Bett, Aunt Bett!" he called as he leaned out the pickup window and beat on the side of the truck with an open hand. She just kept a'goin' in circles, and didn't show any sign of hearing, or even seeing them, so Cord put his truck in park and ran after her. With cautious timing, he jumped onto the tractor when it came around again and brought it to a stop.

"Put her in the truck, Cord. I'll drive the tractor back to her house. Maybe give her one of those orange sody pops."

Cord nodded in agreement. Neither of them even tried to talk to Aunt Bett. Their minds were busy trying to figure out what to do next. Call a doctor? Take her to the hospital? What?

At Aunt Bett's house, both of the men scurried around and tried not to bump into each other in the tiny rooms. Dwayne got his aunt into bed and Cord brought her a glass of ice from the beer chest in his truck with just a little water in it to sip on. She was much too weak to hold onto the pop he had tried to give her. As soon as she went to sleep, the two went to the living room and tried to figure out what they were gonna do.

"Think she'll go to a hospital?" Cord asked.

"Not likely. Besides, at her age, they might scare her to death," Dwayne worried.

"Should we call those girls who are always bringing cakes and cookies over here?"

"Naw. She wouldn't get a lick of rest with those girls in the house. I'm thinkin' I'd better call my sisters. Aunt Bett gets along with them. They've got school coming up. Maybe I can pay them a little bit until Aunt Bett gets back on her feet. They might need some money for school clothes or something."

"What about the fence?" Cord asked. "Are we done for today?"

Dwayne took an exasperated breath and said, "I'll make you a deal. Let's take the rest of the day off so I can get things settled around here. If things go well, we can work real hard to finish the fencing in the next couple of days, and just leave the pond for the fall, when it's not so hot. I won't be here to help you, but Aunt Bett's equipment should be all you need."

"Yeah, we'd better at least get the fencing done. Hadn't had a chance to tell you yet, but we've got three cows missing. Don't know where they went off to," Cord looked down at his feet, afraid to look into Dwayne's eyes.

"Hell's bells, Cord, why didn't you tell me that sooner?" His anger began to well up inside him again.

Cord had stopped listening to Dwayne and was looking around with a worried expression.

"Do you smell something burning?" Cord asked, sniffing the air.

"Jesus Christ, the black-eyed peas!" Dwayne yelled, running to the kitchen.

The next Sunday, Dwayne packed his car in the dark and left early in the morning. Aunt Bett was recovered enough to keep telling

Dwayne's sisters, "Go home. All you're doing around here is eatin' up all my vittles." Dwayne hated to leave her, but Cord promised him that he'd look in on her when the girls left.

They'd managed to get the fencing done. Had to, what with the cows walking off left and right. Dwayne had spent his remaining days at the ranch pushing Cord to his lazy limits. He didn't really have any choice. If he didn't get back to the post on time, that First Sergeant would kick his butt all the way to the stockade. Maybe if he were on better terms with him, he could get extra leave and stay a few days longer, but with things as they were, he knew there was no chance of getting any extra time.

He knew he'd never see Aunt Bett again as he gave her a hug good-bye. There was no way she could hang on for another three years until he got back from Japan. She knew it too. What could he say to her? How could he tell her how much she meant to him? Even if he tried, he knew the tough old lady would shut him down as soon as he got started. Aunt Bett had a heart bigger than a John Deere, but she wasn't one to gush. Life on the prairie had been harsh, and any tears she'd had were cried out long ago.

Dwayne couldn't help but wonder who she'd leave her farm to. She didn't have any kids of her own and his brother never even bothered to come and see her. For sure, she wouldn't give it to her brothers' daughters. He'd never ask her for it, though, because she'd done enough for him when he was a kid. 'Course, if she ever *did* leave it to him, he could sure make good use of it. "What am I thinkin'?" Dwayne mumbled to himself. "As long as she thinks I'll have Grace and Glory with me, there's no way I'll get her farm. The other relatives would dig her up just to skin her if she let Mexicans in here."

Sunday morning, Aunt Bett insisted upon getting up to fuss around in the kitchen and make him some sandwiches for the road and a thermos of coffee. He didn't have the heart to tell her not to bother, that he liked to stop at greasy spoons along the highway. Anyway, it seemed that Aunt Bett was determined to get rid of the Thermos that she had no use for. A lot of her cabinets looked as if they'd already been cleaned out. She'd kept only the cooking utensils that she needed on a daily basis. It was clear the old girl knew that she didn't have much time left.

The last thing he carried to the car was the bag of black walnuts. He cradled them in his arms like they were a piece of Aunt Bett. And, in a way, they were.

When he backed out the driveway, he backed out real slow, so he wouldn't throw dust on Aunt Bett's chinaberry trees.

CHAPTER 10

Guns and Paper Dolls

Grace stopped sewing to wave at Sako from her kitchen window and laughed at her friend's antics with Ronnie. Every time he ran by her, she'd plop his cowboy hat onto his head, and it always fell off by the time he came around again. Cowboy hats made a darn good head cover for Oklahoma, if they stayed on. Unfortunately, the ones for children were woven with stiff straw and tended to bounce off the first time a young cowpoke turned a corner. Finally, Sako threw her hands up in surrender and went in to check on Daniel.

When Glory went out to play, she wore a new cotton sunbonnet. It was a gift from her grandmother after the last cowboy-cowgirl incident when Ronnie forgot that he'd left Glory tied to a clothesline pole in the hot sun.

"Glory, Glory, Gloriiia," Ronnie said as he peeked underneath the deep calico brim. "What are you wearing?"

"It's a hat made for riding in covered wagons. My gramma made it for me." Glory turned in a circle so Ronnie could see the back of the hat. "See the buttons in the back? That's so it can be laid flat for ironing after it's washed."

"That's pretty neat, wonder who thought of the buttons, your Gramma?" Ronnie asked as he examined the hat's structure.

"I don't know. Maybe." Glory was thrilled with the attention she got from her friend. At her window, Grace breathed a sigh of relief. She couldn't hear what Ronnie said, but it was obvious he approved of Glory's new headgear. She knew that if Ronnie teased Glory, the bonnet would never be worn again.

Grace chuckled over Ronnie's reaction to Glory's new hat as she went back to her work.

She drank her coffee while she laid out all of the trims and material she'd collected to go on Frank's shirt. All of it in reds, whites and blues. While she worked with the pieces, she pretended she was a designer in New York, with a whole staff of assistants that waited for her decision on a new line of shirts.

"Miss Grace," they'd say, "would you like to see the new fabrics?" or, "Miss Grace, would you like to have the models come in for their fitting?" or even, "Miss Grace, could we bring you some coffee?"

Between the fantasy and her damaged ears, she almost didn't hear the phone ring. Luckily, she could hear over the phone surprisingly well if she got a good connection.

"Grace, it's Frank." Frank shouted into the phone. "*Cómo ésta?*"

"*Bien, bien*, Frank. I'm sewing your shirt today."

"That's what Momma says. Hey, Grace, you know that last shirt? It's a little tight in the collar…"

"Frank, let me talk to Momma. Momma? Get a tape and measure that cowboy's neck, will you?"

"Momma says sixteen and three quarters."

"Frank, the material hasn't shrunk, you've grown. Better bring it back and let me fix the collar."

Finally, her tall, thin brother was putting on some weight. She was surprised, since he never seemed to stop to eat or sleep.

"You can do that?"

"Yes, I still have some scraps, I'll just cut a new collar."

"I've already washed it a lot. Won't the new collar look funny?"

"You mean look newer than the shirt? No, I'll cut up the apron I made out of the scraps, and it's been washed a lot, so I imagine they'll just about match."

"Sis, you're amazing."

"Yeah? I remember how you used to laugh at me when I first started sewing."

"You were twelve. You sewed a bra and put a big green bead right in the middle."

"That bead is what made the bra glamorous, Frank," Grace said as she remembered her first sewing project.

"That bead was bigger than what you had inside the bra."

"Very funny. No more fancy shirts for you."

Frank's voice changed to a more serious tone as he said, "Sis, Momma has been filling me in on what's been going on over there. Grace, Dwayne's big, but me and a couple of the boys could teach him a lesson or two."

Of all her brothers, Frank was the least equipped mentally and physically to teach Dwayne any kind of lesson that wasn't about music, and Grace knew his heart wasn't in his words.

"No, Frank, he'd have you sent to jail. You know what the good ole white boys would do to you. What chance would you have in the courts if you got caught?" she reasoned. "Besides, Dwayne has a gun now. A big Russian pistol."

"Where the hell did he get the money for a gun?"

"He said he fixed some soldier's car for it. I think the guy he got it from took it off a dead Russian during the war." Grace caught her breath. "You know, I think he's itching to use it."

"Grace, I'll be so glad when they ship him out of here."

"Me too, Frank. Me too." She could have told him a lot more. But the Ramirez men were seldom bothered with details. Women took care of unpleasant things in her family. When she hung up, she imagined Frank still laughing about the bead on her first bra, the offer to beat up Dwayne already erased from the mind of her easy-going brother. Probably, he'd forgotten about Dwayne's new gun too.

Why had Dwayne really bought the pistol? It wasn't for the ranch because when he rushed off for Texas he'd left it strapped with its belt and holster to the wrought iron frame at the top of their bed. He'd already said it wasn't for hunting. *Maybe this gun was for her. Maybe he was thinking about arranging some sort of "accident."*

It would be cheaper to kill her than divorce her because if he divorced her, he'd have to pay alimony. Grace knew that Dwayne would not be an easy man to get alimony from, even if the court ordered it. But if he were going to kill her, what was he planning to do with Glory? The questions spun around and around in Grace's mind, and she'd find herself in the bedroom staring at the gun—not even aware that she'd left her sewing table.

She thought about asking Sergeant Hill to take the bullets out of it, but what if Dwayne noticed the gun was unloaded? What then?

Grace looked down and saw the half-finished shirt on the table. She had to stay on schedule. She'd have to worry about the gun later.

Buttons. She'd forgotten buttons. Plain ones. She didn't want them to stand out because they weren't part of the shirt design. She dialed Pauline's number.

"Hey, Sis, are you coming out today? Can you bring me some buttons for Frank's shirt?"

"Sure. How about some big gold ones?"

"Thanks. But how about some plain white and navy blue ones? Six each."

"Anything else?"

"Could you bring another quart of milk? Have Momma give you some of my money."

"Okay. How's our little toasted tortilla this morning?"

"She's outside playing dolls with one of her friends. I'm thinking about taking her to the doctor today."

"I'll be over after lunch. If you decide to take her in, make it for after that and I'll drive you."

"Thanks, Sis. See you later."

"Is Aunt Pauly coming over?" Glory asked as she cupped her hands by the sides of her face and peeked through the rusted kitchen door.

"Yes, why?"

"Is she going to the store? Could she bring me a turtle?" Glory asked as she clapped her hands, her eyes dancing with anticipation.

"I don't think so, but maybe she could bring you some new paper dolls. But first, come over here and let me have a look at you." Grace saw that the child's skin was beginning to peel, but there was no need to take her to the doctor. With any luck, Glory would be almost healed by the time Dwayne got home, just a lot browner.

"Your Aunt Pauly says you must look like a toasted tortilla. Why don't you call her and ask her about the paper dolls? I'll dial for you, then I'll make you a bologna sandwich for lunch. I want you to play in the house for the rest of the day."

Later, when Glory turned to leave the kitchen, Grace saw that her little back was eaten up with mosquito bites. There must be a whole swarm of them camping out in Glory's room. Mosquitoes liked damp places; mostly, they'd lay their eggs in gutters, fishponds, rain puddles, etc. But if forced to come inside during dry weather, they could breed in a cool dark closet or even under a bed. She needed some bug spray to use in Glory's room.

She wished she could get her hands on some of that DDT the Army used to spray the neighborhoods. That stuff really worked, but the Army would never let the wives have any of it, insisting that the insecticide was too dangerous for private use. She'd have to settle for something at the store.

The phone rang, and the voice on the other end gave her a start. "Sis? This is CG, how're ya'll doin'?" The voice of Dwayne's brother on the phone startled Grace because he rarely called.

"Fine, CG, how are you?"

"Fine. Tryin' to stay cool…do you have Dwayne's phone number down in Athens?"

"No, CG, I don't. I'm not even sure if there is a phone. Is something wrong?"

"Yeah. Well—no. It's just that I've heard on post that he's not shipping out as soon as he thought. I hope he hasn't sold his car."

"No, I don't think he'd sell his car down there. He'd have to take the bus home if he did."

Not shipping out yet? Grace felt a sharp pain in her stomach that doubled her over, and she wrapped her arm around her middle to hold herself up. How much longer was this mess going to last?

"When will he be leaving?" she finally asked.

"Looks like they ship out in August. Have him call me, will you?" he asked politely. There was no hint of disdain in his voice. His sisters used to say the only thing CG could build up a good hate for was deer poachers, chiggers, and the snakes in the lakes that had the nerve to come up to his boat and swallow the fish right off his stringer in one bite.

"All right, give my love to Jewel."

She took a deep breath as she looked at her kitchen with material stacked on every chair. He was a nice guy, she didn't think he'd get her in trouble with Dwayne on purpose, but all he would have to do was innocently mention to Dwayne that Grace sure did a lot of sewing. It was lucky for her he'd called instead of stopping by.

So. Dwayne wouldn't leave until August. This wouldn't be as easy as she'd thought. Even if she baked chocolate cakes, catered to him all day, and pleased him at night, it wouldn't work until the end of August. Dwayne was like a volcano in cowboy boots that blew up regularly and often, without reason or warning. He just blew.

Another thought hit her as she pinned the pattern to the red striped fabric: somehow, she must avoid getting pregnant before he left. She could count on at least two menstrual cycles until the end of

August. She had to talk to Pauline and Vera about this. Her sisters had both been away from home longer than she, and Momma had raised ten kids. It probably wouldn't do any good to ask her.

Frank's shirt was still in pieces when Pauline walked through the door at noon. Grace just couldn't seem to get her fingers and needles to move in the same direction and Pauline could tell when she looked at her sister's face that there was bad news about Dwayne.

"Is he back?" she asked in a low, fearful voice. Cautiously, she glanced into the living room.

"No. But, Pauline, he isn't leaving until late August."

"*Ayyy!* How do you know?"

"CG called, he heard the news on post."

"Sis, can you last that long? Momma isn't going to like this."

Grace had the same thought. Momma had ruled the roost long before Poppa had died, and even Vera wouldn't cross her if she could help it. Whenever Vera thought about a family problem, she took a long drag on her Kool, then she usually started out with, "I'll bet Momma would say…" Momma's advice was almost always good. After all, she didn't raise her kids during the Depression without learning a thing or two. Grace was sure Momma would have something to say about this. She just hoped she wouldn't want her to leave Dwayne before he shipped out. She couldn't do that.

"Let's have some coffee for now, and I'll be back later with Vera and Momma for dinner to figure this out," Pauline said. "It will take all of us together to come up with a plan to keep Dwayne away from you until August."

Grace and Pauline drank their coffee in silence. Even though Dwayne wasn't due home for days, they kept one ear peeled to the outside, and listened for his car. Finally, Pauline's laughter broke the silence. She looked over and saw a frustrated Glory stick a dressmaker pin into her paper doll because the paper tabs had weakened.

"Does she have one of those that's a man?" Pauline asked her sister.

"Shush," said Grace. "There is no such thing as Mexican Voodoo. If there were, I'd have bought some of those paper dolls for myself long ago." They both laughed at the notion that they could solve all of Grace's problems with some paper dolls and a few straight pins.

Pauline reached down and picked up a boy doll and a few pins. She poked the first pin between his legs, right on the zipper. Additional pins on each side of the doll's head didn't satisfy Pauline, so she added some more in the doll's crotch area. In a cartoon voice she cried, "*Ay, ay ay! yi yi!*" as she danced the little man around on top of the table. Glory, down on the floor with the rest of her dolls, gave her aunt a quizzical look; she couldn't see the pins.

"I'm glad Momma isn't here. Shame on you!" Grace tried not to grin as she snatched the doll and pins from her sister's hands. She would have liked to have kept the doll, at least for a little bit, but she removed the strategically placed pins and returned it to Glory. What if Dwayne came in and saw it?

With no warning, the screen door flew open and Vera exploded into the kitchen and started making demands without bothering to say hello.

"Where the *hell* is this damn gun Frank told me about?"

"It's in the bedroom," Grace said, "but don't touch it...it's loaded."

"Not for long it isn't. Give it to me!"

"Gun?" Pauline asked, "What gun?"

In the bedroom, Grace pointed to the pistol strapped to the bed and watched Vera make a dive for it.

"I'll be back in an hour."

"Vera! Where are you going?" Grace asked.

"I've got a guy at the bowling alley that can make sure this gun will never fire even when it's loaded, and Dwayne will never suspect a thing." Vera ran out the door with the pistol in a big shopping bag. Dust flew in all directions as she raced for the bowling alley.

"Can they do that?" Grace asked Pauline.

"I don't know anything about guns, but if Vera says 'she's *got a guy,*' then she's '*got a guy.*' Our sis knows what she's doing. Where did Dwayne get a gun? Did he ever point it at you? And why didn't you tell us right away?"

Pauline was full of questions, but Grace just waved her off. She was much too stressed to discuss it. Minutes went by and Pauline still sat at the table shaking her head. She couldn't think of anything to say. They both watched out the window for Vera's car.

"What are you sewing tomorrow?" Pauline asked to pass time.

"I figure I have time to do one more quick project before Dwayne gets back. I have a size eight pattern and some scraps. I think I'll try to make a dress and sell it at the Post Thrift Shop."

"What if it doesn't sell?"

"Oh, it'll sell, eventually. If I have to, I can lower the price."

"What do you think you can get?"

"I'll ask seven-fifty to start. I'll have nothing in it but time, so I can go down to five dollars if I have to. Once a month, they send out checks. I'll just have them send the check to Momma."

"Let me know when you're ready to go over there. I want to look for some gold brocade curtains with matching valances."

"What makes you think they'll have that kind of thing at a thrift shop? You can't even buy something like that in town."

"Because Vera took them out there this morning after she got her new leopard print ones. And she gets all that stuff from the Ward's catalog, in case you ever decide to redecorate."

Vera was back within the hour. She strutted confidently into the kitchen and headed straight for Grace's bedroom.

"That son-of-a-bitch. Let him try to shoot this gun now," Vera growled as she slipped the gun back into its holster. Then she turned to Grace, grabbed her by the shoulders and shook her. "The next time something like this happens, Grace, tell me right away. Stop fooling around with your life," she ordered. Then she was gone. Numbly, Grace watched the old Cadillac ease down the alley.

As soon as Vera pulled out of the parking lot, Pauline was out the door with barely a goodbye. Grace went back to the bedroom and stared at the gun. Had Vera's friend really fixed it? How would she know?

She got back to the kitchen in time to see the last of Pauline's car disappear around the corner. Funny, but she hadn't mentioned her husband Boyd for days. *Where was he? Come to think of it, Grace hadn't seen Carlos for at least as long. What was going on?*

CHAPTER 11

Flash Floods and Flashing Lights

Grace glanced at the clock. She had about three hours to finish the shirt before it was time to stop for dinner. She imagined her older sister seeing it and using every swear word she could think of to praise it, saying, "God damn it to hell and back on Sunday. It looks damn good, Sis."

As she sewed on the sleeves, she looked up to see that clouds, so dark they were like smoke from a house fire, had rolled onto the sky over her head. The last time she'd checked outside it was while she and Pauline had coffee, and it was sunny. She was surprised to see such a quick change in the weather. The wind picked up, and brought big raindrops with it that slammed onto the dirt like gravel thrown by the back wheels of a road truck. Thunder and lightning came right after.

She tried to count the seconds between the flashes of light and claps of thunder to tell how close the storm was. Her hearing wasn't what it used to be, but she could hear enough to be sure the thunder-shower was moving her way. Out of habit, she looked out the window for any sign of a funnel, but saw none. She knew that didn't mean much; a funnel could develop without warning. She was glad Glory was already in the house.

Out here on the edge of post, it would be comforting to have a storm cellar. Always afraid of storms, Grace would be one of the first ones to grab a blanket and head for shelter. In town, her mother and sisters would head for the church basement if things looked really bad. To them, a storm was just an opportunity to visit and drink coffee with the other parishioners. Vera always took a tote bag full of cards and other games, although she didn't think the card games in the church basement were much fun—her mother never cheated when she was that close to God.

Only the women in the family ever ran to the church in bad weather. Rudolf, Boyd, and Dwayne were needed on post during bad weather alerts, and Ben always volunteered in the senior citizen's home across town. The other brothers were either out of town or reluctant to stop whatever they were doing to go on a funnel watch.

There would be no company tonight. In Oklahoma, even a rainstorm that seemed harmless in one spot could produce heavy rains miles away—rains that could race down dry ravines and trap unsuspecting campers, or carry away cars and wash out bridges with no warning.

The Lawton Constitution always had a picture on its front page of at least one car as it floated down a stream after a spring storm. Pauline swore it was the same photo used over and over again, and Grace had to admit that they did all look alike. She knew that her family, or anyone else she knew, wouldn't venture out tonight; she and Glory would eat alone.

She thought it must be Sako when she heard a knock at the front door. Glory peeked out from behind her mother's legs as she opened the door to find a colored boy about eight-years-old who held a big cardboard box that smelled of barbecue and corn bread. Grace stared at him for a second, and waited for him to realize he was on the wrong doorstep. But no, he broke into a big grin from ear to ear.

"Gracie? Your sister Pauline sent this to you because she can't come over tonight."

"But how? What are you doing out on a terrible night like this?"

"Oh, we do our best business in weather like this." He turned and pointed to a big car parked in front of Grace's. "My Aunt Garnet's trunk is full of barbecue chicken, ribs, and all the fixin's to go with 'em. Gotta go. Food will get cold." He tipped his wet hat and winked at Glory before he turned to go back to the big orange Cadillac. Grace gathered her wits by the time he was halfway down the sidewalk.

"Young man, I don't have any money."

"No need," he called over his shoulder, "your sister already paid for it." Then he came to a full stop and turned around. "Oh, I almost forgot. My Aunt Garnet put something extra in there for you and your little girl."

Grace and Glory raced to the table to open the box that had not only barbecue chicken but cowboy beans and corn bread sticks. Grace found some balloons tucked in the side for Glory that said *Garnet's Lip-Smackin' BBQ—a big bite of heaven for a little bit of money* when they blew them up.

The biggest surprise was a note from Garnet that said she had some new barbecue customers who wanted to start a German square dance club after Christmas. Could Grace make them some square dance skirts? At the bottom of the piece of paper was a name and phone number. Grace grinned and read the note over and over. What kind of angel delivers barbecue, balloons, and sewing jobs out of the trunk of an orange Cadillac on a dark, stormy night?

Then it hit her: Garnet was Pauline's friend who lived next door to their cousin, Tia. She didn't remember that her sister said anything about Garnet making barbecue, but maybe she'd just forgotten to mention it. Pauline must have told Garnet that Grace needed more customers to set up her business when Dwayne left.

Her sister wouldn't come by to get the shirt tonight, but there was little chance that Dwayne would come home a day early in this weather, so it didn't matter. She would just finish it and hide it in Glory's closet. By tomorrow, the sun would most likely be out and Pauline would be by to pick it up.

Grace hadn't seen Vera for days, but that didn't surprise her. Vera was redecorating; Pauline said she'd been holed up for days with the Sear's and Ward's catalogs. The fancy stores in town didn't carry bed and bath linens.

Curtains would have been a snap for Grace to make, but Vera seldom let her sew for her because she loved to shop, even if it cost her more. Eager to make up for years of doing without, all of her clothes had labels from The Parisian and Scott's, the fanciest stores in town. Vera did like Grace to make her costumes for the parties at the officers' club. Her mantel was filled with trophies she'd won with outfits Grace made for her.

Funny, how the Ramirez sisters had zeroed in on different articles of clothing to help them heal the painful wounds of a childhood spent picking cotton. When they grew up, Vera could never get enough dresses from the fancy stores, Pauline always bought shoes, and Grace always shopped for frilly lingerie, although she didn't actually buy much of it. She wasn't sure what her sister Norah liked, but she had heard that Norah, who worked in Washington D.C., had bought a new full-length "mink" coat to wear to work. Norah had kidded Grace that it was "no big deal, I think it's made from monkey fur." Grace knew from her magazines that the coat was most likely not monkey, but squirrel. The wartime economy had impacted even the fashion industry.

Did the brothers have similar appetites for something they'd done without in childhood? It was hard to tell. It was true that Benny always looked like a million dollars when he left the house, but it wasn't fancy clothes he craved, just neat and clean ones. The interesting thing was, he always looked better than the other men who wore more expensive clothing. Lordy, that man could wear clothes better than Fred Astaire.

There was no doubt that Frank had picked up his love of music from Momma and Poppa. They both played guitar. Unfortunately, his music had created a lot of sour notes between him and his mother. They had given up on resolving their differences long ago.

Her oldest brother, Alonzo, had a passion for learning that Grace was sure she could trace back to his yearning for more schooling than was available around the cotton fields. He was always talking about some book he'd borrowed from the library that was so good he'd like to have it for his own.

Before Grace was ready to go to bed, Frank's shirt was finished and on its way to Glory's closet when she stopped to admire it once more. Sewing for Frank was so much fun. She never got to do this kind of work for Aunt Lilia. Unable to resist, she slipped off her blouse and pulled on the star-spangled shirt. She'd gone braless for days because of the heat, so she let the shirt drape over her bare body and wondered what Dwayne would think if he could see her like this. Would he think she was as sexy as that blond who called over and over to leave messages for him at her mother's?

Thoughts about the other women in Dwayne's life used to turn Grace's stomach and make her feel humiliated. This was a small town, and everything Dwayne did was sure to be seen by a friend or relative. And he called *her* a whore. Lately, the humiliation had turned to anger. Anger and revulsion.

This other woman and the others like her puzzled Grace. Did she think Momma was Dwayne's mother? Or did he give her Momma's number because he thought the old lady was too dumb to catch on? If the woman ever got bold enough to actually stop by her mother's house, she'd end up with her face in a tortilla press.

Dwayne kept a scrapbook in his locked footlocker filled with pictures of other women he'd known since he'd joined the Army. All of them were as young as Grace when she first met him. Older women who were more experienced probably spotted Dwayne as a Stetson full of trouble, so they never stuck around. She'd discovered the scrapbooks one day when he'd opened the footlocker and then got called to the phone and forgot to shut it.

"So why do I parade around in a sexy shirt and hope to rope a *vaquero* that I've already got only because everyone else threw him back?" she wondered out loud. If only the buttons in her mind were as straight as the ones on Frank's shirt.

The shirt looked good, and not just because of the straight buttons. Frank would look like a big-time Nashville singer in it, even if he sang in dives with floors littered with broken beer bottles. He loved playing in his band, but his redheaded wife, Bobbi, constantly raised Cain about Frank's travels from joint to joint while he left her and their two boys alone night after night. It wasn't hard for her to get Momma on her bandwagon. Momma wanted every man in the family to be like her Juan. Poppa worked six days a week, and was home seven nights a week. Whenever he didn't work, he sat on the front porch and rocked. But even Momma hadn't been able to get Frank out of the local joints, and Bobbi finally moved the boys home to her mother's. No one knew where Frank slept, if he slept at all.

Before Grace turned off the light in the kitchen, she made a neat pile of scraps by her sewing machine for her dress project. They'd already been preshrunk, so all she had to do was figure out how to get a dress out of them. She knew she could do it. The challenge was to make it look good.

If Dwayne should come home, she could say the dress was for her, made out of scraps from Momma, but chances that he'd come home early were slim; the storm was headed in his direction. On the radio, she heard a woman sing, "*Don't know why there's no sun up in the sky, stormy weather…*" Grace sang along in her flat monotone. That should be her song: *Stormy Weather!*

On her way to bed, she peeked out the front and back windows to make sure Dwayne's car wasn't there. She thought nothing of the flashing red lights down the street. The military police were in the area all the time to break up fights started by men whose war memories were drowning in too many beers. Besides, she'd find out all about it tomorrow from Sako. Her friend always was on top of the neighborhood news. Grace saw her run down the street toward the flashing lights during the storm. She could almost hear Sako's bare feet slap the steaming sidewalk, as the warm rain splashed out behind her heels.

For most of the night the lightning hovered right over Fort Sill. Strike after strike slammed the flat ground so hard that the walls and floors in the area shook. The noise was horrific, like a shell from a cannon that exploded at close range.

She put Glory in bed with her and pulled the covers up over their heads. Glory slept soundly, right through the storm, so there was no need for Grace to act brave. With each flash and crash, Grace prayed beads on her rosary. The rhythm of prayers normally repeated in a monotonous tone took on new inflections: "Hooooly, Mother-of-God" (Boom!) "Praaa-y for us in our hour of neee-d." (Boom!)

She thought things were about as bad as they could get: She was almost deaf, her husband was a terror, she had no job skills, and outside there was probably a funnel brewing that would carry her—and all of her problems—up into the sky to be delivered God-only-knew-where. She was under her covers with Glory and her rosary when the ambulance that carried the body of Sako's friend Meiko went by. She never saw it.

🍁　　🍁　　🍁

Sako got the phone call about Meiko just as she was finishing her supper dishes that night. She knew immediately the voice didn't belong to a friend. It was authoritative. Did he say who he was? Sako wasn't sure…he just kept asking her questions that even people she knew never asked. Somehow the voice at the other end of the line reminded her of Poston. She hadn't been so frightened since she was a child.

"Are you Mrs. Hill?"

"Yes…" Sako answered hesitantly.

"Do you know a Meiko Cushman?"

"Yes…"

"Are you aware there's been some trouble in her quarters tonight?"

"No…what happened?"

"Could you come down and answer some questions?"

"*Aaiee!*" Sako cried out as she hung up the phone. She told Ronnie to stay in the house and watch Daniel. Then she flew out the door and raced barefooted down the sidewalk to where Meiko lived. A block away Sako could see the flashing lights from police cars and ambulances reflecting off the pavement, pulsing with a nightmarish energy all their own.

She was expected. When she approached the front entrance police, medics, and ambulance drivers made a path on the small porch so she could enter. Sako scanned the room. At first she didn't see Meiko anywhere. Then she realized she was looking too high. Her eyes widened when she saw a small form draped in a sheet on the living room floor. Meiko!

Sako tried to run toward her friend but a large uniformed arm shot out of nowhere and blocked her. Blinded by tears, she felt herself being led to the kitchen where a military policeman sat her at the kitchen table and placed a cup of tea in front of her.

"What happened?" Sako asked as she stared at the cup of tea. *How many cups of tea had she had in this cup at Meiko's table?*

"Apparently, Ma'am, there was some sort of argument here tonight, then a fight. The coroner thinks your friend's neck was broken."

"Where is Sergeant Cushman now?"

"Outside in a squad car. He can't hurt you, he's under heavy guard." He took out his pad and pencil and began to ask questions. Questions that made her skin crawl.

"To your knowledge, has this happened before?"

"Yes, quite frequently."

The policeman looked surprised. "Why didn't she report him?"

"I don't know. We all told her she should. I don't think she had anywhere else to go."

All his questions after that made Sako feel even more and more foolish. She felt as if she answered "I don't know" over and over again. This was her dearest friend, how could she not know how serious things were? Or did she know and just block out the truth because it was easier? Why didn't she help her? Why didn't *she* tell someone?

She felt someone wrap a blanket around her shivering body. It was large enough to tuck under her wet, bare feet. It was not large enough to take the chill out of her heart. She'd lost her childhood playmate that she'd known since Poston. Sako had never felt so alone in her life. In the back of her head she could hear girlish laughter from long ago drifting through a wire fence guarded by armed troops.

🍁   🍁   🍁

"*Sako, do you want to get some popcorn? The soldiers are giving it away.*"

"*Let's get some and eat it while we look through the Sear's Catalog and pick out what we'll buy someday.*"

"*Mom's got the catalog. It's our turn to look at it. Let's go to my house.*"

"Meiko, are we ever going to get out of here?"
"Sure we will. Someday, they'll have to let us out to go to college."

Meiko was gone. Somehow Sako thought they'd be together forever. That's the way it had started out. In an internment camp in the middle of Arizona not so long ago…

CHAPTER 12

Japanese Mafia

The next morning, still unaware of the tragedy that occurred the night before, Grace looked through the pieces of material from her scrap box. She had enough leftover material to make the skirt for the dress from small navy blue gingham checks. She'd make the top from a piece of white eyelet that had been in her box for almost a year.

The idea of generating her own business with scraps was appealing to Grace. It would keep her busy when she didn't have any other customers. Hidden in the bed of her machine was the note from Garnet. After Christmas she would have a whole new list of customers.

Only Oklahoma could have a group of German women who wanted to start a square dance club. Grace was willing to bet her last dollar that it was a pretty lively group. She'd pass the word through Pauline that she'd contact the women after the holidays. Even the timing was good. Dwayne would be gone for sure by then.

She sighed as she watched Glory head out the kitchen door to play. She didn't know which was browner, her skin or her hair. Dwayne would have a fit when he saw her, but what could Grace do about it, lock her in her room until summer was over? Of course, even that wouldn't keep her hair blond.

There was a knock at the back door. Grace looked up to see a shaken Sako peering at Grace through the screen door. In her trembling hand, she had a small plate of rice balls with plum centers wrapped in seaweed. Glory loved them, but Grace always had to peel off the seaweed before she ate hers.

"Grace, I made rice balls today. I brought you some for your lunch." Then she asked, "I haven't seen Dwayne for days, is anything wrong?"

"Sako, come in. No, he's just gone to Texas for the week. He'll be back Sunday night. Want some iced tea?"

Sako nodded as she stepped in and gazed at the piles of fabric on the table. "I hear the machine run all the time over here. What are you making?"

Grace tensed. If Sako noticed the noise from her machine, the other neighbors must have heard it too. What if one of them mentioned the machine noise to Dwayne?

"Oh, I just fool around and make things for Glory. Thanks for the rice balls. Glory loves them. She thinks they're vacation food."

"Ah, that's because we take them in the car when we go on trips. They last a long time and don't make a mess.

"That's funny. We take bean burritos in the car when we travel, for the same reason. The only problem is, Glory always eats them before we get to the Texas border."

"What's this?" Sako held up the dress pattern Grace used for the thrift shop dress in her hands.

Grace took a breath and blurted out, "Sako, I sew for people so I can get enough money to leave Dwayne, but please don't tell anyone around here. If Dwayne finds out before I'm ready to leave him I'll be in big trouble." Her hand trembled as she handed Sako a glass of iced tea.

Sako held up her hand and stopped her from explaining further, "I would never say a word to Dwayne. No one would. All of the girls in the neighborhood know what goes on over here," she lowered her voice, "we all worry so much for you."

"Thank you, but it's going to be all right. He's going to Japan any day now."

"I have family in Japan," Sako said, as she did her best John Wayne impression, "good family. Can be trusted." She pretended to pull a gun out of a holster and shoot it. "Bam! Bam!" she shrieked, her voice cracking with emotion.

Grace looked at her friend in amazement. Surely she was kidding—Japanese Mafia? And yet, Sako seemed strangely on edge, despite her John Wayne impression.

"I'm not kidding, Grace. Did you see the red lights from the police cars last night?" Tears began to spill out of Sako's eyes and Grace ran to her side.

"Sako, what's wrong? Tell me. I've never seen you this upset before."

Sako wiped her tears with the back of her hand, and the words tumbled out of her trembling lips. Grace had to listen very closely to understand Sako because her tears flooded the back of her throat and garbled the words.

"My friend. Meiko…" Sako sobbed, her dark lashes were so heavy with tears that the bottom lashes laid flat against the skin underneath her eyes. "Her husband beat her again last night, and broke her neck." Sako looked at Grace with wide eyes filled with sorrow. "Grace, she's dead!"

"Oh, my God." Grace crumbled into the chair next to Sako's and sobbed with her.

"So you see, Grace, you've *got* to leave Dwayne. The sooner the better. Meiko's three children are all alone now. Her husband will go to prison."

"Where are they now?"

"Somewhere on post while they try to find their next of kin. The police took them away. Grace, you should have seen them, still in their little pajamas, holding their stuffed animals. They were asleep when it happened. They had no idea why the police took them for a ride in the police car. They laughed and waved at me through the car window."

"Sako, if that ever happens to me, don't let them take Glory like that. Call Pauline or Vera. Promise me!"

"I'll try, Grace. I would have taken Meiko's kids with me, but the police said her relatives are too far away and it might take days to locate them. They said the kids would be better off with them. I begged them to let me keep them, but one of the MPs said he was sorry but they had to follow regulations. Better off with strangers? I've known those kids since they were babies. We don't even know where they took them. My kids slept in this morning because we were all up so late last night. As soon as they wake up, I'll find some-one with a car so I can go look for them."

"What's wrong with these people? Do they sit around and make these rules up while they play bingo at the club? *Ay, madre!*" Grace hadn't known Meiko well enough to know that they were in similar situations. Now, she wept as much for herself as for Meiko and her children. Overcome with grief, she lowered her head upon the kitchen table and covered it with her arms.

"Grace, I've got to get back home. I just wanted to tell you about Meiko before you heard it from someone else."

"Do you need someone to watch your kids while you look for Meiko's this afternoon?"

"Thanks, but no. I've already asked for someone to come from the hospital to watch Daniel. He needs a nurse. Whoever comes can watch Ronnie too.

Before she went back to her sewing, Grace set the rice balls in the refrigerator; she'd take Sako some tortillas in a couple of days when everyone felt better. Ronnie liked them with soy sauce and bean sprouts.

Later that day she saw Sako's borrowed car pull into the back parking lot when she returned from her search for Meiko's children. She waved to Sako from her kitchen door.

"I'll be over as soon as I check on the kids," Sako called to Grace.

Grace poured two iced teas and waited for her friend. When she picked up her glass to have a sip, her hand shook. She put the glass down and looked at the other hand that was also shaking. She was realizing that she trembled everywhere when Sako rushed through her kitchen door bursting with news.

"Grace, you won't believe this. They put those kids on a military transport this morning and flew them to California. I didn't even get to say goodbye to them."

"Who's going to meet them?"

"Their grandparents. I guess they live close to one of the airfields over there. The social workers gave me their address. I'll check on them the next time I go home. They're probably there already." Sako said as she checked her watch.

"It was nice of the Army to get them with relatives so quickly, but I hate to think of those kids flying all alone in a big plane."

"They weren't alone. They told me that they sent a nurse and a chaplain. I guess some soldiers in one of the battalions heard about the kids and the flight crew almost had to unload some of their cargo to make room for all of the toys the GIs bought them."

"Will there be services for Meiko here?"

"No, they flew Meiko's body home with the kids."

Grace got up and got a box of tissues. Both women had started to cry again.

"I just don't know why these things happen," Grace mumbled.

"They happen," Sako's voice turned hard as she sternly looked at Grace and said, "because women make bad choices and then stick with them. Wake up, Grace, this was no act of God! This wasn't even an accident. And it could happen to anybody, even *you!*"

Grace put her head in her hands and sobbed even more. Sako was right. Her time was running out.

Sako had time before the home care nurse had to go to another patient, so the two women drank their tea in silence. They were both all cried out and there was nothing left to say about the tragedy that had left Meiko dead and three beautiful children homeless.

❧   ❧   ❧

The next day the two women sat again at the same table. Grace hadn't done any sewing on the dress she'd started to make out of gingham scraps. She could remember she washed and braided Glory's hair the night before and read Glory her little books before she put her to bed, but not much else. Grace was numb. Meiko's death had put a harder, clearer focus on her own situation.

Finally, Grace looked over at her sewing and asked, "Do they have gingham in Japan?"

"I don't know, I was born and raised in this country and haven't been to Japan since I was a baby, so I don't remember anything about it. I was going to go back to see my relatives after college, but none of that happened when the war came and they made my family sell everything and sent us to the internment camp at Poston. By the time we got out, it was too late for everything. All of my family in Japan was gone—one way or another—and I never saw them again." She didn't say anything about whether or not any of her relatives were killed in Hiroshima or Nagasaki, and Grace didn't have the heart to ask. *Hadn't they had enough grief the last few days?*

"It wasn't right for the government to make you leave your home, Sako. Are your parents all right now?"

"They're okay, but they never got over #9066. That was the executive order that said we could be rounded up. It came straight from the White House, President Roosevelt signed it himself!"

"Did they ever say why they didn't round up the Germans too? After all, we were also at war with them."

"But they did! Sergeant Hill says they had Germans and Italians stashed in camps all over. I heard they almost rounded up Joe DiMaggio's mother, but the mayor of San Francisco called the White House and said he *really* didn't think the president wanted to have to explain to a nation of baseball fans why our government was holding one of our most famous baseball player's mother in a concentration camp. Actually, I think, they just made the Italian and German men move to a camp. The women and children just had to move away from the coastline, I think…but I'm not sure."

"Sako, why do you always call your husband by his last name? Did you meet Sergeant Hill at Poston?"

"Ah, he was the bus driver who drove us there. The first thing we saw when the bus pulled up to the camp was the fence with barbed wire strung along the top. When my father saw that fence, he broke down and sobbed like a baby." Sako wrung her hands in her lap as the memories rushed back.

"Somehow, he never thought they'd fence us in. My mother will never again live in a house with a fenced-in yard. Anyway, Mother and I could see that Sergeant Hill was crying as hard as we were. For a long time, he refused to open the doors to the bus, even though the military police were beating on them from the outside and trying to force them open. He kind of adopted us, and Mother thinks he's some kind of a god. I first knew him as Sergeant Hill. It's a sentimental thing between us."

"He might *be* a god. It took a lot of nerve to disobey an order. They can put you in the stockade for that. His Army career could have been over."

"Maybe so. Even my brother likes him, and he doesn't befriend most *gaijin*. He's real bitter about what happened to the family farm. He says the whites had us put in camps just so they could get their greedy hands on our land. Before the war, Japanese held some of the most fertile farmland on the coast.

Now that they're back in California, my sister says that Mother asks Father to drive by our old house to see if she can get a glimpse of who lives there now, but so far she hasn't seen them."

"I didn't know you had a brother. Where is he now?"

"Tommy? Oh, he went to fight the war when we went to Poston. Now he's at Ft. Rucker. He's career Army now. A lot of the *Nisei* went to fight the war, they were so anxious to prove they were loyal to this country."

"Well, if the government didn't trust them to stay home, how did they trust them to fight?"

"Who knows? Maybe they thought we'd be easier to control if the young men were gone."

"I just thought of something. Before all this, California used to belong to *my* relatives, I wonder who'll get it next?"

"Maybe your relatives will take it back someday."

"I doubt it. Most of us are too busy trying to keep our kids fed."

"Sooo, who's this dress going to be for?" Sako asked because she was too exhausted to talk anymore about anything serious. She ran her hand over the eyelet and felt the crisp clean texture of the fabric. Next, she ran her hand over the finely woven gingham, almost feeling the deep rich dyes that tinted the smooth navy blue cotton threads.

"Well, actually, I'm not sure. I'm going to try to sell it at the thrift shop."

"What size is it?"

"It's going to be a size eight because that's all the material I have." They both laughed.

Sako ran her hand over the embroidered eyelet again, her fingers traced the pattern of the flowers stitched on top of the fabric. Her mind traveled back to the clothes she wore before the invasion of Pearl Harbor. "You know, I used to wear nothing but silks before the war, when my family owned thousands of acres of prime California farmland." Sako looked down at her faded dress. "Grace, how much will a dress like this sell for?"

"I'm going to try for seven-fifty."

"Grace, can I buy it? I haven't had a new dress for a couple of years."

Surprised, Grace laughed. "Why not? Stand up and let me measure you." Sako jumped up from her chair like a little girl excited about a new doll and raised her arms so Grace could take measurements.

"Grace, I can't believe it. And I just came over to visit."

"I can't believe it, either. I've never thought of my neighbors as customers." Grace quickly measured Sako and jotted down the numbers on her notepad. "Done," Grace said. Sako, giddy from excitement and a little silly, twisted her long, sleek, black pony tail into a bun on top of her head but it quickly fell because she hadn't pinned it. She twirled around in a circle and asked, "When will it be finished?"

"It should be done tonight."

"That fast? It's a good thing I have some mad money. Sergeant Hill's in the field and I don't know what time he'll be home tonight. Sometimes, he doesn't get home until midnight."

"Well, you can surprise him at the door in your new dress. Just don't tell everyone where you got it. Don't worry about Dwayne seeing it, though. He's never seen the material."

"I'll be very careful," Sako promised. Then, she took Grace's hand and squeezed it until both of their hands turned white, "Please tell me you're going to leave Dwayne soon. Someday, he's going to really hurt you."

"I will," Grace assured her, "as soon as I can."

Sako nodded to let her know she understood. To leave Dwayne and survive physically and financially wouldn't be easy with her bad ears and lack of training.

When Sako was gone, Grace looked up at the ceiling and whispered, a prayer for Meiko. To herself she groused, "Stop fooling around and get some backbone, Grace." She went back to her sewing with a new fervor.

While she worked, she thought about what it would be like to live behind barbed wire, and tried to imagine her mother and the rest of her family being taken from their home. Her heart wrenched at the thought of her mother being in an internment camp. She pictured her poor little Momma shuffling off the bus to enter the camp clutching her scrapbook of family photos to her breast.

Sako's family had suffered so much. How awful to drive up to a camp and realize that your children would be kept behind barbed wire. And her poor mother, who went to bed every night wondering who was sleeping in her home—walking in her garden—cooking in her kitchen.

CHAPTER 13

Men See What They Want to See

"Goddamnit to hell in a picnic basket, it's hot."

Grace looked up and saw a strangely rumpled and tired Vera coming through her kitchen door carrying an armload of patty pan squash and tomatoes.

"Uncle Joe?"

"Yep. I took him, Momma, and Aunt Lilia on a ride in the mountains yesterday. It was too pretty to stay home. Momma gave him a bowl of beans and a stack of tortillas and he insisted she take home a trunk full of vegetables."

"Patty pan are my favorite squash and now I think Uncle Joe is my favorite uncle. What's new?"

"I'm here for Frank's shirt and Uncle Joe's pants. Pauline's home with one of her allergy headaches, so she wouldn't come with me."

"Where's Momma?" Grace asked, but what she really wanted to know was where her sister got her latest bowling outfit. The skirt was printed all over in yellow cabbage roses, and the knit shirt had a matching collar. Grace had never seen anything like it, even in a catalog. There was really no need to ask, she decided. It was either from The Parisian or Scott's, they were the only stores in town that carried high-end sport clothes.

"She's at the church with Aunt Lilia."

"Who died?"

"Everyone's still breathing as far as I know. I think they're washing the bingo balls."

"What?" Grace laughed.

"Well, Father O'Sullivan mentioned the bingo balls were getting a little grimy, so they're all over there in the basement washing the *gringo's* bingo balls. Too bad he didn't ask me. I'd have poured them into the toilet, added some soap, and swished them around with the toilet brush—then I would have flushed them. Pauline was so mad when she heard about it that she said she'd have told him what to do with his flippin' balls. Do those priests *ever* do anything for themselves? Some of those women are too old to be racing over to the church in this heat." In the next breath, she asked, "Got any coffee?"

"Vera, it's not like you to drink coffee when it's so hot. I'll make a fresh pot."

"I can't wait. I've been up all goddamned night playing bridge. Couldn't quit because I was cleaning their clocks. Got any old stuff?"

"Vera, you're getting as bad as Pauline. I made the last pot at six o'clock this morning. I'm going to dump it out and make fresh," Grace insisted.

"Dump it into here. No sense in wasting it," said Vera as she held up a cup. "So, when is your son-of-a-bitch Texan coming back?"

"Sunday night."

"Some of the guys at the bowling alley could keep him company when he gets back if you want." All of the brothers and sisters had made similar offers, but Vera was the one who meant it and could get the job done.

"No, I want this all to be over without anyone getting hurt. Besides, I've had a better offer from the Japanese Mafia," Grace nodded toward Sako's quarters.

"Oh, yeah? That'd be okay with me, and the police would never make the connection: a Mexican in Oklahoma hiring a *Samurai* in Tokyo to rub out a Texas cowboy. I like it."

"Auntie Vera." Glory burst through the kitchen door with arms at full stretch, headed for her aunt.

"What has happened to your face?" Vera listened as Glory launched into a full explanation of the joys and traumas of playing cowboys and Indians with Ronnie Hill. By the end of her tale, she had a glass of Kool-Aid in her hand and was out the door as quickly as she came.

"Grace, that kid next door is trouble. You better watch him."

"Vera, did you notice anything else different about Glory?" Grace asked, changing the subject. She wasn't really worried about Ronnie. Besides, she had bigger fish to fry right now. Soon, Glory would be in a new neighborhood. Hopefully one with more girls for her to play with.

"No, what?"

"Her hair is getting darker."

"So what? Most kids' hair gets darker as they grow up, especially when they eat lots of tortillas and beans," Vera kidded as she sipped her coffee.

"But Vera, Dwayne warned me not to let her hair get darker or else."

"Or else what?"

Grace pulled up her skirt, exposed her bruised legs and repeated, "*Or else*." Vera had never met Meiko, so Grace didn't mention what had happened to Sako's friend the night before. There was a good chance Vera wouldn't even read about it in the paper because the Army rarely aired its dirty laundry in the press. Most likely, it would only show up in the police blotter column if the story were ever printed at all.

Vera's eyes narrowed as she looked over her stale cup of coffee at Grace's leg. By the time she'd drained the cup the older sister knew what had to be done.

"What's the latest on when that bastard ships out?"

"August. September. No one knows."

Vera picked up her purse and headed out the door.

"Where are you going? I just put coffee on."

"To the drugstore."

"What about Frank's shirt and Uncle Joe's pants?"

"I'll be back for them—and the coffee."

She left so fast Grace didn't have a chance to ask her about birth control. My crazy sister, Grace thought. What could she possibly be up to? She couldn't do anything about Glory's hair, so that couldn't be it.

The coffee was ready. Grace took the pot off the stove and took a sip of iced water that tasted so heavily of chlorine that she poured most of the glass down the drain and went back to work. Their water was always heavily chlorinated, but in the summer when the reservoir was low, it was almost undrinkable. Grace could never decide if the chlorine was put in to hide the water's muddy taste, or if the mud was added to disguise the taste of the chlorine. She almost threw up when she thought about all the creepy crawly critters that swam around just hours before in the very same water she drank.

Before she cut out all the pieces for the dress, her big sister was back with a purse full of packages. Vera leaned out the door and called, "Glooory, come see your Auntie Vera!" While she waited for her niece, she calmly laid out the contents of the box in the paper sack. When Grace got closer her mouth dropped open. Peroxide!

"Vera, we can't bleach Glory's hair!"

"It's just hair color, and why not?"

"She's just a baby."

"If she were in Hollywood she'd be doing this all the time. Haven't you noticed that Shirley Temple's hair changes color with every movie?"

Glory came in and stood by her aunt. She peered wide-eyed at the brown glass bottles on the counter and the box that had a photo of a beautiful blond on the front.

"Glory, how would you like to play beauty shop with your Auntie Vera? There's only one thing you must know, a lady never tells a man what she's done to her hair, *especially* her daddy."

"This is much better than playing Indians with Ronnie Hill, Auntie Vera." Glory nodded excitedly.

Grace hovered over the two and fretted as they played beauty shop until Vera made her sister to go back to work. Glory was delighted with the grown-up game and listened intently as her aunt told her that the Hollywood stars were always changing their hair color. Giggles hung in the air with the smell of peroxide and Grace couldn't tell which one of them was having more fun.

A few hours later, Glory pranced around the kitchen and tossed her new blond curls. Vera pulled the second bag, filled with Hershey bars, out of her purse and handed one to the new Shirley Temple. While Glory settled down to eat her candy and give her rag doll a pretend hair color, Vera and Grace surveyed the pint-sized blond bombshell from every angle.

"Oh, Vera, what have we done?" Grace worried as she helped herself to a candy bar.

Vera coolly observed her work and replied, "We've colored a little girl's hair and saved you from another beating. She'd rather have roots than be motherless, I assure you."

"When will the roots begin to show?"

"Depends," Vera stalled, "but when they do, we can hide them by cutting her some bangs."

Suspicious, Grace asked, "Vera, where did you learn how to color hair?"

"Oh, shit-the-deer, Sis, I've never done it before," Vera finally admitted after she couldn't hide her face in her coffee cup any longer.

"Vera!" Grace leaned on the stove door for support and stared at her sister with an open mouth. Vera didn't blink.

"I did what had to be done, Grace. That's what life and living is all about."

"But what if all her hair had fallen out?"

"Oh, I was pretty sure *that* wouldn't happen. I *did* think it might turn orange," she laughed.

"Think Dwayne will notice the change in color? Her hair is a lot lighter than it was before," Grace asked as she ran her fingers though Glory's newly golden locks.

"No, men see what they want to see. He won't notice a thing."

Everything was under control. Vera packed up her gear and was on her way out the door. She hadn't planned on staying so long at her sister's, now she didn't have any time to dawdle.

"Vera, I've been trying to ask you, do you think I could make enough money to support Glory and me if I sewed for people when Dwayne leaves?"

"Only if you raise your goddamned prices," Vera answered without hesitation.

Grace was taken aback by her sister's quick reply. Raise her prices? Could she do that without losing business? She took a deep breath and said, "I have something else I wanted to talk to you and Pauline about together. Can you both come over tonight?"

"Not for a few days. I'm all booked up and Pauline is really not feeling well. She was flat on the couch when I left her this morning, moaning something about the pollinating elm trees, although I think it's something else—like the grasses—it's too late for trees to be pollinating. What's up?"

"Let's leave it for later," Grace said, as she rolled her eyes in Glory's direction.

"Can Momma come?"

"Yes. It might be the last time we can be together for awhile. Dwayne will be home Sunday and I have to clean this house and bake a cake so he won't know I've turned my pumpkin shell into a small dress factory."

"Okay, Sis, we'll see you tomorrow night. Guess we better not wait if it's that important. He might get home early."

🍁   🍁   🍁

With a wave, she was on her way down the sidewalk while she mumbled, "Peter, Peter, Pumpkin-eater, had a wife and loved to beat her."

Grace didn't hear her sister's poetry. She had already turned to go back inside.

In her car, Vera took a quick glance at her watch. She had just enough time to rush home to doll up. Luckily, her hair and nails were done. Those were always the two things that took the longest. She pulled into her driveway and raced into the house, tearing off clothes as she went.

What to wear, what to wear? She flew through a cool shower and spritzed on some Desert Ice. Tearing through a closet crammed with at least one of every outfit that a woman who did everything—and went everywhere—would need to get by in the middle of Oklahoma, she finally decided on a conservative sundress with a matching bolero jacket. It was too hot for the jacket, but it wouldn't do to show a lot of skin around the troops. She knew Rudolf wouldn't like that.

For shoes, she chose flat sandals; she might have to do a lot of walking. She applied her Merle Norman makeup with the speed of a professional and was out the door and back in her car in thirty minutes.

When Vera got to the highway she turned toward the mountains. She was lonely, and all of this Army training was driving her crazy; her plan was to put a stop to it. At least for one night.

Opening her purse, she pulled out the sack of Hershey bars she'd bought at the drugstore when she'd bought Glory's hair color.

She smiled and waved at the soldiers who were staked out along the road at checkpoints that led into the military reservation and laughed. Whenever one stopped her to ask what she was doing in a military training area, she winked and said, "Honey, this was *my* training area before you were ever born." Then, she'd toss the soldier a Hershey bar and add, "What goes around comes around. Soldiers used to give *me* these during the war." The soldiers would laugh and let her pass. When she turned up a winding road to where her husband's battalion had set up camp, she drove to where the general's staff car had been parked and fearlessly pulled in right next to it.

She checked her makeup and picked up the bag of Hershey bars, just in case she ran into any resistance.

To the amazement of soldiers she met along the way, she marched right through the camp.

Whenever a soldier looked as if he might try to stop her, she'd wink and hand him a chocolate bar. Along the way, she stopped and asked for directions to her husband's tent, explaining apologetically that "all Army tents look alike."

She was just about to pull Rudolf's tent flap open when he came from out of nowhere and grabbed her arm.

"What are you doing here? And where were you last night? I called every thirty minutes," the surprised colonel asked her.

"I was at a card game with your general's wife. I won. She called to tell old Four Star this afternoon that I'd be here to spend the night and that he and his men had to let me pass." Vera tried again to enter the tent, but was pulled back again.

"Had to? Just who is it wearing the rank around here? You women are getting out of control. Come on, I'll walk you to your car. We can't have civilians sleeping in a military campsite." With a firm grip on his wife's arm, he steered her quickly through the camp to her car.

He paused only briefly to give a quick salute to the general, who by now was outside his tent to watch Rudolf and his wife exit the area.

"You really beat her, huh?" Rudolf grinned in spite of himself.

"Yep. Took me all night, but I did. This stinks. I won you fair and square," Vera protested as he slid her into the front seat behind the wheel. She lifted up her face for at least a goodnight kiss and was startled when Rudolf ignored her puckered red lips. Tears welled up in her eyes so fast she was blinded, so she didn't see her husband go around the front of the car to the passenger door and get in. When she felt his weight on the seat and heard the car door shut, her mouth fell open.

"You're not the only one who can win at bridge," Rudolf winked. "Let's go home. You'll have to bring me back tomorrow morning. Early."

"You got any nylons, soldier?" Vera asked as she grinned through her tears and tossed Rudolf a chocolate bar.

CHAPTER 14

Mexican Birth Control

Grace could have almost finished the gingham dress blindfolded; she'd made at least six from the same pattern in different sizes for other women. By five o'clock, she was at Sako's door to ask her if she could come over to be fitted. Sako sprinted over to Grace's and landed on Grace's porch before she was halfway across the yard. Grace pinned the dress to the perfect length and fitted it a little at the waistline.

"There. You can get dressed. It'll be done before your supper dishes are washed."

"I just can't believe it. Oh, here's the money. Sorry about the quarters."

"That's okay, just remember not to say anything to Dwayne."

As promised, she delivered the dress at Sako's doorstep in an hour, pressed and on a hanger. Sako's husband had come home during the fitting. Grace was sure Sako would try it on so Sergeant Hill could admire it.

Such a nice man, it was too bad about his son. They spent every spare bit of money they had on making him happy and comfortable. But everyone had a cross to bear, she reminded herself. At least that was what she'd always heard. Then examples of perfectly happy and well-off friends began to pop into her mind, and she decided to think about something else.

Pauline called ahead to say they were going to bring dinner and something from Uncle Joe. It was becoming a joke among the sisters. All summer Vera or Pauline came through the door, held up a paper bag without saying a word and put it in the refrigerator. Grace would laugh. Most of the time she didn't even ask what it was. Whatever it was, she knew it would be good. And fresh.

Since she didn't have to cook, Grace spent her time getting a head start on cleaning the house. By six, there were three women and two bags of hot burgers and fries on her doorstep. The burgers smelled so good, and the grease soaking through the Gordon's paper bag just made them taste better. Pauline opened each burger, and cut big slices of tomato and onion from Uncle Joe's garden for each one.

"The onions are sweet, so have no fear." She cut Glory's burger in half before she put the knife in the sink.

The coffee was hot and ready to pour, as three generations of women sat down to figure out life's problems while they passed the catsup. Glory had a carton of milk brought by her Aunt Vera. Chocolate milk.

"*Ayyy!* Vera, you bought *chocolate* milk?" Pauline asked.

"Sure, why the hell not?"

"Chocolate milk has sugar," Pauline scolded.

"Yeah, and so does this. Don't eat this until you've finished your dinner." Vera tossed a Hershey bar leftover from the night before at Glory.

Grace laughed when a big grin erupted from the little face at the other end of the table. She had too many other problems to worry about Glory having a candy bar.

Then, her big sister leaned toward her newly blond niece and said with authority, "Eating chocolate leaves more tortillas and beans for the starving children in China." Glory nodded that she understood.

Grace didn't have to look at her mother to know she had crossed herself—something she did a lot whenever Vera opened her mouth.

"All right, I feel better. Glory, why don't you finish your candy in your room so the old ladies can yak?" Vera asked, after she drained her coffee cup. "Let's bring this meeting to order, girls. What's up, Sis?"

Grace hated to have to discuss birth control in front of her mother, but time was too short to be bashful. "I need advice on how to keep from getting pregnant between now and when Dwayne leaves." She said in Spanish as she looked at Glory. Everyone at the table switched to Spanish automatically even though Glory was already on her way to her room with her Hershey bar.

All eyes flew to Momma and they were stunned to see no emotion at all on her face. Impressed with their mother's composure, the women all looked at each other in surprise.

"Momma, you're hip!" exclaimed Vera.

"I've already talked this over with Father O'Sullivan." Momma took out her handkerchief and blew her nose. "The church supports Grace. Dwayne has no right to mistreat her."

"But Momma, *birth control*," Pauline stammered as she blew her stuffy nose into a tissue.

Gregoria continued, as if eager to get out everything the priest had said before she forgot any of it. "Father O'Sullivan says the baby knows what the conditions are *inside* the body, but it cannot know what the conditions are *outside* the body. So the mom has to decide when it's the right time to get pregnant."

"What else did he say?" Vera asked, leaning forward.

"He said I shouldn't repeat anything he'd just said to the pope." Momma's eyes were misty. Her daughters might have their doubts about religion, but her church and her God had gotten her through every crisis she'd ever faced. How could she ever doubt such love? She added as she blew her nose with her handkerchief and peeked over the top of it with one eye, "And he said if you ever went to mass you would have heard this for yourself."

"I'm waiting for the bingo prizes to get better," Vera teased. They all hooted. Their mother was always trying to get Pauline and Vera to go to church more often, and by her snort, she made it obvious that she wasn't at all surprised by her daughter's flip answer. Grace had been excused because Dwayne objected to her going to mass and because she considered Grace to be the member of her family least likely to be in need of guidance.

"But, what the hell," Vera continued, "if this new priest is so smart, maybe I *will* drop in someday. He's open on Sunday, isn't he? Maybe I can fit him in between bowling and golf. I'll have to hurry because he won't last long if Rome hears what he's preaching."

The chatter had just started up again when Momma motioned everyone to be quiet. As soon as she was sure the sound on the highway was an ambulance's siren, she crossed herself and whispered, as always, "*Via con Dios.*" The girls repeated, as always, "Go with God." Momma's little prayer followed ambulances, fire trucks, and police cars throughout Lawton around the clock like a bass following a Hula Popper fishing plug through one of the local lakes.

"Okay, so how do I do this?" Grace asked. All eyes flew to Vera.

"Damn. Why is everyone looking at me?" Vera asked. "I've never used birth control." Looking at her mother she swore, "I haven't, Momma!"

"I know," Momma said, "and you've never bleached hair before, either."

"Vera, you bleached Glory's hair?" Pauline shrieked. "I thought it was lighter from the sun."

"How did you know it was me, Momma?" Vera asked, ignoring Pauline's question.

"Because only you would be crazy enough."

"You could use the Catholic method of birth control," offered Vera, as she tried to get her mother's attention off of her and back on Grace's problem.

"What's that?" asked Pauline.

"Aspirin."

"Aspirin? Aspirin won't keep you from getting pregnant," scoffed Pauline.

"It will if you hold it between your knees and don't drop it!" Vera snickered and slapped the table, dropping cigarette ashes in her coffee.

"Very funny. They say if you douche with vinegar afterward, you won't get pregnant," Pauline offered.

"Pure vinegar?" Grace asked.

"No, you water it down," answered Pauline.

"How much?" asked Grace.

"I'm not sure."

By the time they'd floundered their way through a pot of coffee, Momma decided it was time to get down to business.

"Grace, at night, before you go to bed," she instructed, "you go into the bathroom and get a wad of toilet paper and push it up inside of you. Afterwards, you go straight to the bathroom and take it out. It's not foolproof, but it's the best you can do." She pointed at Vera and Pauline and added, "You two didn't hear this."

"Momma, you had twelve kids. What makes you an expert on birth control?" Pauline asked.

"Why do you think I quit having kids? Do you think your father and I stopped sleeping together after *Benito*? Raising kids in the Depression with an empty bean pot was hard. I knew I wouldn't be able to make enough milk for a new baby when I wasn't even eating myself." She added, "Your father never knew."

Stunned, the girls got very quiet. All of them had trouble imagining their mother ever using any type of birth control.

"Well. Good," Grace finally said. She was still worried. What if Momma's advice didn't work?

She was glad her sisters hadn't asked her how she'd kept from getting pregnant after Glory. She didn't want to tell them about the other two pregnancies—ones that she'd miscarried each time after Dwayne had punched her in the stomach. At the time, each miscarry saddened and depressed her. It took her awhile to figure out that, with another baby, she'd never be able to get away from Dwayne. As much as she'd like to have another child, having an extra mouth to feed would make it almost impossible for her to be independent. As it was, she didn't know if she could take care of herself and Glory. Besides, another baby would tie her emotionally to Dwayne forever, especially if it were a boy. He might want to be there for his birthdays, holidays, graduations, and vacations. So even if she managed to get a divorce, he'd still be hanging around. Or worse, he might insist that the boy live with him. Then she might never see her son again.

That night, as they left, Momma looked into Grace's eyes and pleaded, "Gracie, I heard that Dwayne has a gun. I know Vera had it fixed, but what if he gets another one? Please come home before he gets back. If we all stick together, he can't hurt us."

"No, Momma, I can't do it yet. There's too much at stake," Grace answered tearfully as she gave her mother a hug.

"This is not good. All the birth control in the world won't help you if you're dead," Momma said as she sadly kissed Grace's tear-stained cheek.

CHAPTER 15

Momma's House

Gregoria told the girls to drop her off at home when the evening was over. She was tired, she said, and wanted to go to bed. It was a lie. She was much too upset to sleep, and she wasn't one to waste time lying in bed counting chickens.

Instead, she went from room to room making plans in case Grace and Glory came to live with her. Which room would be best? It had to be a room with a place for Glory's toys and Grace's sewing. She finally settled on the bedroom closest to the fenced-in backyard. That way, Glory could go out and play while Grace sewed.

The bed and mattress were good. Later on, they could move a smaller bed in for Glory if she wanted it. She had one up in the attic, but it would take a man to get it down.

Gregoria had been in her house for so long it had layers, like a rich archaeological dig. The first layer was the newest. Signs that her children were successfully employed popped up regularly in the old house: a new radio for her here, a new chair there.

One of the girls always noticed when she needed a new coat or purse and the items were replaced with the joy and excitement that women, especially women used to going without, got from something new and pretty to wear.

The second, third and fourth layers were the closets. The closet in the room where Grace and Glory would stay was one of the older layers. There, in neat order, were the coats the girls had given their mother. Going back for years, each had a cleaner's bag over it, and was ready to be worn, if needed. Even the ones that were too worn to ever be used again were cleaned and looked their best.

On the top shelf, Gregoria had all the matching handbags and hats. Each year she gave one coat away to the ladies who sold used clothing in the basement of the church, but it was hard to let go because each one was full of memories. Especially in the pockets. She had put a special memento in each one: a wedding invitation, a funeral program, a faded corsage. All lined up, they were a kind of fabric diary that she didn't have any trouble reading.

Then there was Juan's journal in Spanish she had tucked in one of the coat pockets. She didn't have to read it; she knew the words by heart. They were the only Spanish words she had in the house.

The pages were written during the Depression. They translated to:

> We went through each field twice. The first time, we picked the prime balls of cotton out of the bolls. The second time through, the bolls were much smaller, and it wasn't worth the time it would take to pull the cotton out of the pods, so we just snapped the whole boll off the stem. The rough husks of the plant put blisters on our fingers and ripped the palms of our hands open. The money we made, all of it, went for food and a few extras, like shoes and medicine.

Another page read:

> Some pickers left for the fields in the morning carrying their cotton sacks over their shoulders and were carried back *in* them, dead from a snakebite or just plain cooked to death by the sun. As I work, I hear the moaning of field workers that swells around

their fellow dead picker until the sound gathers and rolls over the fields like a tornado moving low and wide, covering every inch of ground with a roar of sadness. And afterwards, a worse quiet that settles over the field—a quiet born of despair, hopelessness and fear.

The rest of the notebook, too damaged to read, seemed to be a record of hours worked in each field. Gregoria kept the pages to remind her of how far they'd come, the sacrifices they'd all made, and how important said it was that they all stayed together. Juan had said that to her over and over before he died.

The purses that were lined up on the top shelf were also put to good use. One was filled with tithing slips to St. Mary's, going back over thirty-five years. Each bundle was neatly secured with a rubber band. Another purse was filled with old photos. Yet another was filled with newspaper clippings of stories about her three sons. The sons who played football. The sons who boxed. The sons who graduated from college—and the sons who went off to war and never came back. And so, the old purses were no longer handbags, but rather her unique file cabinet.

However, tonight Gregoria was in no mood to be sentimental. Starting tomorrow morning, she'd begin to move her coats and purses—the entire file cabinet—to the upstairs bedroom. It was time to start a new layer.

CHAPTER 16

The Secret Savings Book

Grace knew her mother was upset, but she never guessed the preparations she was going through. Had she known, she might have said that her mother's actions were a little premature. After all, Grace hadn't asked if she and Glory could move in yet.

The last days in Army quarters were full ones and Grace was beginning to crumble from the stress. On Saturday, she woke up with a pain in her stomach before she even realized why. She decided to clean house and get everything else done so that she could try to relax before Dwayne got home on Sunday. Lately, whenever Glory clutched her stomach, Grace looked down and saw that she held hers too. Every time she thought about Dwayne being on his way home, Grace would panic.

About ten times that day she started to shake and break out in a sweat. She wanted to grab Glory and run, but each time she got herself back on track when she looked at the list of things she had to do. She called it her freedom list. Most likely, he'd be in late, but she would fix dinner just in case. She hoped a chocolate cake on the table would get things off on the right foot. It was near the top of her list.

Her plan was to keep two steps ahead of Dwayne's anger. Chances of total success were *nada*, but she had to try. If Dwayne got mad, he could leave her and kidnap Glory, take her to Texas and leave her there, hidden by good-ole-boy Texas menfolk while he went to Japan.

She had heard that threat so many times that she had a clear picture in her mind of just what those good-ole-boys looked like: tall Texans with huge pot bellies who wore straw Stetsons and very pointy cowboy boots. Of course, they all smoked cigars and had huge silver belt buckles with their initials in big ornate letters like CR, or RD. CG, Dwayne's youngest brother, was in the Army with Dwayne, so he wasn't one of *them*.

Grace thought the other brothers used initials because they were so dumb they couldn't remember a real name. Their cars must have those huge, long steer horns strapped across the hood of their Cadillacs that she always saw in parades, although she'd never actually seen any of the brothers' cars. With the courts favoring white men in Texas and Oklahoma, and she doubted if some Texas sheriff would beat the sagebrush too hard looking for Glory on her behalf.

Dwayne could also leave for Japan and put the two in a location far away from her family, and away from the chance of making any income. Or, he could just beat her so badly she would never fully recover. He might even kill her. She feared this man. His temper had become worse and worse, and he had exploded more and more for reasons that didn't make any sense: because he was sure she was whoring around, because her sisters were whoring around, or because she wasted his money—a neat trick since he never gave her any.

Because,

because,

because—because it made him feel good.

Still, she had to hold on until he shipped out. Once he was out of the country, she could start her life over. While she thought about what it would be like to be free from Dwayne, she took out the old pillowcase that held all of her hand washables, rinsed them out, and hung all of her sheer panties in a row on the clothesline that was strung between Sako's quarters and hers.

She didn't have much in the way of clothes, but she was proud of her panties. Full-cut, in pastel colors and made from a pleated sheer nylon, they were quite sexy even though she bought them at the dime store. "Hooray for nylon. For sixty-nine cents, you too can dress like a movie star," Grace said aloud, thinking about an ad she'd seen in a magazine.

She'd never be able to afford this kind of panties if they were silk. She could barely afford the nylon ones. As she turned to go back into the house, the sunlight caught the sheer fabric and sent out pastel rays of light across the hard-packed red clay underneath the clothes-line. She'd have to bring them in as soon as they dried to protect their delicate color.

While Glory napped, she cleaned the house, baked a cake, put on a pot of beans, and washed and rolled her hair in pin curls, securing each curl with two crossed bobby pins.

When she went back to the clothesline to retrieve her laundry, she found each pair with their crotches cut out, their fronts and backs flapping in the wind. Ronnie! It had to be. No one else in the housing area would do something so crazy. But why? Was it meanness? Or some sort of game? Maybe a dare from one of the other boys? Most likely, she decided, it was one of his science experiments. That boy was always running *scientific tests* on one thing or another.

She didn't need this right now, but she knew it could have been worse. She pictured Ronnie making a sling shot from one of her bras. The little squirt. There was an old milk crate under the line. Obviously he'd used it to reach the underwear. Grace stepped around it to grab the cut-up lingerie off the line and headed straight for Ronnie's house.

When she saw him peeking at her from his living room window she was sure he was guilty. She kept eye contact with him all the way to Sako's porch.

When Sako came to her kitchen door, a frustrated Grace held up the panties for her neighbor to see. Ronnie's goose was cooked.

"Ronnie Hill, get in here, now. Front and center!" Sako cried. She followed the command by a string of Japanese expressions that only she understood but which threw both of the women into fits of laughter. They could hardly carry on the interrogation and were finally forced to send Ronnie to his room until his father got home. That night, even his father couldn't get Ronnie to confess. After going around and around the facts and evidence with Ronnie for what seemed hours without any explanation, Grace and Sako decided that Ronnie had adopted a "no-crotch-no-crime" line of defense. Sergeant Hill gladly let the matter drop when Grace said she had to go home to finish her laundry.

Back home, Grace put away what was left of her clean clothes. She hoped Dwayne didn't find out about the panties; he'd blame her for sure. It would be just one more reason for him to be mad. She put in an urgent call to Pauline for new underwear, and got the response she could have expected.

"Does Ronnie have any color preference?" Her sister wanted to know.

Grace sat at the kitchen table doing her nails in bright red when Pauline walked in that evening holding up a paper bag from Uncle Joe that she put in the refrigerator. She carried another bag with the new supply of undies.

Relieved, Grace grabbed the sack and started to pull off the tags, so Dwayne wouldn't know they were new. *Have things come to this? Do I have to be afraid of getting a beating from my own husband over a few pairs of panties?* She felt herself begin to shake and cry as she tore off the tags.

The alarm on Pauline's face forced her to pull herself together. It was almost over; she didn't want her sister to bring her mother over to force her to pack up her things and get out before Dwayne got back.

"What's that, Sis?" Grace asked.

Pauline had forgotten about what she was holding in her hand. "Oh, Gracie, look what I found in the parking lot. It's Dwayne's savings book. I didn't know you guys had an account at First Texas Bank."

"We don't. Let me see that thing." Grace kept flipping back and forth through the check register, checking balances and dates. Then she checked for the name. Only one: Dwayne Tyler.

"How much is in there?" Pauline asked while trying to look over her sister's shoulder.

"It says seven hundred and seventy-six dollars. And look at the amounts, seventy-five dollars a month has been going straight from his paycheck into this savings account." She looked at the checkbook as if it were a poisonous spider. This could be nothing but trouble. Dwayne would be furious if he found out she had seen it. *What was the best way to handle this new crisis?*

"I wonder if he knows he's lost it?"

"Don't know. What are you going to do?"

"I don't think I want him to know that I know about this."

"You could play dumb, say you haven't seen it, and then toss it into the back of his car when he isn't looking," Pauline suggested.

"Yeah, his car's so dirty, he might not find it for a couple of days. Oh, Pauline, I could just kill him; we've lived on next to nothing since we got married. Glory and I have gone without everything. If it weren't for my sewing, we wouldn't have been able to eat some days.

And the doctor—I don't know if Dwayne would have paid for Glory to see the doctor if I would have needed him to." She threw the checkbook down on the kitchen table and continued to fume. Pauline picked it up and started to go through the register, page by page. Her eyes widened, and she handed the book back to Grace, pointing at a scribbled entry.

"Grace, didn't you say you never heard anything from Glory's godparents last year? From this check register, it looks like Dwayne deposited twenty-dollars from them into this account on Glory's birthday."

"Oh, no. No wonder I haven't heard from them. They must think I'm terrible for not even sending a thank you note."

She looked at the book and back at her sister, "Pauline, the money that I knew was going to the ranch was just a drop in the bucket. Here's a withdrawal for Johnson grass seed—two hundred dollars. And fence posts, veterinarians, barbed wire and, listen to this, a custom branding iron!"

"Sis, that man's more pitiful than the topsoil on an Indian farm."

Grace buried her head in her arms on the table and moaned, "You know, for a long time I've been dreaming that he was secretly saving money to take me on a vacation, or even to buy us a little house, but you see where all the money is going. To the ranch."

"What are you going to do with the checkbook, Sis?"

"Can you take it home with you? I don't want him to find it in the house. If he asks about it, then I'll decide what to do." What she wanted to do was rip his head off, but she knew that this was one of those wars that would be won by waiting.

CHAPTER 17

A Delay in Departure

When Dwayne drove onto post the next day, his head was still in Texas, and his thoughts still about his Aunt Bett, his foreman, and the mess he'd found the ranch in. It wouldn't be easy to fire Cord even if he wanted to. Help was hard to get in East Texas. Everyone had enough work of his own to do. Besides, Cord was one of Aunt Bett's favorites, and it was obvious they were close. He didn't want to do anything to upset the only woman he'd ever trusted.

Luckily, he had lots of time to decide what to do about the ranch. He'd stopped by the company headquarters on the way home and found out the departure time for his unit had been moved several times since he'd left. Now, the word was they weren't leaving for weeks.

The extra time also meant that he didn't have to look for a place for Grace and Glory to live right away. He knew she planned on being closer to her family. He'd moved them way out where they were, on the far edge of the post, because it was the nicest place they could afford. It also had an added benefit of being as far away from her family as he could get. But they'd be nice for her to have around if he were gone, and maybe her mother could keep her from whoring. No use having people talking about his ex-wife behind his back. There wasn't much doubt he'd be assigned again to Ft. Sill when his Japan tour was over. He was an artillery instructor, and Fort Sill billed itself as the Artillery Center of the World.

For right now, it'd be a whole lot more peaceful at home if those sisters of hers didn't drive. Officers' wives! They all thought they were so special. He'd let Grace know right up front from the very beginning she was no officer's wife and she would *never* drive a car.

Luckily, with her hearing loss, she didn't seem to even want to get behind a wheel. If she ever *did* ask, he'd give her a lesson she'd never forget, from the top of Mt. Scott. A few turns around that curvy road and she'd realize she wasn't smart enough to drive.

What was wrong with these women, anyway? Even Aunt Bett had told him that she'd taken the tractor to see his Uncle Dick at his farm ten miles down the road a couple of weeks ago. Driving a tractor in a field during planting time was one thing. Driving that thing on the road was something else. That old lady was going to turn that John Deere over in a ditch somewhere. Her and that damned umbrella she'd tied over the seat.

A thick cloud of dust floated toward the housing area and into open windows when he pulled into the back alley and jerked to a quick stop. Raising dust was a very rude breach of Army neighborhood etiquette, but Dwayne never remembered when he was upset, which was most of the time.

By God, he was home, and everything had better be in shape here. He was in no mood for any more aggravation. As soon as he parked, he looked around the corner at the parking strip in front of their quarters to see if they had company. They didn't. Good. All he needed right now was a living room full of women yipping in Spanish and making stuff with those damn crochet hooks of theirs. One of these days he was going to sit on one of those hooks. Then there'd be hell to pay.

"Daddy's home." Glory was the first to see her father's car. She ran to the parking strip to greet him. Dwayne was so pleased that Glory's hair hadn't gotten any darker he didn't notice how brown she was.

"Dwayne, you look tired. How was your trip?" Grace said as she handed him a glass of iced tea.

"Fine. Damn it's hot. Grace, like I always say, you make the best damned iced tea in Oklahoma," he said as he took a big gulp.

Dwayne knew that Grace's iced tea was so good because she loaded it with sugar but he didn't care. Almost everyone else drank their tea with almost no sugar, because they believed that sugar made the ice melt faster. It didn't make any sense to him.

"What did you bring me, Daddy?"

"Gloria, there aren't any stores down there, but Aunt Bett sent you something. Look in my leather satchel." Glory opened the zipper and pulled out the walnuts. Dwayne didn't mention that there were more walnuts in the side pocket of his satchel. He was saving them as a reminder of Aunt Bett and the home he regretted ever leaving.

"This, Daddy?"

"Yes, Gloria. They're black walnuts."

"Can I eat them?"

"Well, you can, if you can get them open," Dwayne laughed.

It took a few minutes to show the excited child how to crack a black walnut with a hammer and get the meat out. Dwayne figured there were enough in the sack to keep her busy for at least an hour. It had the added advantage of being an outside job.

"Take the nuts out on the back porch, Gloria," Dwayne told her.

After Glory was happily started on her project, he turned all of his attention to Grace. Since he'd been away, he'd slept alone. Not only were there not any women that he knew in East Texas that weren't related to him one way or another, but he'd stayed every night at Aunt Bett's to help keep an eye on her after she got heatstroke on her tractor.

"You got a tan, Dwayne." Grace refilled his goblet with iced tea and asked, "Would you like a piece of cake?" Dwayne glanced at the cake and at the little girl who was busily pounding walnuts on the back porch. There should be time to eat cake *and* take Grace to bed. He never answered Grace, but moved to the kitchen table.

Grace cut him a big piece of cake and excused herself; there was no doubt Dwayne had more than cake on his mind. In the bathroom, Grace pulled down her panties and rolled an egg-shaped piece of toilet paper in her fingers. Propping one leg up on the edge of the toilet, she gently pushed the toilet paper far into her insides, being careful not to leave any sticking out where Dwayne might see it. She hoped it would work. Before she returned to the kitchen, she combed her hair and put on fresh red lipstick.

"How was the ranch?" She asked when she came back from the bathroom.

"Grace, you wouldn't believe the mess I found down there. I'll tell you more about it later."

He grabbed Grace's hand and forced it down between his legs. They both glanced at the little girl on the porch. Satisfied that she was busy, they moved quickly to the bedroom. Dwayne's boots and buttons slowed him down; Grace was already on the bed with her dark hair fanned out on the white pillowcase before he was undressed.

Despite the disastrous shape her marriage was in, she was lonely. Even now, she felt the same excitement she felt the first time she slept with Dwayne in the Star Motel, a cheap little mice-infested motor court on the edge of Lawton. Dwayne would never believe her, but he was her first and only man.

He was a poor and inconsiderate lover—but it never occurred to her that she deserved more. In fact, she was sure that anything lacking during their lovemaking must be her fault. In five years of marriage, she'd never had an orgasm, and only knew about them from her sisters. It added to the confusion that every night—even after he beat her—Dwayne told Grace he loved her, so she thought that was what love was. And he probably thought so too.

Grace had pulled on a lacy slip; she'd never had a real nightgown. For years, she'd made do with two nylon slips, one black and one white. Each morning, she rinsed out the slip from the night before and hung it on a hanger in the bathroom to dry. Dwayne was thin, but even the slim weight of his tall frame was too much for the old box springs and mattress. When he stretched out on the bed, she couldn't help but roll over to him. Not one to waste time on foreplay, Dwayne moved on top of her and forced his hardened penis in all at once.

She was uncomfortable and disappointed, but she was relieved to have any physical contact with Dwayne that didn't involve his fists. If only he'd hold her so she could pretend, even for just a few minutes, that she had made a good choice in husbands. What would it be like to let herself float away in the delicious warmth of having him inside of her and the arousal she felt throughout her body?

It hadn't happened yet, but she kept telling herself it might, this time, if she could only do everything right. Maybe tomorrow, she'd have something to tell Pauline and Vera. She closed her eyes and concentrated on something she'd only heard about.

The unpleasant realization her husband hadn't washed for days brought her back to earth. The stink of farm animals, sweat, and cigarettes that mixed together to make a smell worse than cow shit hit her all at once. She completely blocked him out, so that she didn't even realize he'd rolled off of her until the smell had gone away. Grace thought she'd throw up and she could hardly wait for him to get out of the bathroom so she could take out the wad of toilet paper and wash the stink off of her.

Dangling her feet over the bed, she waited for her turn in the tiny bathroom. While Dwayne showered, he was talking to her with the door shut.

"As if I can hear you from the other room," she groaned, "what a dumb shit." She heard just enough to worry her. Something about he wouldn't ship out as soon as he'd planned. She already knew he wasn't leaving on schedule, but had the date changed again?

While she waited, she also wondered why she had so willingly jumped into bed with him. Fear was only part of the reason she had. Why couldn't she stop seesawing back and forth? As she sat on the bed on top of the twisted sheets, she finally realized that she didn't feel good about what had just happened, and that she never wanted to make love to him again.

She didn't ask him what he'd said until she was out of the shower and dressed. She went to the kitchen and sat down at the table. It was easier to understand him if she looked at him while he talked.

On the porch, half the neighborhood kids had joined Glory in the great black walnut massacre, each with his own special weapon, so Grace got up quietly and shut the kitchen door.

"Dwayne, what were you saying in the shower? I'm sorry, I couldn't hear you."

"I was saying our orders are all messed up and our unit won't be able to get out of here until sometime around September. Christ on a tractor!"

It took every bit of composure she had not to show her despair. Instead, she moved to the sink and poured two iced teas. They hadn't remembered to put the leftover ice cubes back in the freezer before they'd left the kitchen, so she rinsed the old cubes off, and added the new cubes. She quickly refilled the trays with the heavily chlorinated tap water and stuck them into the freezer compartment of the tiny refrigerator before she returned to the table. Maybe, with luck, they'd be at least partly frozen by dinner.

"So what does your unit do while it's waiting?"

"Train, train, train, even in this heat, damn it. You can be sure they're not going to let all us troops sit around on our butts while we wait for orders all summer."

"Will you be able to get anymore of your leave?"

"Don't know. At least I'll have some extra time to find a place for you and Gloria to live before I go. It won't be easy; every other soldier will be in Lawton trying to do the same thing. I hear lots of people in town are turning their garages into apartments to try to cash in. Maybe we can find one of those. Then, I might have to go back to Texas."

"When?"

"Don't know. Aunt Bett got sick, and my foreman is keeping an eye on her. I'm not sure if he can handle her, her farm, and my ranch. He's barely handling mine. Grace, I've got three cows missing down there."

Well, they're sure as heck not in my freezer. She looked at the little refrigerator that had only a small freezer for ice cube trays and tried to imagine just what part of the cow would fit in there. The only parts she could think of she wouldn't want to eat.

"How were things here? Anyone stop by?"

Grace knew what he meant: did any *men* stop by? Had she slept around while he was gone? Grace's hands trembled and she quickly hid them underneath the table. It was best to pretend that she didn't know what he was really asking. She didn't want to get into the kind of argument that would cause his temper to explode.

"Just my family, but CG called last week, he'd heard a rumor you weren't going to ship out on time and he was afraid you'd already sold your car." It was lucky for her he hadn't stopped by, because Dwayne had been jealous of his brother for years. Everything, from Army promotions, to friends, to pretty women, came easily to him. A weight lifter, CG moved through life with the style and grace of a man who knew where he was and was happy to be there, even if it was just Oklahoma. It would not have been a confidence builder for Dwayne if CG had stopped by to see Grace when he wasn't home.

"No, I'll hold onto the old Ford until the last minute now. You never know what to expect in this man's Army."

Why can't I keep it and learn to drive? Grace cried, but it was one of those cries that started in her heart and never found its way out. No real sound was made. Even when he hit her, Dwayne would warn her not to cry out, or they might get thrown out of housing.

"Then we'll be in a pretty pickle, with no money and no place to live," he liked to tell her.

Grace sometimes thought *he'd have some place to live, all right: in the stockade.* But he would eventually get out, and then he'd take each day out of Grace's hide. He'd said so.

The one thing Dwayne really feared was jail, and there was no way he was going to serve time just because he beat some little taco and she'd started to yell.

CHAPTER 18

Dwayne

While Grace was thinking about the car, it got quiet. She looked over at Dwayne. He was so beat from mending fences, taking care of Aunt Bett, and the long drive home that he'd fallen asleep with a lighted cigarette in his hand. When she leaned over to take it away before it burned him, he woke up enough to get up and leave the room.

Where did he go? She found him the first place she looked. On the couch, sound asleep. Before he'd left the table, he'd looked like he had something on his mind, but what? Well, whatever it was, Grace was sure she'd find out about it soon enough. *What craziness is he up to now?* She looked at the rumpled form stretched out on her couch.

Few people saw the mean and crazy side of Dwayne that she did. He was smart enough to know his boundaries. He only showed people outside the family the Dwayne he wanted them to see: a tall, good-looking blue-eyed man whose hair was so blond it was almost white. When people talked about Dwayne, they said he was just a good ole cowboy with a Texas twang who was always working on a scheme to make a pile of money.

After they were married, Dwayne came home one day all excited. He had been to a retirement party for one of the sergeants on post.

"Grace, I was talking to an old boy today and he told me there's a fortune to be made in frog farming. Maybe, if the cows don't work out, I could turn the ranch into a frog farm. 'Bout all I'd have to do is dig a pond, fill it with frogs, and wait for the money to start rolling in."

At first, she didn't know what to make of it, but soon, Dwayne was talking about other get-rich-quick schemes, like catfish farms; salmon fishing; and gold, silver, copper, and even diamond-mining. Other schemes included getting a metal detector and finding lost treasure, sneaking into the stock market through the back door, and making a fortune in scrap metal.

After the war, he even had a scheme for making a whole pile of money in the mail-order bride business getting foreign brides for former servicemen who, after their return from Europe, couldn't stand independent American women. He listened to every full-of-baloney story told by retiring sergeants, and Grace shook her head when it was clear he believed them all.

"I want to be rich," Dwayne once told her, "and the only way I can see to get there right now is the ranch." That was before he'd heard other sergeants' schemes. Grace had often wondered how long it would take him to figure out that those mangy cows he had would never turn a profit? If and when he did wise up, which cockeyed plan would he try next?

"Grace, you know, I'm always unhappy," he had said another time after they'd argued about the money he spent on the ranch.

"Dwayne, don't you think it might be because of the awful things that happened in your childhood?" Grace had suggested.

"No, it has nothing to do with my childhood," Dwayne insisted. "I just think I would be happier if I could get more money and be my own boss."

He would never blame his unhappiness on his problems growing up on the ranch with his alcoholic father. It was as if he were still protecting him for what he'd done to Dwayne's mother.

*   *   *

She could never get many details out of Dwayne about his child-hood. When his sisters, Helen and Bertha came to visit, Grace had a long talk with them while Dwayne was at work to see if she could fig-ure out just what had happened when they were kids.

Helen said, "You know, we think that a lot of his problem is that he and his brothers never stood up to our father when he was in his many drunken rages. God help us," Helen cried, "when we girls hid from our father, the boys would hide with us."

She went on to say that when they were kids, night after night, the big farm boys cowardly let their alcoholic father beat their mother in their tiny ranch house. The house was only half as big as it needed to be for a family with five children, so it had no secrets. Whenever his younger siblings asked questions about the beatings, Dwayne told them she deserved what she got, but he never said why.

"That's right. Why, Grace," Bertha said, "Helen and I were getting so desperate we started to say we were going to load the rifle and shoot our father ourselves."

"What happened?" Grace leaned forward, straining to hear every word.

"Luckily, we never had to live up to our threat," Helen explained. "The beatings stopped when our father went out to the range early one morning—still all liquored up—and fell out of the back of a pickup and broke his neck when it hit a bump. No one knew why he was riding in the bed of the truck with his ranch hands instead of in the cab, unless someone back there had a bottle and he wanted to be close to it."

"Oh, no. You poor girls."

"Oh, those were awful days. When he died, he left mother with a stockyard full of debt. Then she lost all of the ranch hands because she couldn't pay them. The next thing she knew, cows just started walking off. Seemed like people were going to take what they were owed, one way or the other." Bertha's voice was full of sadness.

The sisters never had anyone to listen to them before. Back home, relatives didn't believe in spilling the dirty laundry, and the girls found nothing but cold shoulders and hearts when they'd tried to talk about what they'd been through at home.

"Soon after," Bertha continued, "poor Mother was in the state mental institution with a breakdown. They said they had some new medicine for her arthritis and depression. Turns out, they were giving her huge doses of morphine. They thought it was safe back then. She never left the hospital after that."

Grace thought she'd heard it all. She couldn't believe it when they started up again. The girls told her that because the hospital was miles away, their mother never saw the ranch or her family again, except for Dwayne, who visited once or twice when he got his car. After that, the hospital staff asked him not to come anymore because his visits upset her so much it took them days to get her settled down and comfortable again.

Helen said, "We got a phone call one day from one of our mother's doctors saying Dwayne had shown up there that day with a fistful of paperwork on the ranch, turning ownership over to him. He insisted that he had family business to discuss, and kept pushing the papers toward Mother even though she was obviously upset. Finally, the staff told him she'd lost all interest in cows and it was best to just leave her in peace."

"We guessed she was afraid that if she turned the ranch over to Dwayne, she'd have nothing left. No way to ever get out of the hospital because she'd have no place to go if she did get out," Bertha said.

By the time the girls went home, Grace was exhausted.

If the ranch had so many bad memories, why didn't Dwayne just cut his losses and run? Grace wondered after the girls left. But Grace knew that quitting never crossed Dwayne's mind. The worse things got, the more Dwayne increased his efforts to build up the ranch. At the same time, he was shoring up his fantasy of what the ranch was.

Even if he couldn't get his mother to sign papers turning the seventy-acres over to him, he figured it all would be his anyway, some-day, since no one else in his family had any interest in it. His sisters didn't want it and his brothers insisted that there wasn't enough land there to support the number of cows it would take to make a living. CG told him, "Even with supplemental feeding—no, *especially* with supplemental feeding—the ranch doesn't pencil out."

The last few days had made it clear to Grace that the financial security Dwayne craved was for *him*, not so he could provide for his family. It was a realization that was slow in coming, but it did come when Pauline found the savings book in the back parking strip by the garbage cans.

Dwayne was very secretive about his money, so she'd never even known that seventy-five dollars a month was going from his pay-check directly to the ranch.

The money that Grace knew about that went to the cows—the money they'd fought about—was just piddle money by comparison.

CHAPTER 19

A Place to Go

And what about her? What would she and Glory do when Dwayne left?

There would be a lot of expenses. She'd have to pay the divorce lawyer, get an apartment, and pay for all utilities plus all of the deposits. She'd also have to pay for her own health care, although Glory would be covered through the Army until she was eighteen. The three hundred dollars Grace had saved wouldn't cover everything.

If she couldn't make enough money sewing, getting a regular job wouldn't be easy. The plain truth was she was a Mexican woman, without any real skills, who was going deaf in an area where people were still smarting over the Alamo—Fort Sill was just sixty-miles from the Oklahoma-Texas border. She might as well be in Texas.

Even on Sunday drives on the highway to Texas, she and Dwayne had discovered only a few restaurants that would even let her in to eat. Experiences like this made Dwayne angry—with her. She could never understand why they couldn't take their Sunday drive in the other direction, away from Texas.

More than once, Dwayne had taken Glory in to eat and left her in the car because Glory was so hungry she was sick and there wasn't another restaurant around for miles. He always brought something to Grace to eat in the car on the way home, but she was usually too upset and ashamed to eat it.

A white Baptist woman in the same situation as Grace would have had it easier. Being a Mexican and a Catholic in a rabidly Baptist town was a poor position for Grace to be in. Baptists ran all of the big businesses, from the automobile showrooms to the department stores. Grace would have to grovel for a job, but a Baptist woman in trouble would have a job before Sunday service was over at noon.

All of the local politicians were Baptists.

Baptists.

Baptists.

Baptists.

To make things almost hopeless for local minorities, Baptists filled every position on the various educational scholarship committees. Was it any wonder there were no Mexican or colored doctors, teachers, or lawyers in town? Grace wondered why the Indians were still allowed to have their own medicine men? She decided that it was because the city fathers had never felt threatened by them. Years before, the Ghost-Dancers had been banned—and many killed—because they struck fear in the hearts of the settlers.

Nowadays, the white people just laughed at the colorful Indians wearing their feathers and shaking their rattles, until they needed water for their withering crops. Then their memories always got real short, and they would beg the natives to work their special powers on the red dirt. Photographic coverage of these ceremonies always landed on the front page of the paper, and often actually did bring rain, at least a few drops. That was more than the white doctors in town could do.

Vera once came to Grace with an idea to dress up like a medicine man and go from farm to farm, dance, and shake her rattle for a fee.

But Rudolf found out about it and stopped it before she could talk Grace into making her a costume.

To Vera, it was like when she'd dressed up as Dorothy and crashed a bicycle into the crowded dance floor at the officers' club. It was all a lark and she just laughed when Rudolf said he didn't want her out on some ranch where an angry, frustrated farmer might see breasts under her buckskin and beat her up. Vera didn't actually promise she'd *never* do it, and Grace knew the medicine man idea might surface again some hot summer when Rudolf was away on assignment and Vera got bored. Luckily, with a high-ranking officer for a husband, she didn't need to worry about small town politics. Bigwigs be damned. She was free to wear beads and feathers whenever she wanted—as long as Rudolf didn't catch her.

Unless Dwayne stirred up trouble, Grace didn't have to worry about the bigwigs either; they'd think of her as small potatoes. Someday, she knew, they could be a problem. If she got on their wrong side, they could refuse to give her a business license and close her down, disrupt her mail and deliveries, or even lodge a nuisance complaint against her for having customers come to her home, which might be against zoning regulations. For right now, she was just worried about being able to make a living with her sewing. If she succeeded that far, one day she'd have higher ambitions. Then she could worry about town politics.

Right now, all she wanted was for Glory to have the things *she'd* never had: pretty clothes, lots of toys, books, and time to play without stomachaches. Most of all, she wanted someone who would be a real father to Glory.

But that could come later. For herself she wanted a car and a nice boyfriend who would treat her like a lady. She longed for someone who would take her to dinner, and maybe dancing.

Her thoughts turned to her machine; it was an old Singer electric portable that Vera had bought for her from a neighbor. It didn't have a heavy-duty motor and she wondered how it would hold up under the strain of constant use.

But even if she had to buy a new machine, it would be her only big expense. She could buy it on payments from Ramon, one of her cousins who owned a shop that sold vacuum cleaners and sewing machines. Of course, she'd also have to live in a place big enough to house her business. That could be expensive. "*Ay, ay, ay*, I am one Mexican going out on a limb, a *cactus* limb," Grace mumbled to herself.

Thank goodness she had such a good family. Momma's house had a couple of empty bedrooms. She didn't want to have to move back home and admit defeat, but her brothers and sisters moved through Momma's big house all the time, as if it were still their home.

And indeed, it was. Their mother hardly noticed when one of her flock came home; she just rolled more tortillas and cooked more beans. When one of them got back on his feet, it wasn't as if they were gone forever. They were still in and out frequently to visit with their mother and each other.

Like it or not, Grace admitted to herself that she and Glory would have to go to her mother's if things didn't work out. Momma and Momma's house were as solid as the wrought iron skillets she cooked in. They would always have a home there.

CHAPTER 20

School Clothes!

Every summer, the Army warned all the mothers that they should pour lots of liquids down their kids when it was hot and make sure they didn't get sunburned. Grace worried a lot about Glory. The dangers of dehydration and skin damage from too much sun were new and frightening to moms from out of state, but even moms who'd heard the warnings before were cautious.

She couldn't see Glory and she didn't dare call for her and risk waking Dwayne. She gave the clothesline pole a quick check to make sure her little cowgirl wasn't tied up again. At least she didn't have to worry that Glory would go near the tracks. The boys in the neighborhood hadn't left their yards since the rattlesnake incident. After their fathers had gotten ahold of them, they'd lost all interest in straying beyond the boundaries of the housing area.

Before she left the kitchen to fix up a little, she poured a glass of Kool-Aid and set it on the kitchen table near the door. The next time Glory ran by, she'd pour it down her. Later, when Grace came back into the kitchen to start dinner, the drained glass was on the table. Glory must have seen her dad asleep on the couch and had come and left without a word. While Grace fried potatoes, Glory reappeared, all covered with red dirt.

"Glory, where have you been?"

"Me and Ronnie planted the walnuts," Glory answered, her face beaming.

"All of them?"

"No, just the ones we couldn't crack."

"Where did you plant them?"

"Everywhere!" Glory said.

Grace covered the potatoes to steam them as they fried in the pan and started the hamburger, tomatoes, and onions that would be the main part of the meal. In her stone *molcajete*, she ground up garlic cloves until they looked almost like paste, then poured in a little of the juice from the canned tomatoes to loosen all of the garlic pieces from the rock bowl. When the hamburger started browning, she spooned a little of the garlic mixture into the wrought iron cook-ware. Finally, she added a few of the canned tomatoes and cut them up with a knife in the skillet. After she added salt, pepper and cumin, she poured in some water to make a savory mixture that would be scooped up in torn pieces of tortilla and eaten with fingers. Dwayne would eat his with a fork.

This was everyday food of her family. The addition of fried okra added another wonderful aroma to the meal. While the potatoes browned, she stirred the hamburger and minced some hot pepper and onion. She also chopped the last of the canned tomatoes and added all of the ingredients to the leftover ground garlic mixture to make a salsa. The ice was halfway frozen, thanks to Dwayne taking a nap, so iced tea soon filled his goblet at the table.

By the time the meal was ready, the temperature in the little kitchen combined with the heat from outside was unbearable. Neighbors all around her hadn't cooked supper for weeks, and just ate sandwiches and potato salad made earlier in the day. But Dwayne liked Grace's cooking; it was one of the few things she did that he really liked, and Grace was anxious to keep him happy.

He was impressed with her sewing skills, but didn't have much use for them. Grace made him a dressy short-sleeved shirt once. It hung in the closet most of the time because they seldom went anywhere he could wear it. It was too nice to wear fishing, and most of the time around the house he wore a tank-style undershirt and old wrinkled khaki pants.

Once, Grace offered to cut off some of his trousers and make Bermuda shorts out of them so he'd be cooler, but he wasn't about to do anything that would make him look like that German colonel her sister Vera was married to. Rudolf wore Bermuda shorts all the time in the summer, and Dwayne liked to say he could spot Rudolf's little bow legs a mile away when he was mowing his yard. Grace had finally given up. Let the dumb Texan melt.

"So, tell me more about the ranch," Grace asked when Dwayne woke up.

"It was a hell of a trip, before I ever got there, I lost my savings book," Dwayne mumbled, still groggy from his nap, "must've left it in that truck stop."

"What savings book was that?" Grace asked, biting her lower lip.

"Uh," Dwayne stumbled, "oh, an old one I'd had around for a long time."

"Was there any money in it?" Grace forced herself to ask casually.

"Nah. We'd emptied it out long ago."

"Oh." *Then why did you carry it, you dumb-ass? You've got some nerve!* she thought to herself, but said nothing. Instead, she asked, "How's your aunt?"

"Grace, you shoulda seen it. All my brothers' girls are hovering around Aunt Bett just waitin' for her to die so they can get their hands on her antiques, and I swear, she just keeps gettin' younger. She's driving them crazy. They're all fighting over that big, carved, wooden bed of hers. It's gotten so bad Aunt Bett is threatening to be buried in it."

"Shame on those girls."

"Boy, you can't tell her a thing, though. She's mounted a god-damned umbrella on her tractor so she can keep working in the heat."

"How old is she now?"

"Eighty-nine, we think. Could be a lot more. No one has a birth certificate down there. The courthouse burned down years ago. She had a heatstroke while I was down there. Could've lost her real easy."

Dwayne was starting to become agitated. Grace could tell some-thing was coming. Finally, he blurted out, "Grace, I gave our savings to my sisters because they came and took care of Aunt Bett so I could get some work done."

Grace was overwhelmed. "Why? Couldn't Aunt Bett have paid them? She has a good income from the crops."

"I didn't ask her," he said. "The girls both have high school com-ing up and I wanted them to have new outfits. They were nice enough to drop everything and come and take care of her for a few days so I could finish the fence. I'd have you make them something if they were here, but they're not, and don't ask me to take you down there."

Grace just looked at him. *Don't worry about that, cowboy.* Funny, she'd been so occupied thinking about the savings book that Pauline had found, she hadn't thought to look for their joint one. He hadn't left her any grocery money and it was only the middle of the month. *School clothes.* What did he think they were going to *eat?*

As far as Dwayne knew, their savings was all they had for an emer-gency, like Glory getting sick. He'd left them exposed, with no finan-cial backup in case of trouble. It seemed Glory was getting sick more and more. The doctor said it was her nerves. She was the only little kid in the neighborhood who was sick even in the summer. Every time Grace picked up a newspaper there was a story about polio on the front page. Could Glory get polio?

She might need every cent she had hidden away if Glory got sicker. Besides, if she told him she had some extra money, Dwayne might explode again. Even worse, he might take it away from her and give it to his family or spend it on something for his ranch. It had always been clear that his family in Texas came before her and Glory, but this was too much. New school clothes. Grace hadn't even had a chance to go to school when she was a kid, much less with new clothes.

If there were a camel in Oklahoma, this would have been the straw that broke its back. Grace hadn't said anything but inside she was screaming. *What about the savings book you've been hiding from me? Why didn't you take the money out of that?* The sounds never reached her lips, but her face couldn't hide her anger.

There was another message, if only he were smart enough to see it: *he'd had a long ride, but this cowboy's time was just about up.*

Grace got up to clean the kitchen and was aware that Dwayne paced back and forth in the living room while she washed the dishes. She could feel his glare behind her back as she stood at the sink. By the time the last dish was dried, his anger had mushroomed and his strength along with it. As she turned to leave the kitchen, he was waiting for her.

He grabbed her by the arm as he started to pull her to their bedroom and shake her tiny frame like it was a bag of rags. While he pulled her with one hand, he punched her all over her body with the other hand curled into a fist. First he hit her in the ribs, then on the legs, arms, and the side of her head. All the way back to the bedroom, he used Grace's body as a sponge to soak up his anger and frustration. Grace could hardly stand up. She felt the blood rushing through her chest and her head throbbed so much she couldn't keep her eyes open.

"Who are you to tell me what I can or can't do with my money?" Dwayne growled as he hit her.

"Daddy, Daddy. Please stop. Don't hurt Mommy!" Glory cried when she came through the screen door. When she pulled on her daddy's pant leg, Dwayne stumbled and almost stepped on her. Her father was already out of control and hardly noticed her tugs on his trousers or the frightened voice that followed him down the hall. Finally, Grace saw Glory give up and head for her closet with a plate of leftover fried okra.

By now, Grace sobbed uncontrollably. She hurt everywhere. One of Dwayne's slaps to her head pushed air into her left ear; Grace had never felt such pain. She thought for sure he'd broken her eardrum.

He said something to her. What did he say? She was so upset and in so much pain, she couldn't understand the words. She heard "stupid little whore," but what was the next thing he said? Impatient, he sat on the bed, spread his legs apart and pulled Grace down between them. "Suck it." He was saying, "Suck it!"

Grace pleaded, "No, Dwayne, no." He kept pulling her down, as he went on and on about how she was a whore and all of her sisters were whores and she might as well do what whores did. Grace kept resisting. She'd always refused to do this for him. To her, it was a humiliating and degrading act, and she didn't think any other man wanted this from a wife, but Dwayne would not be denied.

As he forced her head down between his legs, Grace's ear hurt and her head began to spin. Without warning, she threw up. Hot sticky vomit spilled all over his male parts and ran down onto the bare oak floor.

Disgusted, he ran for the shower. Grace ran for the toilet. While she threw up the rest of her dinner, Dwayne washed himself. As always, the hot water seemed to calm him down, and by the time he'd shampooed his hair, he'd stopped swearing.

In the shower, Dwayne yelled at Grace, "Damn. I've gone and lost my temper again, but you deserved it. You're just going to have to learn who's gonna be boss, you damn little chili-pepper."

By the time he got out of the shower, Grace was in bed, curled up into a small, tight, frightened ball in her lacy black slip. Her body shook when Dwayne came into the room. He crawled into bed, leaned over and whispered, "I love you, Grace. I'll try to never do that again." Then, his conscience clear, he turned over and went to sleep.

Grace stared at his darkened shape in the darkness. *What kind of a stupid bastard could sleep so soundly after he'd just beat the crap out of his wife?* Grace knew that his family had never been churchgoers, but wouldn't a normal man feel at least a little bit guilty?

She lay very still and listened to his breathing while she felt her pains. Sometime in the middle of the night, Grace dragged her sore body out of bed and emptied her bladder. She tried to survey her bruises in the mirror, but it was small and hung over the sink, too high to see anything.

When she opened the closet curtains in Glory's room to put her in bed, she was hit by a blast of hot air not unlike her oven. Startled that the temperature in the closet was much higher than the rest of the apartment, Grace realized Glory could have died from the heat. The little soft bundle of fear was curled up sound asleep—or was she passed out? on a pile of duffel bags where Grace had found her too many times before. She removed the empty plate of leftover okra, picked Glory up, and moved her to her bed.

After waking her enough to get her to drink some water, Grace sat up on the other end of Glory's mattress, leaned her back against the wall, and watched her all night. "Hold on, Honey," Grace whispered to her sleeping angel, "Mommie's going to get us out of this. I promise."

The next morning at five o'clock, Grace took down the red closet curtain in Glory's room and threw it away. As she stuffed it into the trash bin under the sink, the thought occurred to her that by taking the curtain down, she was admitting that Glory might have to spend more nights in her closet before her father shipped out.

She put on a pot of coffee. Dwayne came in and poured himself a cup and never said a word. As she moved to the refrigerator, he moved to the table. When she moved to the table; he got up from the table and moved to the sink. She felt like she was inside some kind of German clock where dolls moved all around a small space on a track, but never touched.

She didn't offer him breakfast and he didn't ask for any. It reminded her that he'd never called for her to come back to bed last night, either. *Could it be that even he knew he went too far? No, more likely, he'd just fallen asleep.*

They were both relieved when he left for work. Grace looked at the clock; it was too early to call her family. She'd wait awhile. That would give her time to get Glory up, fed, and out the door to play until Grace was ready for them to leave. She also didn't want Glory to relive last night while she listened to Grace talk to her family on the phone.

Grace always wondered how much the child heard before she went to sleep. Glory never said much about the fights the mornings after, except to ask over and over again if her daddy was going to hit her too. Grace always told her no, but she could tell that Glory didn't believe her. She didn't even believe it herself. Maybe he never hit Glory because he knew that would put him in jail for sure. Or, maybe, Glory's time just hadn't come up yet. Dwayne seemed to think all women were whores. At what age did that happen? Seventeen? Sixteen? Twelve?

At eight-thirty, she woke up Glory, gave her a lukewarm bath, put fresh clothes on her, and fed her a fried egg and buttered toast for breakfast. Glory ate slowly but said nothing. Grace guessed that with every bite, pieces of what happened again last night came back to her. When Ronnie showed up at the kitchen door and wanted her to play, she abandoned what was left of her egg and toast and fled out-side.

Grace let her go and called her mother, "Momma? Glory and I are going to come into town today on the bus. Are you going to be home? We will probably spend the night; Dwayne has overnight staff duty." She had no way to know if he really had staff duty or not, but that was what he had said when he went out the door that morning; it was the only thing he'd said. Besides, it really didn't matter where he was going to be as long as he was away from her.

By ten o'clock, she had her house picked up, and was dressed for town. She packed pajamas for Glory and a few Golden Books she'd bought for her at the grocery store. It all fit into a large, brown gro-cery sack; Grace could sleep in something of her mother's. If a neigh-bor happened to see them leave with a suitcase, it might raise questions that Grace didn't yet know the answers to. She hadn't yet decided what she was going to do. She didn't want to come back, but she was afraid she would have to; it wasn't the right time for her to leave Dwayne for good.

There was no doubt in Grace's mind that if Dwayne ever got his hands on their daughter, she'd never see her again. She also knew that if he ever took Glory away from Grace, it would be out of pure meanness, not because he really wanted her. What kind of life would Glory have? Maybe he'd stick her on that stinking ranch of his, miles away from anyone who would love her. What if she became just their little Mexican servant? Grace trembled at the thought.

As she and Glory walked to the bus stop, Grace shivered and stumbled along the broken sidewalk, first aware of a pain here, then a pain there. She had warmed some baby oil to ease the throbbing in her ear; but it had only helped until it cooled off. As she stumbled along, she felt the oil drip from her ear and run down the side of her neck. She didn't bother to wipe it off; she just didn't care anymore.

CHAPTER 21

Downtown Lawton

The old city bus smoked and belched its way down the straight flat road into Lawton. Cement for the road had been mixed with the local red sand that gave the pavement a pinkish tinge. Its surface was veined with hundreds of cracks patched with hot tar that made it look like the scales on a huge pink snake that slithered across the prairie. Each tarred crack jostled the bus as its tires rolled over it, creating a constant chorus of squeaks and thuds. Driver and passengers moved with the jostling, and Grace thought the bumps and twists she felt must be something like the pioneers felt when they'd crossed the prairie in covered wagons.

She had to tell Glory again about the old, brown flagstone stables that were used when the Army rode horses. Even though she explained over and over that the horses were long gone, Glory strained to see into the windows of the dark stables each time they rode the bus.

"Maybe the horses will come back, Mommy," Glory always said.

Grace finally gave up and answered, "Maybe."

An elderly woman passenger was telling Grace how pretty the crape myrtles had been this summer when they heard a squeal from

Glory. "Horses, Mommy, horses." Sure enough, the officers were running up and down on horses and swinging wooden sticks at a ball on the regulation polo field alongside the highway.

"What the heck does polo have to do with Oklahoma?" Grace asked the woman. The woman shrugged and said she had never been big on history, but she was sure the answer was nothing.

It must have something to do with being an officer. A group of officers' wives in wrinkled shorts watched their men from the sidelines. Their sleeveless tops were even more wrinkled than their shorts. They looked as tacky as ever. Why was it they could wear their shorts all over and Grace and her neighbors couldn't even wear them in their own front yards?

Longingly, she looked at the women's cars while Glory's eyes were glued to the polo scene until the ancient scrub oak trees growing along the creek hid the horses and the cars from the highway.

When the bus passed the old, crumbly pink plaster Star Motel and the raunchy nightclubs on Second Street, Grace looked at her watch. It was too early to go to her mother's. She decided to kill some time in town. Lawton's main drag had the local Woolworth's, the City Bank on the corner, movie houses on both sides of the street, a shoe store, and the local bookstore where the kids bought their school-books every fall. That was pretty much it, except for the ritzy department stores, that for Grace, were as far away as Dallas.

Glory wanted to pull the cord that ran above the windows so she could stop the bus and Grace held her up so she could reach it. On the corner, across from the Comanche County Courthouse, an old Indian man gently touched Grace's arm, "Can I give you some money to buy ribbons for your little girl? I used to buy ribbons for my little girl, but she's grown now."

New hair ribbons! She couldn't disappoint either the stranger or her daughter who was so excited she jumped up and down. "That's very nice of you, thank you." Embarrassed, Grace took fifty-cents from the old man and wondered if he thought she was Indian?

As they turned into Woolworth's, Grace let Glory stop long enough to take one last look at the Indian dressed in a print western shirt and twill pants with a big silver belt buckle. His long hair was neatly braided from beginning to end with colorful strips of wool yarn that went the entire length of his braids and brushed the top of his belt. Grace looked to see if he wore moccasins, but no, brown wingtips covered his feet. Glory gave him one last girlish wave before Grace pulled her through the door. Was he Kiowa or Comanche? Grace couldn't tell.

Pauline would know. She'd always been interested in the many Indian cultures in the area. When Grace was small, Pauline had even taught her an Indian song about education that she'd learned while visiting an Indian family with her mother. All through their childhood they'd chanted the words, "…get an education, learn a good vocation…make me proud of you, my son…make me proud of you, my daughter." There was more, but Grace had forgotten the rest. She did remember, though, that Chief Quanah Parker had been so interested in education for his people that he'd sat on the Lawton Board of Education.

Inside the store, Grace looked at the face creams, and saw the hair cream that her sister swore by, but she wasn't in the mood to buy any. Glory couldn't take her eyes off the cobalt bottles of Evening in Paris perfume.

"Buy some, Mommy, buy some," she begged.

Oh, Lordy, Grace thought, *that's all I need.* The cheap, heavy scent of the dime store perfume seemed to intensify in the summer heat, and every bus in town smelled like Evening in Paris, especially toward the back. She did need some clear nail polish and emery boards. She paid for the items at the cashier stand with the cute little redheaded lady. Dwayne said she was a whore because she worked. She'd always been perfectly nice to Grace, and Grace doubted she was a whore at all.

On a whim, before they went out the back door, she bought Glory a beaded bracelet strung on elastic in the toy department for twenty-five cents, and Glory declared the beads to be as pretty as the real thing, whatever she thought that was. Did Glory know about diamonds? If she did, she could thank her Aunt Vera; Grace had never had a diamond. Her wedding band was made from a brass alloy that had its beginning as an artillery shell casing before it was fashioned into a ring by some enterprising soldier who sold it to Dwayne for four dollars.

They decided to buy the hair ribbons at Kress, because they had the best selection. The alley between the stores was cool and breezy, and was a regular shortcut for everyone between Woolworth's and Kress on the next block.

The two stores carried pretty much the same merchandise, except Kress had a counter with two aquariums: one with goldfish and one with little turtles with roses painted on their backs for fifty-cents each. A visit to the aquariums was always the highlight of Glory's trips to town. This trip, she begged and begged until Grace bought her a turtle with a red rose, and a small bag of turtle food.

Then her daughter insisted on buying hair ribbons the Indian man would like. After much thought, Glory finally decided on red and navy blue plaid grosgrain. She pulled Grace to the door of the store so she could look up and down the street for her Indian friend, but he was nowhere in sight. Grace promised her they could look for him again when they walked to the bus stop. She coaxed Glory away from the door with an offer of lunch.

Grace always treated herself and Glory to a hamburger-in-a-basket and a milkshake at the Kress fountain whenever they went to town. Not only were they Glory's favorites, but Grace was always trying to replace the weight that she lost every time she became sick.

The waitress at the counter greeted them both by name and Glory treated her to an introduction to turtle.

"Look what I got, Miss Lorraine."

The waitress looked over the counter, "Why, I believe you got the prettiest one, Sugar. What's her name?"

"Carmen," Glory answered without any hesitation.

"That's a pretty name. Where did you get it?" the waitress asked.

"From the turtle lady. She said she'd already named it."

"You girls want the usual?" Lorraine asked as she wiped off the counter with a dingy rag that looked as if it had once been some man's undershirt.

Glory and her mother both nodded. As soon as the food arrived, Glory held a French fry up to the turtle's mouth and asked, "Want a bite, Carmen?"

"Better put her away, Honey, we'll get thrown out of this joint," Grace kidded her. The waitresses all laughed. Behind the rickety old lunch counter there were gaps between the creaky oak floorboards big enough for a snake to come through—turtles were the least of their problems.

Lorraine mumbled under her breath, "Yeah, Honey, you better put him away before one of our roaches eats him."

"Shall we go to Gramma's?" Grace asked when they'd finished eating. It was two miles, a distance Grace usually walked, but today they waited for a bus. The fare was only ten cents apiece, and Glory looked tired. Grace was worse; she was tired, cranky, and her ear was throbbing. She thought over and over again, *back-to-school clothes for his sisters!*

Normally, Grace would try to figure out how much she'd spent in town while she waited for the bus, but today she didn't care. She was tired and beaten down, but she was also something else. She was angry. Soon her marriage would be over, and she was in no mood to worry about a couple of bucks. She wondered if Dwayne had any idea how she felt. She briefly wondered if he cared, then decided that his feelings didn't matter anymore. *Care, don't care. It was all the same to her.*

While waiting at the bus stop, a gray-haired woman wearing a blue and white striped seersucker suit and short white gloves smiled at Grace and said, "You must be baby-sitting today."

"No, she's mine."

The white woman looked at her in disbelief. It was always hard for strangers to believe light-skinned Glory was hers, but with her new bleached hair shining in the sun like white gold, it was beyond Southern comprehension. The lady hurumphed at Grace and rolled her eyes at the other waiting passengers as if to ask, who did she think she was fooling? She didn't know what the disheveled Mexican woman was trying to pull, but she refused to be drawn into an argument with someone who was so obviously beneath her.

Grace, however, was in the mood for a good fight, and when she moved toward the woman she fully intended to stuff those white gloves of hers down her throat. The woman probably wore them to protect her hands from all the inferior people who rode the same bus she did. *So why don't you drive your own car?* Grace was about to ask as she took another step in the woman's direction. Just before she reached the woman, out of the corner of her eye, she caught sight of a baby blue Cadillac fender pulling up to the curb.

"Hi, Gracie, need a lift?" a voice shouted. It was Bruce Steiner, one of the ballet instructors, in his new convertible. Grace helped Glory into the back seat and then climbed into the front without ever looking back at the gray-haired woman with a dime in her gloved hand and her mouth wide open.

"What was that all about? You're almost as white as I am," Bruce asked as he glanced at the woman in seersucker.

"Oh, nothing. It's just that no one ever believes that Glory is mine. It makes me so mad."

"Calm down—if that uppity woman was confused before, think how she feels now. Maybe she thinks *I'm* the father. So where are we going?"

Grace had to laugh as she answered, "To my mother's on Park-view."

They must be a sight. Bruce's bleached hair blew in the open con-vertible. He wore his light pink silk shirt, open at the collar and pleated charcoal gray trousers accented with a thin, black, snakeskin belt. Beside him, Grace with her dark skin and hair. She wore a faded, full-skirted cotton dress with bare legs and sandals, and car-ried a wrinkled paper grocery sack from The Happy Pig.

"Glory," Bruce called to the back seat, "how do you like my new car?" Glory didn't speak, she just burst out in a grin, so Grace answered for her, "It's beautiful, Bruce, and you look good driving it."

"Thanks. Larry and I fell in love with the color, but I don't know how I'm going to pay for it, if I can't get all of the little girls in town to help me out by taking some classes," he kidded as he looked back at Glory, who still grinned from pigtail to pigtail.

"Glory, keep that turtle in its box…" Grace said to Glory when she saw her pulling the turtle out. Then she turned again to Bruce, "Oh, she'll be there eventually, won't you, Glory? Every little girl in Law-ton has to take lessons at Steiner and Brook, and Glory will be no exception."

"Good. I'm sure Glory will make a great little ballerina, and I'll be so glad to have one student whose mother doesn't whimper over having to sew up a few costumes."

"Bruce, could you send some of those whimpering mothers my way when I move back to town? I could use the work."

"Gladly. Larry will be thrilled, he just hates to have to explain the difference between velvet and velveteen to those helpless women fifty times a day. 'Darlinggg,' he shrieks, 'if you can't tell the difference, just look at the price, one's cheaper than the other.' The other day, a woman asked him, 'Which one?' and he screamed and ran from the studio. Later, I found him soaking in a hot bubble bath with cucumber slices over his eyelids as he sipped white wine right out of the bottle. He still had his toe shoes on!"

Bruce had turned onto Parkview and slowed down when Grace pointed to the big house next to the park.

CHAPTER 22

A Turtle in the Tamales

When Grace and Glory pulled up with Steiner, she was surprised to see Uncle Joe sitting on the front porch swing. She was even more surprised when she saw Steiner wave and call to him.

"Hey, M*uchacho!*"

"How are the tomatoes doing?" Uncle Joe shouted.

"They're *mucho grande*, can I come get some more mulch?"

"*Si*, anytime."

"*Gracias!*"

"Uncle Joe, I didn't know you knew Steiner," Grace said as she climbed the steps to the front porch.

"*Si*, he showed up at my door one day and asked me if I'd teach him how to grow vegetables."

"Steiner?" Grace couldn't believe the two could be friends. Uncle Joe with his khaki pants, tank-style white cotton undershirt, and straw hat, and Steiner dressed like a New Yorker in silk?

"*Si*, I sent him home with some tomato plants and a bagful of my mulch."

"Uncle Joe, you're a jewel. Are you staying for supper?"

"No, I came over for lunch and to pick up some watermelon pickles that Lilia left for me. While I was here, I set up the rain barrels for Gregoria that Vera brought over."

Uncle Joe hesitated, then patted the seat of the porch swing, "And I've been waiting to talk to you. Come and sit by me."

Puzzled, Grace told Glory to go see her gramma.

"Is anything wrong, Uncle Joe?" Grace asked as she sat down beside the man.

"Gracie, I'm an old man, and I've had a good life…"

"Are you sick?"

"No, no, I'm fine." Uncle Joe paused and started over. "What I'm trying to say is I have all I need, and some leftover." He reached over and took Grace's hand, "If you ever need any money, you just let your Uncle Joe know, okay?"

Tears exploded from Grace's eyes. All these months she'd felt so alone. How foolish she had been. She was a Ramirez. A Ramirez! She had family!

"Oh, Uncle Joe, I'll never forget this. Thank you. But I think we'll be all right. The worst is almost over."

The little man eased himself up from the swing and patted his niece on the head. Without another word he headed for his car. He had said what he'd come to say. It was time to get back to his garden.

Grace's mother was in the kitchen and missed the sight of Grace and Glory being delivered to her door by one of the town's most talked about bachelors. Grace was a little disappointed that her mother hadn't seen their unusual arrival, but then thought it might be just as well. It was impossible to guess whether she would have laughed and asked for a ride, too, or cried, saying Grace "had brought shame on the family" for riding with a rich, single man when she was already married to someone else.

If Grace were to have explained that Bruce was *sort of* married—to a man—Momma wouldn't have believed it. After all, she'd say, a gorgeous man could change his mind about whatever he was or wasn't without even a moment's notice. Then she'd say that he just hadn't met the right woman yet.

Grace went into the house and headed for the kitchen. No one knocked when the front door was open at Momma's. Family and friends walked in and went straight to the kitchen, where they knew they'd find every person in the house who was awake. Spouses who'd married into the family joked about the three people in Lawton who never came to the house because they were the only ones not related to the Ramirez family.

Sometimes, on warm summer nights, they'd sit around and guess who those three people might be. Usually it was the Baptist minister, the Methodist minister, and the local "working lady" who stood in front of the bars late at night. "You know, the one who wears the black fish-net stockings and the cowboy boots," someone would say. Even if they weren't related, Grace couldn't think of *anyone* who couldn't come to Momma's door and be handed a plate of food.

"Hello, my little one, are you hungry?"

"Yes, Gramma."

Grace quickly told her mother in Spanish they had eaten in town and they both laughed as Glory gobbled a hot-buttered tortilla as if it were her first meal of the day.

The child was delighted to see the round flat bread served on her favorite plate, pink ironstone in a pattern that depicted Betsy Ross showing the first flag to George Washington, bordered in ornate pink roses. Her gramma had only one of these plates, a remnant of a set she'd had long ago, and it was Glory's favorite.

Grace decided she could eat, too. Maybe it had something to do with this house feeling like her real home that made her hungry. All of the Ramirez sisters married white men, and the homes they'd made with their husbands would always take second place to this one. Here, they could be themselves, speak and act like the Spanish-Mexican family they were, and eat foods that they'd eaten since childhood. They all cooked, of course, but none of the daughters thought their cooking tasted as good as their mother's.

The sisters had long ago given up on trying to watch her mother cook. They knew she liked to be alone in the kitchen, and didn't like to talk about how she did things. Whenever one of them discovered one of her cooking secrets, like when she added eggshells and a little brandy to the evening coffee on special occasions, they couldn't wait to tell the others. But besides the brandy and eggs shells added to the coffee that gave it body, the difference was strictly in the method.

The staples on her mother's pantry shelves were all too plain to draw a gourmet's attention: pinto beans, potatoes, rice, canned tomatoes, onions, flour, corn meal, baking powder, lard, sugar, syrup, raisins, tea, and coffee. And of course, the herbs and spices: salt, chili peppers, black pepper, garlic, chili powder, oregano, cumin, cinnamon, and anise. Out of this very simple assortment of basics came a peasant food that was plentiful enough to feed and comfort nine children, aunts, uncles, countless cousins, and just as many friends. Uncle Joe liked to say, "Each morning, Gregoria casts a bag of beans upon a pot of water and feeds half of Lawton before the sun goes down."

A Coke bottle filled with a greasy-looking red liquid sat on the counter and caught Grace's eye.

"Momma, what's this?"

"Throw that mess out, Grace. It's more of that barbecue sauce that old colored woman gives Pauline every time she goes to visit her. I don't know why your sister goes over there, anyway. The woman runs her business out of her bedroom."

"Where does she live?"

"Next door to Tia."

"Oh. Garnet. She just got me some new sewing customers. Momma, you know Pauline will stop to talk to anyone. Besides, Garnet might have a lot of men going through her bedroom, but we don't know if she takes money for it."

"All I know is if she can buy a Cadillac off the money from her barbecue, I should at least be able to get a Chevy for my *frijoles*."

"Momma, you don't charge for your beans. Garnet charges for her barbecue."

"Yeah, and that's not all she charges for." Case closed.

Grace opened her mouth to argue more and then just shut it. Momma might have a point. That woman bought a new Cadillac each year. But no, she remembered, lots of Negroes bought new Cadillacs every year because they worked hard and earned good money. Still, nobody in Lawton would sell them a decent house in a good neighborhood, so they had nothing else to spend their money on. It suddenly occurred to her that the whites at the top and the blacks at the bottom in town drove Cadillacs, and the people in the middle drove Fords and Chevys. She didn't remind her mother of the facts, however, because they'd had their own run-in with the Ku Klux Klan years ago.

Grace was too small to remember, but she'd heard the story so many times, she felt like she'd seen it with her own eyes. The way her mother told the story, on one hot summer night, when the heat was so stifling it made everyone cranky, the Ku Klux Klan lit their torches and marched down Second Street.

All of the streetlights had somehow gone out, leaving only the light from the torches to reflect off the white robes the marchers wore. Their faces were hidden by more white sheeting that muffled a chorus of low, ugly grumbles that hovered above the marchers, and followed them down the street—like a dark cloud over Joe Bfstplk in a Li'l Abner cartoon.

The hateful group threatened everyone who wasn't one of them. That included the ones who weren't white enough to march with them, and the ones who were—but wouldn't—either out of fear or because they held different convictions.

First, they veered off Second Street and made a run through the colored section of town that was behind the green laurel hedge the city had planted to hide the poverty-stricken area from tourists. There, they clubbed every black man they caught on the street, and even dragged a few off their front porches.

Marching back on Second, they hadn't run out of anger, and as Momma peeked out her lace curtains in the living room, one of them threw a rock through her window, just to let her know they hadn't forgotten she was there.

❧   ❧   ❧

"Throw that sauce out, Grace, before Pauline gets back." Too late. Pauline came through the screen door talking. "Pauline, do you ever shut up?" Momma asked.

"Momma, I started talking before I left my car. You already missed the best part. "*Ayyy*! Glory, you look like a movie star. Who does your hair?" Pauline kidded.

"My Aunt Vera," Glory answered, proudly tossing her bleached curls.

Pauline never missed a step. She picked up the Coke bottle and emptied it into the pot of beans.

Momma didn't see it with her back turned, but Grace did. As her mouth dropped open, her sister winked at her. In Spanish, Grace whispered, "It was great knowing you, Sis." No one, but no one, fooled with Momma's beans.

The old cook, turned to the sink, saw the empty Coke bottle and tucked it into the wastebasket and smiled, thinking she'd pulled one over on her daughter. It was just seconds before the pungent aroma of barbecue sauce began to spill out of the bean pot. She never even considered Grace, her pet, as the culinary culprit. Her glance went straight to Pauline, who was on the other side of the table giggling with Glory.

"Pauline, you've ruined my beans with that old slave's sauce!" Momma started to swing her huge flour sack dishcloth over her head and chased everyone but Glory from the kitchen.

"What's going on?" Pauline asked when they reached the living room. "I saw your paper sack suitcase in the chair by the door when I came in."

"Same thing, Sis. I had everything ready, the house was clean, the laundry was done, I'd baked a cake, and I did my wifely duties in the bedroom. I got a beating anyway."

"What did he say?"

"He said he was sorry and he loved me and he'd try to never do it again."

"He says that every time. What did he say before he beat you?"

"He said he gave all of our money and even our savings to his sisters because they'd helped out with his Aunt Bett when she got sick. He didn't say anything about his secret savings. I'm sure he didn't give them any of that."

"Why was he paying them? His other brothers have money too."

"He said he needed them to watch Aunt Bett so that he could finish the fence. He also said they needed new back-to-school clothes, shoes, and purses."

"In other words, he was being a big shot. Did he ever mention the savings book?"

"Yeah. He thinks he lost it somewhere in Texas, so just keep it, okay? I might need it someday if we ever go to court. Pauline, if he'd had my money, he would have given that away too. I really don't think he wants us to have *anything*. Every dollar we get goes to Texas for that ranch or for his sisters. He never thinks of what Glory and I might need. He hardly ever notices when Glory is sick, and when he does, he blames me. What's wrong with him?"

"First he's a man. Second he's a Texan. They're all meaner than a rattlesnake and dumber than *adobe*. So, are you staying the night, or what?"

"I'm staying tonight because he has staff duty and won't be home anyway. I'm probably going back tomorrow. I'd have to kill him to keep him from beating me, whether I'm here or there. When he swells up with anger, he's stronger than three or four men put together." Grace moaned. "I can't have him over here hassling Momma. I just hope I can hang on until he gets the heck out of here."

"I hear his division isn't shipping out on time."

"You know the Army. If you don't hear a rumor before ten o'clock, start one. But I think this one is true." Grace said.

"We need a new plan."

Glory came into the room with her turtle and the conversation switched to Spanish.

"Yeah. A five-month-keep-Grace-out-of-the-hospital-plan."

"We could have him put in jail, if he were brown, and you were white."

"Heck, Sis, if our colors were reversed, I could shoot him and get away with it."

"And keep custody of your daughter."

"And get all his money. If he had any."

Pauline chirped, "Maybe they'd even give you his sisters."

"He could keep his sisters. I'd like to have that old car, though."

"I suppose he's going to sell it."

Vera came in, and joined the powwow. "We could shoot the son-of-a-bitch!"

"Already covered that," Pauline answered.

"Well," Vera shrugged, "I knew we couldn't do that. We're not Baptists. But I do have an idea…" both sisters leaned forward to listen. Vera was tough as nails. Years of being a minority and an officer's wife had taught her how to survive by making the rules work for her, instead of against her.

"It's so easy, I think. We simply get Rudolf to pull some strings and get Dwayne assigned to the next unit that's leaving for Japan."

"Could he do that?" Grace asked, in awe.

"I think so. If he wanted to."

Vera looked over and saw Glory playing with her new turtle on the couch. "Glory, you'd better get that turtle off of your Gramma's couch before she comes in here and sees it."

"She's clean," Glory softly whined.

"Have you ever heard of that old Mexican recipe for turtle-bean soup?" Vera asked.

"Take your turtle into the kitchen, Glory," Pauline said, "And ask Gramma for a pot—I mean a bowl—to put it in."

Warily, Glory headed for the kitchen.

"Are you sure she doesn't understand Spanish?" Pauline asked.

"Not a word," Grace answered. "She's definitely her father's child. Dwayne insisted from the beginning that I not teach Glory Spanish. He said it would hold her back in school because he didn't think she was smart enough to learn two languages at once. Besides, he likes to say, 'America works in English.'"

"Well, since we can't whisper, it does come in handy that the kids don't understand Spanish. It lets us have some secrets, although Carlos is beginning to pick it up, I think." Pauline turned to Vera and asked, "How long would it take to get Dwayne out of here?"

"I don't know. I'll see what I can find out."

Glory wandered back into the living room with a turtle bowl complete with a green plastic palm tree and a plastic rock.

"Where does Momma get all that stuff?" Vera asked. They all looked at the glass treasure.

"Didn't our little brother Ben have a bowl like that?" Pauline asked.

"Yeah," Vera answered, "twenty-years ago. You don't think?" Closer inspection revealed water lines along the inside of the bowl. The sisters all hooted. Their mother never failed them. When called upon, she had always been able to produce fish bowls in any needed size, turtle bowls, ant-farm frames, bird cages, boxes of colored chalk, bags of forgotten marbles, and jacks.

"Okay," said Vera, winding up the conversation, "what else can we do?"

"Well, he seems to get angrier whenever my family has been around."

"Sure he does, we cramp his style," she sneered. "What we *should* do is camp out over there until the son-of-a-bitch thinks we're Comanches. Build a fire! Put up a tepee in the backyard, stuff a peace pipe with buffalo shit, and pass it around to your Japanese, German, and Italian neighbors," Vera ranted.

"Vera!" Both sisters shouted through their laughter.

"Okay, we'll cut our visits down. You're sure we can't just have him shot? It would be a lot less trouble."

"Let us think about it," Pauline answered.

"Okay, *adios.* I tee off in a few minutes. Then I'll be by here tonight to whip Ben in cribbage, so tell him to stick around."

"No wonder you use the trunk of your car as an extra closet. You never go home," Pauline said.

"No reason to stay home as long as I'm not broke. Rudolf hardly ever comes home anymore, he's so busy training his troops." Then she added, "Good thing I'm so damned good at bridge."

Pauline and Grace looked at each other quizzically, but before they could question their sister about her last statement, she was gone.

Still in Spanish, Pauline commented, "That crazy girl. You know, I never did find those gold draperies she took to the thrift shop. I think someone beat me to them."

"It's just as well, those curtains might have given you nightmares."

"Yeah. Or I might have started craving plaid golf skirts and bright yellow bowling shirts. Momma, is there coffee?" she shouted toward the kitchen.

They heard a cranky voice answer, "I threw it out. I didn't think I knew anyone *loco* enough to want hot coffee when it's boiling outside."

"The beans *sure* smell good, Mom!" Pauline teased.

Grace looked over at Glory, who'd fallen asleep beside her turtle. "How long do you think that turtle will last?"

"Depends on how long she can keep it away from her Uncle Benny."

"What happened to his turtle, anyway?"

"I don't remember what really happened, that was years ago. He probably just died, but I remember Vera told him Momma had added it to the tamales. Benny cried for days and wouldn't go near the kitchen."

By afternoon there wasn't even a hot breeze inside the big house. Grace was grateful for the chance to rest when the women began to find comfortable places to nap until it began to cool off.

Later, they'd eat tortillas and beans and then play bridge, canasta, dominos, and pinochle all night. Players would take a turn choosing their own favorite card game. Sometime during the evening, as always, the cribbage board would be dusted off for the on-going brother-sister cribbage competition between Vera and Benny. Grace would pick pinochle, and then systematically win every toothpick on the table.

As always, she'd have to wait to beat her siblings until Benny and Vera were through squabbling over their cards. Whenever they played, Vera would get mad and make him stand up so she could frisk him. Gales of laughter would roll over the dining room table as extra cards would fall out of every possible hiding place in his clothing. Vindicated, Vera would announce, "I knew it, I knew it!" Few people ever honestly beat Vera at cards. Grace and Vera were the only two who didn't cheat, Grace because she was too honest, and Vera because she was so good she didn't have to. For the rest, cheating at cards in this family was just part of the fun, and was harmless because they only played among themselves. Card parties like this would go on until Momma would get fed up with the bickering, send Vera and Pauline home, and the rest of them to bed.

🍁   🍁   🍁

But for now, it was quiet. The front door was open, and no one heard Benny come in and serve himself a bowl of beans except Glory.

"Glory, where did you find my turtle?" Benny teased.

"It's not your turtle."

"Why, it looks just like mine."

"Mine has a bowl."

"So did mine."

"Mine has a rock."

"So did mine."

"Mine has a *palm* tree."

"So did mine."

"Mine's learning to talk."

"So was mine!"

Smiling, Glory played her trump card, "Mine has a red rose on its back."

Looking closer, Benny agreed, "So it does. Could you ask it if it has seen my turtle?"

"I will as soon as she learns to talk," said Glory, grinning.

CHAPTER 23

The Minnows in the Sink

The next morning, Grace followed her nose to the kitchen where her mother was busy making onion omelets, hot cheese salsa, and Mexican biscuits. They were up so late Pauline had spent the night. Barefooted, she was still wearing borrowed cotton pajamas and had one leg tucked underneath her in the old, white kitchen chair as she sipped her first cup of coffee. Glory had dressed herself in her shorts and halter and was sitting expectantly in front of her favorite pink George Washington plate.

"Momma, I sure wish we had some more of that barbecue sauce to add to the salsa," Pauline kidded. Grace and Glory giggled as Momma gave Pauline the look that she'd spent most of her life perfecting on her children.

"Did you like the beans, Glory?" Pauline whispered to her niece.

"I liked them. They weren't too spicy for me."

"You must have a cast iron stomach, little one. I was up with heartburn all night," Gregoria complained.

Thanks to the shade of an old willow tree, there was a soft breeze blowing in through the kitchen window. Pauline and Grace could feel the cool, clean air lift their loose-fitting cotton sleepwear as the lace kitchen curtain billowed in its own summer rhythm.

Momma had just passed the filled plates around the kitchen table when Dwayne honked the horn of his old car in the driveway.

Pauline ran to the front window to confirm what they already knew. It was Dwayne, all right.

"Don't go, Sis," she begged as Grace turned white and grasped the edge of the kitchen table for support.

"I have to. He'll be gone soon. Then I'll make my move."

Momma took a deep breath, smiled as if she knew nothing of Dwayne's menacing behavior, and went to the door, "Dwayne, come in and have some coffee," she called.

"No, Mom, I can't. I've got live minnows in a bucket on the back seat. They'll die in this heat."

It really irked Grace that Dwayne had the nerve to call her mother "Mom," as if he thought of her as family. She began to throw her things into her paper bag while Pauline followed her from room to room and begged her not to go. Pauline had planned to spend the morning convincing her to stay at Momma's and never go back. But here was Dwayne, pulling her right back into his web before Pauline ever had a chance to state her case.

Momma grasped Grace's hand as she went out the door, and whispered, "*Via con Dios*, my little one," but she wasn't sure if she heard it. "No matter, a blessing is a blessing even if it falls on deaf ears," Momma turned to Pauline and said.

Grace heard it, but she didn't look back. She didn't want her mother to see the terror in her eyes. How much longer could she go on like this? Day after day of stress, pain, and fear were tearing her to pieces. She was beginning to think that Glory wasn't the only one who was going to have a nervous breakdown.

As soon as Glory got into the car, she introduced Carmen to the minnows. Water from the bucket and the turtle bowl sloshed onto the old gray mohair upholstery as Dwayne backed up the car.

"Are you tired?" Grace asked, to make conversation.

"No, I slept in my chair most of the time, except when that crazy German of Vera's came into the office at two in the morning."

"Rudolf? What did he want?"

"I couldn't figure it out. He wanted to know what artillery classes I'd had and when. Then he wanted to know when I was due to make sergeant. He said he just happened to be in the area—at two in the morning! He must have been over at the officers' club playing cards. I sure can't figure out how he ever got to be a full colonel."

"He's a very smart man, Dwayne."

Dwayne shot her a hateful look, so she shut up. Time to change the subject.

"What are you going to do with the minnows?"

"Gonna keep 'em at the house. Gotta keep 'em cool."

"Where are you going to keep them? We don't have any shade."

"In the kitchen sink, I reckon. Major Reid had them in his backyard, but they were dying off faster than chiggers in a bucket of DDT."

Dwayne had no sooner put the minnows in the kitchen sink with the creek water when they heard a car pull up in back of the quarters. Grace looked out the window and saw a car full of captains and majors who were already working their way through a couple of cases of beer while they masturbated their fishing poles that stuck out of every window. Dwayne rushed back in with a minnow bucket, scooped up some minnows, and headed out the door. Before Grace could blink, they were gone.

She looked over and saw her kitchen sink full of stinky creek water and slimy silver minnows. Did he say when he was coming back? If he did, she didn't hear him. They had a place to stash their camping gear down by the creek, so there was no way to tell. They could be gone for days.

Why didn't he just leave her at her mother's? At least then she would have had some company. Annoyed, Grace put Glory in a cool bath and poured some iced tea. *She* knew why Rudolf was there at the battalion in the middle of the night. Luckily, Dwayne didn't catch on. Good old Vera. She drove them all crazy sometimes when she acted like *she* was the full colonel instead of her husband, but she was a good sister. Was Rudolf going to be able to help her? What if Dwayne got shipped out tomorrow? Her heart leaped at the thought, and she imagined to herself just how fast she could pack and vacate Army quarters if given the chance.

She went to put her glass in the sink and stopped when she saw the slimy fish bait swimming around and around, looking for a way to the creek. Shoot! How long would this last? Later in the afternoon, she walked into the kitchen and was hit by the stench of dying fish. The kitchen wasn't even cool enough for creek minnows. Or, maybe they were already half dead when he put them in the sink. She tried to ignore the smell, but it was too much. At first she poured a little water from the faucet into the sink to dilute the stink, knowing full well that Lawton's heavily chlorinated water wasn't good for minnows. Heck, Lawton's water wasn't even good for people.

Dwayne didn't come home that night. By morning, half the fish were belly up, and the stench was hideous. Grace rushed in and dumped a big glob of cleanser into the stinky water. "This won't help you," she said to the minnows, "but it'll sure help me." By noon, the fish were all dead, and she scooped them into an old milk carton and took them to the trashcan in the alley. She scoured the sink out with more cleanser and boiling water. All day, she watched her neighbors go to empty their trash, get a whiff of the dead bait, and run back to their quarters with their garbage cans over their heads.

Dwayne was bound to be furious when he found out that all of his minnows were dead. The thought also crossed her mind she was lucky they didn't fish with snakes. Then, she'd have a real problem in her kitchen sink. She couldn't imagine one of the officers' wives putting up with minnows in her kitchen. Why doesn't he see they're using him?

Grace whipped up a chocolate cake and threw it in the oven, even though it made the kitchen so hot she wasn't sure what she was baking, the cake or herself.

In late afternoon, their car drove up, a back door opened, and Dwayne rolled headfirst out onto the dry grass when he tripped over all of the minnow buckets and poles in the back seat. Dwayne, a non-drinker, was the only one of them who was sober. Why didn't they let *him* drive? When he came into the kitchen, Grace looked into his eyes and knew something was wrong. They had done more than fish on the reservation.

Dwayne was crazed. He hopped around from room to room like a jackrabbit trying to find shelter from a hawk flying overhead. His eyes rolled up and down in his head, and he couldn't stop giggling a nervous giggle that wasn't funny at all. Over and over he looked out the sheer curtain in the front window. *What went on out there?* Grace wondered, but she didn't dare ask.

Later that evening, Dwayne couldn't keep it to himself any longer and began telling her how the fishing wasn't any good—and Major Reid had a rifle—so for hours they had cut through the tall dry grass on the prairie. They took turns at driving while the others sat on the hood of the car to flush out deer and shoot them over and over until their carcasses were almost unidentifiable.

"But it's not hunting season," Grace stammered.

"Oh, they weren't going to take them home, they were just out for the blood," Dwayne answered.

"Where are the deer now?"

"Oh, we left them there. By the time we were through with them, the deer weren't good for anything. It was a lot of fun, but I was afraid we were going to get caught. On the way home, we passed two patrol cars with flashing lights on the highway, and we thought they were probably going to look for us."

So that was why he kept looking out the window; he was expecting the military police! Grace was sick to her stomach. If he were arrested, it could delay his departure or cancel his new assignment altogether. She went to the kitchen window, hoping for a cool breeze, but all she smelled was rotting fish coming from the garbage cans, and it was three days until the garbage was due to be picked up.

She was relieved to walk by the bathroom and see steam as it came out from the cracks in the door. At least he was going to clean up. "Grace," he called to her from the shower, "what is that awful stench?" At least, that's what she thought he said; the water was still running. After his shower, he headed for the kitchen for a glass of iced tea. "Where the hell are my minnows?" he shouted. Grace followed him into the kitchen, and told herself, *don't make a big deal out of this. If you don't, maybe he won't.*

"Dwayne, it was so hot here. They died. I felt just awful."

"Damn, what am I going to tell the guys?"

Tell them to use worms. She waited for signs of anger, but there were none. He took it rather well. But then, dead minnows must have seemed like a minor problem after slaughtering helpless deer from the hood of a car.

The next morning, he was out the door early. Maybe he and his officers were going to have a quick prayer for the minnows before work started. She couldn't believe her eyes when she saw a garbage truck pull up to empty the trash cans several days early just as Dwayne was getting into his car.

Someone must have called and complained. She hoped they didn't know who was responsible for the awful stench. Her standing in the neighborhood was low enough already. She watched Dwayne smile and wave at the garbage collector as he left for work, like he was the one who made the call. Grace shook her head. *What a jerk!*

Later that morning, Vera called. She'd spoken to her husband about Grace's problem.

"Bad news, Hon. Rudolf says Dwayne doesn't have enough schooling to fit into any other slots. There's no place to ship him to."

"Oh, no. Vera, he's really getting crazy." She told her sister about the fishing trip, and about how Dwayne hopped up and down all over the house. "Vera, he'll go along with anything they say and do. He wants to be just like them. Did you know that some of those officers keep their wives locked in their garages whenever they're gone because they're afraid they'll run around?"

"How long do they stay locked up?"

"Sometimes for days. And with no toilets. They can't call for help because making a fuss would put an end to their husbands' careers."

"I'll give Rudolf another call and get back to you."

"But he's already said there's nothing he can do."

"I know. I might have to promise to learn to cook sauerkraut or something."

"Vera, there's nothing to cooking sauerkraut, you just open a can."

"But *then* what?"

It was just too hot to do any housework. Grace decided to join the other wives in the housing area who'd captured a strip of shade on the backside of the building. There was more shade in front of the quarters, but they knew they couldn't sit where they'd be seen wearing shorts. This was, after all, Army housing, and rules were strict where the lower-ranked soldiers lived.

"Grace, hot enough for you?" Sako asked. Grace thought this question was automatically tacked onto the end of every sentence in the middle of summer in Oklahoma:

"You're fired. Hot enough for you?" *or...*

"A hostile band of Apache warriors is holding your wife hostage on the ninth hole of the golf course and they're peeking up her plaid golf skirt. Hot enough for you?" *or...*

"Your whole family and your favorite bird dog were just swept away by a flash flood outside of Tulsa. Hot enough for you?"

She wanted to say that, yes, it was hot enough in her kitchen to boil minnows, but she decided to keep quiet.

"Grace, Virginia here was just saying her daughter's ballet class is looking for a seamstress to make recital outfits and I told her you might know somebody. You were raised here, and we're all new." Sako's expression said: I-haven't-told-her-a-thing-do-what-you-want.

Grace was surprised. "Let me get back to you, Virginia, when is the recital?"

"Not until December, but we thought we'd better start beating the mesquite trees. There are twenty girls, and it'll take some time to find someone."

"What kind of costumes?"

"Well, Mr. Steiner has a picture he tore out of a children's book. It looks like kind of an Arabian top in red with gold rickrack and pink fluffy nylon net skirts."

Good grief. Bruce was still using the same costumes he'd used for the last twenty-years. But then, why change? The kids were different every year and they loved the outfits. When you've found something that works, why change it?

Cautiously, Grace said, "I might be doing a little sewing."

She could never figure out how two bachelors shared a house and managed to make and keep a successful business in Lawton for so many years without being strung up. Male hairdressers had been run out of Lawton just for wearing pink shirts.

Maybe the dancers were allowed to stay because, in the middle of the prairie, Okies needed all the diversions they could get, and Steiner and Brook had been a welcome distraction to many children and their mothers struggling through boring childhoods. The men were good to the kids too.

The hairdressers, on the other hand, were more plentiful than beer drinkers on Saturday night. The town rednecks could run two hair stylists out of town and four more wearing pink shirts would show up the next day.

When the two dance instructors drove through town in their Cadillac convertible with the top down, everyone waved, from Okie rednecks to Catholic priests. Grace suspected St. Mary's was just one of the beneficiaries of the dance studio, although nothing was ever said.

The way Grace had it figured, at five dollars a student a month, thirty students a class, five classes a day, six days a week, the two were loaded. But even if they didn't help the church, she liked the two. They were good people who added a splash of color in a very dull environment. In the middle of her reverie, she heard a woman who joined them exclaim, "The radio says it's a hundred and eight!"

"Don't tell us," several of the women answered in unison.

While she sipped iced tea and visited with the ladies, Grace mentally tallied her prospective list of customers: one dance group, Aunt Lilia, the restaurant, her brother Frank, and the thrift shop. Not enough to strike out on her own, but a start.

Also, Pauline had said her friend Garnet needed some outfits for when she had solos to sing in church. Garnet had put on some weight and had been unable to find a dressy outfit that she could perform in comfortably. Grace looked forward to making her some performance dresses that had room for an expanding diaphragm. She'd already made several outfits for some Methodist singers, so she knew what to do.

A gospel singer! Grace had assembled an unusual list of customers. She loved gospel music, and as she sipped her tea, she toyed with the idea of being invited to Garnet's church to hear her sing. Maybe she'd even introduce her. That would be fun, and good for business.

Garnet's car might be a problem; she was driving a bright orange Cadillac convertible this year; a car like that might be mentioned to Dwayne. Maybe Pauline could drive her over in her Packard. The neighbors were used to seeing Pauline's car in the neighborhood.

While Grace daydreamed, the ladies started to wander back to their kitchens to put their cold suppers on the table. Grace was just getting up herself when Dwayne came roaring up in his old Ford coupe, sending dust everywhere. Frustrated, he got out of the car and slammed the door.

"Grace, the damnedest thing," he shouted, "I've been loaned to another unit and they're on their way to the field. In this heat. God-damnit to hell!"

Grace studied him closely and decided he had no idea who was behind his new assignment. *Maybe he was blaming his bad luck on the dead minnows?*

"That's too bad, Dwayne, when do you leave?"

"Right after supper. Be gone for a whole week, hell's bells!"

She could tell he wanted to kick something, anything, but it was just too hot to waste energy.

"Are my clothes ready?"

"Yes, I starched the last pair of fatigues this morning and ironed them at lunch. What else do you need?"

"That'll do it. I'll have to shine my boots and study this manual they gave me on one of our new artillery pieces. Don't bother to cook; we'll drive into town for hamburgers. Get Gloria into the car." Dwayne's voice had echoed between the buildings and Glory suddenly appeared and jumped up and down as she clapped her hands.

"What an added bonus," Grace said softly. "Get rid of your husband and get hamburgers too."

Half of the carhops at Gordon's were cousins of Grace's. Known for its pretty girls, this was also the cheapest and the best place in town. A bagful of burgers sold for just a couple of bucks and was enough to feed a whole ranch full of little cowboys and cowgirls. There were few Lawton residents who didn't crave the greasy burgers that always soaked through the bag on the way to the car, and some would pick the burgers over Thanksgiving turkey, given a choice.

The parking lot was almost full, although their most faithful customers came late at night. Cars with pregnant women, soldiers and students, all with a hunger for cheap burgers, pulled in and out of Gordon's in the wee hours to pick up the great greasy grub.

Even when Grace was young, she and her cousins would cut their confessions short on Saturdays so that they could run over to Gordon's and get some hamburgers before they were due home. They'd pay for their treat with money they were supposed to give to the church.

Tia used to tell her that, if they didn't, they'd have nothing at all to confess the next week. And it was pretty close to true. Grace and her cousins were kept close to home, and their fathers seldom allowed the girls to leave the house except for school, church, or work. It was out of the question to even think of a date with a soldier. Somehow Grace forgot that when she met Dwayne.

Grace had first met Dwayne at the roller rink during an afternoon skate-in, where she'd gone with her cousins. It was an outing that her poppa had approved, thinking nothing bad could happen to a bunch of girls in broad daylight.

The first time she saw Dwayne, she knew right away he was a soldier because, like most troops, he wore his Army low quarters with his blue jeans, and his blond hair had a short, sheared, military cut. He'd grabbed her when she skated past him, and started to flirt. She had no experience with dating, so Grace was flattered that this good-looking soldier had picked her out of a roller rink crowd. She ignored the calls from her cousins to rejoin their group.

Before long, Grace began to sneak off to meet Dwayne in the parking lots of all the troop hangouts: roller rinks, bowling alleys, and movie houses. Places that were open in the daytime while Poppa worked. The poor man never suspected Grace, his pet, had run off to meet a soldier. Vera and Pauline were the ones that he thought needed watching. The two recklessly flaunted their beauty by wearing the latest makeup, sexy clothes, and high-heeled shoes.

To those two, a little fun was well worth the risk of getting caught and scolded by their gentle father. More than once, they'd barely missed getting into trouble when he would suddenly get off his porch without warning to take a stroll downtown on a hunch he might catch his girls flirting with young men. The girls knew that flirting with soldiers was strictly forbidden, and they rarely stopped to speak to military men who hung around downtown.

Poppa never suspected that Grace, in her loafers, plain clothes, and face stripped of makeup, would sneak around to meet a soldier. *How could she have been so mean to Poppa, especially when he was so sick?*

To Grace's surprise, as soon as Grace and Dwayne were married, the fun stopped. No more roller-rinks, movie theaters, or bowling alleys. Dwayne secured housing for them on the edge of post in the reclaimed frame barracks with peeling Army cream paint, and left Grace there alone much of the time.

🍁   🍁   🍁

At Gordon's, Grace looked around at all of the locals. This was great fun. This was the way she'd always thought her marriage would be. She had never expected a big house with a swimming pool, a Cadillac convertible, or fancy vacations. All she'd ever wanted—or expected—was an occasional night out at the local hamburger stand.

She waved at her cousin Gloria, Glory's namesake. She wished they'd parked in her station but then thought it might have been dangerous; Gloria might have mentioned Aunt Lilia's new dress.

In the back seat, Glory had her hands full. Even a small burger was a lot for her to handle, and her father had ordered her a strawberry milkshake to go with it. Grace was impressed that he never once told her to keep it off the seats. Maybe because he knew he was going to sell the car soon anyway to some other soldier who'd never be able to pay him what it was really worth. Besides, once you've carried rotting fish bait in an open bucket on the back seat of your car, what else could be so bad?

On the way home, Dwayne made a quick swing through the local A&W Root Beer stand and picked up a whole glass gallon jug of root beer. Grace didn't push her luck and ask him to stop for milk; she could have Pauline bring some tomorrow. But Dwayne surprised her when he stopped at Cagle's Grocery and picked up a half gallon of milk without her ever mentioning it. When he started rambling about how they could make ice cream if they had a hand cranker, Grace was stunned. *Was this the same man who went fishing with a rifle?*

He was home just long enough to have a glass of root beer and pack. Before Grace could rinse out the glass, he was gone. The forgotten artillery manual was on the kitchen table. As soon as it was safe, she called Vera.

"He's really gone, Vera, I didn't think it could happen so soon. Please thank Rudolf for me."

"No problem, Sis, what good is rank if you can't pull it?" Then she quickly added, "Don't *ever* tell Rudolf I said that." After a pause, she asked, "How did you say I was supposed to fix that sauerkraut?"

Before she went to bed, Grace cleaned her house. She didn't want to waste good sewing time during the day. Besides, most women cleaned their houses at night this time of year and took their kids to the swimming pool in the daytime. Maybe, someday, she'd be able to take Glory to the pool when it was hot. She could imagine packing little bologna sandwiches, potato chips, and a bottle of juice into a basket to feed Glory and a friend when they got hungry. Someday, life would be so good. If she only lived until then.

CHAPTER 24

New Customers

There were no secrets in military housing.

Grace wanted to spend the day to get organized and sew some leftover material into shorts for Glory, but right after lunch, her porch started to get crowded. It began when, one by one, three women dropped off sacks of pink net, gold rickrack, and red velveteen. Word had spread like chickweed that she would be taking in sewing, and they didn't wait until she moved to town.

Then there was Sako. She had become one of Grace's best customers when she began to bring over pieces of elegant oriental silk sent by her mother to be sewn into kimonos for her family.

Grace breathed a sigh of relief when she found a pattern for the kimono and the obi, a Japanese sash, at the bottom of the package. She had a vague idea of how the garments should look, but the material was real silk; she wanted to be certain she made no mistakes. Later, when she looked at the pattern pieces, she was surprised that the elegant robes were so simple to put together.

Each time a new customer landed on her doorstep, Grace held her breath and kept a worried eye out for Dwayne. Luckily, the women seemed to perfectly time their arrivals and departures, and Dwayne never saw any of Grace's new customers the few days he was home.

There was one close call when a woman with a bag full of net was on a collision course with Dwayne, who'd taken an extra long lunch nap in between trips to the field. He was ready to leave just as the woman was about to walk up Grace's sidewalk, but Sako raced out, grabbed the woman like she was a long-lost friend from Poston, and steered her away from Grace's until Dwayne's car had turned the corner.

Another time, Garnet paid a visit before Grace had a chance to talk to Pauline and parked her bright orange Cadillac convertible right in front of Grace's front door. To Grace's dismay Garnet tested her fitting by filling her lungs with air and bursting out into her solo while Grace measured her. The singer's strong gospel voice belted out, "*Sometimes I feel like a moootherleess child...,*" her strong, vibrant voice pulled people out of their quarters and cemented them to one spot with their toes curled inside their shoes.

What a voice! Grace had assumed Garnet was good, but she had no idea she was *that* good. For days afterward, people in the neighborhood would stop Dwayne and congratulate him on his new phonograph. He complained to Grace that everyone in the neighborhood had gone crazy.

Grace had some fun and asked, "Was it *mariachi* music?"

"Hell, no, they said it was gospel, *nigger* gospel," he emphasized in a low voice.

Grace worked on the recital costumes first because there was too much net and velveteen to hide easily. Anyway, Garnet's solo was weeks away. By the time Grace had measured the last ballerina it was time for dinner.

She surveyed the piles of fabric and notions on the table and decided it was a good night for a picnic on the back porch. After a few quick preparations, she called in Glory and handed her a plate with a hamburger on white bread with mustard, a few spoonfuls of potato salad, and some tomato wedges from one of Uncle Joe's tomatoes. Grace ate her hamburger patty over the sink.

Dessert was a peach because she had a kitchen full of them. Some of the women in the neighborhood had made a trip to an old deserted Indian orchard. Ever since then, there was hardly a child's mouth in the neighborhood that didn't have a peach in it. The fruit was not without worms, but the mothers poo-pooed their presence, telling any child that asked they added protein. Grace never saw an adult go near one of the protein-packed peaches.

The other women complained that it was very time-consuming to cut around the worms to make a cobbler, so Grace hadn't tried it yet. First, she planned to get rid of as many peaches as she could the easy way: from her hand to Glory's mouth.

Peaches, catfish, venison, and even squirrel made up a significant part of the diet in this housing area. Times were tough and each family had its own tricks to fill their children's bellies and at the same time spend as little money as possible.

It made Grace the saddest when the men killed the big turtles in the lakes so their wives could make soup, although she'd made her share of the vegetable broth laced with chunks of turtle meat. Poor little turtles, she always thought, as she put a spoonful into her mouth.

One Italian family made their own noodles, a German woman made black bread, and Grace made tortillas and picked wild persimmons with her sisters and cousins. Once Grace went to the Italian woman's quarters to learn how to make noodles, but it was disastrous. After the women had laughed so hard they cried all afternoon, Maria finally took pity on Grace and just gave her some to take home.

They had even more fun the next week when Maria came to Grace's to learn to make tortillas. Maria rolled and rolled, but she couldn't make the flat bread round. She finally took the ball of dough home and threatened to boil it into noodles.

A lot of the men tried to do their part by fishing, but they weren't as good at it as Dwayne, and all the women agreed the men spent so much on licenses, gas, and gear that each crappie or perch cost them roughly the price of a good steak.

In town, civilian women with more economic means gardened, canned, and made jams and jellies. Canning was out of the question for Grace and her neighbors; water for gardening, canning supplies, and sugar were too expensive. Besides, gardening and canning required staying in one place long enough to produce a harvest, and Army wives were seldom in one place long enough to grow anything more than a sweet potato plant on their windowsill.

Moreover, most of the women didn't even know *how* to can. Grace often wished poorer women had the skills they really needed, like canning and sewing. Richer women seemed to have all of the skills and all of the money.

Grace only knew how to sew because handwork had been a cheap way for her mother to keep her girls busy. From an early age, Momma had put her daughters on the porch and placed embroidery hoops in their hands. All of her girls had started by decorating flour sacks to make dishtowels. Grace was the only one who graduated to pillowcases and sheets.

Vera, Pauline, and Norah found other things to do as soon as their mother wasn't looking—things like cute boys with cars. Cars were a must to the girls, so they could get away from their father who'd never driven a car. A boy with a convertible was one of God's most perfect gifts. But even if a cute boy's car were a real wreck, it would do.

Until Dwayne, Grace stuck to her talent for needlework. When her mother showed her how to crochet a lace edge, she began crocheting bed linens. Whenever she saw her mother coming through the door with a sack full of plain white bed sheets, Grace knew someone was getting married. She took pride in her needlework, and could sit for hours edging a sheet in crocheted lace.

And now, here she was, surrounded by pink nylon net. Brainwashed by Dwayne to believe she was stupid, it never occurred to her she was the only woman in the quarter's area who was skilled enough to make money without leaving her kitchen.

Nylon net didn't have to be preshrunk, and velveteen looked better unwashed, so preliminary work on the dance costumes was practically non-existent. Grace knew the outfits would be worn once, hung in the closet for awhile, and eventually be seen in a sand pile or going down a slide as mothers re-designated the dance costumes as play clothes.

She understood, and wasn't the least bit bothered by it. Mothers hated to see anything go to waste, and little girls were closer to growing out of their dance costume with each peanut butter and jelly sandwich.

For this type of sewing, Grace used her *lick-and-a-promise technique*: no preshrinking, no linings, and no hand-bound buttonholes. The little dancers would look glamorous for one recital and one photo session. After that, the peanut butter would begin to turn the little Cinderellas into pumpkins, and the slide at the park would polish the velveteen seat on the outfit, making it as smooth and shiny as glass.

Anxious to have a net-free house as soon as possible, Grace spent most of her time at her sewing machine. She hardly went back to Glory's room for three days. If she had, she would have seen the turtle bowl set on the windowsill in direct sunlight with its little turtle floating in its own recipe for turtle soup.

CHAPTER 25

Tutus and Four-Fours

"Pauline, thank God you're home. I need another turtle fast. Glory left Carmen on her windowsill and I didn't see it in time."

"Does she know yet?"

"No. She's outside playing. Sis, that turtle water must be hot enough to make a pot of tea."

"*Ayyy*! I'm a coffee drinker," Pauline quickly said, then added, "I was coming over anyway. I'll just swing by and pick one up. Need anything else besides milk?"

"No, just hurry. She hasn't been sleeping and eating well and I don't know how she'll react if she sees her turtle like this."

Within an hour, Pauline rushed through the door with a white paper carton under her blouse and a paper sack in her hand. Grace produced the turtle bowl that had fresh, cool water and rushed the stand-in back to Glory's room. This time, she placed it on the floor out of the sunlight.

"What's for lunch, turtle soup?" Pauline asked. As she was heading for the coffeepot, Glory led a whole stream of kids into her bedroom to watch her feed Carmen.

"Sis, what's the difference between a boy turtle and a girl turtle?" Grace opened her mouth to say something smart, but before she could say anything, Pauline went on, "I mean, does Glory know the difference? I just picked up a turtle with a red rose on its back."

Grace looked toward Glory's room, "I don't know the difference, and neither does Glory. But that Ronnie Hill...if anyone spills the beans, it'll be him."

They both held their breath, but Ronnie was quiet, except when Pauline heard him ask, "Is the rock in the bowl real?"

"Yes," Glory answered proudly, "it's real plastic."

"I'm getting an alligator next week from Florida." Ronnie announced. "I ordered it through the mail." The other children's eyes widened in awe.

Loudly, Pauline repeated Ronnie's announcement in Spanish to Grace who just rolled her eyes. Then, Grace asked, "You don't think he really ordered an alligator, do you?" Pauline could only shrug. The backs of magazines were filled with mail order creatures. Alligators, seahorses, shrimp, turtles, and tropical fish could all be delivered to your door for a just few pennies. "If he did," Grace chuckled, "I want to be there when Sako opens the package."

While Glory was feeding the turtle, Pauline busied herself making lunch so Grace wouldn't have to stop sewing. While she talked, she filled tortillas with mashed refried beans and made fresh coffee.

"Sis, I have iced tea," Grace offered.

"Good. I'll have some with my coffee." She handed a bean burrito to Glory on her way back outside.

"What are you doing with all of this pink net?"

"Making tutus."

Pauline picked up one of the costumes. "Well, this one looks like a four-four."

"I'm gathering the net on elastic, so it'll expand to fit whoever wears it, that way I don't have to worry about fit. Thank goodness for all this work, Sis. I've been working steady every since Steiner gave me that ride to Momma's. Everyone is paying me in cash, so I don't have to worry about their checks being good."

"Do you want me to take the money to Momma's for you?"

"Good idea. I've got it all stuffed in the bed of my machine."

While Grace shoveled out the loose bills, Pauline fiddled with the pincushion on the table. "I've always wondered why this little strawberry hangs down from the red pincushions."

"It has stuff in it to sharpen needles. What, I don't know."

"I lose my needles in the carpet before they ever get dull. Boyd usually finds them for me with his feet. Will you be through with these costumes before Saturday night when Dwayne gets home?"

"Oh, yeah. I've even got some more coming in next week. These things are so easy to sew. Steiner changes the color and the fabric, but he never changes the pattern—by the way, he sure looks good in that new baby blue Cadillac convertible—Momma was in the kitchen and missed it."

"That would have been interesting. With Momma, we never know how she'll react. You know, it's funny, but I never see those dancer's old Cadillacs around town."

"They're probably on some Indian reservation somewhere." They both chuckled at the thought of some Indian chief in full headdress driving Steiner and Brook's old pink Cadillac convertible across the reservation, with the back seat full of calves.

"Hey, Sis, did you hear about all of those houses they built at the edge of the reservation for the Kiowas to live in? Get this—they took money out of the tribe's account without their permission, and used it to buy all kinds of furniture and drapes and other stuff they didn't want or need."

"No."

"Wait, it gets worse," her sister said, "they even put a black grand piano into each house."

"You can't even buy a grand piano in Lawton."

"Some government official must have taken a payoff from a piano salesman. Tia says that, at one house, there's a big nail in one corner of the piano and another big nail on the wall, with a clothesline strung in between. It was the only way they could think of to make use of the thing."

"Those poor people. They won't have a buffalo nickel left by the time the white man is through with them."

"Rosie, that Kiowa who's always at Wyatt's when we go for coffee, told me that when they try to attend the Bureau of Indian Affairs meetings, the bureau has usually changed the schedule at the last minute and they miss them. Then, when they do get to go and ask a question, the BIA officials make the answer so complicated they can't understand it."

"Can you imagine having a bank account and not having any idea how much is in it? Or not even being able to find out where your money goes?"

"They'd be better off letting Momma keep their money with yours in her chest of drawers."

"What's in the box on the counter? I can smell it from here." Grace asked as she saw a leaky box on the counter whose contents were beginning to ooze out the bottom.

"Oh, I almost forgot. Persimmons."

"Oh, good. Where did you get them?"

"I found them on my doorstep this morning. Tia must have gone out on Sunday. They're ripe, so eat them fast." When Grace looked inside, she saw luscious dark orange fruit, and smelled the heavy scent of persimmons ripened by the hot sun. The fragrance of the wild fruit filled the tiny kitchen with an exotic scent as it drifted out of the container. They were almost over-ripe, so Grace put the fruit, box and all, in the refrigerator to keep it from getting too mushy.

Someday, maybe she'd take Glory persimmon hunting in her own car. The locations of the persimmon trees were handed down from mother to daughter, from generation to generation among the locals.

Grace and her sisters knew where all the good trees were. Unfortunately, the wild fruit trees were fewer each year as developers plowed under the prairie to put up housing developments.

One of her cousins had a farm east of town that had some of the best persimmon trees in the state. At least Grace knew those trees would be there someday for Glory. Her cousins loved living on their farm, and had said many times that they couldn't imagine having to sell and move to town.

CHAPTER 26

A Ghost Post

The end of July was usually the worst month for heat, but this year the swelter didn't start to taper off until August, when temperatures still hovered around ninety-eight. Even with no air conditioning, Grace couldn't afford to take it easy like most married women in the housing quarters.

She didn't know why Steiner and Brook had chosen this summer to run dance classes, but she was grateful for the work. Most summers, during the hottest months, the studio was closed. She figured they must have had air conditioning put in.

Not again. Grace went into Glory's room and found the second turtle to go belly up. "Pauline. Guess what? It's going to be a three-turtle summer. The new turtle died."

"Can't you keep those things in the refrigerator?" Pauline laughed.

"This is serious. I need another turtle fast," Grace pleaded.

"Okay. As soon as I get my hair out of rollers, and drop Carlos off at Boyd's mother's house I'll be there. Put the coffee on."

"Sis, I haven't seen my little nephew for weeks, why don't you bring him?"

"He's spending the summer at Gramma Boyd's because she has a pool. Our apartment is unlivable in this heat. You'll see him when it cools down."

Grace hung up the phone. It was odd that Pauline was so worried about the heat now, when last summer Carlos went everywhere with her. He wasn't sick; she would have said so. Did Boyd object to his coming over for some reason? She went back to work still puzzled, but not really worried. She was sure her sister would tell her if anything were wrong. Probably she hadn't seen Boyd because he was just busy training, like all the other soldiers on Ft. Sill.

Pauline hurried in an hour later with a wire-handled white box and a newspaper she bought at Cagle's Grocery on the way over. Grace kidded, "Do you realize that no one in this family has ever had the paper delivered to them?"

"Our family isn't big on long financial commitments. Besides, we always get the leftover ones free from our cousins after they go on their route."

"Yeah. But they're always a day old. We didn't know about Pearl Harbor until two days after it happened."

"This one's new—check out the front page. No. Don't. Check out the turtle first."

"Give me the paper. I've seen turtles."

"Not like this one, you haven't."

"Oh, no, Pauline, what's wrong?" She went to the box and opened it just enough to peek inside. "Sis, what's wrong with you? This turtle has a yellow rose on its back."

"It's the end of the season. It was the only one left. Get me some nail polish, maybe I can fix it."

Grace raced to the bathroom and came back with a handful of red nail polish bottles. All of the sisters had a drawer full of bottles of polish in every color, along with emery boards, removers, and glycerin. There was rarely a chip in any of their manicures.

During the Depression, all of the Ramirez children picked cotton with their poppa. Even Grace went along when she was too small a child to help at home, though all she could do was follow along behind her father carrying the tiny cotton sack he'd hand-stitched for her.

It was really just a way for him to baby-sit Grace so her mother, who was pregnant with Benny, could get some rest.

Every night, on the front porch, their father would rub their sore hands with glycerin to ease the pain and help heal the torn cuticles that were cut and swollen from constant contact with the hard, sharp bolls around the balls of cotton.

Grace would line up with the rest of her brothers and sisters and her father would rub the glycerin into her hands and say to everyone what a big help she'd been all day. In those days, they didn't have any nail polish, but the ritual of hand care remained long after they left the cotton fields.

Now, they were about to take their manicure skills to a whole new level. Grace dug the dead turtle out of the trash so they could match the nail polish in the bottle to the rose on the dead pet. After they'd picked the closest red color, Pauline tried to paint over the yellow rose on a very squirmy turtle.

"Be still," she ordered, "or I'll do your nails, too." Then she said, "I saw Garnet. She says she's already had a fitting." While Pauline chatted and painted, Grace kept a worried eye out for Glory. Thankfully, she was nowhere in sight.

"Yes, and Sis, she's just a little overweight. Mostly, she needs more room in her clothes when she sings. I can fix that easy." Grace opened the paper and gasped when she read the headline. "Is *every* soldier on the fort going to Japan?"

"Just about. Even Boyd. He got his orders yesterday."

"Oh, Sis, I'm sorry."

"It's all right. We're not getting along anyway. I think he's been fooling around for a long time now."

"I've been wondering what was wrong. Why didn't you say something? Is that why I haven't seen Carlos?"

"Yeah, I didn't see any reason to drag him into it, so he's been at Gramma Boyd's. She's good with him, and she really does have a pool at her apartment. I didn't tell you about Boyd because I just didn't feel like talking about it. I thought this guy was gonna be the one, Sis." Pauline tried to focus her eyes, now filled with tears, on the turtle. "Why do we keep falling in love with uppity white men who don't fit in with our family?"

"Because we're related to all the Mexican ones?"

"Funny. But true. It's not just the Comanches who have trouble finding suitable mates. Anyway, after he's gone, I'll probably file for divorce. He says I can keep Carlos, so there's no problem there."

"Carlos will miss him. How long do you think Boyd will be gone?"

"The paper says they'll all be gone at least three years. The mayor was having a fit until the Army promised to move in new troops."

"It says here they're going in stages. The administration people go over first, then the rest as they're ready for them. Is Rudolf going?" Grace asked.

"Don't know. I haven't been able to get ahold of Vera for days. There's some kind of bowling tournament going on. They're even playing at night."

"Maybe he's already gone, and she just hasn't missed him yet."

"I bet she's going to be mad as hell if he goes. Officers usually take their wives, so she'll have to learn to score her bowling and golf games in Japanese."

"Uh-oh, how will she know if they're cheating?" Grace wanted to know.

"She'll be okay unless she plays someone's baby brother named Benny-moto."

Their laughter startled the little turtle that was almost traumatized already by all of the handling and the fumes from the red nail polish.

"You know, Sis," Pauline said, "we should find a big house to rent and split the expenses. Then we could go to the commissary and PX together and split the cost of everything."

"I wonder if we could find something near Momma?"

"I'll start looking on the way home."

"Look for one near a fabric shop with a pool."

"What for, Grace? you don't swim."

"I know, but we can use it to drown our men."

Grace gave her sister a big hug before she went out the door. When her sister left, she scolded herself for not noticing sooner that something was wrong between Pauline and Boyd.

Pauline left Grace's and drove straight home. The smile she had on her face as she pulled out of the parking strip vanished as soon as she turned the corner. By the time she pulled into the alley behind the converted upstairs garage apartment on "A" Street, she was nearly hysterical.

She hadn't seen her husband for days. He had an uncanny ability to come home to shower and change clothes when she wasn't there. Even though his car wasn't parked behind the apartment she raced up the stairs, her hand flying just above the wrought iron railing, barely feeling the roughness of the peeling paint. The cracks in the pink stucco exterior on the stairway jiggled and mocked her desperation as her black patent high heels pounded the stairs and sent spiders racing from their vibrating webs to more secure hiding places under the railing.

"Please, God," Pauline prayed as she threw open the door on an empty apartment. She ran from room to room, inhaled the Old Spice after-shave in the bathroom, and felt the heavy, moist air from Boyd's shower. She'd just missed him. She passed the untouched fruit bowl in the middle of the kitchen table.

Would it kill him to eat just one piece of fruit? Frustration and loneliness overtook her as she threw herself across the chenille bedspread and cried. How could they work things out if she never saw him? He hadn't even told her yet what was wrong. They didn't fight. Why was he leaving her? All Pauline knew was that he had lost interest in everything except Carlos. She knew that he spent a lot of time with their son when Carlos was at Boyd's mother's place. She was grateful for that.

❦   ❦   ❦

Dwayne came home on Saturday just long enough to get his gear together to go fishing with his officer friends. "There may not be any fishing in Japan. No one seems to know. Even if they have fish, they may not cotton to Yanks catchin' them."

Grace wanted to ask if they'd take their poles or their rifles, but thought better of it. She should be glad he was leaving. For the life of her she couldn't understand why she was so annoyed that he was so swept up with his new assignment. This marriage was over. It wasn't even wise to promote a relationship between Dwayne and his daughter, if she could believe the doctor. *Let him go, Grace,* she kept telling herself as he dashed from closet to closet looking for his fishing gear.

"When will you be back?" she asked. She picked up a minnow bucket as she followed him to his car.

"After dark tomorrow. We have to clean up and divide all of the gear we've been leaving down by the creek because we may not be back for three or four years. I'd tell them to store it all here, but we have to move."

Grace counted her blessings. That was all she needed: closets full of moldy sleeping bags, tents, and smelly minnow buckets dripping all over her fabrics and smelling up the house.

Yeah, leave that stuff here. I'll set a big fire in the backyard and add that footlocker full of scrapbooks you have right on top. Dwayne had gotten into his car and started the engine. She leaned into his window, smiled sweetly, and murmured, "Yes, it's a shame, all right."

By the end of August, it started to cool off. "We're lucky," Grace told Sako. "Lots of times, we don't get any relief until September."

"Grace, I can't wait to get out of here and go back to California. What a hellhole this is. Oh, I'm sorry! You're the only person in housing who is from here and I keep forgetting that Oklahoma is your home. That wasn't very nice of me to say."

Grace interrupted her, "It's okay. I've heard it all before. It just doesn't bother us. We're used to it. Is your husband getting out?"

"Yes, we're going back to live near my parents. Sergeant Hill's enlistment is up and we figure Mom and Dad need us more than the Army does. Besides, I could never get used to this, and if they sent us to Japan, I might be in real trouble. The Japanese might look at me as a traitor. So far, only officers' wives have been going to Japan, but we can't take the chance. The Army gets some crazy ideas. It's hard to imagine how things could get worse than having scorpions in your bathtub," she continued, "but I guess they could. Oh, did you ever hear about Millie, a couple of doors down? She found a copperhead curled up on the inside of one of the garbage cans in the alley."

"Tell me it was dead!" Grace gasped. "Glory and the other kids play around there all the time."

"No, Grace, it was alive. When she lifted the lid, it jumped out and slithered away. It must have crawled in there to eat something."

"I don't know about the snakes, but the scorpions come up the drain, somehow. We had a big one in our bathroom and Dwayne chased it around and around the tub with a rolled up newspaper before he finally killed it. I guess the tub was so slick that it couldn't climb out. I wonder if those government contractors never connected the pipes in the tubs and showers to the sewer? What if all of our tub water just drains under the buildings?"

"It would sure explain how scorpions could get in. But then, what keeps the snakes out? You know what else? Sergeant Hill says they used the cheapest material there is for the walls and no insulation at all in these quarters. None."

Grace just nodded and didn't volunteer that she knew this for a fact. Once, Dwayne had punched a hole clear through the wall in the bedroom during one of his fits when he tried to hit Grace in the face and she'd ducked.

Glory was fascinated by hole in the wall, and always wondered how the spiders got in there, and what did they eat? Grace always distracted her when she heard questions like that. Never having been a reader, she didn't know and didn't have any interest in finding out. Why do kids ask so many questions, anyway?

Whenever Glory asked her about birds, Grace answered with whatever came to her mind at the time. There was no impact on her life because *she* didn't know the difference between a whippoorwill and a robin, and she doubted if Glory needed to know either.

What *Glory* needed to know, Grace was convinced, was how to make her way through a multi-cultured game where the whites had all the cards. Maybe her Aunt Vera could give her some lessons. She was an expert at it.

Grace swept the porch while she talked to Sako. She looked down and saw a bunch of gray hard-shelled roly-poly bugs that had climbed up the cement to get into the shade. Without even thinking, she boiled a pot of water on the kitchen stove and poured it all over them. She had never learned which bug was beneficial and which bug might be poisonous, so Grace borrowed Sheridan's philosophy: The only good *bug* is a dead *bug*.

Glory and her friends liked to touch each bug with a stick and then watch as it rolled itself up into a little ball. Luckily, Glory wasn't home.

While Grace was killing bugs, Sako finished taking her laundry off the communal clothesline and started back into her house. On the way in, Grace watched her stop to kick a red anthill that thrived near her porch steps. She let out a stream of Japanese expletives interspersed with English: "Damn bugs. Damn spiders. Damn scorpions. Damn snakes. Damn Oklahoma!" In between the phrases, Grace swore she could pick out "Geronimo! Horse's ass! and Sunshi Bitch!"

CHAPTER 27

Clearing Quarters

All sewing stopped after the last batch of dance costumes. Grace and all of the other wives spent their days preparing to move. Everyone was on the hunt for cardboard boxes; there hadn't been an empty one since the headline about most of the troops being sent overseas had hit the paper.

One day, Grace saw some women at the garbage cans trying to breath life into a flattened cardboard box with a roll of tape. *There might not be an Army if cardboard boxes had never been invented,* she thought. But chances were greater, she finally decided, that the Army would love the simplicity: one soldier, one duffel bag. How uncomplicated!

Each garbage collection day she saw piles of discards in the trash from the closets in the neighborhood. Wives met between buildings and exchanged tips on how to pass the housing inspections. In groups, they went over the *Army way*: no nail holes in the walls, no empty hangers in the closets, and stoves and refrigerators as clean as new.

Grace must have listened for hours as more experienced wives passed along horror stories about families failing their housing inspection when an inspector moved out a stove or refrigerator and found a dust ball, or ran a gloved hand along the top of an inside door frame and found red dust. Imagine that, dust in Oklahoma.

But failing a housing inspection was no laughing matter. Soldiers couldn't clear post to go to their next assignment unless the post housing's crew had signed off on their quarters. If a soldier flunked his housing inspection and was late for his next assignment, he could be demoted, or even face early retirement. Even though the wife was responsible for cleaning in most families, as far as the Army was concerned, the soldier signed off on the quarters. He was the one that passed or failed.

Grace took the inspection instructions very seriously; to her it was a matter of life or death. God forbid that she and Dwayne flunk the quarter's inspection and his departure got delayed, even for a few days. She had the inspection list memorized: knobs must be pulled off the stove and cleaned inside and out; the stove must be taken apart and cleaned piece by piece, and reassembled; the panel from the bottom of the refrigerator in front must be removed, cleaned, the coils must be swept; screens that had pet damage must be replaced; furnace filters must be cleaned. Cat scratches on the government issued furniture were an automatic flunk. Grace had never had a cat—she just had minnows.

Other women complained about all of the work, but Grace joyfully tackled each cleaning job. Every swipe of a cleaning rag, she told herself, brought her closer to Dwayne leaving, and closer to freedom. Closer to having a real life. Closer to having a daughter who slept in her bed instead of her closet.

Grace wondered how she would cover the hole in the wall in her bedroom, but she didn't mention it to the other women. She knew Dwayne didn't know how to fix it; besides, it didn't look like he would be home long enough to even try.

A glance out the window reminded her that the grass in the front yard would have to be cut one more time and the sidewalk edged.

She could do it herself if she borrowed a push mower from one of the neighbors. The sidewalk could be edged with an old butcher knife. Army policy said the sides and back would be left natural to save water.

The brass could have saved themselves the paperwork if they'd just bothered to look at the grass. It was so worn down from being trampled on a daily basis by all of the children in the housing area that mowing and watering were never a necessity anyway.

Pauline stopped by in the afternoon, "Grace, how's the turtle? Turtle season is over, but I could go out and catch a horny toad."

"Very funny. Carmen III is alive and well. Where's Momma?"

"*Ayyy!* She's helping Vera clean out her closets. Our big sis is going to Japan with Rudolf."

"No! How's she taking it?"

"Pretty good. Someone told her she'll be able to buy pearls and china at bargain prices. Let's make some coffee." Pauline always flew in like her sister's coffeepot was the last one on the frontier.

"I take it you still haven't wired your coffeepot into your dash-board."

"I stopped at Vera's for a quick cup, but she and Momma hadn't made a pot since morning. Vera said I could make a pot, then just drink out of the spout all the way over to your house, but knowing me, I'd manage to spill it all over me, anyway."

"How's Boyd?"

"I haven't seen him for days. Garnet told me she heard he's been taking carloads of men to Texas to drink and party with women for twenty-five dollars each."

"Why Texas? We have bars here."

"I know, but the joints here are patrolled by the MPs. Besides, all of the wives know where to look in Lawton."

"Is he making a lot of money?"

"No, from what I hear the money just pays for the gas and his drinks. He's drinking a lot, Garnet says."

"When did he become such a bar-hopper?"

"I don't know, he wasn't that way when we got married. Maybe it has something to do with having to go to Japan. When we were still talking he told me he was real unhappy about it. He said he'd get out of the Army now, if he weren't so close to retirement." Pauline paused, then added, "You know, Sis, that may be it. Garnet also mentioned that Dwayne is always surrounded by women in that bar just outside the main gate. Maybe it has something to do with going overseas."

"Women around Dwayne are nothing new—blond women. With him, it has nothing to do with Japan. Having to go to Japan could be bothering Boyd, though. When does he leave?"

"I don't know, for sure. I don't even think he's going to work right now, so maybe he's burning up his leave."

"How do you know he's not going to work?"

"All of his uniforms are hanging in the closet—dress, khaki, and fatigues. They're all there."

"Have you had a chance to talk to him?"

Pauline shook her head no. "He's never home when I'm home. He made up his mind about divorcing me without my having a chance to say anything. He left me a note!"

"You'll get through this, Sis, you're tough…and maybe he'll be gone soon."

"I hope so. Momma's trying to convince me to get pregnant before he goes so I'll have something to keep me busy for the next three years."

"But you already have Carlos."

"Yes, but he's not a baby anymore. He won't tie me down enough. Momma wants me to be pregnant and unattractive."

"It's the Catholic way. I take it you haven't told her you're divorcing Boyd."

"Yes, I have, she said all that *after* I told her!"

"Okay, so it's not the Catholic way, it's *Momma's* way." Grace shook her head. Momma's advice was good most of the time, but every once in awhile she said something that was leftover from her covered wagon days.

"Speaking of Momma, I found a house for us near hers," Pauline said, her eyes twinkling.

"Oh, Sis, where?"

"It's that big white house down from Momma's with all of the honeysuckle in front and the big weeping willow on the side." The house she'd just described was Vera's house. Pauline continued, "Best of all, the rent's real cheap."

"Sis, what on earth are you talking about?"

"Vera's house. She doesn't want to have to sell it when they transfer to Japan, and she doesn't want renters living in it. She says she'll let us live in it until they get back."

"That would be great, but it won't work. Carlos and Glory are old enough to be rowdy, and Vera's house is full of expensive doo-dads. That house is no place for kids."

"No problem. Vera says if she rents to us, she can have all of her stuff packed and put into the garage. She wouldn't dare do that with regular renters. Luckily, she hasn't re-carpeted yet, so the floors are bare. All we'll need is a dust mop."

"You're serious, then."

"Yep. Got to go. Give me a quarter." Pauline flipped the coin into the air and said, "Call it."

"Tails. What are we flipping for?"

"Well, someone has to sleep in that newly decorated bedroom with the fake leopard fur bedspread. Sorry, Sis, but you lost. It's all yours if she doesn't take it with her."

"Pauline, get your tail out of here."

Grace caught her breath. Vera's house would be perfect for her business because it had a big double-sized bedroom at the back that was separated from the rest of the house by French doors. It even had an outside entrance, perfect for her customers. Also, it was the right location and was sure to be the right price. Exactly what was the price? Oh, well, Vera was family. They'd work that out later.

A neighbor ran over to tell her the latest housing inspector horror story: two blocks over, there was a lady who got in trouble because the clothespin on her mailbox was painted. Obviously, some of the inspectors were drunk with power. Grace added a mental note to her move list: new clothespin, unpainted. She'd have to ask someone who'd cleared quarters before about window shades. Hers were faded and rotted from the sun, would she have to replace them? She hoped not, there were eight of them and it wouldn't be cheap.

Grace moved all the boxes full of sewing materials to the corner of Glory's room and planned for them to be long gone before Dwayne started looking through the closets. It was going to be a challenge to clean the walls because Grace couldn't remember where she'd started and where she'd stopped. They were all so dingy that one wall looked like another, even after one had been washed. Painting was out of the question. Army maintenance men did all painting because only *they* had the approved shades of white.

They also liked to say how the quality of their paint was superior, but Grace and the other women knew better. The first time Grace rubbed against a painted wall, the paint came off on her arm like it was flour. She was always tempted to ask the men, "What did you do with the money our Uncle Sam gave you to buy real paint?"

It looked like Carmen the III would move with them. That reptile had the endurance of some of its bigger relatives. It was almost the end of September, and it was still hot as summer. How was that little squirt surviving the heat for so long?

Grace couldn't see what the attraction to having a turtle was. They didn't learn tricks. They didn't talk. They didn't chirp. The best they could do in the trick department was rollover and die, and they only did it once. So far, Grace and Glory had missed it both times. She didn't know anyone whose child's turtle had made it to its first birth-day.

She assumed this was because of too much handling, the heat, and the lack of natural food. It never once occurred to Grace that the roses painted on their backs might have had chemicals that leaked through the shell and poisoned the unsuspecting turtles. Or maybe, that the poisons in the paints leaked out into the water in the turtle bowl, and poisoned the turtle that way. If so, who could know what trouble was caused by the red Maybelline nail polish that her sister had used to cover the yellow rose?

Grace's only thought when she looked at the turtle was what a good job her sister had done. Besides, it wasn't just turtles that were sacrificed to keep kids busy. Squirrels, chipmunks, wild ducks, woodpeckers, trap-door spiders, scorpions, horny toads, and snakes were regularly loved or tortured to death by bored children. Grace shook herself. She didn't have time to worry about God's tiny crea-tures when her own life was in danger.

The best she could do was feel a small pang of guilt when she opened the cabinet under the sink and shoveled a turtle into the gar-bage. As soon as the turtle was out of sight, the guilt was gone.

Once, a mother had told her not to worry about the mistreated creatures. "When one of them dies," she said, "God just makes another one."

Too bad the turtles and other living animals didn't have the sup-port of a quizzical American born of German parents who was smart enough to become a full colonel in the U.S. Army and even quicker to learn its politics. *If Rudolf could save her, think what he could do for a turtle.*

CHAPTER 28

Camping Trips

Dwayne didn't have much energy to cause Grace any grief when he came home from the field. He was exhausted from fighting war games, and frazzled from trying to figure out why he was living in a Southwest Oklahoma hell. He had mosquito bites everywhere, even between his toes; his light skin was sunburned and peeling; his already-blond hair, and the eyebrows that went with it, were sun-bleached white; and his shoulders and legs ached from carrying artillery gear up and down the Wichita Mountains.

Next, he fully expected to be loaned out to a battalion run by Geronimo and his Apache warriors, or Satanta, one of the meanest war chiefs the Kiowas had ever had.

At first, soldiers from the Northwest and other mountainous areas laughed at the Oklahoma mountain range, but after they'd pulled a cannon up and down some of its mole hills, they gained a new respect for the ancient rocks.

Sundays, Dwayne cleaned and readied gear for the next "camping trip," as Glory called the field maneuvers. Before the first trip to the field, Dwayne went fishing and got back home just in time to throw his gear back in the car and head for the bivouac. But starting the week with dirty gear not only got him in trouble with the brass, but it made for a miserable week. A flash thunderstorm coated Dwayne's already pitiful equipment with thick red Oklahoma mud; he couldn't even keep the red caky globs out of his C-rations.

Sloppy and disorganized by nature, Dwayne was pushed to his limits by added insults like flash floods and high winds. During a downpour, he discovered his portable shovel was rusted shut and he remembered he'd put it away wet after a fishing trip. Unable to dig a trench around his tent to drain water away during a rainstorm made the rest of his gear useless.

His tent was erected with less than the proper number of tent stakes because he'd used some at the creek to anchor a catfish line to the side of the bank and failed to retrieve them. When an unusually high wind blew up and leveled his tent one night in the field, Dwayne was so tired he didn't even realize he was sleeping in a collapsed tent. The next morning, he woke up to the sounds of the other troops laughing at his lumpy form underneath the soggy canvas.

Soon, the men tired of his kissing up to the officers and couldn't get enough of having laughs at Dwayne's expense. For the rest of the maneuver, troops used Dwayne for comic relief. They draped dead rattlesnakes over the guy rope of his tent, left articles of ladies' clothing in his sleeping bag, and warned him about scorpions seen crawling into his duffel bag.

Although Dwayne was sure they wouldn't actually put a scorpion where it could harm him, he could never sleep until he'd emptied out his tent, shook every article of clothing, turned his sleeping bag inside out, and checked his boots.

To make matters worse, a trap door spider jumped on his shoulder from a tree as he passed beneath it. That further frayed his raw nerves and sent his fellow *campers* into hysterics.

They also arranged for the bugler to play taps outside his tent, signed him up for swimming lessons in snake-infested Lake Elmer, and loosened the spark plugs on his Jeep.

Then, they sent him to deliver phony information packets to non-existent officers who couldn't be located even when he drove up almost every dirt road on the Fort Sill Military Reservation. The misfiring engine echoed across the ravines, and could be heard first on this hill, then on that one, as he drove up and down the curvy roads, going from one company to another.

Back at camp, the jokesters sat on the hillside and howled as they listened to the jeep's noisy engine as it misfired up and down the hills. Mountains away, Dwayne thought that he could hear them laughing as he got more and more frustrated. He finally opened the envelope and discovered that he'd been the butt of yet another prank.

Their best gag was when they put a baby buffalo in his tent. It would have been funny anyway, but it became hilarious when the buffalo was discovered during a surprise inspection by the commanding officer. When Dwayne pulled back the flap to his tent, the buffalo strolled out, took a big dump right on the officer's boots, and ambled away to find its mother.

On the other end of camp, the mother desperately called for her calf. No tent or mess kitchen was left standing in her path as she looked for it, an unexpected reaction to a prank planned by men mostly from New Jersey and Delaware, states that had been short on buffalo for years. If they'd considered the mess they were left to clean up, it could have been argued that the plan to harass Dwayne had backfired. But they were having way too much fun to notice they'd been one-upped by a momma buffalo that didn't think it was at all funny that her baby was missing.

Dwayne was a slow learner, but he did learn. When he dragged himself home on the weekends, he made sure his gear was ready to go before Monday rolled around again. This left him little time to have any relationship with Grace, much less beat on her.

Periodically, he made a few threats that they'd better pass the housing inspection on the first go-around. But Grace had always kept a clean house, and he had no idea of the housing inspection rumors circulating the area. Dwayne didn't cope well with pressure, and would have been spinning in circles and bleeding his ulcers if he knew what Grace knew.

He wasn't even worried about the hole in the wall. In his mind, the hole he'd punched in the wall when he missed Grace was her fault—she'd ducked. It was up to her to figure out a way to fix it.

His ranch in Texas worried him more. He hoped his foreman would keep a closer eye on his cows. Dwayne wouldn't be able to go back there at all before he left for Japan, as he'd originally planned. His hired help would have to do the work he paid him to do, or else.

Or else, *what*? He couldn't hit him the way he did Grace; he'd go to jail. Besides, he knew his foreman would hit back, and Dwayne avoided fights like that. His choices really were simple: he could sell his cows or take a chance he would lose them all during his tour of duty in Japan.

Cattle prices were low right now, he might as well leave them there. He wished he could just mix them in with Aunt Bett's cows until he got back. That way he could fire Cord and the Japanese would take the blame for it.

The idea of being able to get rid of Cord without any backlash from his aunt tickled Dwayne. Of course, he knew he couldn't really put his cows in with Aunt Bett's and add to her workload—she wasn't strong enough. Then, too, he might need Cord to help out Aunt Bett if she kept getting weaker.

How much longer could she last? When he got back, Aunt Bett could be gone, and he'd be able to start fresh with a new foreman, if he could find one. If his aunt somehow had a change of heart and did leave the farm to him, he could try to find a family man to manage both places. Aunt Bett's house could be a good draw to a young married man with a wife and family.

CHAPTER 29

One Down, One to Go

"One down, one to go." It was Pauline on the phone, telling Grace that Boyd was finally gone.

"Oh, Sis, how did he leave? Was he angry?"

"No, I just think he was glad to be gone. He said I'd be getting an allotment until I file for divorce. And, of course, he'll send me money for Carlos. All I have to do is send the papers and he'll sign them."

"You don't seem very upset."

"Oh, Sis, I'm just tired. Tired of all our men making us so miserable. Vera got the only good one among us. I think I'll lay low for a long time. I'm sure not anxious to jump into a bootful of trouble with some man again. And poor Carlos, his little heart is broken. I'm so glad we'll both be in Vera's house. I think he and Glory will be good for each other."

"I think so too. They'll be like brother and sister. What are you doing today?"

"I'll swing by and see an attorney on my way to Momma's, then give notice to my landlord that I'm moving. There's not enough time to move to a smaller apartment; I'll just stay here until Vera leaves for Japan. Then, I have to look for a better job."

"I can help you watch Carlos when you have to work. What's Momma doing?"

"She and Aunt Lilia are drying salsa for the winter. Uncle Joe loaded her down with beefsteak tomatoes—the big ones—and Bermuda onions."

"You know, one of us should go with her and figure out how they do that. We might want to know someday."

"Yeah. But I did ask her this morning, and she says they just chop up the tomatoes when they're good and ripe, put the diced onions with them, make flat little patties on wax paper, and let them dry real good on the picnic table in the sun."

"Anything else?"

"Yeah. Make sure it doesn't rain."

"Very funny. What about the peppers and spices?"

"She adds all that when she adds water to the salsa in the winter."

"Are you coming over later?"

"Maybe. Need anything? Turtles? Horny toads? Shalimar?"

"Right. Bring me some of that fancy French perfume and put it on my bill at The Parisian." Then she added, "No, just some boxes, if you have any."

"I don't, but you know Momma can always come up with a couple. The salsa party is over at Aunt Lilia's. I'm going over to pick her up later, I'll bring some out."

"Ask her for an accordion."

"What on earth do you need an accordion for?"

"I don't. I just want to see if she's got one."

"Okay, *adios!*"

Grace thought she might as well read the paper. There wasn't much else to do until she got more boxes. The fabric stores were beginning to clear out their summer fabric. Gingham for forty-five cents a yard! She should go to town and buy some, and hide it at her mother's until Dwayne left. Dwayne wouldn't care that she was sewing for Glory, but he would want to know where she got the money. He hadn't given her any for quite awhile.

A small article about George Watchatooka, a chief and medicine man in the Comanche tribe, quoted him as predicting an early winter. Was there a special dance the Indians do to bring on cooler weather? To get relief from this heat, Grace was willing to put on war paint and dance around the campfire herself. After all, she was Indian too. She was part Aztec or Mayan, or *something* that used to live in Mexico.

Grace read on: Oh, God. Billy Joe, a rich Baptist car dealer, was auctioning off another car for charity. Members of his family won the last two cars; one was his wife. What a deal: have a raffle, get your wife a new car, and take a big tax deduction. Oh, well, that was the type of thing that went on in a small town. No use in fussing over something that was never going to change.

Not much else was news. Even the society column was short today. It must have been too hot for anyone to throw a party. Lawton's version of Hedda Hopper hadn't even done any interviews, she just sent a photographer to take a picture of some garden-club lady frying an egg on the sidewalk in front of her house. At least they were getting smarter. Last summer, some hoity-toity woman had fried an egg on the fender of her car and it had blistered the paint.

In the classifieds, Garnet had a small ad for her Lip-Smackin' Barbecue with just a phone number, since she didn't have a walk-in business. Steiner and Brook had a quarter-page ad with a ballerina wearing a cowboy hat and lassoing a smitten cowboy. Grace tore that ad out and put it in her idea file; it would make a real cute embroidery pattern someday for tea towels or the back of a shirt.

With one hand, Grace reached out and grabbed a pair of gingham bloomers that flew by. "It's too hot to be running around," she told her daughter. She ran a cool bath and plopped Glory into the tub. Then she poured her a glass of Kool-Aid and put her down for a nap.

Grace didn't understand this polio scare that everyone talked about, but they were saying naps might be one of the preventions of infection. It didn't make much sense to her, but it was the only thing mothers had to fight with.

One of the moms in the housing development had heard there was a vaccine on the way and Grace hoped this Dr. Salk guy was working overtime. Every week it seemed, there were a couple of stories about children in the paper whose names Grace, thankfully, never recognized. Children who were stricken by a disease that had no mercy and knew no color boundaries. Seeing pictures of those poor kids in an iron-lung broke Grace's heart. It didn't seem fair for children to have to suffer through that. Their poor parents!

Pauline arrived in the afternoon, dragging four cardboard boxes behind her. They both laughed and didn't even try to verbalize their amazement at their mother, the constant guardian and provider for a large family.

"No accordion, huh?" Grace asked.

"Vera already had dibs on it. She's taking it to Japan."

"While you're here, how about taking my sewing boxes to Momma's?"

"Okay. Did you see in the paper that sale on gingham downtown?"

"Yeah, at that price I could make Glory a dress for under two bucks."

"I'll pick you up some, what color?"

"Blue this week. Last week she couldn't get enough of pink."

"I'll buy a couple of yards and leave it at Momma's. Need lace?"

"No, I have lots of lace and buttons leftover from other projects. She's growing so fast, I won't buy the pattern until I'm ready to make the dress."

By the end of August, the days began to really cool off. Not what the old Indian predicted, but she'd take it. Grace saw the cloud of dust outside her kitchen before she heard the engine on Dwayne's car.

Chances that some big sergeant would come out and flatten the arrogant Texan for raising so much dust all the time were running out. Dwayne was the only driver in the neighborhood who was so inconsiderate. It irked her to think he was going to keep getting away with it, like he did everything else. That man would probably raise red dust when he got to Japan—and later, when he got to hell.

Dwayne came through the door exclaiming, "I have my orders. We're leaving early, around the first of September. I'm going to Japan with the rest of the troops, all right. What the hell is an artillery expert going to do in Tokyo? If we didn't get their attention with the A-bombs, we never will with my cannons." Then, he blurted, "And I got a promotion to Staff Sergeant!"

"Congratulations. Didn't they give you any idea what you'll be doing?"

What she really wanted to know was how much of Dwayne's new pay raise would she be getting for herself and Glory, but she didn't dare ask. All of the other wives knew exactly what their allotment would be. Why was Dwayne so vague about it? The money would be taken out automatically; it wasn't as if he was going to have a choice about it. She would need all the extra money she could get until she got on her feet.

"We're listed as occupying troops. That's all. Jesus, who would have thought a cowboy from Texas would be going to Japan? We only have two weeks to clear quarters and find you another apartment."

Grace sucked in her breath. She knew Dwayne wasn't going to like what he was about to hear. "I've already found a place to live. Pauline and I are going to share Vera's house while she's in Japan with Rudolf."

The thought of Rudolf being in Japan dampened his enthusiasm about his new assignment. Vera's husband was a favorite of Dwayne's only because of his rank. Somehow, now, going to Japan wasn't as special as it was.

He hardly noticed she'd told him she was moving in with her sister. She knew it would come back to him later. She didn't care. He had waited until the last minute to look for an apartment for her and Glory. What kind of place will be left now? *That's okay, cowboy. You mind your little red wagon, and I'll mind mine.*

Dwayne stopped to look at her; somehow she was different, but he couldn't figure out what it was. Maybe it was her expression, or something around her eyes…whatever it was, he didn't like it, but he didn't have time to worry about it now.

"I have to shower, change, and go to an orientation meeting at the battalion this afternoon. I might try to get a set of chopsticks to practice with. What are we having for dinner tonight?" Dwayne shouted over his shoulder as he headed for the shower.

"Tortillas and beans."

Even Dwayne chuckled at that.

*   *   *

In the first days of September, an icy wind started to blow. Unusual for Oklahoma. Grace's housing inspector was in a nasty mood after the cold sleet took the first two layers of skin off his face. He moved around the quarters, from room to room, and paused only to make notes on his clipboard and give Grace long reproachful looks.

He clucked a couple of times, and shook his head as if the quarters had been a palace before this little Mexican moved in. Grace was amazed when he walked right past the patched hole in the bedroom. Sergeant Hill had patched it as well as he could, but the paint he used to touch up the patch was new, and stood out like a noodle on a plate of beans.

The inspector actually did run his gloved hands over the door moldings; he even stopped to pull out the gas stove to check for dirt.

Grace was tempted to call attention to the new clothespin on the mailbox, but guessed this wasn't the right time to make small talk.

"You pass," the inspector grumbled.

Surprised, Grace asked, "Then what about all the marks on your clipboard?"

"Just notes on normal maintenance repairs to be done before the next family moves in, things like new shades and paint."

Without thinking, Grace had stopped in front of the wall patch. The inspector mentally calculated it was right at the height of Grace's face, and closed his clipboard. "Take care of yourself, little lady," he said softly.

He left by the back door, and Grace could see Sako watch him cross to her quarters. Grace gave her the okay sign from her kitchen window just before the inspector reached the Hill's doorstep.

✦   ✦   ✦

Grace turned and surveyed what was left of her little apartment. In the kitchen, just enough utensils and food to serve two more meals. It would all fit into a paper sack the next morning when she and Glory moved to her sister's house. Two dresses hung in Glory's closet and a pair of pajamas lay folded on her bed.

Her room was much the same. She'd kept a straight black skirt and a white blouse to wear to their friends, the Johnson's. They were going to have a card party and Glory would play with children that belonged to the Johnson's neighbors.

Sergeant Johnson was shipping out with Dwayne. His wife, Joan, was going back to Wisconsin to live with her parents and teach at a local elementary school. Although they hadn't seen each other often since the men had started training to go to Japan, she had been a good friend to Grace, and had given Glory's education a head start.

She'd begun by coaxing Glory to learn her ABCs and numbers by giving her a penny for each letter and number she could recite in order each time she saw her. Soon, Glory had a big glass mayonnaise jar bulging with loot.

When asked what she would do with all that money, Glory said the same thing every time: she was going to buy a horse. The thought of a horse on her sister's manicured front lawn, nibbling on her prize weeping willow tree and drinking out of her fancy fishpond always tickled Grace.

Joan also helped Grace improve her English. One of the best gifts Grace had ever received was Joan's old dictionary. At least she said it was old; it looked almost new to Grace.

Once, when she'd told Joan she hadn't finished school, her friend told her that she would have gladly traded all of her knowledge of Chaucer and Homer to be able to use a needle the way Grace did. How often did she use her education on the classics, anyway? she asked Grace. She seemed to be in awe one day when she watched Grace turn a few yards of polished cotton into a pair of curtains for Joan's bedroom. When Grace came back the next day with matching throw pillows for her bed, she was delighted, and it made Grace feel good to see someone so happy.

Grace told her the pillows were filled with old nylons, cut into little pieces. Then she further explained to Joan that she and her sisters sat around a table for hours to cut up old stockings their mother had thoughtfully laundered and put away for just such a project. Money was tight in their circle and this was the way things got done, and they always had a lot of fun doing it. Besides, that kind of stuffing washed and dried in no time at all.

She didn't tell Joan that her family had used stockings since their cotton-picking days when her mother would cut the feet off of old cotton stockings and pull them over Vera's and Pauline's arms to protect them from the sun when they were in the fields. Momma was a smart and resourceful woman. Grace just couldn't imagine how she could tell Joan about the stockings without admitting how poor they had been. How would Joan react if she knew that to survive the

Depression Grace's family had not only picked the cotton, they'd lived in two canvas tents, one for cooking and one for sleeping? Some things were better left unsaid. *Oh, we were living in high cotton, all right,* Grace thought as she hummed a song she'd heard on the radio. *High cotton, high weeds, high snakes, and high spiders.*

Grace was touched when Joan told her she'd miss her and Glory. She and Randy had no children of their own, she'd said, and when she played with Glory it was like playing with the child she hoped she and Randy would have someday. Grace would miss Joan too. It was hard to say goodbye to good friends. After tonight's card game, they would never see each other again. Grace wouldn't travel to Wisconsin, and she was sure Joan would never return to Oklahoma after her husband got out of the Army. Soldiers seldom made sentimental return visits to Fort Sill.

Dwayne was supposed to report to the battalion at 0600. He'd drop Grace and Glory off at Vera's house, and be on his way to San Francisco to catch a troop carrier to Japan with Sergeant Johnson. Joan would leave a few days after that.

Grace's heart skipped several beats every time she thought that Dwayne would leave in a matter of hours. Hours! She couldn't breathe, it felt like someone or something had taken the oxygen out of the air before she inhaled. Her heart pounded. She gasped. She rushed from room to room, and had to stop at the kitchen and bathroom sinks to splash cool water on her face. She felt as if her feet had a mind of their own as they aimlessly paced back and forth in the apartment. All through the summer she'd felt as if the day would never come. And here it was. Almost. In a few hours, she'd be free.

There wasn't anything to do so Grace decided to ride the bus into town with Glory to pick up a cake at the local bakery to take to the Johnson's card party. Vera was at Momma's waiting to leave with Rudolf to Japan. She'd walk over and say goodbye.

On the way to the bus stop, Grace felt the wind whipping around her legs. The temperature was dropping, and all of their warm clothes were at her mother's house ready to be carted over to Vera's. By the time they reached the bus stop, Glory's legs were red and chafed from the biting cold. Grace knew she'd have to stop by and dig through boxes until she found Glory's coat. Dwayne would try to sell his car today, and they might be walking to Joan and Randy's tonight. She and Glory would both need to keep warm.

🍁   🍁   🍁

Vera ran by Grace's place and was surprised to see it all locked up. She peered through the kitchen windows, sure that Grace was there, and just not hearing her knock. Sako poked her head outside her front door and called to Vera. "Vera, I saw Grace and Glory headed for the bus stop about an hour ago." Vera waved a thank you and got back in her car. It was chilly, and she hadn't even left a sweater out when she packed. She'd better run by The Parisian and pick up something to cover her arms.

Vera hoped she'd catch Grace at Momma's, but she wasn't really worried about it. She left for three years in Japan with the same casual attitude she had when she left for the golf course because she was leaving with everything under control. Momma was healthy. Pauline was taking her divorce from Boyd like the trooper she was. Most of all, Vera had even taken care of Grace's problem with Dwayne. That son-of-a-bitch was scheduled to leave right after she did. Good riddance.

CHAPTER 30

A Turtle in the Snow

Grace was going through boxes to look for Glory's coat at her mother's when Pauline raced into the living room. She barely slowed down when she passed her brother who was sleeping on the couch with a quilt her mother had thrown over him sometime during the night. "Guess he was too tired to make it to a bed," Pauline said to Grace under her breath.

Glory was in the kitchen eating a fried egg her gramma had cooked for Benny's breakfast, only he'd never gotten up to eat it. Never one to waste food, Gregoria had set it on the stove. She knew someone would wander through the kitchen and eat it sooner or later.

"What on earth are you doing here?" Pauline asked Grace. "Don't you know there's a big snowstorm coming?"

"I'm getting Glory's coat." Grace turned to look at Pauline. "A big storm?"

"Yes. You'd better find your own coat while you're digging around in there. And hurry up. I'll drive you home. This is no time to be walking from the bus stop."

"But I wanted to wait and say goodbye to Vera."

"I don't even know where she is. She'll probably swing by your place on her way out of town.

Next, Pauline was issuing orders to Glory and Momma. They had to get going and they had to get going *now*. No, Glory didn't have time for her gramma to make Mexican biscuits, one of her favorites.

Grace was grateful for the car that was still warm inside. "It is really starting to look nasty."

"Yeah, I want to be back home before it starts to snow, I've never driven on icy roads."

"I just can't believe this, it's barely September."

"Tell it to that old Comanche who predicted this in July. It's gonna snow, Sis, and it's gonna snow hard. What's the cake for?"

"We're going to go to the Johnson's to play cards tonight."

"Can you walk there?"

"We'll have to if Dwayne sells his car today."

"Good. His tires are slicker than the inside of a cactus."

Grace was glad to be home. Pauline promised to call her the minute she got back to Vera's, their new home. Grace couldn't remember another time when her sister hadn't come in for coffee.

She thought she'd made it home before Dwayne and was startled when she heard Glory talking to someone in the bathroom. He was home—his car wasn't in the parking lot because he'd sold it.

"Did you wonder where we were, Dwayne?"

"No, I called your mom and she filled me in. You got your butt home just in time. What in God's name were you doing out in this weather anyway?"

"Getting a cake. When I left, it wasn't so bad."

She expected a lecture about listening to the weather on the radio, but it never came. She could hear snatches of music, but detailed broadcasts were another matter. She counted on the newspaper for things like weather. But in Oklahoma, where the weather could change from minute-to-minute, that news could come too late to do any good.

There was enough macaroni and cheese for one meal. They ate quickly and Grace put the pan in the sink to soak while they were saying goodbye at the Johnson's. Luckily, they hadn't planned on eating out; there probably wasn't a hamburger joint open anywhere. In a town that rarely had snow and had no road equipment to clear it, even one inch of snow was enough to close everything down. Most likely, the snow would be gone by morning, at least on the roads. Things would get back to normal as soon as the storm front moved eastward in the familiar pattern of weather on the plains.

Pauline called. She'd gotten home safely. Suddenly, Grace realized that snow or no snow, Dwayne hadn't planned to say goodbye to her family. If things were different, Momma would be real hurt. Grace knew that he had not avoided them out of shame, but because he didn't think they were worth his time.

He had no clue they knew about Grace's beatings, so he was unaware of their relief at not having to spend an evening with the tall Texan who always worked overtime to make them feel uncomfortable. The blonds he attracted who called her mother's house made matters worse.

In Gregoria's family, the women had a history of taking action. Her great aunt in Mexico had stabbed her husband when she caught him cheating. Oh, she hadn't killed him, but she'd made her point.

"I'd like to hit that cowboy of yours on the side of the head with a stove lid," Grace's mother had once confided to her after Dwayne had left Grace and Glory at home when he went to Texas.

"No, Momma," Grace had kidded her, "stove lids are becoming scarce and we need them for making tortillas. Could you make do with an iron skillet?"

"I guess so. Might work better, with the handle and all." Of course, violence planned out this way never actually occurred. A couple of rounds of the rosary must have cooled Gregoria down each time. But the anger and hurt over her daughter's treatment was still there, and not very far below the surface.

❦   ❦   ❦

It was the night before Dwayne left for Tokyo, and he was pacing back and forth in the living room. Each time he turned to pace in the other direction, he'd almost stumble on Glory who was following along right behind him in the same nervous path.

"Glory, for Christ's sake, go get dressed."

Glory took off for her room, anxious to wear her little rabbit fur coat with the matching hand warmer that Grace had made from the old stoles from her Aunt Vera. It seemed like she was back in no time, almost stepping on Dwayne's heels again.

"Can I take my turtle, Daddy?"

"Hell, no, Gloria," snapped Dwayne. He was growing impatient and feeling the stress over the past days of getting ready to transfer to Japan. What the hell was a dumb Texan going to do in Japan, anyway? He knew he'd stick out like a chicken in a barnyard of ducks. Yellow ducks at that, he grinned. God, all those Japs were supposed to be unarmed, but Dwayne had his doubts; if things were the other way around, he sure would've figured out how to keep *his* guns.

He didn't notice the tears of anger, fear, and frustration that rolled down Glory's cheeks and hid deep in the fur of her coat collar. Too preoccupied with his own problems to notice that his little girl was about to snap, he'd barely listened when she'd said she didn't want to move, and she didn't want him to go away. She'd get over it.

Certainly he never dreamed that, when she marched back to her room, she'd picked up Carmen, and hidden her in her fur hand warmer. If he had known, he wouldn't have been worried about the turtle; he would have beat Glory's butt for disobeying him.

Outside, the snow glistened. The storm had blown over and bright moonlight slid over the snow-covered roofs on its way to the ground, where it threw long shadows of the bare oak trees across the wintry yards. Glory lagged behind Dwayne and Grace. He thought he heard her talking to her turtle about how pretty the snow was, but he assumed she was just pretending Carmen the III was there with her.

"Gloria, come on. Jesus Christ, why can't this girl keep up with us, Grace?" Glory quickly put the little turtle back inside her hand warmer. "Give me your hand, I guess I'll have to pull you all the way to the Johnson's. Give it to me!"

Dwayne didn't care that the frightened kid had to stumble through the snow to catch up with him; he certainly was in no mood to slow down. Without warning, he jerked her hand out of her hand warmer and Glory's beloved turtle fell into a snow bank. As he dragged her forward, he didn't notice her staring at the little indentation in the snow where poor Carmen III had landed. What he *did* notice was that Glory suddenly lost all interest in walking on her own and had to be pulled all the way to the Johnson's. Furious, he looked into two eyes, soupy with tears, and was surprised to see that they looked back at him with a fury of their own. Assuming she was just upset over being pulled so hard, he growled at her, "Well, that's just too bad. Tomorrow I'll be gone, and you can poke around all you want to."

From the beginning, Grace was completely unaware of the turtle confrontation. She'd been dressing in the bedroom when Glory had asked to take Carmen with her. Even if she had heard Dwayne tell Glory she had to leave her turtle at home, she would never have thought to check the turtle bowl before she left the house. Even grownups seldom challenged Dwayne, and Grace would have never expected Glory to take her turtle to the Johnson's after she'd been told not to.

Grace also didn't have any idea a poor little helpless turtle had been dropped in the snow, not that she would have risked Dwayne's anger to rescue it. That turtle had been through the hottest summer in years, survived handling and mishandling by at least five or six kids and had even been Maybellined with red nail polish. After all that, it was truly a bad omen that it had met its demise in a snow bank.

For Grace, the evening didn't begin to go to pot until they were at the Johnson's. First, the cake turned out to be a white cake with chocolate frosting, and she'd told Dwayne it was his favorite: chocolate. Apparently, she'd misunderstood the person behind the counter. She couldn't miss Dwayne's you-can't-do-anything-right stare across the table, and neither could anyone else.

Then, during a card game, Joan tried to help him pronounce the word *specific*, that he couldn't seem to get out of his mouth. Grace thought this might be the night Dwayne would slip and show his ugly side. His whole mood changed when Joan corrected him.

After that, the fun was gone, and the evening ended early. Everyone was tired and not really in a mood to play cards. When they went into the living room to pick up Glory, they found her curled up in a little ball in the corner, eyes wide and blank. The neighborhood children who were visiting told Grace she'd been there all night, and hadn't even touched the cookies and Kool-Aid that Joan had given them.

"Well, time to go. Say goodbye, Glory," growled Dwayne. Glory mumbled something and struggled into her little coat.

Uneasy about her last evening before Dwayne left, Grace said tearful goodbyes to her friends and walked out into the snow with Gloria and Dwayne. She could hear him threatening a tired little girl who wouldn't keep up. Why didn't he just carry her?

She didn't need to wonder about the grip Dwayne had on her arm. At first she thought he was trying to guide her through the snow, but it got tighter and tighter until she was sure she'd have bruises the next day. Was he still mad over Joan trying to help him with *specific*? Dwayne knew Joan didn't mean anything by it; she was just a born teacher.

Grace panicked when she realized that Dwayne might beat her one more time before he shipped out. By the time they reached their quarters, his grip on her arm had tightened even more and she had no doubt she was going to have a rough night. Frantically, she looked around, but all the lights were out in the surrounding quarters. Everyone had gone to bed. Would anyone even hear her if she screamed?

Dwayne threw her up the concrete stairs to the back porch. Startled, she stumbled and skinned the front of her leg. When he slapped on the kitchen light, she grabbed their daughter and ran her back to her bed. Glory was asleep before she was covered up, still wearing her fur coat. Grace thought she heard her cry something in her sleep about a turtle getting cold, but a turtle's comfort was hardly one of Grace's priorities.

Before she returned to the kitchen, she quickly considered her options and there weren't any—unless she wanted to scream and wake up the neighborhood. And then, what if no one came? Dwayne would be angrier than ever. It was too big a risk. She also knew he would never let her use the phone to call Pauline, and the chances she'd get past him and out the door were nil, that was for sure. Somehow she had to calm him down and get him out of his killer mood.

Sex. That was her only way out. All she had to do was survive until tomorrow morning when they each would go their separate ways. *Okay, so go to the bedroom, get undressed and head for the bathroom. Stuff your insides with toilet paper and go seduce him.* It was a weak plan and somehow Grace knew it was doomed to failure.

She was out of Glory's room and had taken one step toward the bedroom when the full force of Dwayne's arm slammed her against the hall wall. "Dwayne," she begged, "don't do this. You're going to hurt me."

Her begging only made him angrier and meaner. "I'll teach you to laugh at me, you little whore." He pulled Grace to him and threw her against the wall again.

"Dwayne, you know I'm not a whore. What's wrong?" Grace sobbed, but he was already dragging her into the living room by her hair.

"You little bitch! And that know-it-all teacher friend of yours."

"Dwayne, she's your friend, too. You like her."

But he was not to be stopped. "She's a bitch too. Just because she's been to college, she thinks her cunt doesn't stink."

Grace's ribs felt like they were on fire. *He's done it this time. He's actually broken my ribs.* This was to be no ordinary beating. This was the one that could kill her. "No, Dwayne, no," she begged as he pummeled her over and over with his fist and the back of his hand. The tiny seamstress was no match for this artillery soldier who was more than twice her size. She was too weak at this point to even lift her head to focus on the door. There was no way to reach it anyway.

Dwayne's fury grew and she realized he was looking around the room, trying to find something to beat her with, but almost everything had already been moved out. At the peak of his anger, he dragged her down the hall into their bedroom and yanked the pistol out of its holster. She watched in horror as he checked the cylinder to make sure it was loaded. *Oh, my God. He wants to shoot me. What if the gun isn't fixed? What if it fires?* She tried to scream but there wasn't a scream left in her.

"Here!" he exploded. "You're not worth going to jail over. Shoot yourself!"

"No, Dwayne, no," Grace begged. Over and over, she refused to take the gun from his hands.

"Take it!" he insisted. He grabbed her hand and tried to wrap her fingers around the trigger. Minutes went by like hours. Then Dwayne's voice sounded further and further away.

🍁   🍁   🍁

Grace finally passed out. She didn't hear the gun click over and over again as Dwayne, completely out of control, tried in vain to empty the loaded pistol into Grace. Finally, he left her in a lump on the floor.

As soon as he began to cool down he realized he was going to have to call an ambulance or Pauline to come and get Grace. Neither choice was good. If he called an ambulance, he'd go to the stockade, and he was sure to get busted and lose his new promotion. If he called Pauline, she might not keep quiet about it, and he'd go to jail anyway. It really galled Dwayne to have to call Grace's sister, but she was his best chance to avoid getting arrested. An ambulance was out of the question, unless he wanted to run his ranch from a federal jail cell in Leavenworth.

"Pauline?"

"Who is this?" a sleepy voice answered.

"It's Dwayne. You'd better come get your sister," he growled.

"Why? What's the matter?" She was waking up now. Dwayne had never called her before, and it was after midnight. She was too numb with fear to hang up the phone. Dwayne could hear her run around yelling, "Keys, shoes, where the hell's my purse? Oh, my God, he's finally killed her!" Then he heard her pray out loud, part in English, part in Spanish. "Oh, please God, take care of my sister until I get there."

Dwayne finally put the phone back on its cradle. She was on her way. All he could do was wait. Maybe he could knock some sense into her when she got there.

Pauline was frightened and angry when she came through the kitchen door. Dwayne took one look at her face and stepped aside to let her pass. He could forget about trying to bully her. One false move and Pauline would press charges and send him to jail.

She ran toward the bedroom but stopped when she saw the crumpled body in the hallway. She never saw the gun that Dwayne had hidden in the bedroom closet.

"You bastard," Pauline threatened, "you've gone too far this time. I'm calling the MPs."

"Go ahead." Dwayne bluffed. "Call the MPs. That'll fix things for sure. That will leave Grace with no husband and no allotment check. What's she gonna live on?" he threatened. "Just take her and Gloria with you. Tomorrow, I'll be gone and Grace and I will work this out when I get back."

"*If* she lives," Pauline cried, as she turned Grace over and heard her groan. Over and over, in Spanish, she comforted Grace while she tried to get her on her feet.

Meanwhile, Dwayne was busy loading the rest of his family's things into Pauline's car. Glory, sound asleep, made no sound when she was placed on the back seat except to mumble that it was cold. It took both Dwayne and Pauline to get Grace to the car. The panic-stricken sister headed straight for the hospital without ever looking back.

After the car left, Dwayne felt a shiver. This could be the end of all his dreams of having a ranch. Hell, if Grace died, it would be the end of him, period. *Why did he keep doing this to himself? He knew he couldn't beat Grace that badly and get away with it. He should have divorced her long ago. Then she'd be in one piece and he could go on with his plans to live on the ranch. Instead, he might find himself in jail. Jail! He'd heard stories about what happened to good-looking men in prison. Prison was the one place Dwayne had always said he'd never go. Would the military police take him away in irons?*

There was no point in turning himself in. There was always a chance that Pauline wouldn't have him arrested. Or that Grace wouldn't press charges. He'd spend the night at his brother's. If Grace died, the police could find him there. If they weren't there by morning, he'd ship out as planned. Just as if none of this had happened.

He looked around the neighborhood. All was quiet. The pitiful soldier somehow managed to sweat even while he stood knee-deep in snow.

CHAPTER 31

Rough Night

It must have been a slow night at the Fort Sill Army Hospital. When Pauline drove up to the emergency door, several orderlies were hanging around outside, smoking cigarettes, and telling jokes. One of them rushed over, opened the car door, and caught Grace as she fell into his arms. He shouted, "Get a stretcher!" but the other orderlies were already moving.

"Ma'am," one of them said to Pauline, "give me her ID card, and I'll get the paperwork started."

No one asked Pauline what had happened. Accustomed to seeing battered wives on a daily and nightly basis, the medical staff moved confidently through the ugly dance they all knew and Pauline followed along behind them: Chart. Vitals. Blood pressure. "Get her to X-ray while I talk to her sister," someone said.

A nurse snagged an orderly who was on his way down the hall, "Leon, there's a little girl in the back seat of that Packard. Get her, will you?"

Pauline looked back to see the orderly open the back door and find Glory still dressed in her coat and shoes in the middle of the night. "Rough night, huh, kiddo?" the orderly softly asked.

Glory looked up, barely aware a strange man was holding her. Whoever he was, he looked nice. She went back to sleep. Poor little kid, Pauline thought. She should be home in a nice, warm bed.

All in all, the news from the X-rays wasn't that bad. The doctors told Pauline that Grace had a fractured cheek bone, broken nose, sprained neck—could have been broken, the doctor said, with worse luck—four cracked ribs but no lung puncture, a punctured ear drum caused by a blow to the head with an open hand, a sprained knee, and multiple bruises and scratches. One of the biggest potential problems was the damage to Grace's abdomen. Only time would tell if her reproductive organs would suffer any permanent damage.

The doctor said that when she passed out she wasn't any fun to beat anymore. It may have saved her life. He turned to Pauline and spoke with the same ease and friendliness he'd have if he talked to his own sister, "Pauline, there are a couple of military policemen outside the door, could you go speak to them for Grace? She's in no shape to answer questions and I've given her a sedative. The quieter she stays, the better."

Pauline looked at the two MPs in the hall. One was real tall and big, and the other could have fit in the first one's gun holster. Any other time, they would have looked funny. "Ma'am, we need to get some information about what happened tonight. We have a standard report form we use for this sort of, er, occurrence."

"What do you need to know?"

"Oh, the standard questions. Who did it? When did they do it? Where did they do it, that sort of thing."

"And *then* what?"

"Oh, we pick him up and arrest him. I hear it's pretty bad, so he'll most likely be court-martialed and given a dishonorable discharge and sent to prison for awhile."

That was what Pauline was waiting to hear. She wanted to see that bastard locked up forever for what he did to her sister. "For how long?" she pressed.

"Oh, at least a couple of months."

"Months?! He almost kills my sister and all he'll get is a couple of months?" He'd be out in no time and headed straight for them, she realized.

"We know it's not right, but that's the way it works," answered the large MP with a big sigh.

Pauline took a breath and spoke slowly, emphasizing every thought; she had to say this right: "Look, here's how it is. This man is dangerous. Your way, he'll be back to beat her again before Christmas. Tomorrow, he leaves for an assignment in Japan. He's going to be gone for three years. Isn't that better? Can we fix this thing to go like that?"

"Well, ma'am, your sister can refuse to file charges, if she wants. I see your point, but it seems a shame to let him get away scot-free."

The small MP scratched his head and shifted his weight from foot to foot. He seemed embarrassed. Pauline looked down and saw that her coat had come open, exposing her frilly nightgown. She tightened the trench coat around her body and cinched up the belt. Under the circumstances, she really didn't care if her nightie showed. Why should *he*?

"All I want to do is what's best for my sister, I think we can fix it so it won't happen again when he comes back."

"Okay, we'll leave it in your hands." Reluctantly, they headed in the direction of the next battered wife. Pauline heard their conversation trail down the hall.

"Ever beat your wife, Sergeant?"

"No," the big sergeant answered, "my wife says I'm nothing but a big teddy bear. Don't know what gets into some men. Wish they'd try to beat on someone my size for a change."

"Ever had any takers on that offer?"

"Nope, I'm still waiting," the big policeman doubled his huge fist and pretended to polish it on his shirt as both men grinned.

Pauline breathed a sigh of relief. Good lord, they would have kept Dwayne here. In Japan, with any luck, some Samurai warrior would do him in.

❀   ❀   ❀

Glory started giggling the next morning when she woke up and saw she was in her new home. She raced from room-to-room looking for her mother, who had been put into a separate bedroom so she could rest. Pauline was waiting for Glory when she finally found her mother so that she could stop her from jumping on Grace's bed.

She accepted with childish gullibility her mother's explanation of the Army needing her father right away, so he didn't get a chance to say goodbye. She also accepted her story about falling in the snow and needing to rest a few days. That was okay too. After all, she had Gramma, Aunt Pauline, and her cousin Carlos to play with.

Grace was sure Dwayne was gone, but she didn't breathe easily until a package arrived from San Francisco addressed to Glory. "Oh, goody, it's from Daddy," Glory squealed. "I knew he'd send me a present." The two sisters had to laugh at the "Oh, goody!" They both knew she'd picked it up from that Shirley Temple movie their brother Ben had taken her and Carlos to see. Every since, Glory had been trying to look and act like the movie star. For days, she'd been stopping every so often to strike a pose and ask, "Do I look like her now?"

Still in pain, Grace let Pauline unwrap the cigar box filled with Bing cherries, a delicacy almost unheard of in Oklahoma. They only knew of one cherry tree in all of Lawton.

"The woman who owns it must have robbed a bank to pay for all the water it took to grow a cherry tree in a town where water is rationed," Pauline liked to say. "Someday I'm going to stop by the post office to check out the wanted posters and collect the reward. I'm sure her face is up there."

Glory was anxious to share her gift with her cousin. The two women laughed at the youngsters as they ate the juicy cherries under the kitchen table that they'd been using as a pretend fort. Pauline and Grace warned them not to swallow the pits and to look out for "the green cherry quickstep" caused by eating too much fruit, a warning that the two children found hilarious.

Grace's recovery seemed miraculous, thanks to the arrival of those cherries. Now they were all sure there was no chance Dwayne could pop in on them unexpectedly. For days before the arrival of the fruit, they'd checked and re-checked windows and doors before they went to bed each night. Whenever Pauline left Grace alone, she didn't leave the porch until she heard her sister throw the deadbolt.

Momma came in a few mornings after the cherries had arrived and found her daughter struggling to get her sewing machine set up in her new sewing room. "Grace, what are you doing? Go back to bed."

"Oh, Momma, I can't stay in bed forever. I've got to get going." It was apparent that she had been going for quite awhile. Fabrics had been set out on shelves, thread hung from nails on a piece of wood tacked underneath the windowsill, patterns were lined up in old shoe boxes below the fabrics, and sewing gadgets were separated into old cigar boxes.

"That mirror looks familiar."

"It's from Vera's things in the garage. Don't tell her, Momma."

"I won't tell," her mother said, "just remember to put it back. Do you want some coffee?"

"I already made it, it's on the stove. We'll both have a cup."

"Where's your sister?"

"She went to the store. She took the kids with her to drop them off at school on the way."

"Did Glory ever ask you about your bruises?" Momma wondered.

"We told her I fell, but I think Carlos told her the truth. Pauline heard them arguing about it."

"How could he know anything? We've all been very careful not to speak English when we talk about Dwayne."

"Momma, I swear that kid knows Spanish. I know we haven't encouraged it, but he understands; I'm sure of it."

"The white men in the family won't like it. The children won't do well in school unless they speak, think and even dream in English, they all say."

"The only white man we have to worry about now in this family is Rudolf. Besides, how can we keep them from picking it up on their own? That Carlos is so smart. Have you seen his library books? He's always being chased out of the adult section by that grouchy Mrs. Wade."

"That boy reads too much. He should go outside and play more."

"He says his knee hurts."

"How can it hurt? It's only seven years old."

"He says it hurts under the bone."

"Phooey."

She turned to go, and then stopped and asked, "Did anyone ever tell Joan what happened to you?"

"No, and I probably won't write her about it. What good would it do?"

"What are you going to do about Dwayne?"

"I don't know. For sure, I'm going to divorce him, but I don't know if that'll be enough to get rid of him; he may not accept a divorce. If I'm really lucky, he'll be sent somewhere else."

"Just don't *you* leave here, Grace. It would break up the family."

"Leave Lawton? How could I? I just moved to town to find my fame and fortune."

"Fine. Just don't look for your fame and fortune in another man. You girls pick lousy husbands. Why can't you find someone like your poppa?"

Grace moved and tried to put her arm around her mother, only she couldn't lift it high enough.

"Oh, Momma, Poppa was one of a kind. And don't tell me to look at church, either. I've looked, there's no one there worth having."

"I heard those two dance instructors made the mistake of going to the Methodist Church last Sunday. I bet they never show up there again."

"Don't be saying anything bad about my best customers. Besides, I like them. At least they don't go around beating up innocent people."

Momma said, "Maybe that's because they can't catch anyone in those toe shoes they wear." Then she said, "I'm just kidding. The truth is, I like the two as much as everyone else does."

In the kitchen, Grace didn't sit; she stood with her coffee cup in her hand and leaned against the wall. It was obvious Grace wasn't as well as she pretended. "Well, I'm expected at Lilia's, I was hoping to get Pauline to take me over there. Since she's not here, I'd better start walking."

"What's going on today?"

"Lilia has a new crochet pattern for us to try. She says it's more beautiful than the pineapple pattern we did last time. It could take days to finish it."

CHAPTER 32

A One-Buffalo Town

Grace was back in her sewing room separating the buttons and trims when her sister came in and asked, "Was Momma here? I saw the extra cup."

"Yes, she's gone to Aunt Lilia's."

"How?"

"She's walking. I think she was hoping you'd give her a ride."

Pauline turned around and headed for the door. "She can't be very far. I'll go pick her up and deliver her to our aunt's door and be right back. By the way, I heard the kids whispering in the back seat. Something about a turtle in the snow. Did Glory ever say what she did with her turtle?"

"Sis, it's the darnedest thing. She won't talk about it, and she won't let me get rid of the bowl. I know Glory wouldn't do anything to hurt it on purpose; that turtle just disappeared. Do you think Ronnie somehow got in and took it?"

"Maybe. I hope it didn't hitch a ride to Tokyo with Dwayne, she'll be a turtle-in-the-rice."

❈   ❈   ❈

Even though Grace was preoccupied with her own problems, she'd noticed there was something different about Glory. She hadn't been the same since they went to the Johnson's. Grace had the feeling Dwayne had left just in time. Maybe Glory was almost to the point of having that nervous breakdown the doctor had warned Grace about. Whatever it was, Grace was sure the loss of the turtle was only part of it because she'd offered to try to find Glory a new turtle, and Glory had said no. Or, maybe, a new turtle would never do. Maybe she really was grieving over Carmen III. Where was that stinkin' turtle, anyway?

Grace was still putting buttons and trims away when Pauline rushed in and exclaimed, "You'll never guess where I found Momma!" She was talking so fast Grace knew it was big.

"I can't imagine. There's nothing between here and Aunt Lilia's house."

"I found her in the swings at the park."

Grace stopped and looked at her sister as if she had just announced she was becoming a Baptist.

"Momma was *swinging*? I'll bet she didn't even swing when she was a girl. *Que pasa*?"

"I'm not sure, but I think she's worried about us and the stress is getting to her." Pauline poured another cup of coffee.

"Next she'll be in the ditch hunting crawdads with Carlos and Glory."

"Probably that's all her mind will be good for after she learns this latest crochet pattern of Aunt Lilia's. Sis, each line is different, no repeats, and there are hundreds of them."

"What is it supposed to be?"

"Independence Hall."

"On a *doily*? Where do you put a doily with Independence Hall on it?"

"They're going to give it to the church to use as a bingo prize."

"They're going to go through all that work and then *give* it away?"

"It gets better. It's a five-piece set, two for the back of the couch, one for each of the arms, and one for the coffee table."

"When do you pick her up?"

"At six or when they run out of crochet thread, whichever comes first."

"I wonder why they don't crochet burros?"

"Or tortillas?"

"Or chili peppers. Aren't there any Mexican pattern-makers?"

"I guess not. But I haven't seen you sewing up any flamenco costumes lately, either."

"True."

"When are you going to start sewing again?"

"Soon. I had Benny bring in that chair of Vera's that's in the garage. I don't have anything else to sit on."

"*Ayyy*! First the mirror, now the chair. Our sister will have our butts in a taco. We promised her we would leave her stuff alone." Pauline cried as she headed for the coffeepot.

❧   ❧   ❧

The last thing Grace did was put a little handmade sign in the living room window that said: **Sewing & Alterations**, but her first customers in town arrived via the family grapevine. Aunt Lilia needed a dress to wear on vacation; she was going all the way to Colorado to see relatives. Frank needed some shirts to perform in, Benny wanted a pair of winter golf pants, and she had a lot of alteration jobs from other family members. Seemed everyone in her family was either losing or gaining weight.

One day, a young stranger showed up at her door. She'd heard from Garnet that Grace was sewing and wondered if Grace could make a prom dress. Grace said yes. For a week or so, it seemed like every time she opened her door, a beautiful young girl stood there with a big bag full of fabric.

By the end of the week, Grace was begging them to tell their friends that if they wanted a prom dress, not to wait until the last minute, because they were almost as hard to make as a wedding dress and they required three fittings.

Four days before the prom, she opened her door to find a plain, skinny girl with long hair and glasses. At first, Grace thought she must be selling candy, but then she saw a bag bulging with fabric and ribbon.

"Oh, no, Honey," Grace almost screamed. "Where have you been? It's almost prom time!" The girl started crying and Grace could see she wasn't only shedding tears over the dress.

"Oh, please," she begged, "I know it's late, but my mom was going to make my dress and then she got sick and I can't sew."

"Well, come in and let me take a look, what's your name?"

"Shelley. Shelley Wood."

Grace softened, "How much did she get done?" As she spread the dress out on the table, she could see it had been in the hands of a master. The cut job was perfect, and each piece of fabric was still pinned to the pattern piece. "Your mother knows what she's doing."

"She really tried, but she just got sicker and sicker."

"How is she now?"

"Much better, but I don't want her to have to do this."

"Smart girl. There's still a lot of work left to do here. I was just going out, but I'll stay and work on it and at least get it ready for the first fitting by tomorrow. Come back after school and bring your shoes so we can measure the length." By the stricken look on the girl's face, Grace could tell she didn't have shoes yet. "Never mind about the shoes," Grace said quickly, "we'll borrow some from my sister."

Grace had been headed out the door to go to St. Mary's when Shelley had shown up. Some of the women from the church auxiliary were going to clean the church pews with furniture oil. Maybe it was no accident this girl had landed on her doorstep. "God must think this is a better place for me to be," she said in a whisper.

She knew the cleaning at the church would get done without her, but how would an upset teenager with a sick mother get a prom dress at the last minute in this one-buffalo town without Grace to help her?

CHAPTER 33

The Assembly Line

When Pauline returned with Momma later that day, she found Grace surrounded by prom dresses in all stages of completion. Little piles of thread, trims, and zippers lay everywhere.

"Shall I light some prayer candles?"

"Heavens, no. That's all I need is a fire. Bring me my rosary, I'll wear it around my neck."

Their mother went to the kitchen and warmed up a pot of beans and made some fresh salsa and a big stack of tortillas.

Glory and Carlos were in a rush to eat so they could devote their evening to making clay snakes to put here and there around the house. Grace was on the way to the coffeepot and went down the hall just in time to see Carlos put one near the phone that, in the dark, almost looked real. Now, all they needed was their Uncle Ben. He always headed straight for the phone whenever he came over. "Call him," they pleaded. Grace was tempted, but she had too much work to do to socialize with her brother.

"Too bad, kids, but that snake will have to keep until after the prom." After one last look at the clay snake, she headed back to work, chuckling. She knew she could depend on her brother to make a big deal out of being scared when he saw it.

After dinner, Grace's mother joined the hottest assembly line north of the Alamo. Grace sewed, Pauline pressed each piece before it was sewn to the next, and Momma did the hand sewing of snaps, hooks and buttons. They worked late into the night, and when they finally quit, there were seven prom dresses on hangers ready for various stages of fittings. The eighth and latest dress was still in the early stages of completion. One girl's dress called for seed pearls, and they all agreed to call in Aunt Lilia the next day to do the pearl work, even though her only known needle skills were with a crochet hook.

"I can teach her, Momma, and pay her a little something."

"Just tell her you'll make her something later on," her mother suggested.

The next morning after Aunt Lilia arrived, they continued to work with the ease of women who'd grown up together, raised their children together, and were growing old together. Whenever it was time, without a word, one of the women would get up and go make something to eat and a pot of coffee. In the middle of the afternoon, a bread pudding with cinnamon and raisins magically appeared on the table at coffee break, made from a loaf of white bread Aunt Lilia had brought in her huge black purse.

The last four days before the prom, girls with their mothers came and went hourly after school. Grace answered mothers' questions and pinned each gown to fit. Pauline advised on make-up, while Aunt Lilia and Momma sat in the living room doing last minute beading and hand sewing. Grace picked up new sewing and alteration jobs from the mothers and excitedly told her helpers how each job seemed to bring in two or three more.

When Shelley's mother came by to look at the dress it looked so good she was worried. "Grace, how much is this dress going to cost?"

"I'm charging twenty-dollars for each prom dress. They're all about the same in labor. Shelley's will be the same. I won't charge you for the net, because you'd done some work on the dress already, and her dress hasn't required any beading."

"Beading? You've been beading *prom* dresses?"

"Oh, yes," Grace rolled her eyes, "some of these girls have seen too many Audrey Hepburn movies."

"Oh, my," said Mrs. Wood, and they both laughed. "I wish I had been here to help you."

"Well, I might need you next year."

Shelley's mom became very serious, "I would really like that, and please, call me Margaret."

"If I'm still doing this next year, you've got a deal, Margaret." Grace took her into the living room and introduced her to the beaders as next year's relief crew.

"Good. This is the hardest work I've ever done. When you come on board, I'm going to get a job I know something about," Pauline told her. They all laughed when she held up her fingers covered with Band-Aids.

Up until the day before the prom, Grace shoved green bills into the bed of her sewing machine. Friday night, after the last customer had left, she emptied it in front of the women.

"Gee, that looks like more than a hundred and forty-dollars…tips?" Pauline asked.

"I guess so. I never thought about tips!" Grace gave each woman twenty-dollars and the promise of a new outfit if things kept going well. As she passed out the bills and thanked and hugged each woman, it occurred to her that any question about whether or not she could make a living sewing was answered. Oh, she wasn't rich, but the money was good and the job could be done, even with her poor hearing. Moreover, the confidence she was gaining was worth as much or even more than the money.

The women were all tired, but no one wanted to admit their first experience in the clothing business was over. They found themselves around Vera's big dining room table drinking coffee and piecing on leftover bread pudding.

"I thought I'd never learn to bead, I kept dropping them and getting knots in my thread," Aunt Lilia said, "and then, all at once, it was so simple and fun. I might put some beads on one of my hats." Aunt Lilia took her glasses off to clean them on the edge of her skirt and laughed when she found a bead stuck to the nosepiece. While she listened to the other women, she unlaced her orthopedic shoes and gave them a good shake. Beads and sequins fell out and bounced across the wood floor.

"And those snaps! I'm too old to see those things when I drop them. Good thing they're cheap," Momma moaned. Then she said, "I'll be back early tomorrow morning to help clean up, Grace. You can't see the floor in there for the sequins and beads all over it."

"Don't worry about it, Momma, we're all sleeping in tomorrow. You were all a big help and I'm giving you the morning off," Grace said. Then she raised her coffee cup to the group. "I think we make a great team. What would I have done without you?"

"But, Grace, we were so slow," Aunt Lilia said. Then she quickly added, "but we'll get faster, don't fire us!"

"Not much chance, Aunt Lilia. I might fire that old iron, though. I think it's about to kick the bucket," Grace worried.

"*Ayyy!* Don't buy one," Pauline said. "Boyd left one when he went to Japan, I have it in a box somewhere."

Grace looked around the table and realized that she wasn't the only woman who was spreading her wings. For years, Aunt Lilia had been a stay-at-home mother. After the children had grown up and left, she was over fifty and unskilled, so she'd just stayed home. Grace's mother had raised a big family, too, and had never been an outside worker, either. Now, here they both were, in the middle of the most exciting new business in this small town. And all because of her.

"I think I'll go home and bury my crochet needles in the back-yard," Aunt Lilia chuckled, "call me anytime. This was fun!"

"Come on, Aunt Lilia, I'll give you a lift home," Pauline told her.

"Are you going to rest after you clean up tomorrow?" Momma asked Grace.

"I hope so, what's this?" Grace asked, looking at a big sack left on the over-stuffed chair in the living room.

"Oh, Frank dropped that off earlier. I haven't even looked at it."

Grace opened the bag. "Momma, there's enough material in here to make shirts for his whole band. And listen to this note: 'Gary is my size only skinnier. Roger is heavier than I am, Chuck has real long arms…'" She handed the note back to her mother. "Momma, call my brother and tell him to get those cowboys in here for a fitting. It'll be so much easier if they just come over. Then I can read their lips."

CHAPTER 34

A Genuine Grace

Grace had begun to read lips gradually, as her ears failed, so she didn't miss her hearing as much as she felt the pain in her ribs. The bones were taking a long time to heal, and sitting for most of the day was difficult.

She did manage to take some time off from sewing to see a doctor on post about some hearing aids. He'd said she'd need one in each ear, and that they'd be expensive if she got them off-post. Grace knew she would have to order them through the Army before her medical privileges ran out. Anyway, the damage was done when she was an Army dependent, so it was an allowable claim.

Meanwhile, she was so busy she hadn't given much thought to Dwayne, and a letter from him in the mailbox gave her a start. He seemed so far away, not just in reality, but emotionally too. There was no time to open it now. Actually, she had no desire to open it at all; she resented his intrusion into her new life even if only by the US Mail. She went in and tossed the letter on her bed.

There was also a letter from Sako that she read right away:

Dear Grace,

One of the neighbors said there was some kind of commotion at your house the night before you left. I hope everything's okay.

We were glad to get to California after three days of trying to keep Daniel comfortable in the back of the station wagon. The trip was really hard on him.

We're at Mom's now, but will send you a new address soon. Someone told Dad that our old house might be going up for sale. If so, we'll buy it back and we'll all live together; it has five bedrooms and a large yard for Ronnie. We've heard that the last owner took out Dad's prize grape vines and put in a pool, but Dad says it's okay; it'll be good for the kids. I think, really, that he's kind of excited about it himself. Mom is beside herself praying they haven't messed up her kitchen.

Hope all is well, write!

Love, Sako

PS: Ronnie drew the picture for Glory.

The next page was a crayon drawing of a large palm tree with a huge lizard in it. Or maybe it was an alligator. Grace wanted to stop everything and answer Sako's letter, but she'd have to wait until after supper. She had material to preshrink for sewing orders and dresses of Glory's to starch and iron.

Still worried that the other children at school wouldn't accept Glory, Grace was very careful to make sure that Glory's clothes were in order at the beginning of each week. All of her cotton dresses and shirts were starched and ironed. She even starched and ironed her jeans.

When it was time to do the ironing for the kids, she and Pauline would set up the ironing board and have an ironing party, and take turns pressing clothes while they laughed and joked about things that had happened, not happened—and might yet happen in their lives.

Grace liked to imagine the teachers commenting on how nice the two cousins always looked. Every morning, Pauline made sure Carlos's hair was combed and Grace saw to it that Glory's hair was braided neatly by one of the women if she couldn't do it herself.

Glory loved the way her gramma braided her hair. It looked different, somehow, and all the girls at school always commented on it. Her gramma said it was how the Spanish dancers braided their hair. Once, her grandmother even moistened her side hair in front of her ears with soap, and made spit curls, just like flamenco dancers wear, but they washed it out before Glory went to school because Grace worried that maybe the teacher wouldn't like it. Maybe they could do it again for Halloween, her grandmother told her.

All of Grace's dreams were coming true. Glory never seemed to stop giggling; she did well in school, and made at least a few friends. When Grace opened the refrigerator one day to get Glory some juice, she laughed because she realized that even her refrigerator was looking better. There was a package of hamburger and a box of strawberries on the second shelf; Pauline must have gone shopping at Cagle's.

Things were going so well, Grace knew she'd never have to go to work in an office or store, where she'd constantly be afraid she wouldn't be able to hear. What a treat to be here, laying out a pattern for five crazy musicians, she laughed to herself.

The first time Grace came home and saw a driveway full of beat-up pickups in the driveway, most of them with back bumpers replaced with railroad ties, she said a prayer that they weren't some unemployed cowboys that her sis had dragged home. When she peeked through the screen door, she was relieved to see her brother among the group, having an impromptu rehearsal in the living room while they waited for her. She decided things could be worse. Oh, they were still cowboys and still unemployed, but at least they weren't Pauline's new boyfriends!

By the end of the first fitting Grace had a pretty good idea what the rest of her life was going to be like—days after days of stepping over a living room full of musicians in western boots with a guitar in one hand, a beer bottle in the other, and either a song or a joke on their lips. She was in heaven.

As could be predicted, Carlos was picking up impromptu guitar lessons from his uncle and the other musicians as easily as he did everything else he came into contact with. One day, Gregoria showed up with an old guitar she said she'd found in the attic. Carlos was thrilled.

He fit right in with the other kids in the living room who were so excited about getting new clothes that they kept all of the women laughing.

Chuck, the drummer, kept saying he wanted more fringe and sequins than the other guys; Gary, the bass player, wanted his name over his pocket. Did he used to work in a gas station? Grace wondered. Then she thought, no, he just wants to be sure the girls know who he is.

The others were just plain awed that Grace could make something just for them. Roger, the fiddle player, wanted to know if it would be correct to say his was a custom-made shirt. "Definitely. I'm fitting it exactly to your measurements," Grace told him. And, she thought, as she looked at the pile of loud fabric and fringe, I can guarantee you that you'll never see another band that looks like you guys.

That wasn't true for long. In the weeks and months to come, band members from as far away as Nashville found their way to Grace's doorstep. After days of working with bright fabric that practically pulsed in the dark, and dealing with buttons and trims that were either too big or too small or not enough, she was able to convince them to let her pick out the material and design the shirts.

The word was spreading around the bands that if you wanted to look really good, you had to have A Genuine Grace shirt to wear on stage. There was so much business from the musicians that Grace knew she'd sewn her last prom dress; the shirts were much more profitable. Even better, it was a year around business. With every shirt order, she also knew she'd never have to take another beating from Dwayne.

Days after its arrival, the letter from Dwayne was still untouched. Grace finally opened it with the same enthusiasm she opened her power bill. She didn't think that Dwayne had ever written so much to anyone in his life. There was a separate letter for Glory that Grace set aside. Grace leaned back and skimmed over her part: it seemed he was lonely. He was sorry he'd hit her, he loved her, and he didn't deserve her. He wasn't able to please his new First Sergeant, and his stomach hurt from the change in food. He didn't think the Japanese liked him and he was sure they talked about him in their crazy gibberish right in front of him. He talked about the allotment that she was already getting. She was to save as much as she could for the ranch. She wasn't to run around with her sisters because they were all just a bunch of whores and everybody in Lawton knew it. "Oh, bull!" Grace said out loud.

She went back and read the part about her sisters again. That dirty bird. Why couldn't he just say something nice? Why was he so convinced that Grace, her sisters, and all their friends were whores? Sure, her sisters were a fun-loving group, and Pauline loved to go to the USO and dance, but so what? The dances were very tightly controlled. No one went out until the dance was over, and if you did, you didn't get back in. Afterwards, an old bus that belonged to the USO brought all of the women home, right to their doorsteps.

At least that's what Pauline said; Grace never waited up. She loved to dance, and she was good at it if she had a partner who was a strong leader, but her ribs were in no shape to step out onto a dance floor. Maybe later on, she was due for some fun. Maybe she and her brother Ben could go together and show those troops how to do the tango. She needed a dress. Something off the shoulder, with a full skirt, and cut low in the back. Something—red! She'd have to get started right away.

The next morning, she read Glory her letter as she and Carlos ate their oatmeal. Glory held the enclosed slides her father had taken around Tokyo and asked if she could take them to school.

"Sure. You can take the alligator picture from Ronnie too, if you want."

"Why are the pictures so small, Momma?"

"Because they're meant to be put in a machine and shown on a wall, something like a movie."

"Can we get one of those machines?"

"I don't think so. Why don't you ask your teacher if she can show you the slides on the school's machine?" She didn't say so, but she was annoyed. Dwayne knew she didn't have a slide machine. Why couldn't he send Glory prints?

Carlos handled the slides like a pro. Somehow that kid just instinctively knew how things were to be done. If those slides came back today with fingerprints on them, Grace would bet her sewing machine that they weren't her nephew's.

"Aunt Grace, these were taken with a very fancy camera."

"How do you know that?"

"I just know." Carlos shrugged his shoulders.

"Well, it so happens, you are right. Your uncle told me in his letter he's got a Konica now. He says the Japanese make the best cameras in the world."

"Glory, can I have the slides to show to my teacher when you're done with them?"

"Sure."

"I'll walk Glory to school, Aunt Gracie, so she doesn't get lost."

Glory giggled at the teasing. "I won't get lost, silly, it's only three miles."

"That's *blocks*, Glory, not *miles*," said Carlos. He rolled his eyes at his aunt.

Grace and her sister had been right about it being good for them to be together. She wondered how those two would like matching cowboy shirts?

CHAPTER 35

Don't Forget!

By the time Grace got the cowboy shirts finished for Glory and Carlos, the letters from Dwayne slowed down. Apparently he was adjusted to his new assignment. Unfortunately, the letters lasted long enough for Grace to fall in love all over again. When he wasn't talking about her sisters, Dwayne showed a sweet, romantic side of himself on paper Grace had never seen when he was with her. Had he changed? She wanted so desperately to think he had.

He requested sexy photos of her, and she complied, eager to please this *new* Dwayne. The women's whole world stopped while Grace posed in one scanty outfit after another, with Pauline reluctantly taking the pictures. Totally baffled at Grace's turnaround, Pauline and her mother looked at each other and shook their heads.

When letters didn't come, Grace was too busy to think much about it. She took Dwayne's words literally when he said he was sorry that he'd hurt her and that he still loved her. It was easy to believe Dwayne when he was out of sight. She never once considered he'd found someone else. How could he? He was married to *her*. The combination of his letters and her loneliness erased her memory of his past indiscretions.

Meanwhile, Grace busily put money into her account and thought how surprised and pleased this new Dwayne—the Dwayne who was writing about how much he missed her—would be when he came home and found out how successful she'd become. It wasn't a lot of money by some people's standards, but she had proved to herself and others that she could help support her family. She was able to save most of the money from her allotment from Dwayne in their joint savings account.

As a reward to herself, she'd opened an account that held her sewing money in her name. She'd never had a checkbook before. The old Dwayne had always told her she was too stupid to handle money; he kept the checking and savings books. Money was power, and even Grace had always understood that vaguely, but now she was beginning to feel it for herself for the first time in her life. It felt good!

She went to the bank to deposit her checks several times a week, and was probably the only person there who didn't mind waiting in a long line. If someone she knew saw her there, it made her day.

Maybe, she began to think, if she could handle a checkbook, maybe he was wrong about her being too dumb to drive. Pauline started taking her out in her Packard for driving lessons. They decided he might have been right about the driving, and they both laughed after Grace backed into the old peach tree at the end of the driveway for the third time. Prayers and practice spared the car and the old tree, however, and Grace knew she would soon get her own car.

Time raced by, and she learned, grew and succeeded with a speed that would have taken her breath away if she'd stopped to think about it. Other military wives learned to take their car to the mechanic and change their own light bulbs when they were left on their own, but Grace was reborn.

One day, just when things were going so well, a letter arrived from Japan. The women were all working on fringe and buttonholes, so

Grace took the letter back to her room and sat down on her bed to read:

꙾

> Grace, I'm coming home soon. They're not keeping my unit here the full three years. I want you to know that when I come home I'm going to be stopping by to see Gloria. I've met another woman here in Japan and I plan to marry her as soon as I can get a divorce, so get the paperwork started as soon as you can. I'm sure you've been running around just like your sisters always have. I've found me a real woman now who isn't a whore. She's a WAC sergeant who's even had a year of college. Don't worry about us wanting to take Gloria. We've talked it over and we've decided you can keep her. She's over eight now anyway and Frieda figures she's ruined. She wants to bring her kids up from the very beginning so she can control them. I had to have some of my things sent to your house. The Army needed a permanent address. I'll pick them up when I see Gloria. Don't forget about getting the divorce.
>
> Dwayne
>
> P.S. Aunt Bett died. No one knows who will get her farm. Keep your fingers crossed.

Don't *forget?* Grace was stunned. How do you *forget* a divorce? You *forget* to get milk. You *forget* to clean out a closet. You *forget* to put gas in the car. You don't *forget* to get a divorce. She read the P.S. again. "Keep your fingers crossed?" Why should she care if he got his aunt's farm or not?

"Sis, do you know any lawyers?" she asked. Pauline looked at her sister and knew it all without asking. It was an old story among military wives whose husbands were sent away on assignment. Pauline felt an intense relief—her sister was to be spared from her own foolish heart.

"I know the best divorce lawyer in Lawton, Pete Sparks."

"I've heard of him. Do you think he'll help me?"

"Oh, he'll help you. We've been going out for weeks."

"Sis, you're going out with Sparks? Why didn't you tell me?"

"There's nothing to tell. Yet. All he ever asks is to go out to dinner, and the only place he likes to go is Bill's Steak House. I swear, the man's never eaten a bean in his life."

"I've always heard he's the best. Do you think he is?"

"I know he is. I'm using him myself."

"Isn't that a little unethical?"

"I said I was dating him, I didn't say I was going to *marry* him. How can a steak and a baked potato be unethical?"

"I suppose he's really expensive."

Pauline gave her a look that sent all of the women into fits of laughter. "Grace, grow up, for heaven's sake. Let me do this for you. You might as well," she shook her bust, "I'm going to do it anyway!" More laughter erupted from the women.

"He must be married, a fancy lawyer like that."

"His wife died last year. She's probably in heaven having a fit that a Mexican might get her hands on her English china."

Suddenly, Grace felt very tired. She handed the letter to her sister and went to her room. In her half-sleep, she thought she could hear the women shouting swear words and making threats about what they were going to do to that *gringo* if he ever showed up at their doorstep.

One day, he did.

CHAPTER 36

Dwayne's Remorse

Early one morning while Glory was in school, Dwayne hit the door with the full weight of his body, not even bothering to knock. Furious because it was locked, he swore and yelled on the porch, "Why would whores need to lock their door?"

It wouldn't do for Dwayne to get wind of Grace's new business, Mr. Sparks had said, so Grace and the women had run a drill about what they'd do when he got there. They all quickly hid their sewing and sat at the dining room table with a deck of cards. Grace turned in time to see Aunt Lilia hide a few cards under her dress, sticking out just enough for Dwayne to see them. How realistic can you get?

When the stage was set, Grace answered the door. "Hello, Dwayne. I'll get your things. They came on Tuesday," she turned and left the room.

Dwayne could feel Momma's eyes boring into him. "Why do you call my daughters whores, Dwayne? You know it's not true." Surprised and embarrassed by his mother-in-law's question, Dwayne struggled to respond and failed. When Grace came back with his things he bolted out the door.

❧   ❧   ❧

In the weeks to come, Dwayne would be forced by friends and his brother CG to face the truth. His wife was not a whore. His daughter was not ruined; she was a very nice little girl. True, her hair was no longer blond, but what did he expect? Grace had dark hair. Clearly on Grace's side, his older brother told him flat out that he'd been brainwashed by that bullish WAC.

Remorse was setting in. Remorse and regret.

His family and friends described his sexy WAC as homelier than a farm dog with teats sleeping on her back. He had to admit that his military mistress with her pushy personality didn't look like much next to Grace, who was always very gracious and fixed herself up so nice all the time.

Frieda, unaware of the criticism, started to complain about the money Dwayne was spending on his ranch. As soon as he'd come home, he'd had ordered new fencing. He tried to tell her about the ranch he was building up, and the home they'd have on it someday, but that only set her off more. "I am not going to live in the middle of a bunch of stinking cattle with only your stupid relatives to talk to," she spat. She used the word stupid a lot. Especially when she talked about Grace and Glory.

Gradually, when the romance began to cool off, Dwayne realized that he'd again picked a woman unsuitable for the life he wanted to lead. In the heat of passion, he'd believed Frieda when she said she was Spanish, but his friends helped him realize she was just another Mexican, an uppity one at that. Not that it would have really mattered. His family would never have accepted a Spanish woman, either. And Dwayne knew it.

Worse, he'd had a phone call from CG who said Aunt Bett had left the farm to him. It wasn't unexpected news, but Dwayne had been fantasizing that the farm would be his. Did he lose it because of

Grace or because Aunt Bett had heard about Frieda before she died? He'd never know.

There was no way he would ever get Frieda to help him build up a ranch where she wouldn't be accepted. The question was: how long could he keep her from finding out she'd never be welcome in Texas? Could he string her along at least until he got the fence in and the pond dug? How did he get himself into these messes?

On his way home from work, Dwayne began to stop by the honky-tonks again, to look at those long-legged Texas girls. He could have had himself one of those; he began to tell himself again, even though he knew it still wasn't true.

After one of Frieda's tirades, Dwayne tapped on Grace's door. Everyone in the living room had watched him drive up and quietly went to the table and picked up their cards, just as before.

"Want to go to the drive-in tonight?" he asked, "We could take Gloria. It would be fun." Dwayne was beginning to plead. Grace just stared at him. Still outside the door, Dwayne began sputtering, "Grace, I've made a terrible mistake. I don't want a divorce, I don't want to marry Frieda, I can see that now."

"But Dwayne, I've already started the paperwork."

"Why?"

"Because you told me to. I have to go. My iron's plugged in."

With that she quietly shut the door and locked it. A deep anger began to swell inside Dwayne. The bitch wasn't going to take him back! Well, she'd just see who would be sorry when he built his new house. If he married Frieda, their combined incomes would build a hell of a house in Lawton, where housing was already a good deal.

Marrying Frieda would have its drawbacks; that was for sure. For one thing, she insisted she handle the money because she said she was better at it. She also said he spent too much money on that piece of crap he called a ranch. Her bitterness really surfaced when she found out how much allotment the Army had made Dwayne send to

Grace while he slept with her in Japan. Why hadn't he divorced Grace right away?

One day, when she was rifling through his bills, she found his savings book. "Dwayne, you haven't made an entry in this book for almost two years. How much money is in here?" Dwayne had forgotten all about it, and had to admit he didn't know. Grace had made all of the deposits while he was in Japan. "I want you to go get her savings book right now. We'll need all the money we can get for our new house when we get married. Tell her that. And don't take no for an answer." Frieda pounded on the kitchen table for emphasis.

Dwayne was still angry over Grace's refusal to take him back, so it didn't take much to get him started. He tore over to her house determined to get what Frieda told him was rightfully his.

❧   ❧   ❧

Not thinking, Grace didn't check to see who was at the door when she answered it and Dwayne grabbed her arm and pushed her inside. Grace was frightened; he was all pumped up like he used to be when he beat her. The other women were in the back, cleaning up the sewing room from their latest shirt order. She tried to call out to them, but he grabbed her by the throat, silencing the scream.

"I want my savings book," he sneered.

"Dwayne, it has both our names on it; even *your* lawyer says it belongs to both of us and will be divided between us," she whispered through her closed throat.

"I said I want it. I earned that money, you don't have any right to it."

If Dwayne hadn't gotten into the house, Grace may have resisted, but she knew she was in danger of getting beaten again, and she was no longer willing to put herself in that position; it just wasn't worth it. Even if she *could* yell, he might end up hurting someone in her family.

When Grace opened the desk drawer to get the savings book, she saw the secret one he'd dropped in the parking strip months before. She handed both of them to him, looked him in the eyes, and said very slowly and clearly, "Here's the book, Dwayne. And another one I found that I'd like to jam down your throat. Take them both. I don't need them anyway. In fact," she said, with her voice getting louder, "I'll never need *anything* else from you, you son-of-a-bitch! Now, GET OUT!" This time, when he left, she slammed the door. Hard.

Stunned by Grace's reaction, Dwayne thought the two women in his life were making an awful lot of fuss over a few bucks. He tossed the book in the front seat of his new Dodge sedan, and then picked it up again. He was curious to see just how much money was in there—over eight thousand dollars! His foot slipped off the brake and he backed into the same old peach tree Grace backed into when Pauline had taught her how to drive. What did she live on all the time he was gone? One thing for sure, she hadn't been pissing away all of his money like Frieda said she had.

He couldn't go home. Not with this much money in the savings book. If Frieda got ahold of it, he'd never see it again. He had to go to the bank, get the money, hide most of it in a separate account, and then open a new savings account in his and Frieda's names. He didn't want to open an account with Frieda, but he knew she'd throw one of her frequent fits if he didn't.

He smirked when he looked at the other book. He'd just throw it away. He'd gone to the bank and withdrawn all of that money before he'd gone to Japan. Yes siree, that money was long gone, Grace would have had a hell of a time getting her hands on that. He wondered briefly how she had gotten the book in the first place, but forgot about it when he glanced at the savings book with the money in it. There was enough in there to make some improvements on the ranch, dig that pond, and even buy some new cows, if only Frieda didn't find out about it.

🍁   🍁   🍁

Inside, Grace leaned against the door for support and closed her eyes. It was finally over. It had to be; there was nothing else he could want from her. She wished she'd remembered to tell him that she had a secret savings account too. There was enough in it to buy two or three more cows for his precious ranch, not that she'd ever give it to him.

It saddened her to think she'd never have a chance to share with him her excitement over her sewing business because her lawyer had counseled her against it. Her successful enterprise, he'd said, would not work to her financial advantage in a divorce court.

Who cared? Later on, after she settled down, she'd call Sparks and tell him she didn't want any alimony. She didn't want anything from that bastard except for him to go to hell and eat barbed wire.

In the meantime, she had a business to run; she went back to her shop and tried to pretend nothing had happened. She looked over her sister's shoulder and calmly said, "Needs more sequins, Pauline." Grace turned to walk away but started to cry. Pauline sensed more trouble with Dwayne, and tossed a box of loose sequins at her to break the tension. A war broke out, Aunt Lilia threw buttons, and Momma threw pieces of leftover trim. The sewing room erupted into a free-for-all full of laughter that escalated when Momma pulled out Carlos' squirt gun from out of nowhere and showed no mercy.

Later that day, Grace found a postcard in the mail from Sako saying they'd gotten their home back, that Ronnie was in the pool with Daniel, and that her mother was in the kitchen. The best news was that the kitchen was almost the way she'd left it. Grace smiled and went to tell the others that things had worked out okay with Sako and her family. Better than okay. Momma crossed herself and said a quick prayer. Grace smiled and wondered if she were giving thanks because Sako got her family together again, because they got the house back, or just because Sako's mother got her kitchen back?

Grace left her co-workers and called her attorney. "Mr. Sparks? Grace Tyler. How are you?"

"Fine, Grace. We're just about ready to go to court over here. Are you ready?"

"Yes, but listen, I've changed my mind about wanting alimony and half of the savings. Let the bastard have it all. Let's just push the paperwork through as fast as we can."

"Grace, you'd better think about this for awhile. Half of that money is rightfully yours, and you might need it someday. If not for yourself, then for Glory."

"I appreciate your concern, but I know now that I'll never be rid of Dwayne until he has all the money. Let him have it all. I'll take care of this family from now on."

Epilogue

Not long after that, Pauline came home with a tale from Garnet about Dwayne beating Frieda. As it turned out, his new girlfriend wasn't nearly as docile as Grace. After the first few fights, she told Dwayne she fully intended to go to the hospital and have each bruise and cut documented. Then she followed through with her threat. After the first few times she got in her car and drove herself to the hospital, she had his attention.

Dwayne knew that if he kept it up, he'd be out of the Army pronto, and lose his retirement. There was also a story that Grace had heard from her ex-sister-in-law, Jewel, that Frieda fought back. Jewel also said that once, when Dwayne hit her, she jumped up on the bed and furiously swung a pair of combat boots by their shoe-laces around her head. Grace didn't believe that. Who would be brave enough to fight back with Dwayne?

There was even *another* rumor, one Grace just couldn't believe: Frieda was as dark as Grace! Grace had yet to set eyes on her, but everyone else said she looked enough like Grace to be Grace's ugly sister.

Weeks went by and Grace was so immersed in her business she seldom gave Dwayne and Frieda a thought. One day, she went to the door with a cup of coffee in her hand and had a clipboard shoved in her face. "Sign here, Mrs. Tyler." Assuming it was a fabric delivery, she signed. It was too late to call back the driver when she saw the name on the crates: Mrs. Frieda Tyler.

"Pauline!" Grace screamed. Her sister ran to the front door wrapping a Japanese kimono around her from Vera that stuck to her just-showered body; it failed to cover all the important parts of her damp skin.

"Gracie, what is it?" She looked down at the address on the crates. "*Ayyy!* Help me get them inside." She ran to the kitchen and came back with an old butcher knife. "Let's see what's in here."

"Look, Sis, china!"

"Wow! Wonder which one of them paid for this stuff; it's Noritake. How many place settings?"

"Let's see. Twelve!"

"Twelve! What is she going to do, have her whole battalion over for dinner?"

Just then, the phone rang. Pauline picked it up and handed it to Grace because she couldn't stop laughing. Grace knew it had to be Dwayne.

"Grace, Frieda wanted me to call you and tell you to let us know when some crates arrive for her. I guess she didn't have a permanent address so she used yours," Dwayne shouted into the phone.

Dwayne's voice was loud and Grace heard every word. "They're here, and did you know they're addressed to Mrs. Frieda Tyler? A little premature, don't you think?" She tried to be serious, but she couldn't stop smiling. It just didn't matter anymore. She could swear she heard scuffling on the other end of the line as she hung up.

A few minutes later, the phone rang again. This time it was a very frantic Frieda who shouted at Grace. "Grace, I want my crates and I want them now. Dwayne and I are coming to pick them up."

By now, the two sisters were laughing hysterically, "Why, Frieda, the only crates here are addressed to a Mrs. Tyler. Right now, *I'm* the only Mrs. Tyler, so the crates must be mine. *Adios!*"

Grace looked over at her crazy sister who held a huge platter above her head doing a victory dance around the wooden crates of china in a sashless kimono that billowed and flowed around her naked body. She picked up a soup tureen splashed all over with a pattern of matching shocking pink chrysanthemums, put it over her head, and joined Pauline. She held the china high, like a soldier proudly showing off her spoils of war. The china was ugly, and she didn't really want it, but that didn't matter. She had won the battle and she had the war trophy to prove it, with service for twelve.

Best of all, she had Glory.

0-595-24375-4

Manufactured by Amazon.ca
Acheson, AB

11479454R00196